Typewriter Pub, an imprint of Blvnp Incorporated
A Nevada Corporation
1887 Whitney Mesa DR #2002
Henderson, NV 89014
www.typewriterpub.com/info@typewriterpub.com

ISBN: **978-1-64434-088-2**

DISCLAIMER

This book is a work of fiction. The characters, incidents, and dialogue are drawn from the author's imagination and are not to be construed as real. While references might be made to actual historical events or existing locations, the names, characters, places, and incidents are either products of the author's imagination or are used fictitiously, and any resemblance to actual persons living or dead, business establishments, events or locales is entirely coincidental.

A DIAMOND IN ISLAM

S. NAHAR

To my closest friend, Ethar, for always standing by this book.
In a time of darkness and fear, you were the friend who put your faith in my works and in me, and for that, I will always be thankful.

FREE DOWNLOAD

Get these freebies and more when you sign up for the author's mailing list!

s-nahar.awesomeauthors.org

CHAPTER 1
Not an Ordinary Day

AMIRA SARKER

A usual morning for most American teens consisted of cereal, light-hearted conversations and continuous complaints about school, however in my household, it was never that casual. Any child born in a Bengali household knows better than to expect such a simple, perfunctory morning.

"Tanwir! Don't roll your eyes at me," Baba yelled. "Other kids aren't always staying at home, gazing on their laptops. They go out with good friends or help their parents. All you do is ignore your family. Does it hurt to answer your phone, once in a while, when we call?"

Mom and I sat and ate our breakfast quietly while listening to a father and son argument. My twenty year-old brother still had not learned how to stay silent when being scolded at. His nostrils flared as Baba's words stung before his eyes.

"Maybe if you stopped comparing me to others, I wouldn't act this way!" Tanwir countered back.

Baba sighed. "Tanwir, please, just listen to us. You don't even talk to us anymore. Did you even pray your daily prayers lately?"

Tanwir stayed silent.

"Tanwir! *Allah* doesn't teach us this in the Quran. We were made to worship Him. Stop taking advantage of life in this *dunya* (world). Your time here is limited. You can't guarantee that you'll be alive tomorrow morning," Baba said.

"I've been busy," he mumbled.

"That's no excuse! On the Day of Judgment when *Allah* asks you why you didn't pray, 'I'm busy' is not going to be a good reason."

"All you do is criticize me," Tanwir said. "You never listen. Comparing kids is one of the reasons why Muslim kids turn away from Islam."

"*Astaghfirallah* (May Allah forgive you)! Don't say that."

"But it's true. You know what? Just forget this. I can take care of myself," Tanwir ran up to his room, seething.

He slammed the door loudly. Baba sighed, sitting down at the table with his head in his hands. He was mumbling a small *duaa* (small prayer) for his son.

"What are we going to do with this boy?" he asked Mum wrinkles showing on his brown skin.

"I don't know," Mum replied. "How did he end up this way? I miss my quiet little boy."

She was absentmindedly stirring the sugar in her tea, her dark eyes holding deep sadness reflecting my father's.

Tanwir attended to a college near home, so he didn't have to move into the campus living areas. He was a straight A student, but had a nasty attitude that emitted fear to anyone he walked by. His rage was unbearable at times.

I looked at the clock on the wall. It was 6:45 a.m. and school started at 7. Knowing I had to run, I grabbed my backpack, and prepared to head out.

"*Assalamualaikum* Mum and Baba," I said, opening the door.

"Waalaikumusalaam."

I stepped outside and felt rain drops on my *hijab*. Great. Nonetheless, I walked to the bus stop.

*   *   *

When I got to my locker, I saw my friends Tasneem and Lucy waiting for me. They were both Muslim students, but Lucy converted two years ago saying Tasneem and I inspired her. She found Islam to be fascinating and logical. It fits her moral values, which ultimately led her toward the path of Islam. Unfortunately, her family disowned her, so she moved out and lived with her aunt. As Muslims, my friends and I wore *hijabs* around our heads.

"What's up?" Tasneem asked.

"Not much," I replied, shuffling through my things to find the correct textbook. "Did we have any history readings?"

No one knew how rocky my brother was with my family and his faith, and I had no intention on telling my friends everything. Some secrets were better left untold.

Tasneem shook her head. "No history homework this time. Thank *Allah* for that. I was so busy."

Lucy had her eyes glued to the phone; her light-colored eyes reflected a popular social media app. She seemed indifferent, scrolling through the mindless stream of updates and shallow posts. Suddenly, her eyes brightened, and she showed her bright screen toward us.

"There's a new guy at school. One of the girls took a picture of him," Lucy said, shocked at the gall that our classmates had. "That poor boy is already stuck with a paparazzi."

"New guy?" I asked.

"Oh yeah. Apparently, that new guy in school is really hot," Tasneem gushed, but quickly straightened herself when I raised a brow at her. Clearing her throat, she continued talking.

"I heard that he's a complete genius, but hardly acts like it. There was a rumor at his previous school that he moved out because he had gotten into a fight with a Muslim! Can you believe that?"

At this point, I was intrigued. *He had troubles with another Muslim? Why would he be at our school where the Muslim population was greater than in other areas?*

"Yeah. I think his name is Derek."

"No, it's not. It's David."

The girls bickered while I rolled my eyes. A new boy in town just meant another person for me to avoid. Given what I'd heard about him, I wouldn't want to start a feud.

Suddenly, a tall, intimidating, fearful and towering shadow loomed over me. I knew it was a male student before I even turned around.

"It's actually Damon, ladies," a deep voice rumbled from behind. His voice was oddly sensual, as though he was trying to provoke something within us.

Tasneem and Lucy instantly stopped fighting. I turned around and crashed into a wall of a human being, inhaling a deep breath as a strong scent of cologne winded through the air. My caramel brown eyes met his dark shade of green eyes, emulating an evergreen forest with the harshness of his gaze. He had thick, dark brown hair and perfect lips that slightly parted.

I lowered my gaze.

For a moment, he stood silent as if he was the judge and I was a witness on the stand. He scrutinized my behavior, but I didn't dare to react. When I stole a glance I noticed his sharp gaze on me like he hated me without even knowing who I was.

This time, I didn't back down and met his eyes with the same fervor. Perhaps, he really did get in a fight because the student was a Muslim. For all I knew, I could have been completely wrong, but the way he stared at me gave me a feeling that I wasn't.

"Hey Damon. Come hang out with us. Not with these terrorists," Maya said with disgust, another student who was far from being comfortable with Muslims. No one really cared though.

I broke myself from my daze, frowning at Maya. "Excuse you. Unless you catch me in the act of terrorizing somebody, don't you ever assume that I'm a terrorist just because of my hijab. At night when you're asleep, I'll assume that you're dead and bury you," I said calmly. In fact, I was waiting all day to say it. Some of the perks of being a minority student were all the snarky comebacks one could come up with. There were no limits, so I took full advantage of that.

The new guy, Damon, seem slightly impressed. A ghost of a smile feathered his lips; I thought I could have been wrong all along.

"Oh, shut up. You think you're so smart, don't you?" she hissed.

I laughed.

"I do in all honesty. Thank you for noticing. I appreciate the compliment."

Maya was fuming red at this point; her tan skin burned with a red coat of embarrassment.

"You're a feisty one, huh?" Damon winked. "That's a favorable quality."

Maya, who felt threatened by my presence, stood to whisper into his ear and smiled devilishly. His eyes brightened, and they turned to a corner only *Allah* knew where.

"Boys get turned on too easily in this school," Tasneem said, shaking her head. "Did I mention that Damon is an absolute flirt?"

"I wonder what gave that away," I muttered sarcastically.

*   *   *

Seated in my history class, my non-Muslim friend, Aria, was smiling brightly when she entered the room, and sat in front of me. I had no idea why she would be so perky on a Monday morning when nothing but stress outlined the rest of my day.

"Hey," she said.

"Why are you so happy this early in the morning?"

"Because a smile a day keeps everyone happy."

"That's absolutely atrocious."

She threw her head back in a soft laugh. Her silky brown hair was moving effortlessly as she did. At times, I wondered how people would react if I ever took my *hijab* off. I wondered if they would silently admire my own hair.

Stop these thoughts, Amira, I told myself. *Your beauty does not have to be advertised for everyone. It's personal.*

Aria broke me from my thoughts. "Did you hear about the new guy?"

"Yeah. He's a charmer," I said, rolling my eyes.

"Got on the rocky road with him?" she laughed.

"Please. You know I don't do boys. Besides, *Islam* doesn't allow dating," I shrugged.

"Hey, babe," Mark, Aria's boyfriend, interrupted as he walked into the classroom.

"Hey," she said, as she pecked him on the lips.

They had been together for a year now and were a cute couple. Just then our teacher, Mr. Well, walked into our class right when the final bell rang, indicating to start the class. He was an elderly man with gray hair, but slim enough to infer that he cared at great deal about his health. His blue eyes gleamed with wrinkles creasing around them as he addressed the class.

"Alright, guys, settle down. Today, we have a new student named Damon. Please treat him with your best behavior," he announced while ushering Damon to come in.

My eyes widened. *You have got to be kidding me? The new jerk in town is in my history class?* I groaned.

"Let's see. How about you sit behind Amira? The girl in the peach colored headscarf," Mr. Well pointed on my direction.

Damon nodded, and walked to the seat behind me. He lightly brushed his arm against mine, causing goose bumps to appear in that spot. I inwardly groaned, *not this guy again.*

I took a couple of deep breaths. If I continue ignoring him, then I'd never have to talk to him.

* * *

When Mr. Well partnered us up with people to do a project on a leader, I knew all chances of ignoring Damon would fly out the window because, lo and behold! Damon became my new partner. Given our earlier interaction, I dread the flirtatious conversation that I knew for sure would bother me.

"So, who do you want to do the project on?" I asked, turning in my seat to face him.

He looked more bored than a student watching an ecology documentary. "I don't really care. As long as I get a good grade on it," he said.

I thought for a while, knowing he'd be no help. Damon continued to stare at me, silently observing my every movement once again. I noticed that with every gesture of my hands, he would visibly tense as if awaiting a punch or hit.

"Are you okay?" I questioned. "You seem oddly… nervous."

"I'm fine."

I hesitantly let the topic go, thinking back to our project. "Let's do it on Prophet Muhammad (peace be upon him). He changed the world and was a wonderful leader, the start of the Islamic Empire."

"Okay, but you're gonna need to tell me more about him."

"How about afterschool in the library tomorrow?" I asked.

"Deal."

He changed the topic to our project and I momentarily forgot all about his odd behavior. We reviewed the structural format of our project, assigning each other with roles and responsibilities. Him being cooperative this morning, seemed like a faraway dream. Damon wasn't being overbearing or strange, but focused on our presentation completely.

That was until he decided to bring up a small talk.

"So, where are you from?" he casually asked, scribbling a quick note down.

I couldn't tell if he genuinely wanted to know or was just trying to be nice and failing at it. "Guess," I told him, curious about what his answer might be.

Because of my *hijab*, I would always get the most random Muslim countries from the Middle East. For some reason, people always assumed that all Muslims came from the Middle East and no other country.

"Saudi Arabia."

I shook my head.

"India."

"Close," I replied, mirroring his note-taking.

"Just tell me," he sighed, exhaling a defeated breath.

"My parents are from Bangladesh."

He nodded. He kept asking me questions until he brought up a dating matter.

"Do you have a boyfriend?"

"No. Islam doesn't allow us to date."

He glanced at me, amused. "What a darn shame, huh?" he mocked. "Luckily, I wasn't interested to begin with."

"So, why ask then?"

He shrugged. "For amusement, I guess. That's what Muslims enjoy in their own twisted ways."

His words angered me. I had no idea why he insisted on a passive-aggressive conversation with me when he could have just easily ignored my presence. He had no right to say such a disrespectful comment. I knew there was more to his fighting rumors.

"Listen here," I whispered, leaning close so only he could hear, "I don't care whether you choose to ignore or hate me for the rest of the year, but keep religion out of it. Have some decency to be at least respectful to other people's beliefs."

"Aren't you a little fireball?"

"Whatever."

He was about to say more until the bell rang. I was the first to get out of class. The nerve of that guy! I wanted to punch him. He had to get off his high horse, as he wasn't the king of this school. I hated those types of people who acted like the world revolved around them, especially this guy who was the epitome of an arrogant high school senior.

* * *

Lunch came around fast. I went to sit at my usual table that consisted of my awesome but weird friends.

"Trouble in paradise?" Aria teased.

"What?" I asked, confused.

"Don't play dumb with me. Damon seems to be all over you," she giggled.

"Yeah, no. I don't have time to waste on that fool. We were just talking about the project, and then he started to subtly insult me," I huffed. "The nerve of that boy disturbs me."

"Doesn't everyone?" Tasneem smiled, as she fixed her *hijab* using her phone camera.

Everyone laughed because she was partially correct. Many students did get on my nerves, but Damon pulsed the venom through my veins with his hateful words. Although it was a subtle comment, it weighed a lot heavier on my shoulders. Muslims at our school were already struggling through their days, but adding someone like Damon to the mix only made things worse.

My laughter ceased after seeing a displeasing sight. Across the lunchroom was Damon, with Maya, sitting on his lap. They were whispering only *Allah* knows what to each other. I could only imagine. I was deep in thought until someone snapped their fingers before my eyes.

"Amira, are you even paying attention to the conversation?" Tasneem asked.

"Sorry. Could you repeat that?"

She sighed.

"I was saying that Damon is a known flirt. Don't get too fond of him. He crushes a girl's heart, and then moves on to his next interest. Don't fall for it."

"Who said anything about falling in love? I already have too much on my plate to deal with him."

"I had an older brother to worry about," I added silently.

Damon could rot in the darkest depths of hell for all I care.

CHAPTER 2
Story Time

AMIRA SARKER

I woke up to yelling, and groaned at having to get up at five in the morning. I already prayed, so I tried to catch a little more sleep before school. Desperate for more sleep, I covered my ears with pillows, trying to muffle the voices.

It didn't work.

Finally deciding to find the source of the yelling, I stood up, determined to give them a piece of my mind. Opening the door, I saw Baba and Tanwir arguing again.

"How could you come home so late last night? You had us worried sick!" Baba exclaimed.

"I was just out with some friends, playing soccer," Tanwir mumbled. Man, he could be so stupid sometimes. Who in their right minds would go outside in the middle of the night and play soccer, especially in a Bengali community?

"At midnight? Are you crazy? Do you even know how unsafe America can be during night time?" Mum shouted. I flinched at her tone. It's like five in the morning and my parents were already shouting.

"I know what I'm doing, Mum. You guys are just worrying too much," Tanwir shrugged off. *Bad move, buddy.*

"Worry too much? You didn't even tell us you would leave! Where is the communication?" Baba yelled.

"You guys should have just called," Tanwir muttered.

I face palmed myself. He was asking for more trouble than he already was in.

"But you never answer! Tanwir, I don't want you going outside at midnight. You could have been reading *Islamic* books to increase your knowledge," said Baba.

"Yes, Baba," Tanwir rolled his eyes.

"Don't roll your eyes at me, son. Your time here in this world is limited. You should be trying to increase your *iman* (faith) during this time," Baba glared.

Tanwir just glared back at him and went to his room, slamming the door loudly. *Geez, what's his problem?*

Baba sighed and went up to my mother. Mum hugged him and sobbed a little. I hate seeing how depressed my parents are and I could feel their pain.

"Mum, he's just having a tough time now. I once went to this Youth Conference, and one of the speakers said it was normal for young Muslims between the ages of eighteen to twenty-five to lose their faith. Just don't stop being the good Muslim parents you are. *In Shaa Allah* (If God wills it) he will come around," I said softly, and went back to my room.

It was already six. I got ready for school, carefully pinning my scarf around my head, ensuring all hair had been hidden under the cloth. When I was done, Baba came into my room.

"I'll drop you off to school today. I have something I need to talk to you about," he said, before walking out.

A dread feeling came upon me. I felt as if I was in trouble. My parents had never asked me for a talk, and the idea of being trapped in a moving vehicle with them as they yell at me, terrified me to no end. *Oh Allah, save me.*

* * *

"I'm very impressed by you and so is your mother. What you said today gave us an idea," Baba started as he drove the car, his Bengali accent occasionally slurring over his words.

"What kind of idea?" I asked.

"Did you know that in most Muslim families, it's the older sibling who finds the truth of Islam and becomes the role model to their younger siblings?" he questioned.

I nodded my head.

"Well, in our family, it's you. You found peace and guidance in Islam, and saw what a wonderful religion it is. You're the role model to Tanwir now," he sighed.

"What do you mean?"

"Meaning, I want you to help him," he stated calmly.

"But—"

"He listens to you. He has a very strong love for you as his sister. Have you ever noticed that he calms down as soon as you enter the room? You're the one who can reach out to him better. That's why I want you to help," he cut me off.

"Okay," I answered, getting out of the car.

Giving me a responsibility really scared me. I wanted to help Tanwir with all my heart, but would he actually listen to his little sister? It almost seemed unbelievable that he would or even attempt to acknowledge my advice. I sighed, as I entered the school doors. Perhaps one day, *Allah* will show him the right path.

* * *

I walked to my history class after taking my things from the locker room. Of course, Damon was there, talking to his friends. For a new guy, he sure fit in really quick. My footsteps echoed as I walked, allowing students to glimpse at me for a moment. Damon's gaze, however, lingered longer than the rest. I ignored his burning gaze, wishing he'd stop. He had that same cautious look that swirled around his green eyes like a glowing ember. Something about me bothered him, and I was betting a lot of imaginary money that it was my beliefs, judging from his comments in class.

Snapping himself back to reality, he caught up with me. "We're still meeting at the library, right?" Damon asked.

"Huh? Oh yeah. Right after school. Don't forget," I said.

He nodded, and walked off to his group of friends. Something about him made me feel odd, almost a little pressured when he stared at me. I shook my head*; he was just another guy*.

* * *

Damon was in four of my classes; English, History, Science, and Gym. I saw him more often toward the end of the day. His mere presence in multiple of my classes was starting to bother me. I didn't want to see him at all; I had an instant dislike toward him.

Spotting my group of friends at a table nearby, I waved and joined them for lunch. I had to stop bombarding my mind with Damon because he was irrelevant to me. I tuned into my friends' conversation.

"Have you guys ever read *The Mortal Instruments*?" Aria asked.

"Yeah, I read the first two books. Why?" I asked.

"In the fourth book, two of the characters named Jace and Simon go into a market. There's this girl who come up to Jace and was like 'Can I touch your mangos?' and she wasn't talking about the fruit," Aria smirked.

We all laughed except for my other non-Muslim friend, Meredith.

"Oh my. That just ruined mangos for me now," I grinned.

"I know right! I was like that girl has some naughty thoughts going on there," Aria said as she wiggled her eyebrows.

"Wait, I'm lost. Why is that so funny?" Meredith asked, confused.

We all looked at her. "Mangos, as in a guy's jewels," Tasneem said.

It took a while for Meredith to realize what that meant until her face twisted in disgust.

"That's gross."

"It is, but hey! That's how messed up society is nowadays," Aria shrugged.

"True, but seriously, I will never look at mangos the same way again," Meredith groaned.

We erupted into a bubbling laughter once again, enjoying each other's company. Friends were the real reason I came to school, because it didn't matter if I was having a horrible day. They always reminded me that everyday could be a great day with the right people.

* * *

Before I knew it, it was time to tell Damon the *Seerah* (biography) of Prophet Muhammad (peace be upon him).

I packed up my things and went to the library, impatiently waiting for Damon. Glancing at the clock, I wondered, *where in the world is he?!* I had studying to get to. After a couple of more waiting minutes, he came in.

"Alright, let's start this thing."

"Okay, so Muhammad (peace be upon him) was the last prophet of Islam-" I started, but was cut off by Damon

"This isn't going to be another religious lecture. Is it?" Damon groaned.

I rolled my eyes. "Shh. Just listen. Anyway, He's a leader because he brought a new light to the people of Mecca. He was an honest man and acknowledged the equality and brotherhood of men. Some of his oldest companions were an African slave, Bilaal, an Iranian called Salmaan, and Suhayb of Rome. All of these men came from different places with different culture. However, in his company, they were equal to each other without distinction."

"What else did he do?" Damon asked in bored tone.

"Prophet Muhammad (peace be upon him) went through many struggles in life, and lead people on the right path. He was sent with a message from God, but he didn't just preach it. He practiced it. The moral values and life lessons he taught and showed are important things for all mankind to follow. He also gathered an army to fight in the Battle of Badr. Lastly, Muhammad (peace be upon him) would listen always to the people of Mecca and Medina. He would listen to their problems, and help guide them through it. He was the ideal role model for all mankind," I finished.

"Impressive. I didn't know you knew so much."

"I do try my best," I shrugged it off.

"Since I don't have anyone else in mind for this project, let's just go with this holy guy."

I nodded, making a couple of side notes for our work. As I was writing, I noticed Damon's blank expression as he watched the movement of my hands again. He seemed so cautious like a bird without its wings, flapping with all its might to survive in a dangerously cruel world for the weak and helpless. I wondered if he truly feared me.

Were the rumors true? Did he and a Muslim student really fight over their beliefs?

Like a nail shattering the glass of tension between us, "Why do you wear that?" he asked, pointing at my *hijab.*

"I wear it because my Lord commands it," I simply replied.

Damon scoffed in disbelief, crossing his arms over his chest. "Are you telling me that your Lord commands you to hide your beauty away? That's so stupid."

"No, it's not. The *hijab* is a promise and a reminder. It shows the world I'm a Muslim girl. It also shows my dignity and is an act of modesty," I stated confidently.

"Still, shouldn't the girl be free?" he asked with a curious gleam in his eyes.

"The girl is free, but she's very precious in Islam. Women in Islam are considered the diamonds of Islam. When she is a daughter, she opens a gate to *Jannah* (paradise) for her father. When she is a wife, she completes half the faith of her husband. And when she is a mother, Jannah lies under her feet. That is the status of a Muslim woman in Islam," I said.

"But still..."

"Think of it this way. She is giving herself self-respect through her various acts of modesty. It's no secret that there are men who see women as objects of sexual pleasure, but in Islam, the *hijab* prevents a woman from being ogled and judged purely on her appearance. A *hijab* is more than just a piece of cloth."

The fire of ignorance still flared within his eyes, closing the gates to open-mindedness. "Islam treats a woman exactly like an object. Don't even pull that bullshit on me."

My defensive walls arose, towering over my tired form with its own magnitude of energy. I was prepared to defend my morals, my beliefs, my *Islam.*

"Damon, I suggest you stop spewing nonsense," I said each word, slow and steady as if he was the tiger and I was the trainer. "If you truly understood Islam, you would know that women are not seen as toys in my religion. Historically speaking, it was the first religion to truly give women rights for divorce, court systems, and property. Muslim women had the most freedom."

His jaw clenched, a vein beginning to pulse on his smooth, white neck. "Islam is a religion that just hurts innocent people. Look around you, Amira. Look at all the destruction and pain Islam has brought to your nation. Look at all the lives that have been lost in wars against the Muslims!"

"Those wars were fought due to nationalism and superiority! Wars don't happen, but religion tears people apart. It happens because people are imperfect and flawed. It happens because of greed and power. Religion is a barrier that they use. It's shown throughout history that people of power take advantage of those below them, and crave to dominate inferior people. They also used religion as an excuse when it had nothing to do with it!" I argued fiercely.

Damon stood abruptly, his chair shrieking against the tiled floors. His height dominated me from my seated position, as his piercing glare cut through me like a double-edged sword from ancient times. He practically growled like a beast.

I didn't back down.

When he continued to stay silent while seething at me in distaste, I began to puzzle some pieces of the rumors in my head.

"Did you get in a fight at your previous school with a Muslim student?" I asked quietly. "Was that why you switched schools?"

His shock was evident in his crumbling visage. "H-How do you know about that?"

"Rumors fly fast."

"Just… just go away," he mumbled, as he grabbed his stuff and ran away from me, leaving the ripped pages of his story untold.

Well, that was interesting.

CHAPTER 3
Mystery Behind Eyes

AMIRA SARKER

When I went home, I caught Tanwir eating my soft chocolate chip cookies. *This jerk had the nerve to eat my cookies.* I shook my head before I ran up to him, glaring.

"How dare you eat my cookies? They were mine," I whined.

He took another cookie and put it in his mouth, chewing thoughtfully. I crossed my arms over my chest, waiting.

"I didn't see your name on them. Besides, sharing is caring little sister," he smirked.

"Since when do you share? You never share with me so you can't say that," I retorted.

Just like that, his smirk dropped, and he glared at me. I took the chance, and grabbed my cookies back, taking him by surprise.

"Wha—?"

"You snooze, you lose. Now leave me and my cookies alone," I huffed.

"Pig," he mumbled, as he walked away from me.

"Excuse you mister, but that is not the way to talk to a lady," I said in a fake British accent.

He just ignored me, and walked off to his room. I took my cookies into my personal den and started to do my homework. After an hour, Aria had texted me.

Aria: *Can I ask u* something?

Me: *Sure.*

Aria: *Do u think Mark still likes me? I feel like he's avoiding me. I mean, I feel like he's lost interest in me.*

Say what now? The perfect couple was having relationship issues? That was unexpected. I thought Mark was crazy about her.

Me: *Where is this coming from???*

Aria: *He ditched me for the last few days to hang out with a girl, his childhood friend and… I feel like he has some sort of strong feelings for her.*

Me: *I think he just wants to be around her for a while. Don't stress it. I know he really likes u. I doubt that he's gonna leave u for her.*

Aria: *Idk anymore. I really like him. But I'm also kinda hurt that he just ditched our plans and went with someone else.*

Me: *I agree that it wasn't right for him to ditch both of ur plans like that. Just give him some time. Give him space until then. Boys r idiots at romance. But ur quiet attitude should snap him out of it.*

Aria: *I'll try and thanks :)*

I smiled; feeling satisfied that I could help my friends. Dropping my phone, I continued writing mathematical equations onto my notebook.

*   *   *

Deciding to reward myself for my productivity, I went downstairs to watch a movie. I was turning the television on, when I heard Tanwir's footsteps thundering against the staircase like a storm had followed him all the way down. He was about to walk out the door when I stopped him.

"Where are you going?" I asked, suspicious.

"Outside with my friends," he responded bluntly.

"You shouldn't go outside now. Mum and Baba will be worried."

"I'll come back. Just don't say anything."

"Tanwir, you can't be serious? You're making Baba even more stressed than he already is. Can't you just listen to him for once?" I said, staring at him directly in the eye.

He walked a few steps closer to me until he was towering over me. I looked up, not lowering my stance. *I'm not going to let him scare me.*

"You don't know shit. They never stood by me, so why should I stand by them? You don't know what I'm going through. I suggest you shut up or else," he whispered harshly.

"You've just misunderstood them. They're trying to help you, and you keep pushing them away. You keep throwing your religion away!" I yelled.

Mum and Baba weren't home. They went shopping, so they weren't going to hear this.

He roughly grabbed my arms. "I'm not throwing my religion away! You don't know what I'm going through. Go back to your princess life. Go back to everyone giving you all the attention, and just shut up!"

"No! I won't! You're my brother. I'm supposed to help you. We're supposed to be there for each other. Why won't you let your family help you? Why do you keep pushing them away? One day your family won't be there anymore. One day they will all die and be gone—"

"Shut up! Don't say that! You know what? Just shut up. No one else has an annoying sister like you," he glared.

"I'm trying to help you, but all you do is yell at me and hurt me! Can't you see that?" I desperately pleaded with him.

None of the worries of my day like my argument with Damon even mattered anymore. I just wanted my older brother to be as kind as he was when we were kids, when we were too pure to be tainted by harsh reality, when we still had everyone in our family. I wished things would go back to normal again before that incident had happened.

He twisted my arms, making me wince in pain. It hurt and I was holding back sobs. Pain erupted under his grip and I tried to pull away. He was stronger than me, making my struggles useless. I bit my lip to hold back a cry, holding myself to stay strong. He didn't know what he was doing, I had to be calm.

"I hate you. I don't need your help. Don't ever ask or try again. This is a warning," he seethed, letting me go.

I fell to the ground and he left, shutting the door. I let the tears fall. I sobbed quietly and let out harsh breaths. He hurt me again and this time, he gave me a threat. *Why was he doing this? Oh Allah, please help me reach out to him.* I was so scared for him and myself. *Would he really hurt me more for helping him?*

I wrapped a scarf around my head, and went outside. I walked to a lake where no one goes, and sat on the bench where my quiet spot is. I let all the tears out, all the pain and misery, all the aching need for my old life. It had been years, yet the pain still throbbed against my chest.

Death always rendered the weak in a state of mindlessness.

I cried and looked at my arms. Bruises were beginning to form. I was not going to give up. I was going to help even if it was the last thing I do, but at what cost?

CHAPTER 4
Terrorist Control Central

DAMON WINTERS

I had stormed off after an argument with Amira, and allowed the gentle wind to caress my worries away with a kiss of a breeze. The world had spun out of my control since we moved. My mother forced me here because she thought, being around with a diverse set of students would allow me to adapt better.

But, I didn't want to adapt. I didn't want to like the people who had wronged me, who had hurt me, and who had absolutely betrayed me.

The rumors had been true. I did get in a fight with a Muslim student, and it wasn't a regular high school fight either. The emotions between the two of us were too complex that physical dominance had been the only rational option, but it didn't make things right.

The thing that wouldn't get out of my mind was her eyes. As my anger intensified, and as the minutes went on, so did her defensive walls. They rose higher with every second that skimmed past the two of us. As I stood before her in the library, I realized that Amira was not somebody to reckon with. She would defend her beliefs through every type of accusation no matter how true they were. As much as I hated to admit it, Amira's quick responses fueled a part of me I hadn't known.

It was free will and debate.

I didn't agree with her religious beliefs, but she argued so fiercely and strategically that I had been lost for words. I admired her bravery to stand up against me like that.

Sighing, I spotted a lake up ahead, feeling a flood of relief wash over me. I needed a minute to sort through my conflicting thoughts. I had seen Amira when I first moved in and I remembered how different she was. How she acted like an ordinary American teen does, finding her way through life.

But why is she different from the rest? What makes her special?

When I reached the lake, I heard sobs. I looked around until my eyes landed on one beautiful creature. It was Amira. Tears streamed down her golden cheeks like a waterfall, her body was shaking as she heaved deep breaths to calm herself.

What happened?

I walked a little bit closer to her and I saw her eyes and gasped. The hidden emotions in them started to show themselves, but I couldn't read them.

"Amira? Are you alright?"

She looked up at me with her lips trembling. My heart broke looking at her. Her cheeks were flush and damp with tears. Sniffling, she vigorously wiped under her eyes.

"I'm fine. Don't worry about me," she forced with a tight smile.

She was about to walk away, but I grabbed her arm. She winced the second I touched her. *What the hell?*

I pulled her arm towards me, pulling her sleeve back and saw bruises, dark and tender. "Who did this to you?" I asked, harshly. I may have had different beliefs than her, but it didn't make me completely heartless to a girl who needed a shoulder to cry on.

My chest ached, seeing her pain-ridden eyes with a mixture of fear and heartbreak. This was the same girl who matched my fervor in argumentative debates, the same girl who challenged me in a way that no one had ever dared, and here she was completely shattered beyond recognition.

She pulled her arm back and looked back at me. "Nothing. I just hurt myself," she said calmly.

"That's bull. I know you're lying. Why were you crying, and why do you have bruises?'

"Nothing happened. Just leave me alone," she mumbled.

"Amira—"

"I'm sorry but I have to go," she whispered, running away.

I called after her, but she disappeared. *What the hell?* Something about this girl had me going for her, and had me feeling sympathy for her. That high school fight became a lost memory as I tried to search for the reason of her distress.

I didn't even know why I cared for a girl associated with a terrorist religion.

She's not a terrorist. She's different. My inner thoughts contradicted.

Yeah, right. They were all the same. They tricked people with their amicable ways, and pounce when someone's guard was down. After all, that was exactly what happened at the school where I came from.

CHAPTER 5
Just the Beginning

AMIRA SARKER

I was on lunch, talking to my friends as if yesterday never happened. I was very good at concealing my feelings. I didn't want to burden my friends with my problems when they were going through their own. Plus, it felt nice to forget about yesterday and enjoy myself.

"*Theo James* is so hot. I'm not joking," Meredith gushed.

I raised my eyebrows. *Theo James* was the actor who played *Tobias Eaton* in *Divergent.* I admit he was cute, but I wouldn't go crazy about it.

"I swear you are too obsessed with him. You barely know the guy for heaven's sake!" Lucy laughed.

"I agree. Sure, the guy is cute, but not crazily hot," I said.

"Oh, shut up. A girl can dream," Meredith playfully glared.

"Hey! Telling people to shut up is my thing!" Tasneem exclaimed.

"Oh whatever. Everyone tells people to shut up," Lucy remarked.

"Yeah, but the way I say it, is way cooler," Tasneem argued.

Tasneem and Lucy continued their silly argument. Meredith and I just laughed at their comebacks. I noticed that one member of our group stayed silent, and looked as if she was in deep thought about something. Aria, who was sitting next to me, was looking across the room. I followed her gaze, and saw her looking at Mark's table.

He was laughing with his friends with a girl seated right next to him. She touched his biceps, twirling her hair, and giggling at whatever he says. Mark didn't seem to realize her obvious attempts at flirting.

I looked back at Aria. Her once electric blue eyes turned stormy and were glistening, clouded with hurt and betrayal. I grabbed her hand which seemed to get her attention.

"Talk to him," I whispered.

She rubbed her eyes to rid the tears. "He really is losing interest in me, isn't he?" she asked, broken.

"I can't say, but if he does, it's his loss. You're an amazing girl. You have a kind and pure heart. You're selfless in your deeds, and you do your best to become a good person. If he doesn't see that, then he's an idiot. Talk to him about it, and see what he says," I told her softly.

She nodded her head, but kept her head down. Her light brown hair covered her face. I saw a tear slip on her hand and I squeezed it in reassurance. My heart was aching in pain for my friend of many years.

"Some guys aren't worth the tears," I said.

I gazed around the pantry, and my eyes landed on Damon. He was wearing a plain shirt with jeans, an outfit too casual than I expected from him. For a guy who had a whispering rumor about a major fight, I expected more of a bad boy look; wearing a leather jacket, driving a motorcycle. Damon was full of surprises.

I really hoped he forgot about yesterday, but only *Allah* knew. Damon was staring at his food, picking at it as his mind waivered. He seemed lost in thought about something. I turned my eyes away from him, and paid attention to what my friends were saying.

Damon was just another boy; he isn't worth my thoughts.

*   *   *

Lunch was over and I was walking to my science class. Science was my favorite subject. It always fascinated me, especially how the body worked. Human health was interesting. Maybe that was why I wanted to be a doctor or a biomedical practitioner. Organisms and microbiology really heightened my interest in learning their complexity and their ability to regenerate easily, only if the cells were healthy. *Allah's* creations were indeed perfect and beyond amazing.

As I was walking, Damon ran up to me.

"Hey," he smiled.

"Hi," I replied.

"Are you going to tell me what happened yesterday or not?" he asked, seriously.

"Nothing happened," I responded, firmly. I was hoping that he forgot about yesterday.

"Don't give me that crap. If nothing happened, then why were you crying, and why were there bruises on your arm?" he asked with raised eyebrows, like he was challenging me to tell him otherwise.

"I hurt myself really badly," was my simple reply. I thank *Allah* that I didn't stutter. It wasn't a lie. Not exactly. I pushed Tanwir to his limits, so part of it was my fault.

He gave me the 'are-you-kidding-me' look.

"A likely story," he remarked.

I shrugged.

"Tell me the truth now. What happened? I know you didn't hurt yourself. Did someone hurt you physically? I want to know. Are you in an abusive relationship?" he demanded.

"I don't know what you're talking about."

"The hell you don't. You know exactly what I'm talking about, so I suggest you spill the beans," he retorted.

We walked into the classroom together, and were the only ones at the moment. Placing my stuff on my desk, I turned to him with my most expressionless face.

"There are certain things in life that are meant to stay under lock and keys. It's my personal life and I suggest that you," I said, while pointing at him, "stay out of it."

"I'm trying to help you," he said with a determined look in his forest-green eyes.

"Why? Why do you care so much about it?" I asked.

"Because... well because," he paused, shifting on his feet uneasily. That same tension coiled around him it seemed, immobilizing his train of thoughts. "Well… I'm not quite sure."

I was shocked. The new guy treated me his friend! "Well, I don't need your help," I scoffed, taking my seat. My next words flew out without my consent. "I doubt you'd want to help a girl you deem incapable in her beliefs."

Offense crawled over his features. "Hey, we don't have to agree on every little thing. I'm not a heartless person, Amira. You can trust me."

"It's not a matter of trust."

He sighed. "Damn. Why do you have to be so secretive?"

"Secrets are meant to stay hidden," I smiled tightly.

"You are a mystery behind eyes, Amira Sarker," he grinned, slowly easing the tension away. It seemed like he was warming up to me.

I felt my face heat up at the comment and I thanked *Allah* for my tan skin. It was harder to notice my blush, which was a trait many would wish to have.

I watched, as Damon engaged in a conversation with some of the other guys. His eyes suddenly gleamed with newfound brightness and luminosity which occasionally landed on me. Lost in my own world, I didn't notice that my science partner, Anna, came and took a seat beside me.

"Are you blushing or is that just makeup?" she asked while squinting her eyes, looking at my face closely.

"When do I ever wear makeup in school?" I answered back with a question.

"The great Amira Sarker has actually blushed for the first time in forever. Who's the lucky guy?" she asked.

"No one."

"Liar. Someone has set their eyes on you, huh?" she winked.

"Oh, shut up. That's not true," I laughed.

She just grinned and wiggled her eyebrows at me. I was about to tell her to quit it, but the bell rang and cut me off. Everyone took their seats, and our teacher began the lesson.

"Today we are going to start with the research presentations. First up is Anna and Amira," she announced.

"Ms. Lyon, I need to log into my email to open up the power point since I saved it online," I said.

She nodded her head and I got up with Anna, following behind me while Damon sat near the computer. I quickly logged in and opened up the presentation, ignoring his burning gaze on my back.

* * *

I arrived home, and placed my stuff on the counter. Walking over to the sink, I washed my hands, and saw Mum putting a bowl on the counter.

"It's macaroni and cheese, so enjoy! The kids are about to wake up. If you need anything, I'll be downstairs. Oh, and when you're done with your homework, come and help me take care of the kids," she said, and headed downstairs.

Mum was a babysitter. She ran a family day care so we all pitched in to help. She made a daycare out of our basement. It was like a child's dreamland down below.

I grabbed the laptop, and checked my email while eating my food. It had been a long day. Damon kept glancing at me in all our classes together, and no matter how hard I tried to ignore it, I just felt even more hot and bothered. His sudden act of kindness had painted his personality in a different light.

He was willing to put our differences aside just to help me. As much as I'd like to ignore it, my body felt warm and fuzzy like I rested upon a cloud of loving embraces.

Sighing, I opened up my Google chat, and saw something that made my body freeze.

damonwinters@gmail.com would like to chat with you.

CHAPTER 6
His Messages

AMIRA SARKER

What the heck? Is it really Damon? I didn't know his last name, but it could be him. If it is, then how did he even get my email to begin with? I never gave it to him. After thinking for a few moments, I replied.

Me: *Who are u? And how did u get my email?*

It couldn't really be Damon. It just couldn't. It didn't make sense. No boy had ever, and I mean ever, gotten any of my personal social media accounts. I'd always turn them down or never even answer.

Damon: *It's me. Damon from school. Ya know? We're partners for history. And I saw u type in ur email in science.*

So, it is him. Why would a guy like him be talking to me through chat?

Me: *Stalker much?*

Damon: *XD well yeah. I mean this way I can annoy u when ur at home 2. I forgot to bold their names here.*

That made me smile before mentally hitting myself. What was wrong with me? Talking to the opposite gender in such a playful manner is *haraam* (forbidden), yet I feel so tempted to. *Shaytan* (Satan) makes the forbidden seem attractive when it really wasn't. *Allah* told us to stay away from these things, so why am I going to do it? Why should I go against my Lord and His commandments?

I really did want to talk to Damon though. I guess I felt something for him. *No. Stop. This isn't right.*

Damon: *What r u doing?*

Maybe if I keep the conversation from getting playful, it wouldn't be so bad.

Me: *Doing my homework.*

Damon: *Ur such a nerd dude. Live a little.*

I snickered. I had the perfect comeback for that one.

Me: *Oh yeah, I should totally forget about my future and become a bad girl with no future -_-*

Damon: *Ur still a mega nerd.*

Me: *I would rather be a nerd than a dumb bimbo duhh.*

Damon: *U make a compelling argument.*

Me: *Don't I always?*

Damon: *I wouldn't go that far, genius.*

Me: *Thanks for the compliment.*

Damon: *U always seem to trap me like this, don't you?*

Me: *I wouldn't be Amira if I didn't.*

Damon: *Guess ur right.*

My heart rapidly thumped against my chest and I had no idea why. Here I was, ignoring my assignments and to-do-lists, simply because I was too distracted by a boy and his messages. The same boy who insulted me too, nonetheless. *Honestly, what is wrong with me?*

Me: *Oh my. The great Damon I-don't-know-ur-last-name admitted defeat. Shocker.*

Damon: *My last name is Winters. My email username kinda gave that fact away.*

Me: *Well, how was I supposed to know that?*

Damon: *It's called using ur brain, idiot.*

Me: *I am not an idiot! How dare u?!*

Damon: *I dared myself.*

Me: *If anyone is an idiot here it's u, playboy.*

Damon: *Playboy? Yeah real original.*

Me: *Y thank u. I do try.*

Damon: *XDDD*

I smiled. It was fun talking to him. Who knew he was such a weirdo? I couldn't help but feel a little guilty though. I knew I wasn't supposed to do this. Heck, I never even had a conversation like this with the opposite sex. I didn't have any males on my contact list. *Why is Damon on it then? Why couldn't I just ignore him?* I was praying to *Allah* that whatever these stupid butterflies in my stomach were, they should be gone soon.

There was also a matter of his previous inhibitions toward me. Not knowing what compelled him to spark a conversation with me; I wondered if there really was more to be explored when it came to the curious case of Damon Winters. His kindness proved that there was more to him than his arrogance and negative perception with Muslims.

Damon: *U there???*

Me: *Yeah.*

Damon: *So, do u wanna tell me what happened that day when I saw u crying?*

I sighed, not this again.

Me: *I already told u.*

Damon: *U told me a crap of a lie. Tell me the truth.*

Me: *I did. Deal with it and move on with ur life.*

Damon: *Y don't u trust me enough to tell me?*

Me: *It's not about trust.*

Damon: *Then what?*

Me: *It's personal.*

Damon: *I hate u.*

Ouch. Well, that hurt.

Me: *Just because I won't tell u about my personal life? Ur crazy.*

Damon: *I hate u. I hate u. I hate u.*

Me: *Fine. Whatever. I already knew u hated me.*

Damon: *What do u mean? I was joking. I don't hate u.*

Me: *It seems like u do.*

Damon: *I really don't.*

Me: *Whatever. I have to* go.

Damon: *Bye :(*

I logged off. I leaned back against my chair and sighed. *Why am I even talking to him?* I knew it was wrong. *Allah* said not to even go close to *Zina* (unlawful sexual intercourse). I wasn't going to have sex, but talking to him casually was wrong, and might even lead to something like that one day. I shivered, praying that it would never happen.

Realizing that it was getting late, I prayed *Isha* (night prayer) and went to bed. That night, I wondered if talking to Damon would really lead to something more.

* * *

After praying *Fajr* (dawn prayer), I walked downstairs and found Mum sitting and drinking some tea. Desi people loved their tea. They couldn't function without it. I shook my head at the thought.

"Morning, Mum. Where's Baba?" I asked, as I kissed her cheek.

"Oh, your father went to work early today. If you want, Tanwir can give you a ride to school since it's all wet outside," she said.

I felt like all the blood in my face dried out. I didn't want to talk to Tanwir, but I knew I couldn't avoid him forever.

I sighed. "Okay. Only if he'll take me though."

Mum nodded. "Tanwir! Come down here!" she yelled.

I heard a groan followed by heavy footsteps coming down the stairs.

"What?" he asked, sleepily.

"Take your sister to school."

"Can't she just walk going there?"

"It's all wet outside. Just drive her there."

"Fine," he said. Tanwir turned to me. "Hurry up and eat, tubby".

I was already dreading the fact that I would be trapped in a moving vehicle with him.

Save me, Allah.

*   *   *

We drove in silence. The tension wasn't thick like what Damon and I had at the library before; in fact, this silence was comforting in a way, knowing that Tanwir would not confront me about that night. I saw sadness lurk his eyes whenever I saw him, but it seemed like we promised to never talk about what happened, upon witnessing the destruction it had caused.

Sometimes, secrets were better left untouched. Nothing ever harmed people from not knowing or understanding.

I finally decided to break the ice. "So, what's up?"

"Are you really asking me that?" he answered.

"Just trying to make small talk," I muttered.

"Well, you suck at it. Try something else to make small talk."

"Since you think you're so good at small talks, why don't you start it?"

"Alright, fine. Do guys stare at you in school?" he asked seriously.

My jaw dropped. He thought this was small talk. "Wait what? I said small talk not big talk," I spluttered out.

"So, guys do stare at you?" he said slowly with a hint of anger.

"What? No! Of course not!" I exclaimed.

"Good. I thought I was gonna have to beat someone up."

"Typical brothers," I mumbled, under my breath.

He glared. "Oh, shut up. Get on with your life, tiny."

"I'm not short. I have a pretty good height, you know," I argued.

He pulled over in front of the school.

"We'll discuss this later. Now get out. I wanna get some sleep before going to college."

*   *   *

As I was walking to my locker to prepare for the first period, Damon ran up to me with his black backpack hung over his shoulder, and a stack of books in his arms. His tousled brown hair stuck up from all over the place like he had spent a night of endless tossing and turning, yet his eyes remained a bright evergreen.

"'Sup, cover girl," he smiled.

"Cover girl? You're so lame," I said, as I rolled my eyes.

"It was way better than playboy."

"It totally was. You *are* a playboy," I scoffed.

He placed a fist over his heart. "I am offended," he acted with a fake hurt.

I stuck my tongue out at him which only made him chuckle at my childish antics. Speaking to Damon without our differences hanging over our heads like bullet targets, felt so surreal compared to when we first met. Although I knew about his fight, I tried my best to not bring it up. I didn't tell him my secret, and he didn't have to tell me his. It was a silent pact.

As we were talking about our project, Maya walked into our conversation, bursting our dreamlike bubble.

"Hey Damon," she purred, as she twirled a strand of her hair.

Damon looked at her with a disgusted expression. "What do you want?" he grumbled.

"I thought we could hang out tonight," she said while glaring at me.

Whoa. Bratty attitude much?!

"Sorry, I'm busy tonight," he told her.

Maya's face turned red. "Don't tell me you've gone soft already?"

I was about to say something but Damon protectively stood in front of me, and beat me to it.

"Watch your mouth, Maya. She has done nothing to you. Stop picking fights when nothing concerns you," he spat out angrily.

She stood shocked, fumbling for words. "Do you know you're defending a Muslim right now? Or did you get brainwashed, too?" she questioned, sparing me one nasty glare.

Damon froze like an iceberg had crashed upon him, stuck in a moment of time, where for a split second he had defended me. He had his prejudices and I never properly addressed them after the library. We both pretended as if that moment never happened. When Maya pointed out his stance, I felt certain that Damon would now ignore me for the rest of the year. Our conversations wouldn't change a stoned heart in an instant.

He straightened his spine, his chin slightly jerking up, as he stared down at her blankly. "Amira is... my friend. This has nothing to do with religious beliefs," he said with a passive voice. Without waiting for her to respond, he turned to me. "Come on, Amira. We have a class to go to."

I followed him, reeling in shock. He had established our friendship not only to Maya, but to everyone around us. Damon had spoken the words with such ease that it was hard to believe he was the same guy who claimed I was blinded by my religion.

"You didn't have to do that. I could have handled it," I said, approaching our class.

Today was our presentation day, but I was still too curious. "But why did you do it? You don't even like me?"

He shrugged. "Friends can have differences, too. But I still don't like your beliefs, so don't get any ideas."

I only smiled.

CHAPTER 7
Gym Class Horrors

AMIRA SARKER

Once classes were over, I decided to head out to school immediately until Aria stopped me in my tracks.

"Amira!" she called.

I swung my backpack on my right shoulder, and turned around to face her. "Yeah?"

"I was wondering if you wanted to hang out. I have a lot of stuff in mind, and you're like the first person I go to for advice," she admitted, sheepishly.

I felt pride at her words, but I didn't want to brag about it and be conceited. It was nice knowing that I could give good advice. I just didn't want to think of myself better than everyone else because I probably wasn't.

"Oh, well… sure. I'll call my mom, and tell her I'm going to your house," I said while reaching for my phone in my pocket.

"Cool, I'll be waiting outside my car. Meet me there," she said.

I dialed Mum's number, and she answered on the third ring.

"Assalaamualaikum."

"*Waalaikumasalaam.* Mum, I'm going to Aria's house for a while," I said, already knowing what her reaction would be.

"What? No! It's not right to be going to someone's house on a school night."

I rolled my eyes even though she couldn't see it. Mum was very protective of me. She wasn't quite fond of the idea of me hanging out at a friend's house for too long. I understood why she was all jumpy about it. Girls lied to their parents to hang out with boys where she grew up, and a whole lot of "things" happened after that. Anyway, she trusted me, but not other people easily. She trusted Aria though, but it's her motherly nature to question me.

"We need to talk about some things, so I'm going to meet up with her at her place. If it gets too dark, Aria will take me home."

"What are you girls going to talk about?" she asked, suspiciously.

Even though I understood her reasons, it didn't make it any less annoying to my teenage mind. *Oh Allah, grant me patience.*

"I don't know. She just wanted to talk and hang out. Don't worry though, Aria is a good girl. You know that," I persuaded.

She sighed. "Alright. Just don't forget to pray."

"Okay. *Assalamualaikum.*"

"*Waalaikumasalaam,*" she replied, hanging up.

I slipped my phone back into my pocket. I started to walk towards Aria's car. As I neared Aria's silver vehicle, I saw Damon chatting with his friends outside of his black car. He casually leaned against its frame; his arms crossed over his broad chest, as he threw his head back and laughed, a deep, sensual rumble that delivered shivers down my spine.

His emerald green eyes lifted up to see mine, locking our gazes. I wasn't sure where we stood with each other on terms of friendship. Regardless, I hesitantly lifted a hand to wave, offering a small smile.

He only nodded in acknowledgement before tuning into his conversation again, instantly smiling at whatever his friend had said. *Ouch*, I thought with a slight wince, *he could have at least waved back. He's acting like we're strangers to each other.*

We were strangers though. Sure, he defended me once, but that didn't mean anything. Nothing could melt a frozen heart like Damon's. He decided to close the shutters on being open-minded and hearing me out when it came to religious explanations. He established that we were "friends," however; friendship came in many different forms. Judging from how coldly he dismissed my wave, I wasn't very high on his friend chart, probably just above the thin line of being an acquaintance.

I sighed. Boys were a waste of time, and I was a fool for dwelling too much about it.

There is a reason why Allah says to lower your gaze. Easier said than done, but I still have to try, I thought.

*   *   *

We were seated on Aria's bed. We had just finished our tedious homework questions before we collapsed on the bed, allowing schoolwork to slowly drain our will to be productive again. After a couple of light-hearted conversations, Aria began to confess her worries.

"I really like him, Amira. I never really felt this way about a crush before. Could this be love?" she asked me.

Love. That was a thing that I've been yearning for. When I was younger, I even dreamed about having my future spouse until now. There were all these stereotypical concepts of love. Many people thought that love was making out, touching, and a whole lot of sexual actions. They threw the word 'love' around like a toy, messing with another's feelings like it was a game. It was absolutely disgusting and demeaning.

Love was supposed to be someone who would always be there for their significant other, and support them through their good times and bad times. They wouldn't be perfect, but they still accepted their flaws. That person was not only a lover or spouse, but also a best friend.

"Well, that depends. Are you only attracted to his body or looks? For example; you guys mostly just flirt when you are together, and you enjoy his presence because he's always touching and kissing you," I said.

Aria thought for a while before responding. "Actually, we haven't had a lot of big make outs. We kiss and all, but we mostly just talk and hang out. It's not really an intimate kind of sexual relationship like most people at our school do. I just like talking to him, but of course I like it when he kisses me. I mostly like his presence because he brings out a lot of good in me," she smiled at the thought.

"Then, it looks like you might be in love," I grinned.

Her smile fell as her gaze lowered, eyes brimming with the misery of a one-sided romance. "But he doesn't love me," she whispered.

I scooted closer, wrapping my arms around her. "You don't know that just yet," I tried to reassure her.

"He doesn't seem to notice me anymore or want to hang out. I might be in love with him, but he probably just thinks of me as an average girlfriend who he doesn't love. I don't even think he likes me anymore."

"Shh. I know he's been acting like a jerk lately, but guys are like that. They don't know how to express their feelings. I'm sure he does like you a lot."

"It's like I don't know him anymore," she mumbled.

I pulled away from her. "Hey, just talk to him. If he doesn't feel the same, then he is an idiot. Don't waste your time giving love to someone who doesn't deserve it. Okay?"

She nodded her head.

I checked the time, realizing that it was getting late and I still had to pray. "I got to go, but you know I'll always be here if you ever need a shoulder to cry on," I smiled, voice as soft as the roses that decorated her bedroom wall.

She sniffled. "Thanks, Amira. I don't know what I'd do without you."

"Don't mention it, but I seriously need to go. I might miss my prayer," I rushed in a single breath as I practically ran out her bedroom door.

In a Muslim's life, prayer would always come before everything else. It was the very essence of a Muslim soul, the sustaining portion that kept a stable mind away from insanity.

Salah (prayer) was supposed to help ease, and relax a Muslim through the most difficult parts of his or her life, and I relied on my prayers heavily. Hearing Aria talk about her love life falling apart made me wonder about the day that I would meet the perfect man for myself, the man *Allah* created to be paired with me. A part of me longed to be like Aria or any of the other high school girls.

But the other part knew that all good things came with patience.

*　　*　　*

"Alright guys we have a special announcement to make," Baba said to us.

We were eating dinner when Baba decided to tell us something important. I wondered what the special announcement was, but my mind faded back to Damon. *Why am I even thinking about him?*

"What?" asked Tanwir.

"My parents are coming to America from Bangladesh. They got their visiting visa," Mum smiled.

I blinked, coming to terms with what my mother had just said as Damon's image evaporated from my eyes. "Wait, what?" I questioned, confused. "They're coming here?"

Mum nodded excitedly.

I felt my lips curl upwards, mirroring my mother's happiness. My grandparents and I were separated by an entire ocean and continent. Visiting them was costly, so we only went back every couple of years. It hurt to not see my family during Eid or on the weekends like other kids. I would only hear their voices over the phone, but now I would finally be able to hold my elderly grandparents in my arms, hugging them close like I did as a child.

I hadn't seen *Nanu* (grandpa) or *Nani* (grandma) for four years. Nanu had a broken hip from falling off his bike, so he could barely walk now while Nani had bad hearing. It would be a blessing if they came, we could actually help fix some of the burdens they were given.

I glanced at Tanwir, noticing his expressionless face as a dark scorn traced his lips, cold and unforgiving. He wasn't exactly on socializing terms toward any part of the family.

"When are they coming?" Tanwir asked while keeping a straight face.

"In a few weeks. *In Sha Allah* (If Allah wills it) when they get here, we can get them better medical attention," Mum replied, and seemed to be studying Tanwir's face. Just like me, she was trying to figure out his emotions.

Tanwir abruptly stood, and without saying another word, he ran up the steps, slamming the door shut behind him. The crackling of the harsh noise crinkled across the thin air, and my parents were exchanging worried looks with one another. I felt my own concern claw at my chest. *Why did he seem so upset?*

*　　*　　*

My parents assured me that they would handle all the immigration paperwork, so I didn't have to worry. My only focus should be on my grades, my father had said, and that was exactly what I did.

I was in our gym class, prepping for a huge chunk of my grade. The plan was to get graded on how well our field hockey form was and our ability to communicate game strategies with our teammates. The coach paired the groups together. We needed a team of six, and of course we were not allowed to pick our own team members.

"Team Seven is Damon, Maya, Alexis, Priya, Ryan, and Amira," Coach Jackson announced.

Oh great. I'm stuck with the two barbies, Maya and Priya.

They were always flirting with any guy. It sickened me at how these girls threw themselves on any guy, as if seeking validation through their lustful comments while kicking those below their status even lower into the muck of high school hierarchy. They were the queens; we were the peasants.

Ryan, the other teammate, was a pretty smart guy. He was that quiet mysterious kind of guy in school. I'd seen him play in sports before and he was incredible! *Watch him be a famous athlete in the future.*

Alexis and I were good friends. She was a hipster. She had good taste in music and was always up for a challenge. She supported her friends through anything, no matter what the situation was. *At least I have her,* I thought with relief.

"Alright guys, we are going to crush the other teams," grinned Damon.

We all nodded. Maya and Priya started whispering and giggling with each other. Damon and I sighed. Those girls seriously annoyed me. Ignoring them, I turned back to Damon with a raised brow.

"So, what's the plan? Who's on defense and offense?" I asked.

Damon scrutinized us before speaking again. A competitive gleam entered his evergreen eyes, igniting a drive towards victory, and a burning need to crush those who opposed it. He was playing for a win. "I'll be on offense with Ryan. Alexis, Priya, and Maya can be defense. Amira will be goalie."

"What?" yelled Alexis and I simultaneously.

"Why do you guys get to be on offense while we're stuck on defense with *them*?" Alexis whispered the last part.

"That's because we're awesome and way better at this," smirked Damon.

I was about to protest, but Ryan beat me to it.

"Dude, we can have alternating players. Alexis and Amira can switch positions. Alexis can help with offense. Amira, you can switch your goalie position with Maya or Priya and then become an alternating player. Only come when we make eye contact with either one of you. Got it?"

Alexis and I nodded. I put on my hockey mask and gloves. Alexis and Ryan were talking strategy with each other while Maya and Priya gossiped, checking their nails. We were up against a pretty decent team. They had two good players, so we had to be alert for them. As I was thinking, Damon came up to me.

"Nice mask," he teased.

I glared even though all he could see were my narrowed eyes, since the mask covered my face. "Oh, shut up. This is very uncomfortable."

"I can tell."

As I was adjusting the mask, I couldn't help but feel his stare on me like he was a scientist observing an experiment. My body heated to a degree from being under such meticulous eyes.

I cleared my throat. "Staring is rude, you know," I mumbled.

"I wanted to talk to you."

This perked my interest. "About?" I pressed.

He sighed, stuffing his hands into the pockets of his Nike sweatpants. "Listen about that day in the library, I'm sorry if I offended you."

To say that I was shocked was an understatement.

"I really did mean what I said to Maya. You are my friend, even if I don't agree with how you choose to live your life."

"Wow," I said, "I wasn't really expecting an apology after all that."

He shrugged. "I figured it sounded really cold-hearted of me to treat you like that, and I'm sorry. I may not like a lot of your people-" he started.

"You mean Muslims?"

He winced at my disappointed tone. "Yeah," mumbled Damon, "but can we just agree to put our differences aside now, at least for the sake of this game?"

I smiled. At least he apologized for being a jerk. I didn't expect groveling, although, it was a favorable scenario. "Agreed."

Damon visibly brightened, eyes lighting with elation when we made our truce. "By the way, you look good today," he winked before catching up with the rest of our teammates to get into position.

My cheeks heated with a blushing ember.

Coach Jackson blew the whistle, and the game started. Team Three was better than I thought, and from the looks on Alexis, Ryan, and Damon's faces, they were shocked as well. Regardless, they continued with their plan.

Team Three managed to use passes to make sure Damon and Ryan couldn't get the hockey puck. Ryan made eye contact with Alexis and she nodded as she went straight to them. Alexis stole the puck, and passed it to Ryan. He caught the puck, and protected it as he made his way closer to their goal, passing the puck to Damon.

I was in my goalie position and couldn't see anything because Maya was in front of me. I mean, I was crouching down and her tanned legs were blocking my view. I looked up at her.

"Do you know how to twerk?" she asked me.

"I should answer this question because..." I trailed off.

She rolled her eyes, and turned to Priya. "I wanna show you how *I* twerk," Maya said to Priya.

Oh no. I didn't know if she realized she was in front of me, but she started shaking her bottom around, moving her hips as if a drum had thumped to the rhythm in the background. My eyes widened, instantly closing. *They were supposed to be on defense, not shaking their behinds!*

I heard Priya laugh. "Maya, you're making her uncomfortable."

"What do you expect from *virgins*," she huffed before walking away and leaving us defenseless.

I didn't say anything since I had a million rude things to say to her, but all I did was narrow my eyes at Maya, a lethal glare staring like daggers at her back. Just then the puck went into our goal, giving Team Three a point. I exhaled a frustrated sigh.

"What the hell?" Damon yelled.

He ran up to me with Ryan and Alexis following close behind.

"How did the puck get passed you?" demanded Damon.

"I was distracted," I mumbled quietly. *By the two annoying girls you forced me to work with.*

Damon closed his eyes, pinching the bridge of his nose. Ryan turned to Maya and Priya, who were snickering at me. "Why were you two not doing your job as defense?" he asked.

"We were, but that terrorist was being a bad goalie," Maya scoffed.

"What did I say about calling her a terrorist, Maya?" Damon growled.

Maya rolled her eyes.

"You two weren't doing your jobs. You were busy twerking in front of Amira," Alexis glared.

Priya gasped. "How dare you?" she screamed while getting in Alexis's face.

I stepped between the two. "Stop it! I'll take the blame. I was distracted when I should have been focused. I'm sorry!" I yelled in an attempt to get the girls to calm down.

"Guys, we need to score so we get a tie. Come on and this time, everyone should focus on their jobs," Ryan said, giving the girls a pointed look.

I sighed, walking back to the goal. I was disappointed in myself for letting my team down. The guilt ate at my flesh, as a cloud of darkness loomed over me. I had a duty to my teammates, an important role in their plan, yet I screwed it all up. I was too focused on my disgust and had easily been deterred from my position. I might have cost my team not only their victory, but their grade as well. Before I could get to the goal, a hand clasped onto my wrist.

"Cheer up, it wasn't your fault," Damon whispered softly, making sure only I could hear him.

He let go of my wrist, and went to stand next to Ryan. A weird feeling erupted in the pit of my stomach again. He comforted me. Damon barely ever comforted or apologized to anyone, even if he was a jerk to them.

CHAPTER 8
Playful Tease

AMIRA SARKER

As soon as I got home, I checked my Google chat. Damon didn't chat with me. I felt a tinge of disappointment in my chest before I mentally slapped myself.

What the hell is wrong with you? Stop craving for his messages, nitwit!

I closed the laptop, and went upstairs to my room to do homework. As I finished half of my work, Tanwir barged into my room.

"Sup Tubby," he said, as he laid himself on the bed. Tubby was a nickname he always called me.

"What do you want?"

"Nothing," he said while getting comfortable on my bed.

"Then get out. I'm doing homework. Now leave," I commanded, as I tried pulling him off.

"But I'm too comfy," he playfully whined.

It was funny how he could go from the worst to the best. He sure was bipolar.

"Get off, you pig," I grumbled.

"Nah. I'm enjoying myself here."

"Mum! *Bhaiyah* (brother) won't get off my bed and he's annoying me!" I yelled.

Either she didn't hear or she didn't want to deal with us.

"You annoy Mum too much, Tubby. Give the woman a break."

"Look who's talking? You're the one with bipolar moods," I stated, as I crossed my arms over my chest.

"I have my reasons."

"Care to share?" I asked.

"Nope. Stop pulling me," he ordered.

I didn't stop. This time I took a pillow, and started hitting him with it. He kept dodging my hits, laughing at my weak attempts.

"Get a life, you weirdo," I glared.

"I have a life. You don't," he smirked.

"Get off my bed!" I whined, as I pulled at his legs. He didn't even move!

"Hey! What's going on in there?" Mum yelled, as she walked into my room. She saw the scene in front of her and sighed. "Grow up you two! You act like five-year olds."

"He started it," I said, as I pointed a finger at Tanwir.

"She's disturbing peace, Mum. Make her shut up," he groaned while placing a pillow on his ears.

I gasped, exaggerating how offended I was of course. "*You* came into my room and *you* lay on my bed. *You* disturbed the peace not me."

"Both of you stop it! Tanwir, leave your sister alone. Amira, respect your brother," Mum scolded us before walking out.

Tanwir got up. "See ya, tubby," he said, as he left.

"Jerk face," I mumbled to myself.

When Tanwir left my room, I felt ease crawl back into my heart, witnessing how easygoing he was today without bursting in rage. He was unpredictable at times, but today, his mood was different and oddly reassuring. On a normal day, we would have bickered nonstop until eventually someone left either in tears or in rage. Today neither of us erupted like volcanoes at one another, which was a step towards progress.

Then again, maybe I was over analyzing the whole situation.

I decided to check my Google chat on the laptop. As I expected, Damon sent me a message. I felt excitement rush through my veins. Geez, I needed to calm myself down. *He's just a guy, nothing special.*

Damon: *I can't believe they did that 2 u in the gym.*

Me: *I know right! So messed up. But eh, I've seen worse.*

Damon: *Can I ask u a question?*

Me: *Sure.*

I wondered what he wanted to ask me, anxiously waiting for his reply.

Damon: *Y do Muslims have to have an arranged marriage?*

I knew what he was thinking. He thought Muslims were forced into a marriage with a complete stranger. I shook my head. Society made Islam sound like a prison when it really wasn't.

Me: *It's not the type of marriage u think. It's not a forced marriage. It's actually haraam (forbidden) to force a person into marriage. The girl or guy has the choice to refuse the proposal. And the point of not dating is so we stay pure for our spouse and vice versa. We believe that self-respect for ourselves mean not flaunting or using our bodies in inappropriate ways.*

Damon: *Y does a girl or guy have to follow that guideline?*

Me: *Allah knows what's best and for those who keep themselves pure, it's rewarding for both parties. A man and woman are each other's first, so the experience is different. It's really about self-respect. For example, I don't waltz into any guys arms because a lot of people are just looking for casual relationships with no indication towards a married life, which is why Muslims wait.*

Damon: *But u still have to marry a stranger. That's dumb.*

Instantly, I felt my defensive side rise. I didn't like it when people insulted my religious beliefs and Allah's word, but I understood where Damon was coming from. He, like many others, didn't know the truth behind everything. It made them blind towards Islamic teachings and a complete victim to falsehood.

Me: *Actually, the guy and girl meet up with each other in a public place to get to know each other before accepting the proposal and everything. There is a supervisor who makes sure things don't go out of hand with the guy and girl when they meet up so, they r not completely strangers.*

Damon: *Oh. Well, I still prefer to have my sexual freedom. It's the twenty first century after all.*

Me: *You do have a reputation that precedes you.*

It was silent for a bit, and I wondered if I took it too far with the subtle comment.

Damon: *Well, at my previous school, I did have a lot of friends with benefits, but idk, I'm trying to focus on just school now. My mom would kill me if I didn't.*

Me: *Y would she do that?*

Damon: *My mom wants me to get into a good college before my dad gambles everything for addiction. I'm basically relying heavily on some scholarship. Money and fooling around with girls aren't going to give me that.*

His dad was a gambler. I couldn't believe it.

Me: *Your father gambles?*

Damon: *Yeah. He does it behind my mom's back sometimes, but it's usually not too much money.*

Me: *Damon, I'm so sorry you have to go through that.*

Damon: *Don't worry about it. It's no big deal.*

Me: *But that still doesn't explain why ur so tense around me.*

Damon: *U know the rumors of a fight make an educated guess.*

Me: *I don't want to believe in all rumors.*

Damon: *I don't want to talk about it then.*

I didn't need to be told twice to drop that conversation, but it still made me wonder. What did that Muslim student do to Damon for him to be so untrusting toward any Muslim? Questions flew around my thoughts like a flock of birds but I didn't act upon my inquisitive nature, it was just too personal.

The only way I could show Damon that not all Muslims were horrible was by being a good Muslim myself.

Me: *What r u doing?*

Damon: *Watching Pretty Little Liars.*

Oh, my *Allah*. Guys watched *Pretty Little Liars* too? I thought girls watched it mostly because it was all about how pretty girls find themselves in the middle of a murder mystery.

Me: *OMG I love that show!*

Damon: *Lol yeah, it's pretty great. My little bro and I watch it 2gether.*

Me: *U never did tell me about ur family. How many siblings do u have?*

Damon: *I'm the oldest. I have 2 little brothers. One is in 13 and the other is 10. The 13-year-old watches it with me.*

That was so cool. I wondered if they look like Damon. I never would have guessed that he had two younger siblings.

Me: *Cool. I just have an older brother. He's so rude. Like today he just sat on my bed and wouldn't get off. I even pulled him! And then he said, "I disturbed peace." Can u believe that?*

Damon: *XD Lol I can believe that. U do disturb peace.*

Me: *Ur so mean!*

Damon: *Don't u know it sweetheart ;)*

Me: *What's up with u and ur nicknames. I have a name ya know?*

Damon: *But I like teasing u.*

I didn't know why, but that comment made my stomach clench. I shouldn't feel this way. It never ended well.

Me: *Another reason on y ur mean.*

Damon: *U know u love it.*

Me: *Y are you suddenly being so nice to me?*

Damon: *To be honest, I felt a bit guilty after that library day. I was out of line.*

Me: *Really? What brought the sudden change? No offense, but you always seems so cautious around me like I'd bomb you or hurt you.*

Damon: *That's because I believed one day that you would.*

Me: *Should I be worried?*

Damon: *Probably not. U don't seem threatening.*

Me: *I'll take that as a compliment, but u know that not all Muslims are terrorists, right?*

Damon: *I don't know what to believe anymore.*

Me: *What do u mean?*

He was quiet again for a brief moment as if he was contemplating whether or not to tell me what really happened in that fight, something that other students didn't know. In that regard, Damon and I weren't that different. I had a secret I concealed my whole life, a trauma that I hid behind my writings or my complete focus on my schoolwork.

Sometimes, I wondered why death had taken such an important person away from me, why I was meant to suffer while others lived happily. Death didn't discriminate against who it takes, but I knew it was all a test from Allah, a test of patience and healing, a test of my faith.

Damon: *It's nothing. Just personal things honestly.*

Once again, I dropped the issue, not wanting to pry.

Me: *Thanks for the compliment and the apology today. I really appreciated it.*

Damon: *It's all part of the charm sweetheart.*

I rolled my eyes. He was such an arrogant jerk. Here I was, offering my gratitude, and he was praising himself instead.

Me: *Ur too cocky for ur own good.*

Damon: *Am not.*

Me: *Yeah u r.*

Damon: *No, I'm an irresistible member of society who has the ability to make a girl weak at the knees.*

Me: *Whatever playboy. I know the truth.*

Damon: *XD*

Me: *I need to go to bed. Bye.*

Damon: *Sweet dreams sweetheart ;)*

I giggled a little, before I stopped myself. *What was wrong with me?* He was bad news, a walking disaster. Falling in love was something I refused, especially to a boy like Damon. He was not someone who would learn about Islam or go through all the processes just to get married. I mean, the guy wasn't a big fan of Islam to begin with.

Although, the thought that he would never like me did sting a little, but I felt relieved. I had nothing to worry about. *I'm sure he'll get bored and stop talking eventually.* That however, did nothing to ease the guilt that began to blossom in my heart.

Sighing, I rose from my seat. *I'm sure praying would ease my anxious mind.*

*   *   *

I was about to sleep after I praying, but got thirsty. I walked down the stairs, and stopped as I passed Tanwir's room. He was most likely downstairs fixing a midnight snack, and being the annoying sister I was, I went inside his room.

I was looking at all the cool books he had and the heavy textbooks, completely astonished at their size. My fingers gently brushed against the side of his shelf before my eyes landed on a small stack of notes on his desk. I looked closer and saw that they were notes to himself.

Remember to pray on time.

Not sleep late.

Work on controlling anger.

Maybe he wasn't as bad as my parents thought he was. He was at least trying. Didn't that count for something in the eyes of *Allah?* Sometimes people had a bad attitude on the outside, but their relationship with *Allah* could be closer than it seemed. Not many people remembered that and just judged the person straight on.

I put his notes back, walking back to my room with a small smile playing on my lips, as pride bloomed within me. My thirst was forgotten. Tanwir wasn't a bad person. He was trying to change. He just needed a push and I was going to be the one to deliver it.

*   *   *

I was in English class with Damon where we were typing up an essay about a book we read in class. My brain hurt from trying to formulate complex sentences and finding perfect examples. We only had one class period to write the whole thing and I was determined to get a high grade.

Of course, Damon sitting next to me was nothing but pure distraction.

"Hey, check this out," Damon said, nudging me.

I turned towards his computer screen. He finished his essay and was playing on the computer. It was a game called *Happy Wheels*. He purposely killed his players by flipping them over. I cringed in disgust.

"Ew, Damon. That's gross," I winced, as I watched the guy lose his arms.

"It's just a game," he chuckled.

"It's still disturbing, to say the least."

"You're just too innocent," he shook his head with a smile.

"At least I have standards in games," I playfully glared.

"Whatever you say, sweetheart," he winked.

I gave him a blank stare before heading back to my essay. I was almost done. After writing the last paragraph, Damon nudged me again.

"What now?" I snapped.

"I'm bored. Entertain me," he pouted.

"Damon, get a life."

"I have one and it involves you," he winked.

"Flattering," I said, sarcastically.

He leaned back in his chair and stretched. His shirt outlined his muscles, and for a moment, my eyes gazed at the flex of his muscles before I turned away, feeling my cheeks heat up. Shaking my head, I looked back to my screen, and printed the essay out. I was about to get up and get it, but Damon stopped me.

"I'll go get it," he said, as he got up.

"Thanks," I murmured.

Damon came back after a few minutes. "Looks good. You're very talented at writing, Amira," he said while handing me my paper.

"I guess."

"No, really. It's really impressive."

"Thank you," I smiled.

I walked over to one of my friends, Alexis, who wiggled her brows at me. Damon was still distracted by the game, finding more creative ways to kill off the characters which disgusted me even more.

"Want to explain how Damon and you got so close?" she asked playfully.

My eyes went wide. "No, we're not. He's just an annoying jerk that won't leave me alone," I scoffed.

"I'm not annoying. I'm charming," Damon's deep voice spoke behind me.

I jumped. "What in the world do you think you're doing?"

"What does it look like I'm doing? I'm defending myself. And here I thought you were the smart one," he teased.

"Damon! Go away!" I exclaimed, frustrated, flopping down in my seat.

"Nah I like it here," he smirked, as he leaned against the wall.

"Damon," I growled through gritted teeth.

"Amira," he grinned.

"I give up. Forget it," I sighed, falling into my chair.

"I think I'll be going now," Damon said.

“Oh, so now you leave?” I said sarcastically.

He just chuckled, walking towards his friends. I turned back to look at Alexis, whose grin reminded me of Cheshire Cat from *Alice in Wonderland*, surprisingly widening when my scowl deepened.

Alexis patted me on the shoulder. “And you wonder why I tease you about Damon,” she laughed.

“Whatever,” I muttered.

I took a glance at Damon. I didn’t feel any romantic feelings for him, but could I guarantee that it would stay that way?

Oh Allah, please protect me from Shaytan’s (Satan) evil doings, I silently prayed.

CHAPTER 9
A Blast from the Past

DAMON WINTERS

I was walking toward my locker when a voice stopped me.

"Damon Winters!" she yelled.

I felt a smile creep its way onto my lips. I turned around to face her.

"Yes?"

"You're such a jerk. You know that?" she glared.

I had teased Amira too much during English. "It's okay, sweetheart. We all have those moments," I winked.

Her glare became even more intense. If looks could kill, I would be dead by now.

"Moments? You just teased me for the whole hour! And they were all about my handwriting. I told you it gets worse the longer I have to write!" she huffed.

I laughed even harder.

Amira looked confused as hell. "What?" she asked, placing her hand on her hip.

"I can't take you seriously. You look adorable when you're mad."

She rolled her eyes. "Bye, Damon."

"No! Wait! Amira, come back!" I called out, but she already walked away.

I shook my head. That girl was something else, whether it was good or not, I still hadn't decided. We had gotten closer over the days, finding similar interests among each other. We still didn't talk about religion as much because it was a sore topic for the both of us. I wasn't sure if I could let myself trust another Muslim again, but Amira definitely made me doubt my previous inhibitions.

She had given me no reason to fear her. My guard was still up in case she did, and I refused to allow her to crumble my walls through her kindness and generosity. She hadn't judged me when I told her about my father's gambling addiction, nor had she spread rumors to me. Instead, Amira confronted the inner demon that lurked inside, desperate to find answers to her unanswered questions.

I wasn't sure if I was ready to share that part of my life yet. Not until I knew the past wouldn't repeat itself.

"Yo, Damon!"

I closed my locker, and found Tye walking down the hall towards me. He was one of my new friends at this school. Coming from a Japanese family, his parents were quite strict, especially when my mysterious rumors had whispered into their ears about that 'fight.'

I wasn't even sure if 'fight' was the correct term. It was a piercing betrayal, deliberate and concise. He meticulously planned for those guys to jump me. He wanted to see me suffer.

My abdomen churned painfully at the thought.

"Hey, man," I greeted, tying to ease my tense mind.

"Why are you so busy all of a sudden? I see you always on that phone of yours," he asked, wiggling his brows in suggestion.

I had been spending a lot of time talking to Amira on Google chat. I could never get bored of her. Every conversation was different, a window to her world, and a door to her heart. Slowly, I felt as if I was being pulled to her through an invisible string. She was alluring like a goddess from all of those mythology books, the ones who lured men with their beauty only to crush their hearts in the end.

I still had doubts about her.

"Nope, just this one girl."

"Who?"

"This girl," I simply replied, not wanting to dwell on the subject any longer. "What brings you to my locker, anyway?"

"So, the guys and I are heading over to Jacob's place to play Call of Duty. Wanna come?"

"Sure."

"Now about this girl. What does she look like?" he asked, grinning too widely for my liking.

Tendrils of qualm circled around me from his questions. *Why was he so persistent about her?* "She has pretty good looks," I said, swinging my backpack over my shoulder. I stared into his small eyes. "Why do you ask?"

He shrugged, blowing the black strands away from his eyes. Tye was a typical Asian, who put all his efforts into his schoolwork. His pale skin was whiter than mine which made him almost looked like a vampire from *Twilight*.

I pushed down the anger that was bubbling deep in my chest. Tye's questions about Amira irritated me; she wasn't an object of sexual satisfaction. Amira was worth more than that; she was meant to be respected and adored.

"I can't believe you're talking to a girl and not actually trying to get laid."

I frowned. "I told you I'm focusing on school now."

"You never did tell me what happened at your previous school."

"Trust me, it's not worth knowing. What's done is done."

Tye had gone silent, eyes squinting at me like I was a puzzle he had yet to solve. Everyone knew that there was something 'badass' about Damon Winters, but they didn't know the full story of why I had gotten transferred, while the other kids involved in the incident were expelled. Not all Muslims were terrorists, but not all Muslims were saints either. Some were as malicious as history itself, people who reveled at another's misery.

*   *   *

An hour later, I had beaten the guys in the game.

"Damon, you suck. I can't believe you won again," Thomas groaned, another close friend of mine. His tousled auburn hair knotted even more during the duration of the high stakes game.

I grinned. "You snooze, you lose. Deal with it."

"Hey, I'm going to fix up some snacks. Anyone want to come?" asked Jacob, standing up from his beanbag chair.

Thomas and Tye ran to the door. *Those pigs*, I thought.

Jacob and Thomas quickly built a friendship with me, knowing it best not to bring up my previous school. Thomas was a blue-eyed devil in my eyes when it came to video games. I had never seen someone so dedicated and bloodthirsty for a win against me. I always did love a competitive match up.

On the other hand, Jacob was a lot calmer and more composed. With his curly brown hair and pasty skin, he was a girl magnet, a gentleman from another time period despite his preppy style. Jacob came from a religious Jewish family, so he didn't endeavor in female company when he could be studying religious texts instead.

Jacob turned to me and said, "Set up the game. Rematch."

I set up the game and sat back down. *I wonder what Amira is doing.* Pulling out my phone, I saw that she sent me a message.

Amira: *What did u write for the English hw?*

I rolled my eyes. Of course, she was doing homework. That little nerd.

Me: *U already know that I don't do homework this early.*

Amira: *Ur useless to me then.*

Me: *Ouch. That hurt my ego :(*

Amira: *And I should care because......?*

Me: *Because I'm ur friend.*

Amira: *What else u got?*

This was what I loved about Amira. She was fresh with conversations. She knew how to talk to someone in a way that never got boring.

Me: *Harsh. I thought we had a thing.*

Amira: *Ur dumb.*

Me: *Says the one in the lower classes.*

Amira: *Hey! We r in the same classes! Just different periods!*

Me: *Oh right. Ur worse XD*

Amira: *Damon!*

Me: *Amira!*

Amira: *Ugh why r u so difficult?!*

I couldn't help, but smile. I loved getting her angry. I was going to reply, but the guys came in.

"Alright, let's kick some butt!" Tye yelled, settling himself in front of me with a sandwich in hand. "I feel good about this game."

"No way! Food first," Thomas argued.

"I second that," I replied.

"Tye wasn't kidding when he said you use your phone a lot now," Jacob muttered.

We all turned to him.

"What?" he shrugged, as he took a seat next to me.

"His eyes are glued to his phone." He's probably right.

"I was just texting someone," I shrugged, trying to get Jacob's suspicions off my back. "Why are you guys so up on my case about this?"

Tye and Thomas exchanged glances with one another. Tye was biting his lips as if he was nervous to bring a subject up again. His eyes sought assistance from Jacob, who sighed knowingly.

Glancing at all of their expressions, I wondered what ailed them so deeply that they were nervous to even bring it up. A pit of dread settled in my stomach. I knew they were going to confront me about something I wouldn't want to talk about.

Jacob cleared his throat. "Are you talking to that Muslim girl again?"

"How would you know?" I shot back a bit too aggressively.

"Well, it was an educated guess. You have been getting close with her lately."

I scrunched my eyebrows in confusion. "I fail to see why this is a problem."

This time, Thomas spoke. "Given what happened at your previous school, are you sure you're okay with talking to her?"

I nodded.

None of them seemed convinced. All three of my friends saw nothing wrong with Muslims. They had been around them since elementary school, but they didn't know all Muslims. They didn't know the bad apples of the bunch and the horrid intentions that lurked behind their eyes.

Amira's different, a voice in my head reminded me. *She's not like the rest. You enjoy her company.*

"Look, Damon," began Jacob gently, "I know what happened at your old school was horrible-"

"You don't know the whole story," I cut off.

"Regardless of that, something bad happened to you. A Muslim hurt you, but if you're going to get involved with Amira, you shouldn't hurt her in revenge. Not all Muslims are like that guy form your school," he continued, dark eyes searching for a way to get through to me.

The shutters of my mind shrieked, covering my eyes with memories of my old friend, Luqmaan. He betrayed me. He destroyed my trust. Maybe if he didn't jump on me that day, things would have been different. I could have trusted people easily, could have told my parents everything from beginning to end. No one knew the whole story, no one but me.

"How would you know?" I croaked into the silence that engulfed us. My voice was hoarse as if the memory hurt too much to think about.

Jacob smiled tightly. "Just because one Muslim commits a crime doesn't mean they're all the same. People are flawed, Damon. Some are worse than others."

I opened my mouth to argue, but Tye had beaten me to it.

"We're just telling you to be careful. Amira's a nice girl. If you're going to make her feel bad about her religion, then maybe it's time to abort that mission, and spend time with other Muslims. Isn't that why your mom brought you here? To learn how to be more accepting?"

I felt myself shrink into the beanbag at the mention of my mother. She had so much on her plate especially with my father's gambling addiction, yet she was still determined to raise me to become a better person, a more honorable man. She would have said the same thing.

"Yeah," I mumbled. "I guess you're right."

Perhaps my friends were right. I may not trust Muslims yet, but I shouldn't shun all of them, especially someone as sweet as Amira. We made a pact to keep our differences aside so we could get along for all our assignments together, but I was slowly starting to regret that decision.

CHAPTER 10
Taqwa

AMIRA SARKER

A conscience of guilt pricked against my soul, gnawing and biting down on the tender parts of my heart like the guilt would slowly suffocate me. Damon was becoming too addicting to ignore and lovable to hate. There was more to Damon and his life than all those rumors.

Rumors seemed like nothing but a loose string in a ball of yarn. They had no meaning, no significance when there was a far greater story beneath it all. The truth is, Damon and I had quirky conversations and at times borderline flirtatious. He would tell me about his day and I would tell him about mine from the most exhilarating to the most frustrating parts.

We shared countless laughters together, but deep down I knew it was wrong. I was allowing myself to become vulnerable to him, an action I swore off the day that death kissed the lips of a loved one. I didn't want to disobey *Allah*, yet here I was continuing to speak to Damon as if it was no big deal.

My family and I sat in a car, heading out to dinner. I had automatically agreed to come because I needed some time away from my phone screen and laptop. I needed to get away from Damon and his addicting personality. My parents had noticed my odd silence, occasionally calling my name to make sure I was still a functioning human. It was common knowledge that parents had a sixth sense when it came to their children, and mine were no exception to that rule. My mother and I, sat in the backseat, and her hand reached to grab mine, squeezing it tightly.

Even Tanwir could sense that something wasn't right about me.

Instead of prying, my father did what he usually thought was the best option. He told us a story, one with Islamic significance. It was more like giving us an Islamic lesson.

"Do you guys know what Taqwa is?" he asked.

"Isn't it like fear of *Allah*?" I questioned, hesitantly.

"Not entirely. There's more to it. There's not an exact word in English or any language that can describe Arabic words. Taqwa is a high state of heart, which keeps one conscious Allah's presence and His words. It motivates one to do righteous deeds and stay away from the forbidden," said Baba.

"What do you mean, Baba?"

"Let's say that you are watching T.V. Then the *athan* (call for prayer) goes off, but you're still watching the show. The show you are watching is bad. Your mind is not telling you that it's wrong and you don't feel guilty. That's how you know that you don't have Taqwa. But, in this same scenario let's say that when you are watching this bad show, your mind goes off in alarms. Telling you that it's wrong and keeping you aware of Allah's presence. Then you feel guilty. That means you have Taqwa. Do you get it?" Baba asked Tanwir and me.

"Yeah," we both said.

I looked at Tanwir. He looked like he didn't care, but his fearful brown eyes showed otherwise. They were swirling with guilt as he seemed lost in his own thoughts.

Did I have Taqwa? I mean, when I do something bad and it's against the teachings of Islam, I feel pretty guilty. I thought about it for a while.

When I talked to Damon, I did feel pretty guilty. I needed to stop talking to him. As the days went on, my feelings for him got stronger, and I didn't see him as "just" a friend. It scared me.

I had no idea what possessed me to even start talking to a boy who was weary of my community, and my heart didn't abide to logical reasoning. It had its own eyes, its own ambitious needs. It lurched for a man who was out of my reach, who couldn't understand why I chose to believe in *Allah*.

There was no happy ending to this tale. We were too different and our personalities surely clashed against one another. *Allah* was my priority because without *Allah* I had nothing. Without *Allah*, I was alone. My spirituality meant more to me than a high school romance.

I knew that if I was patient, then *Allah* would reward me for it. There was a man out there for me, one who would marry and cherish me till the day I die. Damon would not be that man.

I shook my head. *He doesn't even like me and here I am thinking of what if I had a future with him. What is wrong with me?*

As I stared at the blurry scenery while our car zoomed through the interstate highway, my thoughts continued to wander to a green-eyed boy. I never had this problem before. What was this test? How could I control my heart?

I'm going to stop talking to him starting tomorrow. Just today and that's it, I promised myself. Deep down, I knew stopping it altogether would be much more complicated than it seemed.

CHAPTER 11
Temptation

AMIRA SARKER

I was watching an episode from the anime *Fairy Tail.* It was the weekend and this was my idea of chilling, until my phone beeped. I fished my phone out of my pocket, and saw I got a message from Damon. I hadn't talked to him in three days, trying to stay true to my promise.

Damon: *What did I do wrong? Why are u ignoring me?*

To reply or not to reply, I wondered. The answer to not reply was ringing in my ears, but another voice in the back of my mind begged me to take the risk. The thing about risks was that sometimes they weren't worth it. I cringed as I thought about what to do.

Come on, Amira. You've been strong the last few days. Stay strong, I reminded myself.

Giving myself motivation, I quickly put my phone down and continued watching *Fairy Tail,* but I kept on glancing at my phone throughout the episode. My fingers were itching to open all of the new messages, to resume our light-hearted conversations, and to dig deeper into who Damon Winters really was.

No. Stop it, Amira.

My brain kept nagging me and the temptation was so strong. It was an alluring force that beckoned me like a siren's call.

The phone was pulling me to it. My shoulders started to weigh a ton, and tension was coiling around my neck, forcefully pushing me toward sinful desires.

Oh Allah please give me strength to walk away.

"Amira! Come help me!" Mum called from the kitchen.

I jumped up. *Thank you, Allah. This should keep me busy.*

"What is it?" I asked while I entered the kitchen.

"I need you to cut the onions for me."

I glared at the onions. Darn. Those things always make my eyes burn. I slumped my shoulders and sighed. It was better than fighting a lure to my phone.

"Alright," I answered.

"Before you do those, call your brother to come downstairs," she said while preparing the chicken.

I ran upstairs to his room and knocked, but got no answer. I knocked harder. "Open the door! Mum is calling you!"

I heard a low mutter as the door swung open, revealing less than pleased older brother. His disheveled black hair stuck out from all sides, deep purple bags lined under his eyes, and his lips were set in deep frown. "Knock lightly next time," he growled.

"Well, maybe next time you should open the door and not be lazy," I mumbled.

Tanwir turned his head toward me slowly with a murderous look on his face. "What did you just say?"

"Nothing," I chirped quickly.

He gave me one last dangerous look before walking downstairs.

I let out a breath that I didn't realize I was holding in. *Are brothers supposed to be this scary to sisters?* I always read stories about how the older brother was always that overprotective, an awesome guy who wasn't moody and loved his sister to pieces. He even showed it to her!

May Allah guide him. He may not have been the best all the time, but there were his good days. Some kids probably had it worse.

I entered the kitchen and was met with Mum and Tanwir arguing. I silently watched, frozen in my spot.

"Why should I bring the box inside? It won't break!" he yelled.

Mum sighed. "Tanwir, it's raining outside. What if the wind blows the box down?"

"You're being paranoid," Tanwir snorted.

"Please, Tanwir. I would feel much better if you just brought it inside."

"No! It won't fall," he protested.

Mum huffed. "Fine, I'll get it myself then."

Tanwir was raging.

Was it wrong of me to just be standing like a statue? I finally decided to cut in. "Tanwir, just bring the box inside. Her hand is hurting for cleaning so much."

He gave me a blank stare. Now, he was getting me angry. She had been cleaning all day, and her hand wasn't supposed to be sore from all the work. Honestly, what planet did he live in? I managed to keep my anger intact.

"Come on. Just bring it in," I persuaded.

He sighed, and brought the box in from across the street while muttering a few unpleasant words. One of our neighbors had gotten rid of daycare items since they were retiring, and they sold the items to my mother. After Tanwir brought the boxes in, he went back into his room, slamming the door so hard that I swore the walls cracked in fear.

"I can't believe him sometimes. I truly hope *Allah* guides him," Mum said, resuming her cutting.

I chose to stay silent. Tanwir wasn't all bad. He just needed support, even if he acted like a jerk.

*   *   *

Damon: *Stop ignoring me! I'm sorry if I said or did anything to hurt u.*

My fingers were twitching by now. To walk away from temptation was not as easy as it sounded. I put my phone down quickly. *I won't do it. I won't. I know this is wrong for me, so why am I craving for it?*

I couldn't help but want the forbidden, just to experience a little bit of what other girls experienced with their crushes.

Ya Allah, these thoughts I was having were very dangerous. I felt like I might actually do something *haraam* (forbidden) which had never tempted me before. Small things lead to bigger things.

I glanced at the phone. Time seemed to have been going slower. I started to feel anxious. I couldn't sit still; again, the tension was killing me. Anxiety was spreading through my system like a virus. Finally, I picked up the phone and responded.

Me: *Sorry I was busy.*

I groaned. After two days of staying strong, I gave up because he was pleading for me. I wanted to slap myself.

Damon: *Y did it take so long?!*

Me: *Sorry.*

Damon: *It's fine. At least u responded.*

Me: *Yeah. What r u doing?*

Damon: *Being forced to dance.*

Me: *XD Do tell the story behind that.*

Damon: *My cousins came over and forced me to dance. I hate dancing. It's just not my thing.*

Me: *Same here.*

Damon: *One day I'm going to force u to dance.*

Me: *U wish hun ;)*

Damon: *Did you just call me hun?*

Uh oh. Probably shouldn't have sent that.

Me: *I say that to everyone.*

Damon: *Not to me.*

Me: *Well ur a jerk.*

Damon: *Then y did u call me 'hun' hmm???*

Darn, he got me. How would I fix this mess now? Come on, Amira. Think.

Me: *Because.*

Damon: *Because what?*

Me: *Because it slipped out.*

Damon: *Sure it did.*

Me: *Hey! Watch it buddy! I'll hurt u physically.*

Damon: *Nah. Ur too nice for that.*

Me: *Nice?*

The chat went silent again as Damon typed and deleted whatever he was trying to express, before typing again. The seconds felt like hours, anticipation building around the serenity of our conversation. It was light, soft as a feather, our bond strengthening. My faith screamed against it, yet I couldn't stop myself.

It was such a feeble excuse, but it was the truth.

Damon: *Yeah. I've told u before that u seemed different from the rest.*

Me: *U mean other Muslims? I thought we were going to leave our differences aside.*

Damon: *Can u blame me? We're friends, Amira, and friends don't run away from their flaws.*

My defensive side rose. How could he call my testament to *Allah* a flaw? My religion was not a flaw. Islam had always been perfect, and it always will be. People were not, but that didn't give Damon any right to criticize Islam the way he did. *Allah* knew us best. After all, He was our Creator, the Lord of the universe.

To me, my relationship with *Allah* meant everything. There was a different love when it came to religion. As my mother had always said, people always leave. No one could stay with us forever because one day, they would be called back to *Allah*. They would be in their graves, but *Allah* would be timeless. He alone could comfort all my worries away, and I knew that no matter what, I would always have *Allah* on my side.

Even if everyone was against me, *Allah* would never leave. Believing in *Allah* was a strength. It was faith.

Me: *My religious beliefs are no flaws. They made me who I am, they shaped my character.*

Damon: *That came out wrong. I didn't mean to offend u, it's just hard to suppress that side of me.*

Me: Why *do u suppress it?*

Damon: *I may or may not have had a bit of an awakening. I value our friendship and all our witty conversations. I don't want to make u feel uncomfortable in my presence.*

Me: *I think ur more uncomfortable in my presence. I assume it's because of ur old school?*

Damon: *Seems like I'm really labeled for that, huh?*

Me: *Ever wonder how Muslims feel when u label them because of one incident?*

Damon: *Not really.*

Me: *Next time, think about it.*

Damon: *That school thing is a lot more complicated than just that, Amira.*

Me: *Talk about it to someone. Talking helps.*

Damon: *How would u know?*

Me: *It helped me.*

Damon: *Had it rough?*

Me: *Yeah.*

Truth be told, I never really talked about it with anyone. My family kept our sadness concealed from the world around us. We helped each other through the tough times, but there were still days where my mother would spend entire nights mourning or my father would pray long hours just to ease the pain that still lingered in his heart. After all these years, we were still healing.

Damon: *I got to go. Parents r fighting again.*

Me: *Sorry to hear that :(*

Damon: *See ya at school.*

When we were done, I felt the small pricking of guilt. I sighed; *I can't believe I failed a test from Allah.* I couldn't resist the temptation. I couldn't stand not talking to him and it had only been a few days. Talking to Damon was a bad habit that I couldn't get rid of, and it seemed like there was nothing I could do to stop it. No matter how hard I tried.

CHAPTER 12
Temptation

AMIRA SARKER

My alarm started beeping. I groaned as I gazed at my clock. It was *Fajr* (dawn prayer). My eyes still felt drowsy, maybe five more minutes would be okay. My head fell back against my soft fluffy pillow.

I hugged the comforter closer to my body. As I felt sleep overwhelm me again, a voice in my head wouldn't stop alerting me of prayer. I tried to ignore it and immediately felt the guilt creep up on me.

I jolted up. I was a Muslim. I was made to worship *Allah*. I mean, how was I better than a non-believer if I didn't pray my daily prayers? I could go to sleep right after.

I dragged my feet to the bathroom, and made *wudu* (ablution), then brushed my teeth. I yawned as I pulled a prayer mat out and wrapped a scarf around my head, and started my prayer.

*   *   *

I decided to stay up because I couldn't fall asleep. The house was quiet, only soft snores were heard while small birds chirped outside. They sang their morning melodies, awaking the world around them. I looked out my window, and saw the sun rising. Its orange color filled me with warmth.

"Beautiful. Isn't it?" a voice said behind me.

I turned around and came face to face with Baba. His beard was getting some gray hair in it. It saddened me how he and I got older. Soon he would be gone, and away from me. Baba walked to stand next to me as he stared out through the clear glass.

"I always found it spectacular on how only *Allah* could make such perfect creations. We, humans, try to recreate them, but tell me. Are they ever equal to this beauty?" he asked, looking at me with a soft gaze. "Do we ever appreciate life when it is beautiful?"

"I suppose not."

"Nothing is truly ugly in this world, Amira. Allah has made all his creations perfect. Always remember that," he said, as he turned around, getting ready for work.

I looked back at the sun. He was right. Only *Allah* could create such perfect things, not even humans could recreate it. It reminded me of the words that *she* used to tell me long ago.

From my father's light sniffles, I knew he was remembering his lost child again, his eldest, his once pride and joy. A void burned darkness through all of us, but we knew this was a time of tests. *Allah* gave those he loved the most difficult trials of faith, to test their limits, to see how far their faith in Him could go. *Allah* would never give his servants a task they couldn't handle.

This trial of mine was something I could handle as well. I just had to keep trying.

*　　*　　*

Damon: *I'm bored. Entertain me peasant.*

My jaw fell. This boy was always full of surprises. First, he was cautious and almost fearful of me; then he insulted me, and now he was as carefree as every high school senior. There were too many sides of Damon.

Me: *Excuse u? How dare u call me a peasant?*

Damon: *I dared myself. Now entertain me.*

Me: *Forget u.*

Damon: *What the hell is wrong with u?*

Me: *Nothing?*

Damon: *Never mind. Today my 13-year-old bro challenged me to a soccer match. Guess who won.*

Me: *Ur bro XD*

Damon: *Do u really think a 13-year-old could beat me? Come on sweetheart. Use that pretty little brain of urs.*

My heart did a little flip. *Darn the ways he makes me feel.*

Me: -_- *my brain is not little.*

Damon: *;) suuure.*

Me: *How did things go with ur parents.*

Damon: *They made up as always. A toxic relationship in my opinion, but that's what love does to people. They easily come back.*

Me: *It sounds like u don't trust ur dad much :/*

Damon: *I have trust issues, I digress.*

Me: *I feel like there's more to the story than u let on.*

Damon: *Nice deductive reasoning. Good use of that brain ;)*

Me: *Shut up.* R *u going to tell me the rest?*

Damon: *Honestly, there's not much to the story. My dad has always gambled. It's never been too much money, but it gets to my mom sometimes, and it gets to me.*

Me: *Understandable. You feel helpless, don't you?*

Damon: *All the damn time. It fucking sucks. My brothers don't even understand any of this, but I do. I've lived through it far too long.*

Me: *I'm sorry. I'm sure it'll all get better soon.*

Damon: *I hope so.*

Me: *I know so. I have faith.*

Damon: *In God? No offense, but that's pretty bull.*

I knew he wouldn't understand, but I wanted to share a special part of me with him, hoping it might ease some of his qualms about his family.

Me: *In Islam, we believe that Allah tests those that he loves the most. All this is part of a bigger plan, one that benefits us in the end. Sometimes, you just gotta have some faith.*

Damon: *That's a dead concept to me.*

Me: *I'm not forcing u to believe what I do, but that's a thought that helps me when I'm down. Maybe it'll help you.*

Damon: *Even after all the times I disrespected u, ur still looking out for me. How r u and other Muslims the same?*

I rolled my eyes. Repeating the same defense was getting tiring, but it seemed like my words had fallen to blind eyes. Repetition might be his only cure at this point.

Me: *U haven't met enough Muslims to really make a generalization like that.*

Damon: *Ur right. I haven't.*

Me: **gasps* is the great Damon Winters surrendering his pride to little old me? What a historic event, ladies and gents!*

Damon: *I've been doing that a lot with u, kinda freaky.*

Me: *I wonder why.*

Damon: *Ur quite the special one, Amira. I mean it.*

I smiled; feeling the warmth crawl up my cheeks till a prominent blush kissed the apples of my cheeks. He was so smooth, and I wondered if he even knew how he made me feel.

Even though I got the tingles and butterflies in my stomach, I couldn't help but feel a heavy weight on my chest. It was suffocating in a way. My heart felt heavy and tired like I had run a marathon, emulating the sluggish nature of my body. What was this feeling?

Could this be an effect of desire for a bad thing? I felt absolute discomfort at the moment. Instantly, I wanted to get rid of the feeling.

I looked at my clock. It was *Asr* (afternoon prayer) time, so I got up to pray. As I stood for prayer, I noticed something I didn't notice before. The discomfort I felt before started to slowly leave. I felt some sort of a calm state flow over me. I focused on my prayer.

The beautiful verses that slipped from my mouth sunk into my heart as I thought of the meanings of the verses I recited. This was what people meant when they said focusing on prayer would relax one's soul. I finished up my prayer, and felt fulfilled.

"Amira! Tanwir! Come on and eat so we can go to the airport!" Mum yelled from downstairs.

Oh, right. My grandparents were supposed to be coming today.

*　　*　　*

We were currently in the car, the only place where my father could confront us, and we couldn't run away.

The airport was an hour drive from our place. Tanwir and Baba were in the front seat, Mum and I were in the back as usual. According to Mum, people in the front were more prone to serious damage during an accident than in the back. She wasn't wrong in that regard.

"Baba, if a Muslim does something wrong because it fulfills their desires, and after doing the deed they feel discomfort; why is that?" I asked.

"Do you know about the signs of *Allah's* love?"

"I might, but could you explain it just in case?" I said.

"Tanwir, I want you to listen as well," Baba said, sternly.

"I'm listening," Tanwir mumbled.

"*Allah* says in the *Qur'an* that there is nothing more beloved to Him than the acts that he made obligatory (fard) which are the things that a Muslim must do. For example, the *hijab*, the five daily prayers, the fasting in Ramadan, etc., *Allah* made them fard because he loves these acts, and he punished us if we don't do it because he refuses us to drift away from Him. That's how you stay close to *Allah*. By doing those acts, we keep closer to *Allah*. A Muslim keeps doing all this until *Allah* begins to love him or her. Do you understand?"

I nodded my head.

"When Allah loves His servant, he becomes the ears that you hear with, the sight which you see with, the hand that you touch with, and the legs that you walk with. Do you know what that means? It means that your ears should only listen to good things. When you listen to something like pop music, you will feel discomfort. It is the same thing with the eyes, legs, and hands. When you do something that *Allah* disapproves with you feel discomfort. That's how you know that *Allah* loves you," he concluded, and I could only nod.

Does Allah love me? I thought as I leaned my head on Mum's shoulder. I gazed Tanwir, who had a distant look in his eyes, reflecting from Baba's words. I knew the words had touched him on the inside, and I felt proud. He really was trying to change. Maybe I could, too

CHAPTER 13
The River of Denial

DAMON WINTERS

Amira still hadn't responded to my last text. *Why won't she freaking answer me?* This girl was slowly becoming a drug for me, one that I needed more of everyday just to sustain myself. She was an addiction that I never wanted to overcome.

"Damon! I need help with the math homework," Tye whined beside me.

Tye was hanging out at my place, so we decided to finish some homework. I looked at his paper.

"The answer's four."

"You're a lifesaver, man," he grinned.

I chuckled.

"So, how's Amira?" Tye asked, as he wiggled his eyebrows. His eyes were a deep sienna with a healthy dose of mischief.

I gave him a blank stare. "How should I know?"

"Sure, you don't. No guy would spend all his time texting some girl if he wasn't interested in her," he snorted.

"Hey, I don't have to be romantically interested in her," I defended.

"Is Damon in a relationship?" my thirteen-year-old brother, Daniel, questioned as he walked into the room. Like me,

Daniel had my brown hair that created waves like the ocean on our head, but Daniel could go tan and I couldn't.

"I don't have a girlfriend!" I exclaimed. "How many times do I have to tell you that I'm just trying to focus on school right now?"

Daniel and Tye cracked up laughing, holding onto their stomachs as the tremors of ineffable contentment swarmed over their hearts, a gentle rhythm of guys enjoying each other's company.

I exhaled a deep sigh, realizing there was nothing I could say to save myself from the situation. As the boys laughed, I openly glared at them, crossing my arms over my chest in an attempt to look threatening.

"He really is blind," Tye chuckled.

"I know right," Daniel smirked.

I wished that I could slap them without getting in trouble.

"What are you idiots talking about?" I glared.

"You're denying a very strong affection towards this girl, dude," Tye said, patting my shoulder.

I rolled my eyes, pushing Tye's hands off me. "I don't roll like that. She's just a friend. Nothing more and nothing less," I stated in a confident voice.

"That's what you think," mumbled Daniel.

"That's what I *know*," I retorted

Daniel shrugged innocently, a smug smile playing on the corners of his lips, emerald eyes glinting like a devil planning a bargain.

"Get out, Daniel," I scowled.

He threw his head in a small chuckle, winking at me as he walked out the door, shutting it behind him.

Once he was gone, I sighed, sliding to the floor, leaning against the side of my bed. Tye sunk down next to me, offering a small smile to ease the annoyance that littered around me from their constant teasing.

The atmosphere between us was shifted by a gentle rush of wind outside my window. The blue curtains flowed, flying with effortless ease. I felt myself move with it, my mood immediately lifted from the stillness of nature.

I couldn't like Amira romantically. We were just friends, something that she made very clear to me. She was a Muslim, I had despised Muslims, hating the cruelty they brought to the world, and to me. It wouldn't make sense if I actually fell in love with one.

The irony of that situation would kill me. Guys like me didn't have to fall in love, especially with Muslims girls. I could not fall in love with Amira. It *wouldn't* happen.

"Hey, Damon?"

"What?"

"Why are so against the idea of liking Amira as more than a friend?" Tye asked, quickly shifting his gaze to the carpeted floors like he was uncertain of my response.

The question caught me off guard. "I guess… I guess it's just hard to overcome what Luqmaan did."

He scrunched his eyebrows in confusion. "Who?"

"Luqmaan," I winced slightly at the very mention of his name. "He's the guy who hit me first and started all this. He pretended to be my friend for *three years*, Tye. Three years."

"For what reason?"

"My connections with other people. Luqmaan was heavily involved in some shady things, stuff I shamefully participated in," I sighed with disappointment clouding over me. "I still can't believe what he did."

Tye nudged me again, smiling sadly. "Hey, man. You don't have to tell me everything. I know it must hurt."

"It does."

"But Amira and most of the Muslims at our school are nothing like Luqmaan. You came to our school for a clean slate, right?"

I nodded.

"Well, this is your chance, Damon. You don't need to keep hurting yourself with the past. It's time to move forward."

"I don't know how," I whispered a bit too brokenly for my liking.

"Stop all these doubts with Muslims. You're giving yourself unnecessary amounts of stress. I've lived by them my whole life, and yeah, there were bad apples among the community, but doesn't everyone have that?" he asked gently.

"I've never heard you sound so wise," I lightly joked, trying to lift the mood.

Type scowled. "Really? That's all you got from my deep, moving speech? Honestly, Damon, you give me senior depression."

I chuckled. "Thanks, Tye. It sounded exactly like something Amira would say to me."

"She's right, you know."

I knew Tye wasn't encouraging me to date her or anything because Tye and I knew well that Muslims didn't fool around in relationships. Either I was in it forever or for never. Tye wanted me to open my heart to the community just like my mother, but I wasn't sure if I was ready to.

I wanted to change. I wanted to be a man that Amira could be proud of, that my brothers could admire. I wanted to free myself from the chains of prejudice. I just didn't know how.

How could I trust those who have wronged me? They came from the same seedling of beliefs, yet contrasted in their practices. Luqmaan lied with such ease and poise.

Amira also plays that same role. This time, I was cautious. This time, it would be different. She may not be like Luqmaan, but she definitely wasn't off the hook. No amount of attraction could change that.

CHAPTER 14
The Storm on the Sea

DAMON WINTERS

Thunder roared outside. Lightning flashed throughout the room like harsh needles piercing against the window. The winds howled, whistling its dangerous tune to all those who dared to step in it. Animals scurried away into their hiding spots and I found myself distracted by the loud screeching from my window, the game in front of me was forgotten.

"You did what?" exclaimed my mother from the kitchen.

My head shot up. Daniel and I, were playing video games, up until we heard Mom's screams and shouts. The shouts were followed by a loud crash. I jumped a little. *What on earth was going on?*

We ran toward the kitchen. The screaming and crashing didn't stop as we entered the room. My parents had argued before, but none were as violent as this. There were never night piercing shrieks, only mild yelling or a couple of curses thrown around, but they always made up before the sun rose and streaked the sky in its brilliant rays of radiance.

Although I hated how easily Mom forgave him, I knew that I couldn't deny the longing I felt for my father to be just like other American fathers, ones who became role models to their children, ones who were always there, ones who brought out the best in me.

My father wasn't like that. He was distracted by money with constant unstable jobs, relying heavily on my mother.

The first thing I saw was Mom's tear streaked face. Dad was kneeling beside her, as she leaned against him on the floor.

Dad wore a tired look on his face. His hair was messed up, sticking out like static and stress mixed together. There were dark, deep purple bags under his eyes and his forehead was creased, lips thin from shame.

Mom looked broken. She screamed and thrashed against him, hitting his chest repeatedly. Her blue eyes were glaring ice shards at my father through her bloodshot tears and heart wrenching sobs. Her cheeks were flushed as she continued insulting Dad.

"Mom? Dad?" my ten-year-old brother, Percy, asked with fear in his eyes.

Through all the commotion, I didn't even notice that Percy entered the room. I stared horrified at my parents, and their eyes were not meeting ours. They were absorbed in the fire that had ignited between them, and their love was going in flames from the mere sight. Mom pushed Dad off her with a strong force, making him stumble back. She stood up and openly glared at Dad, clenching her fists at her sides.

"Would you like to tell the kids, or should I?" she seethed in distaste. Her eyes had an unusual flare to it. It was cold like an iceberg prepared for destruction. I've never seen such anger radiate from Mom ever before.

"Lauren, please—" Dad begged.

"How could you? Did you ever once think of your kids and their well-being? Tell me! Are you really that blind?" Mom screeched, pushing his chest.

Another clap of thunder echoed through the room as a hushed silence feel upon us. Mom's heavy breathing and choked sobs were all that was heard. I tried to speak, but I was frozen.

Fear overwhelmed me at my mother's state. I opened my mouth, but words didn't come out. My mind swirled with all the stupid things Dad could have done. I tried to move, but my limbs and joints stayed frozen to the floor. Dad looked at me, his pleading eyes made me snap out of my trance.

"Dad, what is she talking about?" I asked slowly.

Dad opened his mouth, but Mom beat him to it. "He gambled eight thousand dollars last night!" she yelled.

My jaw fell open as I stared at Dad. He had his head held down in shame, not able to face us after what he had done. The weight of his actions laid heavy on all of our shoulder. The force threatened to shatter the strength this family had built for years, cracking the thin glass inside us. After the shock wore off, my fists clenched at my sides as I felt my blood boil.

"What the hell, Dad? Why? Just tell me why? Damn it!" I practically growled.

"Damon, I didn't mean to," he reasoned.

Mom let out a humorless laugh. "Yeah right. You had full control of your actions. I thought you would have thought of your family first, but I guess I was wrong," she sneered.

I felt Percy tug my shirt. I turned to him, and saw he had tears in his green eyes. My heart instantly softened at this sight. He was terrified, paralyzed from the toxicity in the air that my parents had created, more importantly my father.

That God damned bastard.

"Daniel, you and Percy, go to your rooms. Stay away from the kitchen until this is sorted out," I ordered.

Daniel glared at me. "No. If you get to stay here, so do I."

I looked at him with a fierce expression. "Daniel, it wasn't a request. It was an order and I expect you to follow it," I said coldly.

Daniel was about to talk back to me, but Dad stopped him. "Please Daniel. Don't make this harder than it should be," he pleaded.

Daniel sighed and took Percy away. *Stupid thirteen-year-olds can't even listen to simple instructions*, I mentally huffed. I turned my attention back to my parents.

"Dad, I can't believe you did that. I agree with Mom. How could you not think of your family? Are we really not that important to you? Wow. What a great dad you turned out to be," I sarcastically said as I headed for the door. "Maybe next time you should think like a father and not an asshole," I said over my shoulder and then walked out.

I headed to my room, and slammed the door shut. *That asshat!* That man was supposed to be my father. I groaned in frustration. Dad just wasted so much money. *What are we going to do now?*

I felt anger build up inside me as I thought more about the situation. The sparks were burning within me, my mind was ripping the image of my father. There were no heartfelt memories, no sweet moments, no words; just a hollow black hole seemed to fill that void. My fist collided with the wall. I felt a burning sting on my knuckles, but I couldn't care less at the moment.

The surging flare crept up my body as I hit the wall with more force, letting all of my frustrations out of my system. I finally felt a terrible sting on my hand, but I kept going punch after punch, yell after yell, kick after kick, and I didn't stop till my body was completely drained of the poison my father had implanted within my heart.

I stopped punching the wall and looked down at my fists. My breathing was heavy and there was sweat trickling down my neck. My knuckles were red and swollen with a few blisters and blood was seeping from the busted skin. I slumped against the wall in defeat. No matter how long I punched my anger out, I knew that it would never erase Dad's mistakes.

A small buzz came from my back pocket. Reaching out to grab it, I unlocked my phone to see a message from Amira. *Man, how I wish I could hear her voice now.*

I wanted to hold her tight against my body, to feel her soft body mold perfectly against mine as I embrace her. I could see her breathtaking smile shining down on me. Sighing in content, my mind drifted off to the thoughts of her, needing to feel the warmth that I desired from her. How was it that the mere thought of her calmed my senses down?

Amira: *I am so sorry that I didn't respond. My grandparents were arriving today and I had to go to the airport. Again I am so sorry.*

She was so innocent and adorable.

Me: *Don't worry. I figured u were busy. Don't beat yourself about it.*

Amira: *Sorry I have this guilt meter thing inside me. If my mom asks me do the dishes and I refuse I feel so bad afterwards. It's how I was raised.*

Me: *ur too cute.*

She didn't respond for a while. My mind felt numb, no energy to even feel a slight inclination to her. I was desperate for a release, desperate for comfort, desperate for an escape from my torturous reality.

Amira: *Did u just call me cute?*

Me: *yeah.*

Amira: *oh.*

I could almost see her perfect lips form an 'o' shape. Leaning my head against the door, I closed my eyes with a smile. My tense back relaxed as I took deep breaths. Trying to ignore the tremors of fury, I focused on Amira. The voices outside my door erupted with harshness like a double-edged sword in an argument between two people who were supposed to take care of me, to maintain a stable home for me.

My world was crumbling and I was falling with it into an abyss of negativity.

Me: *how do u deal with the urge to punch someone until they black out?*

Amira: *well, I usually walk away from the scene and calm myself down before I react.*

Me: *I should just punch the bastard to get it over with.*

Amira: *What happened?*

Me: *My ever so idiotic father gambled $8000.*

Amira: *omg that's horrible!*

Me: *I know.*

Amira: *It'll be okay. Life throws things at us when we're not ready but it works itself out.*

Me: *how would u know?*

Amira: *bad things happened and r happening in my life. A lot of things happen, but u just have to be patient.*

Me: *What if I don't want to be patient?*

Amira: *Then I don't know what to tell u. Things won't always go ur way, Damon. I suggest that u learn the value of patience for ur own benefits.*

I slammed my phone to the floor, not appreciating the advice that she'd given me. *Patience? What a laugh!*

I had gone through hell and back. I had lived through an unstable household where my father's gambling was always a topic of discussion at the dinner table. I had gone through a backstabbing best friend, who spat slurs at my face as he repeatedly punch me, calling me an infidel who would never deserve love.

I believed him. Luqmaan was right.

Amira's words echoed back to me. *Patience.*

Could I really be patient? Would the results be better for me if I was?

Closing my eyes, I wandered myself searching for answers, for a way to help my family, especially my mother. I was her eldest son. She had sacrificed so much for my growth as a student and an adult.

Her own cries brought tears to my eyes. It tormented me, chasing my soul until the pressure's finally settled against my chest, clawing at me like a demon sent to take me away. I was blinded by my own doubts.

Why, Dad? Why did you hurt us?

*   *   *

Knock! Knock!

"Come in," I feebly mumbled from my bed.

My father's disheveled body stepped into the room. His dark silhouette against a soft moonlight highlighted his sunken eyes, red and tired like he hadn't slept in days. Slowly, I sat up with eyes glaring like daggers at him.

He awkwardly stood by the door, scratching his neck. "Could we talk?" he asked hoarsely. I only nodded, not trusting my voice.

Dad sat down on the edge of my bed with hands trembling, as his lips opened and close like he wasn't sure where to begin with his explanations. I'd heard so many excuses that I wasn't sure if he could create another one. They were all the same mistake, the same story, and it always happened *again.*

"Just tell me what I did wrong." I spoke into the silence with a dull voice from the pain I felt. "Why did you do it?"

"Damon," he began softly, "none of this is your fault or Percy's or Daniel's. It's all my fault. You share no blame in this."

"Yet, you still did it again. This time was worse, Dad," I croaked, staring deep into his eyes. "This time, you gambled savings away, money that was supposed to go to your children. How can you claim to care about us when you pull shit like that?" He was stunned and completely speechless.

"You can't claim to care for us when you don't care enough to stop your addiction. What is so important about gambling that you don't even think for a second about your family? Why do you insist on hurting Mom for some cash? Just be honest with me," I pleaded, gripping the bed sheets under the covers. "No more excuses this time."

"Damon… I —"

"No more excuses," I repeated, firmer than before.

He sighed, holding his temple as if the stress had shot a bullet through him. "I'm sorry. You're right. I should have thought about you guys. I should have been a practical adult with money, and I wasn't. You all deserve better than that. You deserve better than me, Damon."

"Just be my father. Be someone I can rely on."

Uncertainty lined his eyes like a pool of guilt and shame swirling in the same waters, reflecting his inner conflicts. "I'll try. I… I promise," he whispered with a hint of nervousness as if he was unsure of keeping it.

Somewhere deep inside, I knew the same story would replay again. This wouldn't be the last time. He knew it too. Dad was hiding something from all of us.

He was lying.

CHAPTER 15
Armed in Friendship

AMIRA SARKER

I walked into history class and was met by Damon. He was sitting on his seat, tapping his pencil on the desk. He looked bored as hell. I looked around the room, and saw that it was only us, a predicament I did not want. Trying to be as discreet as possible, I put my stuff on my desk quietly, walking out to get some water before class started.

As I leaned down to take a sip of the water, I heard a voice right next to my ear.

"Hey there, sweetheart."

I jumped backward and crashed into a hard chest. His arms immediately wrapped around my waist, steadying me. I turned around and saw Damon, his eyes gleaming down at me, making my heart beat faster. How was it that his eyes seemed to get brighter every day? The touch of his hands on my waist snapped me from my thoughts. *Allah* would not be pleased with me.

I glared at him, but was still tense. He just shrugged and let go.

"You know if you were less of a jerk, you wouldn't have to deal with such hatred from me," I said while crossing my arms.

He rolled his eyes. "I totally feel the love."

"You should, if I had any for you," I retorted.

"Oh please. I have *plenty* of love from *plenty* of people including you," he huffed.

I shook my head with a smile. "You're too arrogant for your own good."

"Yeah, but hey it's part of my charming figure," he smirked.

"That's what you think," I coughed quietly.

He gave a throaty chuckle. That one sound was so hot. *Curse my female hormones.* I really needed to get a grip on my emotions, pulling onto the reigns of my self-control. I could not fall in love. His presence allured me in ways that scared me, tempting me closer to a point of no return.

I remembered last night, how Damon's life had taken an unexpected turn, and I felt shame for not asking him sooner.

I bit my lip, wondering if it was a good idea to bring this up. "Damon, how did everything go last night?" I asked.

Immediately, his features darkened, and his smile dropped. "I don't want to talk about it," he mumbled.

His lips told me "no", but his eyes tell a different story. Those forest green eyes were as bright as an evergreen field, yet they pleaded for help with fresh crystal tears. He refused to let them drop, and then he broke our gaze, knowing that I could read him like a book.

I knew that my next words would be were wrong and I felt despair at seeing his struggles. His life was in shambles; his heart was broken repeatedly from those he loved. I wanted to help. I wanted to save him from destruction.

"If you ever need to talk," I started as regret pooled in my stomach, "I–I'm here for you."

As I prepared to walk away, leaving him in his silence to collect his thoughts, his meek voice called out for me barely above a whisper, but the hoarseness told me of his inner turmoil.

"Amira, wait," he said. "I need to talk to someone right now."

I slowly turned to face him. "About last night?"

He shook his head. "About all the other nights when the same thing happened. I just… really need a friend."

I nodded and followed him back to the classroom. *Oh Allah*, I thought, *what have I done? Why did I allow myself to fall victim to this?*

Perhaps if I kept the conversation from ever getting too intense or too playful, I would be fine. The only problem was I wasn't sure if I could control my own desires, and keep *Allah's* words as a continuous echo in my mind, to remind and advise me.

I can do this without crossing boundaries.

* * *

"So, what happened?"

Damon exhaled a shaky breath like the mere thought of his father constricted his airways. "He always gambles money. He's been doing it since my youngest brother, Percy, was born. He never tells us why, except that he loves the thrill and that he needs it."

I let the words sink in. "So, he didn't gamble when you or your other brother was born?"

He shook his head. "No, only after Percy," he whispered. "It was like he wasn't ready to have another kid. Maybe that's why my mom and I try to shield Daniel and Percy from all this because we know that it would crush them if they knew the whole story."

"So, you decided to carry the burden for them," I finished for him. "That's really honorable of you, Damon."

"It doesn't feel like it."

"Sometimes, we don't see how much of an effect we have on others. We're blind to it because we only think about how it affects us personally," I said softly. "Trust me, you are a father figure enough for them."

He gazed into my eyes, searching honesty from the sincerity in my actions. I knew he had doubts. I knew he feared that

I would one day betray him like his old friend did at his old school, but I wouldn't.

Silence ruled between us where neither of us intended to break our locked gazes. He tried to puzzle through me, and examine my true intentions. He had doubts, and in his darkest hour, he felt as though I would take advantage of it.

Part of being a good Muslim came from showing kindness to others because in return, they would see the error of their ways, knowing that Muslims were just like other people. They were humans that tried to live everyday like it was their last.

Maybe my own kindness would break through to him.

"Why are you being so welcoming toward me?" he asked. "After all the things I've done and all the times I made disrespectful remarks, why are you still so kind to me?"

I smiled. "We're both humans, Damon. We all have feelings."

His body relaxed as his own lips curved upwards. "Thanks. I've thought about your little text speech from yesterday. You know about patience and faith?"

"Yeah?"

"Well, I hate to admit it, but you're right," he paused, chuckling to himself. "Man, I say that so much to you."

"Don't worry about it," I waved off. "Think of it as me bringing your ego down a notch."

Damon narrowed his eyes, a small smile still playing on his lips. "I truthfully think I don't deserve that."

"I beg to differ."

That was when Tye and Thomas decided to walk into class with other classmates behind them. Damon and I turned around when we heard singing.

Thomas was singing some perverted song that made me roll my eyes. Tye was right next to him, cracking up. Damon looked at his friends with a grin, but didn't make an attempt to get up and talk to them. He stayed seated in front of me. I found the gesture sweet, and then thought I was over analyzing the situation. He probably was just too lazy to get up.

My classmates started filling the classroom and giggling at the fresh entertainment for the day. I even laughed as it was amusing to watch. Never did I believe that Thomas was ever going to sing some perverted song in school. He didn't seem like that type of guy.

I saw Aria, in the corner of my eyes, looking down at her notes. Her hair covered her face, but even from my seat I could feel the intense emotions radiating off of her. I frowned as I saw Mark talking with some girl.

It was like he didn't care that his girlfriend looked as if she might burst in tears. I stood up, and walked over to Aria's seat. The whole way felt like a weird feeling of being watched.

"Hey," I said softly, as I took a seat next to her.

She looked up at me. I narrowed my eyes as I tried to read the hidden emotions in her eyes. She bit her lip, looking at me with a sorrowful look. Her eyes glazed in unshed tears. Her eyes were stormy and clouding with despair. There was no spark in her eyes; nothing seemed to make her feel alive. She was empty like a hollow shell of a human being. The first thought that hit my head was Mark. It had to be him.

"Mark?" I asked.

She didn't say anything. She looked down at her notes and mutely nodded her head.

I sighed as I looked at Mark. How could he let such a beautiful girl go? She had done nothing but love him. Didn't he see that? How could he break such an innocent soul? This was something that scared me the most in life.

Love can bring out the best and the worst in a person. I knew that Aria loved Mark. I could see the emotions that flew through her whenever he walked in and the way she looked at him like he was the only guy in the world. She smiled all the time when they were together, or at least she used to.

"What happened?" I whispered.

She sucked in a huge shuttering breath before speaking. "We broke up," she said brokenly as she winced at her words.

I stared at her in shock. "Tell me exactly what happened," I said.

"I called him up two days ago, told him about how I was wary of his childhood friend getting so touchy with him, and he laughed it off. He said I was being silly, and assured me that they were just friends. Then I asked if he wanted to hang out, and he declined because he wanted to spend time with her. I got mad, and said that he never spends time with me anymore, and it's been several months since we hang out. He got mad, told me that I was being too clingy that I needed to open my eyes, and see that the world didn't revolve around me. Then I told him that if he hated me so much, then we shouldn't be dating. After that, he said he was happier without me," she said the last part so quietly that I almost didn't hear her.

I felt rage burning my blood. *That idiot!* Of course, Aria would ask why he distanced himself from her. She was his girlfriend for goodness sake! Any girl or guy would feel threatened if the person they were in a relationship with suddenly spends more time with another person. It was common sense.

Aria slightly shaking, snapped me out of my thoughts. Her breathing became rapid, as her hand covered her mouth to stop any sound. She sniffled once more before looking up. The tip of her nose became slight pink, and her eyelashes were glossy. My heart ached for my friend. I could only imagine how it must have hurt.

I grasped her hand, and said, "Listen, he's an idiot for letting such a beautiful girl go. He should know that he won't find a girl like you. You had the right to be mad. Don't feel bad about yourself."

She nodded limply, and looked back at her notes. I took the gesture as a sign that she needed her space. In the corner of my eyes, I saw Damon looking at me. I fidgeted under his heated gaze, but I shook it off as I made my way toward Mark.

Mark was chatting with that childhood friend of his. What was her name again? *Linda... Laura... ah yes Leah*! When I reached them, Leah glared at me.

I ignored her, and turned to Mark. "Can I talk to you?" I asked.

He scoffed. "You're talking to me right now."

The jerk of the day award, goes to Mark, everyone!

"Yes, but I would like to say this to you without your friend hearing," I retorted while crossing my arms across my chest.

"So be it," he muttered, as he ushered for Leah to leave. She pouted, but left. Then he turned to me. "What do you want?" he asked, annoyed.

"Why did you do it?" I asked bluntly.

"Do what?"

"Break Aria's heart. Why?" I demanded.

"It's none of your business," he snarled.

Whoa, what happened to the playful Mark that I knew? This was an entirely different guy.

"You're right. It is none of my business. Just know that you'll never find a girl like Aria. You ignored her for so long. She's a beautiful girl who deserves to feel loved," I said calmly, with a hint of anger. I turned around, and glared over my shoulder. "What comes around, goes around, Mark. Just a good life lesson to know," I said, and walked back to my seat.

Damon looked at me with admiration, as if he couldn't believe what I had done.

"What?" I snapped, still angry at the sight of Mark. That boy fueled my blood with fury, and an overwhelming urge to slap him came to mind. *Take a deep breath, Amira.*

"Do you stick up for all your friends like that?"

I nodded, curious to where he was taking this. *Wasn't it natural to stand up for those you care about?*

"You really are nothing like Luqmaan," he muttered to himself.

"Who?"

"It's… no one," he said, quickly covering it up with a grin. "So, how about you help me stay awake during class today?"

I knew for a fact that Damon was lying. *Luqmaan*, I thought. *He was the Muslim friend who betrayed him.*

CHAPTER 16
Observing Beauty

DAMON WINTERS

I tapped my pencil against the scratched desk with rapid rhythm mumbling against a wooden surface, following the ticks from our clock. Sighing, I leaned back; borderline insane from the slow ticking of a clock, telling me that time was just as slow as my mind was processing it.

We were currently in science class taking a test and I finished early as usual, but I still had a lot of time left. I looked at Amira across the room. She was writing fast, and kept looking at the clock, trying to race against time. I looked around me to see if anyone was looking, but there was no one. Turning my attention back to Amira, I found myself getting lost in her little testing antics.

She pulled her bottom lip into her mouth; her subtle brown eyes were wildly searching for answers on her sheet. Amira seemed as lost as a bat during daylight hours, wondering what her mistakes were and whether her certainty was accurate.

Testing was always easy to me. There was a technique to all, and once I figured it out, there was no holding back to my perfect scores or the close to perfect ones. My SATs were even outstanding.

However, my above average test scores didn't make my life any better.

I'm sure, my education was set to go, ready to face all the intellectual obstacles that would cross my path, however, my determination vanished. My mind harassed me late at night about Luqmaan and my father, two men who managed to scar my life without knowing it.

Luqmaan made me doubt myself. My father made me pull out hairs. Both damaged and complicated souls that roamed the Earth in hopes of finding their purpose. I was becoming just like them.

Now is not the time for this. I thought, as I brought my eyes back to her.

I couldn't bring myself to look away from her. She was wearing a blue scarf with a loose gray sweater that hung at her hips and jeans that hugged her thighs. Amira would never wear something that purposely attracted men to her figure. She didn't need a man's validation or compliments.

She looked absolutely beautiful in anything she wore like she was the sun herself; radiant and pure, spraying the bright rays against my cold-hearted self. Even when she didn't try to look good, she still looked good.

I sighed, leaning my cheek against my hand. Amira let go of her bottom lip, licking them when the dryness got to her. *Man, I really wanted to kiss her sometimes.* I knew I couldn't and I knew I shouldn't feel this way, but she had me falling hard for her. I wondered if all I felt was lust.

How could I, Damon Winters, a self-proclaimed hater of all things spiritual, start liking a girl who was the exact opposite of me? Sure, we had similar interests. Sure, she understood me and knew how to comfort me, but she was a Muslim.

I couldn't trust her yet. My brain refused to, but my heart leapt towards her whenever she was within my presence. I had no idea when these feelings started, yet denying them for such a weak reason wasn't going to work out anymore.

Amira was untouchable, clean of any other man's touch. Her chastity was guarded by an unbreakable force that refused to open the gates for anyone. I knew many other guys at school had spared Amira a couple of glances, thinking the same as I do, but there was no way of getting close to her. She was protected from our prying eyes, hunger and thirst.

Suddenly, I felt an eraser chuck my head. I turned in my seat, and saw Tye and Thomas with grins across their faces. I glared, flipping them off with my finger. It was as logical and immature as it seemed.

Turning back to Amira, I watched as she turned in her test and sat down. She cupped her hands, and started mumbling something into it. *I wonder what she's saying?* Then she blew into her hand.

"Alright, you guys can talk for the rest of the class while I organize the tests," Ms. Lyon said.

I got up and went over to my group of friends, who were close to Amira's table. I did a mental cheer in my head. *Perhaps I could trick them into walking over to Amira.*

"Damon, why so rude?" Thomas teased. "We were just trying to grab your attention."

"You deserved it for chucking the eraser at me," I scoffed.

He chuckled. Tye looked towards the direction of Amira and her friends. Anger bubbled within me as I tried not to think about Tye being interested in Amira. I took a deep breath. *Chill the fuck out, Damon.*

"You guys wanna annoy the girls over there?" I asked, while tilting my head towards Amira's group.

Tye and Thomas shrugged and went with it. Surprised, I followed them, momentarily forgetting about Tye's stares. As long as I could spend more time with Amira, I was okay.

As we walked over, I noticed that her friends were laughing about something Amira had said, reminding me of the first time I saw her. Her laughter was a melody that played a constant crescendo in my head, never letting me forget about the Muslim girl who thought of me a nuisance.

"Hey, weirdos," Thomas smirked at Anna and Alexis.

"Why are you guys here?" Alexis asked, confused.

"We wanted to bless you with our irresistible presence," said Tye, bowing slightly with an exaggerated British accent. "M'ladies, could I offer thou some divine assistance?"

"Aye, my companion, I shall join you," Thomas continued, as he bowed as well, tilting his head towards me. "Sir Damon, these ladies deserve some respect."

"That's King Damon if we're playing this medieval game," I said.

Tye and Thomas straightened, both exhaling deeply in disappointment for my inability to follow their impromptu acting. The girls had erupted into a fit of laughter, especially when Thomas and Tye managed to attract the attention of other classmates. With their confidence at high spirits, they continued playing along with their jokes.

While our class became immersed at Tye and Thomas, I couldn't help but keep my gaze on Amira, copying Anna's notes for some class. Amira bent over the desk with her grey sweater falling loosely at her curves.

She looked so perfect. Her long, thick eyelashes hid her big brown eyes from me. Her gaze was purely focused on the paper, glazing over the notes in a rushed manner. She lifted her head, and locked our gazes.

I swore that time halted at that moment. I desperately wished that I could take a picture of her, making the moment last longer. Millions and billions of thoughts rushed into my mind, as I tried to imagine a future with her. Amira tilted her head at me, like she could read my thoughts. Her lips parted as she stared at me with a shocked expression. Even though it only lasted for a few seconds, the image was everlasting in my mind.

What the hell is wrong with me? When did I turn into such a love sick sap?

Amira looked at the clock on the wall beside me in a calculating manner. I never noticed how timely she was. Time was the essence to Amira's being. She lived and breathed in time because there was always an aura that she was running out of it. I wondered what event in her past must have caused that fear in her, that habit that she had.

"Sir Damon!" exclaimed Thomas, a knowing gleam in his bright cerulean eyes. "Doth thou find a fair maiden?"

My cheeks burned with embarrassment. "No. Why would you say such a thing?"

Amira momentarily glanced up, a coy smile playing on her features, ripe with her own amusement.

Thomas wrapped his arm around my shoulder, pulling me to him. We were roughly the same height, but I did not appreciate the closeness. "Oh, Damon. Love has bitten thou with its cupid bow."

"Get away from me," I muttered, pushing him away.

"You wound the brethren," said Thomas, pouting like it would get him anywhere with me.

The class' laughter echoed off the walls, even our teacher thoroughly enjoyed the free entertainment. He went back to acting with Tye, thankfully keeping me out of it. Amira focused on her homework again, isolating herself from the world around us. She had the dedication and drive that I dreamed of, the pen of her future in her hands.

She was so focused on the paper, attentive to every last detail. Her fingers gripped the pencil harder as she continued pressing her pencil down on the paper. I was surprised she still hadn't noticed my gaze.

"Damon, I can see you looking at me. You're not very slick," she said, without looking at me.

I paled, *Spoke too soon.* Amira looked up after closing the notebook. She smirked up at me.

"Oh, shut up, Amira. God, you're so judgmental," I scoffed embarrassed, as I turned away.

"Aww. Did I embarrass the little guy?" she laughed.

"I am not little. If you haven't noticed, you're shorter than me!" I exclaimed.

"Why are you so defensive?" she shook her head, amused.

"Me? You're always defensive! What the hell?" I defended.

Amira softly laughed at my weak attempts at defending myself. I found myself relax to the sound of her laugh. I smiled along with her. Something about this girl kept me happy all day. Something about this girl erased all my worries away. Something about this made my insides melt form the mere sight of her.

She was so bubbly and cheerful towards people. It was such a welcoming gesture. Her parents did a great job at raising her. *Are all Muslims like this? I hadn't met many.*

"Damon, it's okay to be shy sometimes. Don't be so blue," she pouted.

I froze.

Images of taking her lips into mine, capturing them with my dominance, and tasting the sweetness of Amira overwhelmed me. I felt a familiar heat crawl up my neck, making the small hairs on my arm stick up. With the innocent glint in her exotic eyes, I wasn't so sure if all Muslims were as awful as I thought.

She wasn't Luqmaan. No, Amira was better than him in a thousand different ways. My heart had known that a long time ago.

CHAPTER 17
Family Comes First

AMIRA SARKER

I walked outside the school building, welcoming the gentle breeze that blew softly on my *hijab*. I looked up into the sky, watching the large fluffs of white clouds float among the ocean of blue, slowly drifting as the world turned on its axis. A flock of birds followed the motion of the clouds, flying far away to a place where the weather would welcome them with open arms.

Smiling, I continued walking as I ignored the obnoxious students around me. The boys were tackling each other in an attempt to show off their strength. The girls giggled, winking at a boy that might catch their eyes. I rolled my eyes, *teenagers*.

"Amira!" a voice called. I turned around and saw Damon, jogging up towards me. "Do you need a ride?" he asked.

"Nah. I'm taking the bus," I told him.

He gave me a blank look. "You're riding with me. Come on."

I shook my head. A part of me wanted to follow Damon to wherever he would take me, to allow him the freedom to venture my body, mind, and soul, but I knew it was wrong. An alerted bell rang in my mind in warning, screaming at me to turn away. *Allah* came first, not boys or materialistic things, not even grades.

"Damon, no. Thank you for the offer though."

"Amira, come on. I'll get you home faster. I'm not exactly fond with you riding the bus."

"And why is that?" I asked with raised eyebrows.

"Because I'm more trustworthy than a dumb bus. You know how many fights go on a bus?"

I raised a brow. "If I remember correctly, you were once a part of those fights."

"I'm reformed, aren't I?"

"I'm not sure if 'reformed' is proper word choice," I remarked.

He sighed. "You really antagonize me, you know that?"

"Of course, I do," I said proudly. "If I don't keep you grounded, then who will?"

"You make a compelling argument, but seriously stay a while," smiled Damon.

My body suddenly felt cold, a chill running down my spine in warning. He wanted to ride with me to have time alone with me. Texting and real-life conversations were two different types of communication. When we were texting, I could easily leave the chat whenever I wanted without burying myself into the depths of Damon's life.

In real life, there were no barriers between us if we were alone. I could surrender to desire; forget all my values in the heat of a moment. There was peer pressure and the need to be like everyone else. There were guidelines to interactions in *Islam* to prevent a time where my vulnerability allowed someone to take advantage of me.

Damon sensed my ambivalent thoughts. "We could talk out here. When is your bus coming?"

I checked the time on my phone. "In a little bit," I replied.

"Do you think you could spare me a little time?" he asked, shyly at first. "I just really wanted to talk."

My heart warmed a little at his words. They were so sweet, luring my heart closer to the gates of no return and I allowed it. It wasn't right, but we were in public where there were other students. *It couldn't be that bad, right?*

"Sure."

His smile had brightened, lifting his spirits almost immediately. The joy stretched his cheeks until I wasn't sure if I had ever seen him that pleased before.

"So," I opened the conversation, "what did you want to talk about?"

He settled himself on a bench outside the building, patting the seat next to him. Hesitantly, I sat on the far side, clutching my textbooks to my chest. My nerves bundled together, warnings flashing through my mind, my breath quickening. *Relax, it's not a big deal. Just chill.*

"Anything to keep you here a while longer," he winked.

"Anything?" I tested.

He nodded, eyes glimmering like emeralds and the sheen of morning dew. He couldn't stop smiling, nor could he keep his eyes away for a second almost like he was hypnotized.

"Well, who's Luqmaan?"

That was the key to dropping all progress between us. A frown painted his lips, dark and distant. "That's a little sudden, don't you think?"

I shrugged. "You said anything."

"That didn't include this."

"Like you said, anything," I emphasized, gazing at his with suspicion. There was a secret hidden behind his eyes, no matter how hard he tried to hide it. "Why do you always do this when I bring up about that fight or Luqmaan?"

Damon exhaled, pinching the bridge of his nose. "He was a friend of mine from my previous school. We were best friends to be exact."

"What happened?"

"Amira-"

"Just forget I asked," I mumbled, beginning to stand up.

"No, wait!"

I paused, knowing I was being unfair to him, but the curiosity suffocated me, narrowed my airways, and burned me at the thought of the real reason behind Damon's dismissal of *Islam*.

I could hear shuffles behind me, and he stood up as well. "Amira, Luqmaan was a horrible person," he whispered, taking cautious steps to walk around me until we were face to face again. My books couldn't even hide me this time. "It's not that I don't want to tell you, it's that he's not worth remembering."

"How could you say that?" I asked, my own voice barely above a whisper. I retreated a few steps from him. "He was the guy who made you so distrusting. He's the reason why you don't trust me or any Muslim at this school. If he's not worth remembering, then why do you let it affect you?"

"It's more than just that."

I shook my head. "No, Damon. You haven't gotten over the fight, have you?"

He looked panicked as if I had cornered him into a wall, and trapped him among feral beasts. His hands clenched into fists, body tensing as his shirt seemed tighter against his chest. Damon looked terrified and I wondered if I went too far.

"I haven't," he croaked.

Sympathy wrapped around me. "Luqmaan isn't a representation of all Muslims, Damon. You say we're friends, but friends aren't afraid of each other. I don't want you to fear and not trust me."

"Do you trust me then?" he asked.

"I... I..."

He raised a brow.

From all our personal conversations and all the times we had been there for each other, I knew I trusted him. The only obstacle that punctured that trust was whether or not he could ever see me as his equal, whether he could see me as a human being, whether I was good enough to be remembered as Amira to him, and not just another Muslim set out to destroy him.

"Yes, I do," I said firmly. The bus had pulled over on the side of the road. "I have to go."

"I can still give you a ride."

"No, thanks."

I could feel Damon's gaze on my back the whole way until I was out of his line of vision. I wondered if he liked me. I knew my feelings for him were growing stronger and uncontrollable. The idea of being with Damon wrapped around my brain like warm gloves on winter days, yet the rest of the cold days face the heat eventually.

* * *

When I got home, I saw my very ill *Nanu* (grandpa) lying on the couch. Nanu had a very bad leg injury, preventing him from walking. It brought tears to my eyes to see him in such a condition. Wrinkles creased the soft skin of his eyes and lips, making him even older and look tired. His lips pressed to a thin line, perhaps angry at the situation of his weakening body.

"Mum! I think something is wrong with Nanu," I called out.

"I know. I'll take him to the doctor as soon as your dad comes home," she said softly.

"But, Mum, he's really not looking good. You need to take him now," I insisted.

She sighed. "Who will take us now? I still have the kids to watch and Tanwir isn't home. We'll go as soon as your dad comes home, but for now, can you make him some tea?" she said gently.

I nodded my head, went to the kitchen, and started brewing the tea. *Oh Allah, please let Nanu be okay. Please Allah. He only just got here. I just got to see him after all this time. Please help him.*

"Amira? Are you making tea?" Nani (grandma) asked. Nani had bad hearing. Years and years of poor living conditions in the villages of Bangladesh were starting to take a toll on herself.

"Yeah I am," I responded.

"What?"

"Yes, I am," I said, louder.

She nervously laughed. "Repeat, that for me."

I shook my head and sighed. I turned around and pointed to the teapot, hoping that she would get the memo. Seeming confused for a moment, she finally understood the gesture. I smiled at her, letting her know that I wasn't annoyed. She nodded at me before turning away, going to comfort her husband.

My phone beeped, alerting me of a new text.

Damon: *Y didn't u let me give u a ride home?*

Me: *It's not proper for a Muslim girl to get in a car with a boy who is a non-Mahram.*

As I waited for his reply, I stirred the tea. Almost a few minutes later, he responded.

Damon: *What's a Mahram?*

Me: *Didn't I already explain this?*

Damon: *Explain it again.*

Me: *A Mahram is a blood relative to a Muslim girl, but not all blood relatives qualify. A Muslim girl can only show her hair to a relative, her husband, father in law, all girls and her grandpa from both her mom and dad's bloodlines. A Mahram is a person the girl can't marry. A non-Mahram is a person the girl could potentially marry, make sense?*

Damon: *Yeah, so I'm a non-Mahram?*

I bit my lip, realizing that he was right. Guilt gnawed at my conscience.

Me: *yupp, pretty much.*

Damon: *I trust you.*

Well, that was random.

Me: *Um what?*

Damon: *Earlier in our conversation. U asked me if I trusted u, so I thought it over and I do.*

Me: *Really?*

I fixed the tea and walked towards the living room. I gave Nanu the tea, but he barely looked up. My phone beeped, but I ignored it and pulled out the Qur'an. Sitting beside him, I unlocked my phone to tell Damon I was busy.

Damon: *Yeah. Ur the only person that I have no doubts about trusting. Ur perfect.*

The words sunk in, his admiration lightened the heavy ache on my chest, knowing that Damon was really changing. Although I wanted to continue, I knew my grandfather needed my attention more than Damon. A boy wouldn't come in between my family and I.

Me: *I gotta go. My grandpa needs me. Talk to u later.*

I began reciting, watching my grandfather's eyes close at the sound. I let the words fly through my tongue in a slow rhythm, resting on each syllable. Nanu relaxed and smiled a little. Although it was a weak smile, it still made my heart flutter because I knew I was making him happy. He drank some tea as I recited.

Homework can wait. Family is more important than work.

Family was irreplaceable. I could always make up another assignment. I could always get another good grade. I could always succeed again, but I couldn't get my wasted time back. My family needed me, and they needed my attention more than anyone else.

"One of the baby's moms will take us to the hospital. I'll go with them. Take care of your Nani please," she told me.

Her caramel eyes stared at me with fear. I realized that she feared for her father's life, feared for heartache, feared for the destruction of her family. She needed her father as much as I needed her.

"I will," I responded.

She kissed me on the head. "Thank you. Be careful, okay?"

I nodded. How could I not? The last thing I wanted to see is another member of my family hurt.

CHAPTER 18
Party Disasters

AMIRA SARKER

After I prayed *Maghrib* (sunset prayer), I sat and read another thriller book. Although thriller books terrified me to my core, I couldn't stop my curiosity from reading more. I had an insatiable taste in scaring myself and I needed books to breathe.

As I read, I couldn't help but think how Nanu was doing. *Was he okay? What about Mum and Baba?* They were still not at home and the thought alone scared me. Tanwir came home an hour ago. He seemed dreadfully angry, and went straight to his room. I wondered what got him so mad.

Nani lay in bed ever since Nanu left for the hospital. She only got up to pray, and she spent a long time in worship. I couldn't help but admire how hard she was focused on only *Allah*. She would spend so long in worship that it made me ask myself what was stopping me from doing that.

My phone beeped and I checked to see if it was a message from Damon, and indeed it was. I felt a smile climb onto my lips.

Damon: *Hey u going to the Tye's party tonight?*

Tye was having a party today as a cheer for the start of winter break. He invited our whole class since his parents were out, but they let him have his party because who wouldn't throw parties in their huge house when their parents aren't around? I obviously didn't go to those high school parties because it was just a red zone to *fitnah* (temptation). As tempting as it may have been, I loved *Allah* more.

Me: *Nah. High school parties aren't my thing.*

Damon: *Well that sucks. I'm gonna miss ur presence there ;)*

Even when he wasn't next to me, he could still make me feel like I was on cloud nine. My stomach turned in ways that I never felt before. The fact that he could make me feel burning sensations all over my body, scared me to no end. Damon was the forbidden apple that I desired, the one *Shaytan* (Satan) kept urging me towards with promises that were weary.

I couldn't be attached to him. Whenever a girl became attached to a guy, the romance collapsed. I wasn't naive to reality. The world was harsh, pushing me past my limits more than once, and through it all I was strong in my faith towards *Allah.* I was firm in my belief.

Me: *I hope you have fun.*

Damon: *it won't be much fun without u.*

I desperately wanted to go to the party. Damon was going, but I knew that would be a terrible idea. I promised to take care of Nani while Mum and Baba were at the hospital with Nanu.

I sighed, leaning back against the sofa with my eyes closed. Every other girl had a boy attached to her hip, free to kiss whoever she wanted, and not conflicted between right and wrong, where the wrong looked most appetizing.

Allah tested those who were strong in their belief to make sure that their faith was true. I believed in *Islam* with all my heart. I understood the warnings but I was young and vulnerable to mistakes. *Allah* was privy to my scandalous thoughts, but I knew *Islam* was a religion that taught self-control.

Allah is saving someone very special for you. Just for you. Those romances are full of crap. You know pure hearts are for the pure. Be patient, and you'll get the best romance of them all, I reminded myself.

Me: *How sweet of u.*

Damon: *Don't u know it XD*

Me: *Get going u big goof.*

Damon: *Only if u come with me.*

Was he asking me to go with him? An unfamiliar pounding clammed itself against the mental walls that I spent so long to build. I could feel my mentality cracking slightly.

Me: *What?*

Damon: *I better get going. see ya later?*

Me: *Yeah, bye.*

Maybe he was kidding about me going with him. Yeah, he probably was. I put my phone down and checked the time. I bet Nani was hungry right now, so I got up and made tasty tuna paste to put in a sandwich.

* * *

I climbed the steps towards the guest room, and knocked twice. She obviously didn't hear, so I slowly peeked in.

Nani sat on her bed while reciting the Qur'an, her frail voice shaking over pronunciation and her lips murmuring softly. I quietly shut the door behind me, and brought the food to her. She noticed me and frowned.

"What's this?" she asked, eyeing the sandwich.

"Food. It's bread and fish. I made it myself and thought you were hungry," I said loudly hoping she heard.

"What?"

I sighed and tried again. "It's bread and fish."

She tilted her head sideways and I knew she had not heard. I was getting really frustrated, so I took a few deep breaths. *Calm down she can't hear correctly.* I tried one last time, and repeated what I said, even louder.

She finally heard me, and thanked me for the food. I smiled.

"Amira! Be quiet!" Tanwir shouted.

I glared at the wall. "She couldn't hear me, smart one," I shouted back.

Stupid jerk. Who would have thought that trying to help a person would be so difficult? This was not only a test to his faith, but my faith as well, as I had to be patient with his tantrums and use proper Islamic manners.

My phone buzzed, much to my annoyance.

Meredith: *Hey could u call me when u get my text?*

Sighing, I quickly dialed Meredith's number, and she answered after the third ring.

"Hello?"

"It's Amira."

"Oh, hey. Um... I kinda need a favor," she trailed off with uncertainty weaving through her words like yarn.

"What kind of favor?" I asked, suspiciously.

"Well... uh... you see... my guy friend took me and Aria, to Tye's party so we could help her get over Mark, and let's just say it didn't end well," she mumbled, timidly.

"What happened?" I breathed out, anxious to know.

"We caught Mark making out with Leah, and Aria kinda lost it. I don't want to stay here, and let Aria sit in misery. Plus, my guy friend is drunk, and Aria is lightheaded, so my only ride is gone and I just really need you to come pick us up," she rushed over the roar of the music.

How do teens even get access to alcohol? Society is screwed up.

"But I only have my learner's permit. What if the cops catch me?" I asked nervously while glancing at Tanwir's door. He'd surely kill me if I took his car.

"Please, Amira. We really need you. I promise the cops won't come. Tye isn't that stupid of a party thrower. He keeps things organized," she tried to reason.

"You don't know what will happen," I sighed.

"Amira, please. You're my only chance. Think of Aria. I can't let her suffer like that. We're her friends. She needs us the most right now. I'm not good at making people feel better, but it comes naturally to you. Please, come," she begged.

I thought my choices over in my head. *I'm a Muslim. I'm supposed to help others, right?* Meredith was right. Aria needed her friends.

"I'm on my way. Just go get Aria."

"Thank you. You're a lifesaver."

"I know," I smiled, hanging up.

Now, my only problem was to get a car. Tanwir was home, so maybe I could get his car, and leave Nani in his care. I went to his room and knocked twice. I heard him grumble and thought that was my signal to come in.

"Can I borrow your car?" I asked.

"No."

"I really need it. Please, Tanwir. It's really important that I get it."

Oh Allah, please let him agree.

"Who's gonna take care of Nani?" he asked, as he raised his eyebrows.

"It won't be long, Mum and Baba will be here soon."

"No, Amira. Now, can you please leave."

"Tanwir, I am begging you to let me use your car. Nani is in her room, and won't bother you I promise. And if you really don't want her here, I'll take her with me. Just know that she's your family member and she's sick. She took care of you when you were little. Think what the Prophet would do," I said softly.

"Shut up and take the car. I'll watch over Nani. You better be back soon," he stared at me pointedly.

"Thanks, bro. I promise I'll be back as soon as I can," I smiled appreciatively.

I hoped Meredith and Aria didn't do anything they would regret before I got there.

* * *

Meredith texted me the address of Tye's house and I reached it in no time. Music vibrated from the huge house. A strong scent of alcohol hit my nostrils, making me scrunch my nose in disgust.

I regret coming here.

A pit of uneasiness formed in my stomach, as I walked towards the front door, each step was heavier than the last, restricting my ability to get in and get out.

I swallowed my fear and knocked on the door. *This is for Aria. I'm doing this for the sake of helping my friends,* I reminded myself. No one answered, so I tried again. Finally, Maya opened the door.

"Who invited you?" she scowled.

"I'm here to pick a friend up. Last I heard it's a free country," I retorted.

"Don't outsmart me. Get out of here. You're not welcomed," she glared, as she turned to shut the door.

Alright, Amira time to swallow your pride. I put my foot in before she could close the door. "Please Maya. I really need to get in," I said, gently. She looked at me once before letting me in. "Thank you," I smiled as I walked by.

The music was so loud that I wanted to just turn it off. I hated these types of parties. Girls wore skimpy, skin-tight dresses, grinding against a half somber guy, who looked as if he was personally enlightened. I shivered at the crudeness of the party. I started searching for Meredith or Aria. They weren't picking up their phones, so now I had to look around this place. *Just my luck*, I thought.

I saw a couple kissing their life out of the each other, the boy licking around the girl's lips and groping her in different off-limit zones. The girl didn't mind, smirking against the guy's lips as she tugged his hair. I resisted the urge to gag.

My Lord, this is disgusting. Have these people never heard of a room? The smell of sweat crawled up my nose. *Gross. Oh Allah, please protect me from all of this.* As I almost gave up, I saw something that made my stomach turn.

Damon was leaning against the wall with his hand on a girl's hip. His hair looked like fingers ran through them, and he was wearing a plaid shirt with jeans. The girl next to him placed one of Damon's hands on her behind, whispering into his ear as she giggled from intoxication.

Anger welled within me, my frustration rising to the surface as I glanced at them. I knew he wasn't different. He was just like all the other boys in the world, full of empty promises and broken words.

Guys like Damon lured a girl into their trap, ushering them with gifts and kindness, telling the girl that she was special just to rip open her chest, and stomp on her heart.

Damon always was and forever will be just a crush. I meant nothing to him. I was just a girl who was a victim to his playful ways, to his breathtaking smile, to his alluring charisma, and that was my fault for not seeing through it. I wiped the angry tears from my eyes.

He was just another boy who meant nothing to me.

CHAPTER 19
Self Control

DAMON WINTERS

This party was outright horrible as I imagined, but I think I would have liked it better if a certain beauty were here.

I sighed. Amira would probably hate this party; the grinding bodies did no justice to that statement. A couple of months ago I wouldn't have cared about people showing public "affection," but now I saw how disturbing it was to watch.

It felt like I was intruding.

"Damon, man, what's got you in the blue? This is the type of party you live for," Tye said, while giving me a glass of water.

"Just thinking of someone."

"Would this someone happen to be this girl you keep texting?" he asked, with raised eyebrows. "Perhaps maybe Amira?"

I gave him a blank stare. "No."

"Lying is a bad look for you," he smirked. "Let's skip the middle school crush game and just be honest this time around."

"I don't like her," I scowled.

Even I knew I was lying. There was no point denying it anymore. I liked Amira. I liked her a lot, but there's no way in hell I'd be telling her that. She hated me. I didn't blame her because I was not the most welcoming.

Amira was a girl who deserved a man who stayed faithful till his last dying breath. She needed a man who could argue back and forth with her, but never lost interest. Amira's love was not something to be won, but a prize to be earned through all the obstacles she threw. From her sweet smile to her jovial laughter, there was no other girl like her in the world.

"Didn't you ask her to the party? Did you tell her about how you feel? ?" Tye pushed before finding the error in his words. "Ah, not too many Muslims like to put themselves in a situation like this. Man, that means I can't play Cupid for you."

I forgot he was here for a second.

"Maybe you should pretend to be Cupid on Halloween, Tye," I chuckled, grabbing his arm, and pulling him into the dance floor. "Right now, let's enjoy the party."

Some girls came up to Tye and me, asking if they could dance with us. I shrugged, figuring why not. A party was called a party for a reason, but I couldn't ignore the pang of guilt I felt.

When that girl, Kaylie, touched her hip against my groin, I felt the strong urge to push her away. When her arms wrapped around my neck, I felt like screaming in frustration.

She wasn't Amira. She wouldn't satisfy my undying thirst for a girl who could never be mine.

"Want to hang out away from these people?" she asked, seductively.

I nodded, realizing I needed distraction, anything to get my mind off Amira. It was remarkable how one girl managed to consume my every thought. I had practically memorized her facial features and the soft curve of her lips that made my jeans become tighter.

The idea of Amira suffocated me, killing me from materialistic gain, and setting my eyes on the rarest gem of all, a diamond that shone in the moonlight. *My Amira.*

"Didn't know I had such an influence on you," she purred.

She's still here? Whoa, get a grip, man!

I could smell alcohol on her, so I knew she was a little drunk. *Damn it. Why couldn't Amira be here? My God, what could have I done with her.*

We could have danced like there was no tomorrow. Her hands wrapped around my neck, as she kissed me hard on the mouth. She pulled my hair so gently like her teasing did. If only she could hear my thoughts now, her cheeks would have surely turned red from the explicit details that my mind refused to forget.

I leaned against the wall. I saw a few of Amira's friends tonight. Meredith was frantically talking on the phone, while Aria walked off outside. I bet it had to do with that Mark thing. What a prick that guy was. Now, he was making out with that girl, Leah, even though he knew that his ex-girlfriend had been watching.

Mark was a prime example of a man I didn't want to become. That was a heartless act, something that couldn't be easily forgiven, and I never wanted to become that type of monster. Mark took a young girl's fragile heart, and crushed it without a second thought. He plundered through the gift of love just to rejuvenate his expanding ego.

Breaking away from my distasteful thoughts, I realized that Kaylie was trying to make small talk, but the alcohol was getting to her. She put her hands on my chest to steady herself. *Damn, this girl only had one shot.*

Tye even made sure the alcohol wasn't too strong. It was just a *sprite*-type drink, and barely had any alcohol in it. But some people sneaked into other people's drinks, so who knew what this chick even drank?

I placed my hand on her hip to steady her. Trying to force myself to become somewhat aroused by the more than willing girl in front of me, I couldn't stop my straying mind from thoughts about Amira and her smiles. I squeezed my eyes shut, needing to pretend for once that the girl in front of me was Amira just to ignore the slashing pain on my chest.

When I opened my eyes again, I noticed a navy-blue scarf behind Kaylie's massive curls. *Did my eyes deceive me? It can't be her.*

My heart drummed loudly against my chest in anticipation as I pushed Kaylie away, and was meet with the sweetest little eyes. "Amira," I breathed.

I couldn't stop the smile from coming onto my lips. She was here. She stood there standing in purple floral pants and a navy-blue button-up shirt. It only made my mouth drool to see what was underneath even though she was thoroughly covered, but most of all it made me want her cuddled up next to me. The primal urge to claim her as mine was overtaking my senses.

Her eyes were cloudy with a mixture of emotions. Hurt, anger, and betrayal? My smile dropped. *Why did she feel that way? Why wasn't she happy to see me?*

"Amira, what's wrong?" I asked, as I took a step closer.

She took a step back, and raised her hands as a sign to show me to stop. "Sorry I interrupted. I didn't know you were busy," she said with irritation.

"Busy? I wasn't-oh," I realized. "Amira, no, it wasn't like that."

"It's cool, Damon. Sorry I even bothered," she whispered the last part in hurt. She turned to walk away.

"No, Amira. Stop," I begged.

I needed her to listen to me. I didn't want her to think of me as a player anymore. I wanted her to like me the way I liked her. I wanted Amira, not Kaylie. I was not letting her get away from me. Not tonight.

Amira stopped walking away. She stood breathing heavily. *Was she crying?* Guilt stabbed at my chest, knowing I was the cause of her tears. I had hurt her, something I did not want to do.

"Amira, why does the thought of me being with Kaylie bother you?" I whispered, quietly.

"It doesn't. You like her, so what?" she spat out with anger lingering in her eyes.

"I don't like her."

"Damon, you need to stop using girls for your pleasure. You promised your mother and yourself that this year would be different. It's not fair to anyone involved," she scolded while glaring at me.

I didn't want anyone, but you. It wasn't fair to you, I wanted to say. "You're right," I admitted, while paying more attention to her beautiful face. Her lips looked so soft and inviting.

"Then, why do you keep doing it?" she asked with crossed arms.

She was so freaking cute. I couldn't pay attention to her without wanting to kiss her worries away. I wanted to claim her badly as mine. I wanted to reassure her that I was all hers and nobody else's.

"We were just talking. I had no intention of using her, Amira. I wasn't going to go back on my word," I stated.

She was taken aback by my response. "Really?" she questioned with curiosity.

God, her eyes were beautiful. How did God create such a pretty being? Even her *hijab* showed how beautiful she was. So innocent, so pure, I wanted her bad. I wanted her to be mine.

"Amira, are you jealous?" I asked, with a smile tugging the corners of my lips.

"What? No! Of course, not," she huffed with a faint blush covering her cheeks.

"Sweetheart, I would never do such a thing if I knew it bothered you so deeply," I kept my voice low and deep.

I saw her body tense with how husky my voice sounded. I didn't want Amira for sex. I wanted her to be my girl. I learned to love her personality. She was my addiction, much more than a friend.

She was beautiful to me because of how chaste her heart was. She told me that her *hijab* represented a symbol of modesty, and that if she wears it, she also has to play the part. She played it very well.

Her purity rang bells to those around her, forcing evil eyes to stay below the white exterior of her chastity. Her heart could not be tainted with immorality because Amira was moral with strong beliefs that echoed within my mind.

She didn't have to wear revealing outfits for my gaze to be only on her. To me, she was the most beautiful woman in the world. Amira's presence just screamed respect and love. It took everything in me not to push her against the wall and claim her lips in a mind-blowing kiss.

"Go back to partying, Damon. I have stuff to do. Wouldn't want to break in on your parade," she said with a hint of anger.

I was getting angry. Couldn't she see that I just wanted her?

"What the hell, Amira? Can't you see that I just wanted to party with you? And you lied to me. It's not fair if you get to be angry and I can't," I glared.

Even though I was getting worked up, her flushed cheeks and fiery eyes had me harder than ever. The need to crush her body to mine was overwhelming.

"What do you have to be angry about?" she challenged.

"You said you weren't coming to the party and here you are," I said.

"How dare you accuse me of being a liar? Have I ever lied to you, Damon? I wasn't going to come. I only came to pick up my friends," she spat out.

"Oh."

"Yeah. 'Oh'," she mocked.

"Why are you being so rude?"

"Why are you flaunting around with another girl?" she retorted.

Damn, that hit a nerve.

"I freaking told you I wasn't going to use her," I said exasperated.

"Then I have nothing to say."

"But you're still talking!"

"Cause you keep arguing."

I chuckled. "Okay, okay. You're right. I'm sorry. Am I forgiven?" I smiled, raising my hands in surrender.

She sighed. "If my Lord can forgive, then who am I not to?"

"So, is that a yes?" I asked.

"I guess it is."

I walked closer to her and raised my hand to touch her cheek, but she flinched and moved back.

"Why won't you let me touch you?" I asked gently while grabbing her wrist.

Tingles shot through my arm at the feel of her smooth tan skin, but before I could do anything, she closed her eyes and pulled away. She was breathing heavily and I knew I had an effect on her. She wanted me like I wanted her.

"I'm saving myself for someone special," was her simple reply.

"And I'm not him?" I smirked.

"I don't know. But I'm not taking risks," she said.

While I had the courage, I should tell her that I really liked her. After what happened today, I wanted her to know how much she means to me. I was positive that my feelings were real. No other girl made me feel this way.

"Hey, Amira. I really l-" I started but was cut off.

"Amira! Finally! We need to leave now. Aria looks like a lost soul right now," Meredith yelled, as she came close to us with Aria right behind her.

"Oh right," said Amira, seeming a little distracted in her own thoughts. "Bye, Damon," she waved over her shoulder.

I waved back as she took her friends away. I sighed, being left bothered, and the one girl who could fix that was gone. After waving my friends off, I decided to go home. I felt no reason to stick around without Amira.

Everything seemed bland and dull without her calming personality.

"Stupid feelings," I muttered, as I stepped into my car.

CHAPTER 20
Subtle Confessions

AMIRA SARKER

After I successfully dropped Meredith and Aria home, I headed back to my place. I couldn't help but think of Damon. His touch burned me, igniting an inner flame that awoken dormant desires. Every second that he was so close to me, I felt my body go into alarms, warning me to step away.

I sighed, *the things that boy did to me.* How could something so wrong feel so right?

I was longing to be loved, to feel the comfort in a man's arms, the gentle press of his lips, to be close to him in every possible way. It was almost as if I was open to the idea of breaking all the walls of moral beliefs I built up just to get with Damon. As much as I wanted to, I knew I couldn't.

I had to be patient. Surely, the pure hearts were for the pure. I had to trust *Allah.* This was a test that I have to pass, but so far, I looked pretty average.

I parked Tanwir's car and got out. I really hoped Tanwir kept good to his words because although I trusted my brother, there was a small tinge of fear for what he was capable of.

Oh Allah, please don't let his anger have controlled him while I was gone. Fear settled deep in my stomach as I unlocked the door. I felt guilty that I was thinking so low of my brother, but what if something bad happened?

"Assalamualaikum," I called out, as I walked in and shut the door behind me.

"Amira?"

"Oh... uh... Mum?" I stuttered, realizing that I had been caught.

"Where were you?" she asked, suspiciously.

"I had to pick up some friends because they didn't have a ride."

"From where?"

"Uh... a person's house?"

"Whose house?"

Oh Allah, this feels like an interrogation.

"A classmate's. Don't worry. Nothing bad happened and I safely came home. I wasn't even gone too long. Less than an hour," I reassured her.

Mum stared at me with a hard gaze that made me shift in my position. *Lord, she's scaring me.*

"Amira, don't leave without telling me next time. It's not a good behavior," she sighed.

I looked at the ground. "I know."

"Go to bed now. We need to go to the hospital in the morning."

"How's Nanu?" I asked.

A look of despair crossed Mum's features. Her eyes dulled down and her lips were in a thin line. "The doctors don't know yet. They're still running tests."

"Oh."

Mum walked up the stairs and I followed after. Poor Nanu, he didn't deserve this. Not even Mum.

I remembered how I used to sing *nasheeds* (Muslim songs) to Nanu whenever we went to Bangladesh. He took me to the marketplace and bought me anything in the bazaar. Even though I only saw him for two months every few years, I still felt a connection towards him.

I still had a strong love for him. He was a special person in my life that contributed to helping me become who I am today. *Oh Allah, please protect and save him. Please help my Nanu.*

I shut the door to my room and took my *hijab* off, changing into more comfortable clothes. I laid on my bed, and pulled out my phone, feeling the urge to talk to Damon again.

Lucky for me, I had a new message from Damon. I bit my lip. I shouldn't talk to him anymore. I had to end this before these feelings grew even more. He didn't feel the same and he never would. I knew this, yet I kept hoping that it was a lie and he really did like me.

I groaned. Why couldn't life be simple? Why couldn't he be mine? I had to stand on the side lines, as he flirted with whoever he wanted. This wasn't fair! I sat straight and clutched my head.

I felt tears prick my eyes but I held them back. I felt a heavy weight on my shoulders, dragging me into my sin to an even darker abyss, reminding me of all my faults, and all my imperfections were written in ink. On the Day of Judgment, I had no excuse to give *Allah.*

Slowly, tears began to streak down my cheeks, rolling down the smooth surface. "Oh Allah. Hear my call. Please help me understand my feelings. Please protect me from the forbidden desires I'm holding deep in my heart. Help me, *Allah.* Only you can help me," I whispered into my pillow.

Damon didn't feel my struggles. He would never understand why *Allah* put restrictions on Muslims in an effort to protect their hearts from heartbreak and impurity. He would never understand my love for my Creator, and why I always put *Allah* first.

"I'm so scared, *Allah.* I know this is a trial, but it's getting to hard to pass now. I'm scared I'll do something I'll regret. I'm afraid of my desires. Help me, please. I beg you, Allah. Save me."

This was too hard. I bitterly laughed at myself. We're not even together and I'm acting like this is a break-up. How pathetic of me.

Stop, Amira. Calm down. Don't do this to yourself, my thoughts chimed me.

I took a shuddering breath, sitting up and wiping the tears with the back of my hand. I heard a beep from my phone.

Meredith: *Thanks so much for picking us up. But we really need to make Aria feel better :(*

I flipped through my contacts till I found Aria's.

Me: *How u holding up? U can talk to me if you like y'know. I'm here for u :)*

I leaned back against the headboard of the bed. *Allah, why do you give so many trials in life? It's so hard and I know I should trust You, but it's so hard.* These feelings inside me were almost deadly, stabbing me with knives threatening to shatter my form. Damon was a temptation, an attractive face behind a mask.

Another beep sounded from my phone.

Aria: *To be honest I feel like crap. I want him back, but it's too hard. I hate him, yet I still love him. What do I do?*

Me: *Aria, guys don't think with their heads now. We're young and can be stupid. ur a very mature girl and some guys take longer to get on our level. I know heartbreak isn't easy to get over, but take things slow with urself. Have patience in life because with every hardship comes ease.*

I reread what I sent. I had to be patient as well. I trusted *Allah.* He would never give me a trial that I couldn't handle.

"Whoever puts his trust in Allah, He will suffice." (Surah Al Talaq 65:3)

The ghost of a smile feathered my lips, as I thought of the verse. I was going to be okay. I had to be. I had *Allah* with me. At that moment, I felt as if a weight was lifted off me, as I began to feel the seeds I planted grow inside me in an effort to stand bolder, stronger without any force dragging me down because I had *Allah's* radiance protecting me.

I pitied the people who didn't have *Allah* in their hearts. How could they not? I couldn't imagine losing my relationship with *Allah*. He was the only one I can count on to help ease my pain in life.

No medicine in the whole world could make me feel better the way *Allah* could. Drugs distracted the pain, but they could never get rid of the roots of the pain. Only Allah had the power.

My phone buzzed beside me, and I saw it was a text from Damon, making my heart flutter in my chest.

Damon: *Did u get home safely?*

Me: *Yeah.*

Damon: *Can I tell you something?*

Me: *Sure, what is it?*

Damon: *There's this girl who's really amazing. She doesn't see it, but everyone around her does. She can break my heart if she wanted to. I don't know how but she put a spell on me, and the girls can't even compare to her. I trust her with all my heart, and the fact that she might not feel the same kills me. What do I do?*

I felt my heart drop. He liked someone. The green vines of jealousy wrapped around my form, choking my insides in a deadly grip that threatened to escape me.

Me: *She must be pretty special.*

Damon: *Oh, she is. I could lose myself in her beautiful eyes every time I talk to her. She doesn't even know how the smallest movements she does manage to kill me inside.*

Who was this girl?

Me: *Is she pretty?*

Damon: *Absolutely beautiful but that could just be because of how amazing her personality is.*

Me: *She sounds great.*

Damon: *Who do u like?*

I wanted to tell him that I liked him, but now he liked someone. It was a lost cause.

Me: *Y do u care?*

Damon: *Because ur my friend. We trust each other.*

Me: *I don't like anyone.*

Damon: *Ur lying.*

Me: *I'm not.*

It was quiet for a while. How I wished I was the girl he was talking about, but if I was, it would be dangerous as well because I would be heartbroken in the end. Damon and I couldn't be together.

As harsh as it sounded, we would never work out. I was a Muslim. *Allah* told us that we should stay away from these relationships because he had someone special saved for us. I trusted *Allah*, which was why I'd try my best to stay away.

"Oh, *Allah* please forgive me," I whispered.

After several minutes, Damon responded.

Damon: *I have to tell u something.*

Me: *What?*

Damon: *I like u.*

CHAPTER 21
Difficult Pathways, One Destination

AMIRA SARKER

Those words three letter words kept replaying in my head.

I like you.

Butterflies erupted in my lower region. Joy overwhelmed me. He liked me. Damon liked me. I couldn't help but be satisfied that he felt the same as I felt for him. I was about to type back and tell him that I'm feeling the same way too, but of course the harsh reality hit like cold water.

I can't do this. I can't tell him.

It would only cause Damon more pain in the end realizing that we couldn't be together. I wasn't stupid to believe that we could be together just because I liked him. It felt like a knife stabbed me in my chest, a familiar pricking of a tragic love story too soon to take flight.

Our mutual affections were like clouds on a stormy day, reckoning chaos everywhere it went, and not caring whose lives would be spared. It was dangerous, vigorous, and most of all, breathless to be a part of until it ended, and all that was left were the fragmented pieces of a once secured heart under locks.

With a shaky hand, I picked up my phone. I didn't want to hurt Damon. I couldn't let myself do that to him. Each word caused a swelling of grief on my wounded heart.

Me: *Damon u shouldn't like me.*

Damon: *Don't u get it? It's feelings and not an object that's easily gone. I really like u Amira. I'm serious.*

His words made me feel even guiltier.

Me: *We can't be together. I can't date u.*

Damon: *I know.*

Me: *Y do u like me? I'm not hot or pretty.*

I felt regret staple itself to me, biting my nails nervously as I waited for his response.

Damon: *Ur right, ur not pretty.*

Ouch. He didn't have to be so blunt.

Me: *I know.*

Damon: *Ur beautiful. That girl I was talking about, was u.*

The butterflies in my stomach grew stronger for calling me 'beautiful.' Not hot or sexy, but beautiful. I stared in awe at my screen. For a high school guy, calling a girl 'beautiful' was a whole new ball game, a new uncharted territory.

Me: *Y are u telling me this?*

Damon: *Because I needed u to know. I can't keep these feeling inside anymore.*

I bit my lip. I had to stop this thing with Damon before one of us got seriously hurt. *Allah* came first. Just because I had a crush on him didn't mean that I should disobey *Allah,* and secretly be with him, but that thought alone didn't stop my scandalous imagination.

My fingers typed on their own accord, desperate to know why Damon felt the need to tell me. There was more to the story, but he kept it hidden and locked like he was afraid of fully trusting me. He guarded himself carefully, and the more that he slowly opened up to me, the more I pushed against his defenses.

Me: *That doesn't explain why. U know we can't be together. U know that there is no future for us, so why even confess?*

I tried my best to be harsh, to repel him from like I was a flame sent to burn his skin. If I could keep him at arm's length, then I wouldn't have to worry about disobeying *Allah* or following through with my desires.

Damon: *I'm not sure.*

Me: *People don't spontaneously confess.*

Damon: *Y can't you just accept my feelings without question? Y does it have to be a reason for me to like u?*

Me: *Because I know you, Damon. You don't trust easily. You're weary of me. You're afraid to love anyone because you don't want to be like your mom where you forgive everything for the sake of love. I know you, and I know there's more to all this.*

He was silent for a moment, letting the words sink in before the typing resumed.

Damon: *U really do pay attention to my stories.*

Me: *We are friends.*

Damon: *I'm not sure if I want to be 'just friends' anymore.*

My cheeks heated in a blushing ember, burning up to my ears. The sizzling sensation on my face refused to cease. His effect on me was unmatched. It was solely Damon's ability to make me stumble over my words and to worry for him whenever something went wrong in his household.

Me: *What?*

Damon: *The real reason I had to tell u was because it felt wrong to hide how I felt. Don't ask me why, but for some reason, u appealed to me. U were there for me when no one else was. U stood by me even when I was a complete ass. When I needed comfort, u were there, Amira.*

Me: *U needed someone. That's y.*

Damon: *I needed someone when Luqmaan allowed his friends to jump me, but he wasn't ever there for me like u are.*

Me: *I'm not him.*

Damon: *I know.*

Me: *Then y do u keep bringing him up?*

Damon: *Sometimes I can't help but compare. I still don't understand why u two are so different but follow the same religion. Maybe that's why I like u. Ur different from other Muslims.*

I began to feel slightly annoyed. He still compared me, and believed that I was what the media labeled "terrorists."

Me: *Damon, u can't claim to like me, and then compare me to a guy who physically and mentally scarred u. He and I might share the same religion, but we are two different people. Not all Muslims are the same. They are people just like u and me. They're capable of their own mistakes.*

Damon: *I know. It's just that, it still hurts sometimes. I told u that I trusted u, but I'm afraid to be hurt by u or betrayed in the same way.*

He kept bringing up betrayal, yet I had no idea what had happened. All I knew was that Luqmaan and his friends fought with Damon at his previous school, and no other details were given. Only Damon and Luqmaan knew what happened that day, and Luqmaan was expelled according to the rumors.

Me: *What did Luqmaan do? U keep bringing up this betrayal, but u never say what it is?*

Damon: *He jumped me.*

Me: *Why?*

Damon: *Because he was using me the whole time. Luqmaan didn't care for our friendship. He needed the connections that I had, the bad connections I had to be exact. When I refused to keep his little business going, he planned for an attack.*

Me: *He didn't hold onto ur friendship. That hurt the most, didn't it?*

Damon: *Yeah, it did. I had put everything into our friendship, stood by him through every type of trouble, yet he left me when I needed him the most, and he never looked back.*

Me: *What happened to him afterwards?*

Damon: *Expelled. Never saw him again.*

That confirmed the rumors. I felt sympathy toward Damon. This one Muslim had completely deterred Damon away from the Muslim community. This one man's action shattered his perception of an entire religion, making him more vulnerable to the misconceptions that the media had fed.

Damon knew that not all Muslims were horrible, but the stigma was deeply rooted in him, planting its seeds right where his wound opened. The root of his problems was the trauma of a heartbreaking betrayal. No amount of physical pain could hurt more than losing his best friend.

Damon: *Amira, ur more than my best friend. Ur a girl who I can't live without. I don't even care about our differences; I just need u in my life. There's so much shit going on, and if I lost u too, I don't think I could ever trust anyone again.*

Me: *Damon, u can't like me. We discussed this.*

Damon: *I want to learn about the real Islam. I don't want to be afraid anymore. I don't want to keep doing this to u.*

He was tortured by the past, trapped by it in every way where he was chained to his memories. Damon was a prisoner to himself. In a way, we weren't that different. I, like him, was also trapped by the vortex of time.

Me: *Then maybe u should start by opening ur mind.*

CHAPTER 22
Awakening of Inquires

Damon Winters

I desperately wanted to tell her. I wanted Amira to know how badly she made me want her, how her smile brightened up my day and how her eyes seemed to beg me to hold her and lavish her. She was too irresistible.

I sighed as I leaned back against my headboard. She was a Muslim and I was an atheist. She couldn't have a date with me.

Religion had no meaning to me; especially that I found the idea of a religion stupid to begin with. My parents weren't religious either and I had never grown attached to the idea of God or spirituality. I preferred to live in the moment, in the absence of all chains of restrictions that religion imposed on helpless souls.

Islam had always been a religion I was weary of, unsure how anyone could follow a religion where terrorism reigned like a second nature, where anger overtook humanity. How Amira became a part of that religion, I had no idea.

Me: *Why does Islam allow terrorism? Why are u part of such an oppressed religion?*

Amira: *Islam doesn't allow terrorism. Islam is totally against it. Also, women are not oppressed. I speak from experience.*

Me: *Doesn't jihad mean terrorize? And how are women not oppressed?*

Muslim women had to cover everything, hidden by layers of clothes in order to oppress them from society, keeping them away from basic social interactions. It was saddening to see. They didn't even get to marry four husbands unlike their male counterparts. That wasn't even fair.

Amira: *Jihad means struggle like this is my jihad right here. It's my jihad (struggle) against ignorance. There r some Muslims that twist up the truth for their own advantages just like in any other religion. It's not just Islam that has people like that. There are a lot of serial killers that are from other religions, but they get to hate like Muslims do because they are told they have mental illnesses. That's the same with the other terrorists. Some have mental problems while others just use religion to cover crimes.*

Me: *I see ur point but u still didn't answer y women aren't allowed to have multiple husbands, but men are? Islam sounds like a religion that only fulfills men's need. It's filthy.*

As I sent the message, I felt a little bit of fear in the pit of my stomach. If there was one thing that I learned about Amira, it was that I should never underestimate her knowledge. Why did I have a feeling that she's about to put me to shame? Considering how long it was taking her to type this I knew that I was doomed.

Amira: *Damon, don't say anything about a religion if u don't understand it. When learning about Islam, don't listen to the crap that the media says cause there is a lot of falsehood behind their words.*

Secondly, in Islam, it is believed that women and men have different roles that they fulfill. Men are the protectors and sustainers of women. Their role is to provide and protect their families. Women are the ones who help raise her family, and support them. She also is the one that keeps her husband in check from doing wrong as her husband does the same for her. Men and women are like puzzle pieces that fit together to create a loving family.

Since men are the protectors and sustainers of women, how can a woman fulfill that role if she marries more than one man? That creates more stress for her. As for men, it says specifically in the Qur'an that if the man is not capable of taking care of another women, yet he still decides to marry a second wife and is bad at taking care of his wives, Allah will punish him because Allah warns us in the Qur'an about it. You don't believe me? Check Surah #4 A Nisa is about women and men's rights.

She totally just won this debate, but I was not about to admit that.

Me: *But still...*

Amira: *Actually, a lot of girls convert to Islam compared to men. They're not oppressed and if they were these women, wouldn't be converting. Also, Islam limits the number of wives one can have while other religions don't.*

Me: *Really? I didn't know that.*

Amira: *It's true.*

Me: *And u wonder y I like u so much;)*

Amira was quickly becoming so much more to me. I never felt so affected by a girl, especially one who didn't show anyone her beauty. It was so unlikely of me, but Amira somehow crawled her way into my heart, breaking all my previous standards with a mere smile.

Me: *Do u like me?*

It was quiet for a while with no response from her.

Amira: *it's complicated. Let's just say that u don't want to like me Damon. I don't want to hurt u.*

Me: *Ur gonna hurt me more if u don't tell me.*

Amira: *U won't understand these feelings.*

Me: *I could help u go through those feelings. Amira, what are u so afraid of?*

Amira: *Of this. Damon please.*

I didn't understand. Was she afraid of her feelings for me as well? It couldn't be just due to religious differences. There were tons of people who dated outside the constraints of traditional beliefs.

Me: *Are u ashamed of me?*

Amira: *No! It's religion. I don't know what to do right now. I don't want to hurt anyone.*

My heart broke into tiny pieces, shattering around me in sharp shards. She didn't want me like I thought. My chest felt tight, squeezing my heart, and making it beat out of rhythm.

It was getting hard to breathe as I let the rejection set in. The girl that I thought was perfect didn't want me. *Why?* She had to have liked me. She acted like she did. I was the first guy she ever texted, something she'd never done before. I was her first.

Me: *I just wanted to tell u I liked u. It's okay if u don't like me. We can still stay as friends. Nothing will change.*

Amira: *No, Damon, that's not it. It's just I can't like u. We can't be together. I want to, but I can't.*

If only she knew how much I wanted her. Surely, there had to be a way for us to be together. I couldn't lose her. I couldn't suffer the same fate as before.

This time, I wouldn't be able to survive another tragedy.

CHAPTER 23

Snow Drugged Emotions

DAMON WINTERS

It was finally March. Sunlight poured from the sky, touching the soft ridges of branches that were covered in a blanket of snow. White specks of dust fluttered towards my window as I squinted my eyes on the road.

The shimmering snow glittered, untouched and begging for attention. The air was frosty and freezing to the point that I could already see my breath, but nonetheless, was a sight for sore eyes. Bits of green peeked through their winter caps, a sleek glaze of white frosting the suburban roads as fur-lined coats populated the streets.

Every time I stopped by a red light, I found myself admiring the crystal flakes that drifted with the wind, following a gentle wind through denuded trees. I found comfort in the soft bits of snow we had received, relishing the peace that came with a gentle storm.

As I drove through lanes, all that was on my mind was Amira. I couldn't get her out of my mind anymore. It was not just attraction toward her, but it was so much more. She wasn't perfect, but she was perfect for me. Just like the flurries outside, Amira eased my worries away. She was the calm to my chaos.

She was smart, sweet, caring, had strong morals, modest, and had the most beautiful eyes. A strong string pulled us toward each other, where everyone else became a blur. It was only Amira who consumed my thoughts and mind like a drug. I sighed. *Oh Amira, you have no idea how much I want you,* I thought.

After parking my car, I walked to my locker before heading towards my first period class. As I walked into history, I saw Amira's maroon colored head scarf elegantly wrapped around her head. Her fingers vigorously scribbled something down, her head bent low and face twisted in concentration. Without realizing, I walked toward her. She didn't notice me as she was so engrossed into what she was writing.

"Hey," I said softly.

Amira jumped and looked up at me. Her warm brown eyes looked so welcoming like they were beckoning me towards her, tempting me with an aching need to be loved. She quickly averted her eyes to the ground and muttered to herself.

"So, what are you writing?" I asked as I leaned over her desk to look.

Her body tensed, clenching her hands into fists. Breathing in deeply, she sighed, her long eyelashes covering the eyes that haunted me in my slumber. I couldn't help but want to wrap my arms around her and pull her closer to my chest. I was just about to do that when my eyes landed on her writing, and I froze, suddenly catching every word.

Whisper, whisper,
In through the ears,
Right to the heart,
Quiet as can be,
Lips that never tell,
A fragile girl,
Covered in another's tale,
Acts as if she is at ease,
But it's a lie,

Worries surround her,
Pain chases after her,
She has no idea how to escape,
Secrets cover her,
Her soft lips seal them away,
No one knows,
What's hidden inside.

I stared at Amira in shock. She looked away from me, almost embarrassed at the pure masterpiece that she created. This girl in her poem reminded me of her. There were so many secrets to Amira that I had yet to discover. Could it be that Amira's past was really rough? What were the secrets that she concealed so easily?

"I know it's pretty bad writing, but this is the way I escape from the troubles in life. This and praying," she said with a faint smile that reached her eyes.

"Bad? Are you nuts? This is heart touching, Amira. Why have you never shown me your writings before?"

"I thought they weren't that good," she muttered.

I chuckled deeply, and pulled out a chair next to her. "Sweetheart, you're excellent at so many things. It's one of the many reasons why I admire you."

She looked up at me, and gave me a breathtaking smile that made my heart stop. Her soft lips were tempting me to taste them. They were begging to be caressed by my lips and tongue. Her sun-kissed skin was making me clench my fists to refrain from pulling her head toward me, and smashing my lips against hers.

Amira's lips were moving, but I couldn't pay attention to what she was saying. All I could think of was how she would feel against my body and how she tasted. I could already imagine her cuddled up next to me as we watched a movie or just talked.

I wasn't after Amira for sex. Something that other girls never could give me. It was the love and care she provided me with. She made me feel protected by her warmth. It felt as if I could do anything with her by my side. She made me feel euphoric. When she wasn't around to talk with me, I felt restless and unable to function without her attention on me.

I needed Amira in my life. *Whoa*, I thought. *This girl hit me way too hard with shivers.*

"Damon!"

I snapped back to reality. "What?" I asked innocently as if I did nothing wrong.

Amira glared at me with her eyes pointing like daggers and lips pressed. Even her facial expressions brought joy to my usually dull, gray life. Every second, every minute, every hour with Amira was a burst of colors, a new world that I had to discover.

"Is there ever a day where you don't glare at me?" I laughed.

"Keep dreaming, jerk," she huffed.

"Are you seriously mad?"

No response.

"Amira?"

Silence.

"Come on, Amira. Don't be so childish," I teased.

She just leaned her head onto the palm of her hand as she looked at me with a smug look.

"Okay, you win. I'm sorry for not listening," I sighed.

Amira brightened immediately, flashing me her pearly teeth. "It's all good."

This time I was the one glaring at her.

"Now, Damon, is there ever a day where you don't glare at me?" she mocked.

"Damn you," I mumbled under my breath.

"Damon! Profanity!" she exclaimed.

I rolled my eyes at her. "We're in high school," I said, as I gave her a blank stare.

"Still profanity," she argued.

"You say shut up all the time. Isn't that profanity?" I asked amused at her argument.

"No. That's child profanity. Those are allowed."

I laughed and some of my other classmates that came early turned to look at us like we had lost our minds from our contagious laughter. "You're weird," I grinned.

"And you're insufferable," she smirked.

"Oh, big words. I'm so scared," I said sarcastically.

"I would be if I were you. Never go against a linguistic person."

"And I'm not linguistic?" I asked with raised eyebrows.

"Aw, you, poor soul. I know you wish you had my skills, but we all can't get what we wish for."

I leaned in close to her until we were inches apart, my voice dropping very low for her ears only. "The only thing I wish for, Amira, is you," I whispered.

She tensed. I could sense the inner battle in her from the way her hands shook, the way her eyes widened in disbelief, and the guilty bite of her lips.

"Why do you get so tense every time I'm close?" I asked.

"I'm not used to guys being so close to me," she answered.

"Oh, well you better get used to it, sweetheart. I'm starting to crave for you," I replied, keeping my voice low and husky.

A barely noticeable shade of light pink stained her cheek. Amira sighed. "I'm sorry, Damon, but we can't be anything to each other. You're going to get hurt."

"Look me in the eye, and tell me you don't want me," I dared. *I refuse to let her get away from me.*

"Damon," she started.

"Do it," I demanded.

"I can't," she sighed defeated.

I smirked. "Stop fighting this, Amira. We can still be together. Please, be with me," I pleaded, as I grabbed her hand.

She shook her head and looked at me with a pained expression. "I have to fight it, Damon. I don't have a choice."

"We all have choices, Amira. What's your choice?"

"You don't understand," she gasped.

"Then make me understand!"

With a quiet, shaking voice she said, "We have choices in life, but those choices can do worse if we don't follow what is right. I don't have a choice if I know what the right choice is."

"Amira," I whispered.

She was in pain. My sweet, pretty girl was in so much pain and I couldn't help her. I had never felt so helpless in my life. In that moment, I realized that Amira was hiding more than I ever thought.

She hid her emotion and I felt terrible for doing it to her.

"Do you like me?" I asked, as I tilted my head.

She mutely nodded her head.

The realization hit me harder than I thought.

CHAPTER 24
Puppy Love

DAMON WINTERS

At lunch, I could barely focus on the conversations around me. Amira once again consumed my mind. She liked me, but she couldn't be with me. I didn't know what would hurt more, her not liking me or her not being with me when she liked me.

We were trapped in an endless cycle of pain, neither of us knowing which way to go. I was pushy in my advances, and was always rejected by Amira, a girl who prided herself in her beliefs. Most guys would have been repulsed, but her piety brought me closer to an inner comfort I never realized had existed.

The space around me was a distant buzz as I softly gazed at her. She looked down at her journal and started writing. That notebook was what she always wrote in. I could sense that there was something special about that journal.

I knew it wasn't a diary because I read a page from it, and it didn't read out as a typical teenage diary. No, Amira's journal was as complex as she was, filled with poetry and musings about snippets of her daily life. She was secretive in every way possible.

Amira bit her lip, and my eyes followed her every movement. I was finding it harder to control my urges for her. How could someone be so close to me, yet so out of reach?

After lunch, I ran to catch up with her, suddenly trying to find any excuse to start a conversation. My distracted mind made me blind to the girl in front of me, who I accidentally crashed into, making her drop all her stuff.

"Shit," I muttered, reaching down to help her pick up her stuff.

"Watch your profanity, stupid," a velvet-like voice scolded.

I looked up from my crouched position, and couldn't stop the smile from forming onto my lips. "Well, well, if it isn't my little beauty," I grinned.

Amira rolled her eyes. "Well, well if it isn't the little jerk."

I scoffed. "Little? Sorry to break it to you, sweetheart, but I'm several inches taller than you."

"Oh, shut up."

"For a girl you sure know how to hurt a guy's ego," I winced.

"Please, I was just warming up the insults. Don't be such a wuss."

I pouted.

"Damon," Amira said in warning.

I gave her my puppy dog face, which she merely stared at, clearly not amused.

"Puppy dog faces don't work on me," she taunted. "Try again."

"Damn you," I mumbled under my breath.

Amira sent me a coy smile, sly and elegant like she found my scowling more entertaining than anything else. I scoffed; feigning hurt as I glanced away from her.

"Damon," she tried, "Stop being such a child about this."

"I feel bullied. I want to file bullying and harassment reports now," I said with a hint of humor in my tone. "You wound me, Amira."

Amira walked ahead of me, laughing softly to herself as she left me trailing after her. It was like she had me on a leash, dragging me wherever she went. All the worries, stress and heartaches disappeared the second I heard her lilting voice; the minute I heard her breathtaking laugh.

"Wait for me!" I called, running to her side. "Why do you insist on insulting me on a daily basis?"

She shrugged and kept walking. I walked in pace with her, and looked down at where her hand and mine almost touched. All I had to do was move my hand a little more. I shifted my fingers to grab her soft hands. My fingers lightly brushed against hers. Amira looked up at me as she stopped walking, and I paused with her.

Those eyes, that captivated me since I first met her, stared at my deep emerald colored ones. The corners of her mouth tugged upwards into her beautiful smile that always knocked the breath out of my lungs. I took this moment to firmly grab her hand without hesitation, blocking my actions.

"Damon," she breathed, shaking her head in remorse.

"Please," I begged. I didn't want to let her go. A flash of the past burned the back of my mind, and I genuinely believed that letting Amira go would lead to that same feeling of emptiness and despair.

She was my best friend. I couldn't lose her over a couple of silly feelings.

I pulled her towards me, and she crashed into my chest. Something seemed to click in Amira's brain and she tried to pull away from me. My hold on her tightened, having her so close to me felt so very right.

"Damon, I can't. I'm sorry," she said with such sadness in her voice that I had to loosen my grip, not wanting to force her into anything.

"Just a few more seconds?" I tried to reason with her. Her hands rested on my chest, a feather like touch that made the skin underneath ignite even though we were covered in clothing. My hands fell down to her waist, loving the sensations it felt.

"No, Damon. I can't do what you want me to do. It's against *Islam,* and everything I've always believed in. I'm truly sorry but I can't," she stated firmly and successfully pushed me away.

To say I wasn't pissed was an understatement. There was so much I wanted to do with Amira, but she was a Muslim. Never in my life did I think I would fall for a girl who was so devoted to God. It was a trait I admired. The amount of self-control Amira had always seemed to surprise me.

"It's fine."

She seemed hesitant, staring at me uneasily. "I…"

"Yes?" I asked eagerly.

She shook her head with a nervous smile. "It's… nothing."

"You know you can tell me about anything."

"Yeah, I know."

"So," I drawled, leaning closer. "What's bothering you?"

She exhaled deeply. "This isn't right, Damon. I don't want to start something."

"What are you saying?"

"I'm saying that I want to be just friends. I have boundaries in Islam. This *hijab* is a testament to my beliefs. I can't be like all those other girls, Damon."

As I opened my mouth to argue that I didn't care if she couldn't be like other teens, a familiar girl with brunette curls accidently bumped into Amira, causing her to drop her binder and her other materials fell out of her hands.

"I'm so sorry," the girl said.

Oh, I remember now! That was the girl from the party. Kaylie.

"No, it's fine," Amira reassured and smiled at Kaylie.

Kaylie walked off, giving me a longing glance. Amira seemed to have noticed, her cheeks flushing with silent anger. I didn't want Kaylie, but I did like how jealous Amira could get. If the roles were reversed, I would have punched any guy who gave Amira a wistful glance.

Amira picked the last of her things. "Come on, we'll be late if we don't go now," she told me as she walked off.

I was going to follow her, but something got my eye. Amira was scurrying away in an attempt not ruin her attendance record, and left her journal laid limply on the ground. I picked it up, staring at it as if it was the most valuable thing on Earth, and in a way it was.

I held the journal tightly as I thought about what to do with it. Surely Amira would be pissed as hell if I read it, but at the same time I wanted to see what secrets it held inside to make me understand Amira better. Suddenly, I got a text.

Mom: *Come to the front office. I just talked to the attendance lady and we're going home early. Be quick. Your father and I need to tell you and your brothers something important.*

Amira's journal could wait.

CHAPTER 25
Drainage of Years

AMIRA SARKER

Damon unexpectedly left. I felt a tug on my heart throughout the whole day. As much as I would hate to admit it, I missed Damon but I couldn't like him though. If I started admitting my feelings for Damon, they would only get stronger. I couldn't take that risk.

I knew Damon would never understand how I felt. He wouldn't understand my decision of choosing my religion over him. As much as my mind and body wanted to leap into Damon's arms and kiss him senseless, I knew I couldn't.

Deep in my heart it felt wrong. In my heart, I felt the remembrance of *Allah*, knowing that my ongoing courtship with Damon in such circumstances only left me more vulnerable to a broken heart. I shouldn't have even talked to Damon secretly, but somehow *Shaytan* (Satan) got a hold of me. He kept on whispering and now I was in too deep, unless I stopped everything now.

The whispers taunted my mind like a damaged record player, whining from overuse, and laughing at my foolish mistake.

I mentally groaned. Damon relied on our friendship as much as I did. He trusted me with secrets and feelings he'd die before admitting to anyone else. My insides suddenly felt like fire.

My heart burned against my chest as I felt the constriction of pain in this life. It was like a warning.

I shook the feeling off. *I'm Amira Sarker. I can handle this. I can make Damon move on and still be intact with my faith. Everything is going to work out,* I reassured myself.

These days, I wasn't so sure anymore, but I knew that I had to try. I had to keep *Allah* as my priority, my *deen* (religion) as my focus. This life was temporary, a speck of dust compared to the endless amounts of joy in *Jannah* (Paradise).

Surely, those who struggle in this life were given the greatest blessings afterwards. I just had to keep my head on and my hormones away from logistics.

* * *

I took a bus straight to the hospital. Nanu's condition was getting worse. His once colorful eyes were now dull and blank, swirling with masked pain.

The man I saw five years ago was happy and optimistic. The man on the bed was depressed and ill, his condition overtaking his entire life, and leaving him in the wake of something worse. How could five years do this much to a person both emotionally and physically?

It made me wonder. Could this happen to me after letting Damon go? As I walked into the hospital, I searched my bag for my journal. I felt nothing, panic suddenly arising.

My eyes widened as I paused my steps, and frantically looked in my bag. *Oh Allah, where could that journal be?* I wrote in that journal since I was in third grade. It meant a lot to me and reminded me what I learned about life in the past. That journal was my life written in ink and numerous linguistic puzzles; I couldn't just lose it.

I took deep breaths to calm myself. *I probably left it at school. I'll find it tomorrow.*

Nanu's coughing form filled my senses, and the journal was forgotten, my heart was impatient against the rise and fall of my chest and the worry that settled behind my eyelids. I blinked back the tears.

He was going to be okay. *Allah* will take care of him.

The sight in front of me made my heart clench in an uncomfortable way. Nanu had IVs pierced into his arms. He had dark bags under his eyes as if he didn't sleep well for days. His lips were dry, cracking a little with dried blood resting against dead skin.

The feature that struck me the most was his eyes. They looked lifeless, hollow, empty. When his eyes met mine, a gasp escaped my lips, my lips trembling at the frail man that rested on a bed that wasn't his own but at the hospital's.

Thoughts about Damon flew from my mind; my eyes were blurring as I watched my grandfather smile tightly at me, never minding his own misery at being imprisoned in a hospital bleeding through. His pain mirrored mine.

I walked towards him, gently grasping his hand in mine, and holding it between my palms. Nanu jolted a little before relaxing under my touch once he noticed how badly I had to reassure myself that he was still alive and well.

Mum told me this morning that Nanu was going to get surgery due to his broken hip bone. The doctors said he had a blood clot forming.

A few months ago, Nanu rode his bike in Bangladesh, and fell on his hip. He didn't get it checked for a long time until now. He had so many health problems that I wasn't even surprised he needed surgery for it along with the numerous amount of pills he was given.

Even though I expected this to happen, it still hurts to see him like that.

Sighing, I took a seat on the chair beside the bed, letting the hand go. Silently, my grandfather watched me with knowing eyes, meticulously following the movements of my limbs.

It wasn't just him I was worried about though.

Too many things were happening at once. Sometimes, the stress of life was just too much, forcing irrational thoughts to form into webs of problems. There was never a solution because all humans really cared to think about were endless problems until a mountain of them formed.

I had Damon to worry about, how to break his heart in a way that wasn't harsh. My grandfather was struggling to recover on his hospital bed, worried for his family that he left in Bangladesh just for the treatment, and I found myself chasing after my spirituality.

That was something I could never lose, my religion. Without *Allah,* I was nothing. I had no purpose. I needed *Allah* more than I needed love in my life because Allah was the one who *guaranteed* that love.

My thoughts paused as Nanu tried to sit up. I scrambled to my feet to help him, resting my hand on his back as he hissed in pain from the searing torment of his hip bone. Glancing at the pillows, I grabbed a couple to rest the injured part of his body on, which he graciously accepted.

"What will the doctors do to me?" he whispered.

"They will take good care of you *In Shaa Allah*. You're going to be okay," I reassured, embracing him in a small hug.

Nanu's raspy voice spoke again, cutting into the perfunctory noises that filtered through the hospital halls from computer beeps to the click of a nurse's shoes. A couple of murmurs surrounded adjacent areas, but my grandfather's voice managed to mask all that.

"You know," he began with a faraway look in his coal-like eyes. "When your mother was your age, she used to always worry about everyone whether it be her siblings or your grandmother and I. She would worry about everyone and their well-being."

I stayed silent, intrigued by the story. My mother clearly hadn't changed.

He threw his head in a small laugh, dry but soft. His hand reached out to stroke his graying beard, a memory overtaking him. "She would always stress herself with the concerns of others, never wanting to take time for herself. Even now, she still sacrifices all her youth and time to help me."

"Well, you're her father," I said gently. "She loves you."

His eyes met mine, a mist of flurries and masking his despair at having his daughter sacrifice everything for him. "Being selfless isn't always going to be rewarding. Putting other people's needs before yourself is harmful to not only your body but your mind as well."

"What are you saying?"

"I'm telling you to not be entirely like your mother, Amira. Her life has drained away through stress and worries. You're still young. You need to think about yours, too."

A cold chill rushed through me, knowing that my grandfather's words hit too close to my nerve. "But what about everyone else-"

He put a shaking finger to his lips. "No," he said, "everyone else is not always important. Yes, you should be selfless, but not if it hurts you. Take a moment to breathe, Amira. *Allah* will always know your intentions."

Of course, he was right. I wanted to do the right thing, *Allah* knew that, but I was also conflicted. I didn't want to hurt anyone or forget about how much my family needed me.

Although it had only been a couple of months, being a senior felt like years had flown by without my realization. I was getting older, reaching the age of young adulthood. Life wouldn't get easier, and if I kept worrying about others, I too would have my life drained before my eyes.

I'm going to be okay as well, I thought, *Allah will take care of me and my family.*

CHAPTER 26
A Storm of Woes

DAMON WINTERS

I followed Mom and Dad into the house. I wouldn't lie and say I wasn't terrified about what they want to tell me because I was. After Dad's gambling incident, Mom hadn't gotten along with Dad really well, not that I blamed her.

I took a seat on the couch with Percy and Daniel. Percy was fidgeting, while Daniel didn't seem to care. I rolled my eyes. *Rebellious teens these days,* I thought. Percy was only ten, so it made sense that he was nervous. I didn't blame him either. The last few weeks have been rough on not just our parents, but us kids as well.

Mom took a deep breath and then looked at me. "Your father and I are getting a divorce."

Silence.

The shock shook me. My first reaction was denial. It couldn't be true, not after their almost two decades of marriage. It had to be a lie. I looked at Dad, and he was expressionless. I felt my skin starting to boil in heat. The shock that I felt disappeared and was replaced with anger.

"What the hell? Why now? Like I get that Dad gambled a lot, but we're family. Can't we just help each other out?" I seethed.

"Damon, please just listen to—"

"No! You listen to me, dad. Did you ever think of the impact that you two arguing did to your kids? Percy and Daniel are reaching that critical age. Stuff like this affects them in negative ways!"

"Damon, listen to me! What about how I feel about this marriage? Did you ever think of that?" Mom glared.

I crossed my arms over my chest as I stood up. Anger was traveling throughout my bloodstream as I saw a raw emotion flash through my mother's eyes.

"What's going on? There's more to this divorce than what you're telling me."

"We just fell out of love," Dad argued.

I laughed bitterly. "Oh really now? You just 'fell out of love'. That's crazy right there. After all those years of being happily married, you decide the one problem that can be easily fixed is going to end your relationship? Did I mention how happy you two were just a month ago?" I gave Dad a blank stare. "I can tell a lie when I see one, Dad."

"Damon, calm down," Daniel whispered behind me.

I turned toward him. "Calm down? Daniel, they're not telling us the truth. We're their sons, not their puppets. We have the right to know."

"Damon, that is the truth. Now, calm down," Dad said sternly.

"You can't expect me to calm down when my parents are getting a divorce! Damn it! Just tell me why you two are actually separating," I exclaimed.

Silence surrounded me as Mom and Dad exchanged glances nervously. I was breathing heavily after my outburst. My body was tense, muscles straining against each other as my veins pulsed. The air was blocking my lungs. I already knew that what my parents would say next would be a displeasure.

Finally, my mother broke the silence. "Your father had an affair with another woman years ago," she said in a shaky voice.

I felt my anger halted along with the rest of the room. My eyes widened, and my throat felt dry as I took the revelation in.

"Wait, did he get her, you know, pregnant?" Daniel asked, nervously.

Mom mutely nodded. I heard gasps from my brothers. Mom's head was down, her shoulders shaking as a sob ripped through her. I couldn't comprehend it. I couldn't believe Dad. He cheated on Mom. He broke her. He broke our family.

My head snapped toward Dad. I looked at him directly into his dark green eyes. "You're no father of mine," I seethed, running towards the door.

I heard my name and shouting, but I just ignored them, and kept running. I needed to get away from here.

*　　*　　*

Running away, my legs brought me to the lake where I first saw Amira crying. I sat against the trunk of a tree, ignoring the pricks of the barks behind me. My eyes burned, but I refused to cry over my scumbag of a father. *I have a half sibling.* That thought just seemed to echo in my mind. All I could think about was Dad's mistake.

I buried my head into my knees. *I can't deal with this. I'm not strong enough. Why did life hate me?* This void in my heart just pained me. I felt so helpless. The deed was done and I couldn't do anything about it. I felt a knot in my throat.

As I tried to relax my breathing, I heard gentle footsteps come toward me. I didn't lift my head up to see who it was. The wind whispered against my shirt, blowing the creases. The calm breeze eased my tensed body a little.

A couple of stray brown hairs fell across my forehead, bristling from the gentle winds that pulled me away from my dark abyss of sorrow. The footsteps stopped in front of me. After a few moments of silence, a familiar velvet voice cut through the thick air.

"Damon?" she asked, softly.

I slowly lifted my head to gaze at Amira. She had an olive colored scarf on with a loose black sleeved shirt and plaid pj bottoms. Her eyes were sketched with deep concern.

"Damon, are you alright? You look like a mess," she said.

I snorted. "Gee, thanks," I muttered sarcastically.

Amira put her hands up in a type of surrender. "No, I didn't mean it like that. I meant you look kind of depressed," she amended.

I sighed. "That's because I am."

Amira sat across from me on the bed of grass. "Wanna talk about it?" she asked.

I leaned back against the tree. "What can you do about it? It's not going to help me," I spat out bitterly as I ran a hand through my messed up hair.

Amira looked down at the ground. "Sometimes bad things happen in life that makes us feel different emotions. Battling up with those emotions for too long can leave one's soul to be restless," she looked up at me with those warm melted eyes, "It's not easy to carry those burdens alone. Sometimes you need an extra shoulder to cry on. I should know."

There it was again. That thump in my heart that squeezed painfully as I thought of Amira's struggles.

"Yeah I guess I just figured that out," I said.

"Please tell me. Whatever you're going through right now, you don't have to do it alone. I'm here for you," she reassured me.

I took a deep breath as I prepared myself to tell Amira what happened. "My parents are getting a divorce," I said. She gasped, but I continued on. "Ever since my dad gambled so much money away, Mom hasn't gotten along with him. They constantly argue every night, but this is different. All I heard when I tried to sleep were the screams and yells from my parents. I felt so... alone. If their arguing hurts me this much, I can only imagine how bad it is for my brothers. They're still young, Amira. They're just reaching that critical age in their lives and stuff like this can emotionally scar them, especially after what my dad had done," I whispered the last part as I gazed at the lake. I couldn't look at Amira as I felt my eyes sting.

"What did he do?"

"He... he had an affair with another woman and... impregnated her," I forced out.

"Oh my God. That's terrible, Damon!" she exclaimed.

I laughed humorlessly. "You know what sucks the most about this? That I am so useless. I feel so damn weak. I can't do anything to stop this all from happening. My parents are getting divorced and there's nothing I can do to stop it," I growled lowly as I felt a tear slip my eyes. "Who knew the past could hurt this much?"

"Oh, Damon. Look at me," urged Amira. I looked up at her. "This is out of your control. I understand how helpless you feel. It's not easy finding all this family history out in one day. Damon, you're an amazing individual. You will get through this trial in life. I promise you. I'm going to be here for you as you go through this. We're in it together," she smiled.

That was when I moved closer to her warmth, wrapping my arms around her. She was the constant thing in my life, the one person who didn't change or turn into a monstrous human soul. A few tears spilled onto her scarf and my shoulders shook uncontrollably. Amira tried to pull away but I tucked her back in my arms.

"I know that I shouldn't hug you, but please just this once. I need this right now. I need you," I begged.

She paused. I breathed in her delicious scent and felt her hands on my chest. I pulled away and gave her some space. She breathed in deeply.

"Amira, can I ask you something?"

"Of course."

I locked gazes with her. "Will you ever leave me?"

She smiled up at me. "Never. I will never leave you."

"Good because I won't let you leave."

"Damon, relax. I'm here for you. I'm not going anywhere," she said softly.

I smiled. We sat there and talked for a while. She told me about her grandfather's surgery. I could see the pain in her eyes as she recalled his physical appearance, his words of wisdom, and his fragile state of mind. It was evident that she deeply cared for him, more than her own life struggles it seemed.

I couldn't bear to see my girl like that. I couldn't bear to see how distraught she was and how her own tears lined her waterline as she blinked back her own tears. We both had problems. We both were stumbling through life with certain blindness. I had no direction while Amira had too many to follow through.

"He's going to be okay, Amira. I'm sure."

"Only *Allah* knows," she sighed.

I stayed silent. *Allah*. Amira sure did put a lot of trust in *Allah*. But why? What made her believe in *Allah*?

Amira didn't say much about her grandfather. She just seemed so deep in thought. The silence was peaceful as we gazed at the lake. I glanced at Amira. Her eyes were trained on the shimmering water. Her cheeks had a light pink to them. It was at that moment that I felt the emotion I thought I would never feel. *Love.*

CHAPTER 27
A Touch of Hope

DAMON WINTERS

When I arrived home, I went straight to my room. I couldn't bear to see Dad's face. I was hoping Mom would divorce him for all he did to our family and all the pain he made us go through. I never would have thought that my life would have taken such a bad turn.

Everything was so fine. It wasn't a perfect life, but I was contented with it. Now, I realize how much I took my life for granted. Those sweet memories of my life meant so much more to me now.

I stripped my shirt off when I heard a knock on my door. I stayed still; not daring to move. More knocks followed after. I still didn't move until I heard a frustrated grunt from the door. It sounded like it came from a little kid.

I quickly threw my shirt back on, and opened the door. Percy stood at the door, fidgeting and shifting from foot to foot. His dark curls were messy, and his eyes were puffy. My heart softened at his state. *This divorce must be difficult for him.*

"Um... could we talk, please?" he asked.

I nodded and ushered him into my room. Percy sat on my bed and I sat beside him. He was fiddling with his fingers unsure of what to say. I sighed.

"Percy, what's wrong?"

"Mom and Dad."

"Percy—"

"No, Damon. They're separating. I may be ten, but I'm not stupid. He got someone pregnant! I-I can't believe it!" he exclaimed. "Why couldn't he just keep it in his pants? Better yet, why didn't he stay faithful to Mom? Or even-"

I covered his mouth with my hand. Now that my anger subsided, thanks to the help of Amira, I could handle the situation in a more mature manner.

"We don't know why he did it. We can't just accuse Dad so blindly right now. I mean, yeah, we're pretty piss— I mean mad. Still, we should at least ask him," I advised even though my words stabbed at my conscience.

Percy let out a deep breath. "I know, but I just can't believe it. No... I don't want to believe it. This isn't true. Right, Damon?" he asked, while looking up at me with those identical dark green eyes of Dad.

Everything about Percy reminded me of Dad. His dark brown curls, his crooked nose, and his eyes. He was the mini version of Dad. As he looked up at me, I couldn't help the pain that swelled my chest. *He's scared, just as I am.*

I wrapped my arms around my little brother. I rested my chin on the top of his head as I whispered, "I wish it wasn't true, Percy. I really wish it wasn't."

Percy's arms tightened around me. He was silent for a few moments. "Sometimes I wish I was never born," he mumbled into my chest.

I pulled back to stare at him with wide eyes. "Don't you ever say that! Just because Mom and Dad are arguing doesn't mean you should lose your will to live. Whatever Mom and Dad are going through now is just a new chapter of their life. Pretty soon, the next chapter will be written."

He shook his head. "I don't want new chapters. I want the old ones back. I want my family back!" he yelled, tears crawling down his rosy cheeks.

Although Percy felt really bad about our family's situation, I felt it even worse and the burden of my brothers was on me now. I was responsible for them and I couldn't even take the pain away from them.

As much as I would hate to admit it, I wasn't stable enough to take care of myself. Teenagers these days were reckless. They didn't care about the world and were only out for worldly pleasures in the comfort of warm arms, but life had thrown my old life into a bin. I was no longer responsible for myself alone, but for my brothers as well.

"I want them back too, Percy. I want them back so bad, but that's not how life works. Mom and Dad may argue more than ever, but I'm not going to leave you. I'll always be here for you, little bro," I smiled.

I will never leave you.

Amira's words echoed into my head. The words were so simple and effortless, yet valuable. Her words lifted the weight off my shoulders, the pressure sank, and the world seemed right again because at least, I still had one person who was willing to stay.

"Damon, why did you run away?"

I sighed. "I was scared."

"Of what?"

"Of losing my family."

Percy went silent and I immediately panicked. I didn't want him to think depressing thoughts after our entire conversation. I should have been giving him hope, I should have been his light, but how could I if I was scared, too?

I knelt in front of Percy as he put his head down. I was pretty foreign of giving affectionate gestures to my brothers, but this just came as an impulse. It was like my body had a mind of its own. I cupped his cheeks so he would look at me. His deep green eyes bore into mine like a hurricane in the depths of wilderness.

"I'm scared too, but we're going to be okay. Alright?"

He nodded his head before reaching up to wrap his small arms around my neck, pulling me towards him. The gesture shocked me, but I quickly recovered and returned his hug, feeling as if we had the strength to overcome this obstacle in our life.

*   *   *

Percy and I sat in my room for a while, playing video games. Daniel joined us afterwards as we tried to ignore the fear we all felt. I let the boys just crush each other in the games as I thought of one certain girl.

Her inviting lips seemed to taunt me every time I was around her. Her smile always made my heart do weird flips. Her voice lightened even the darkest day, expelling all the clouds away from her radiance. Her touch melted the ice that surrounded me, allowing me to drown in of her essence.

She was more than a friend to me.

I was attracted to her since the first day I met her, but it wasn't as strong as it was now. I found myself missing her presence whenever she wasn't around. I loved the way she laughed and how she always had a smile on her face. I even loved the harsh glares she gave me.

Her light touches made electricity surge through my veins. The sound of her voice was a welcoming melody to my senses, a symphony that I never wanted to end. *Damn, I'm so whipped.*

I loved her.

I have never been so sure of anything in my life. I knew I loved her for a while now, but I didn't really take notice into the emotion. The urge to tell her has been bugging me, but I didn't know how. How would she react? I knew Amira liked me. I just didn't know how strongly she liked me. She concealed her emotions all the time. I could barely figure her out.

"You should really tell her how you feel," a voice interrupted my peaceful thoughts, dragging me back to the hell I had been so kindly blessed with.

I saw Mom leaning against the door frame with a small smile. I rolled my eyes. "It's nothing."

"I may be getting a divorce, but I know that my son has a crush."

I got up. "Mom, go to bed."

Instead of leaving, she settled herself next to me on the bed but I wasn't in the mood. The shackles that strained me seemed to get tighter; my inner demons poking through, telling me I was worthless. I was a mess and my family would never be like other families. Love wasn't a force strong enough to hold two people together.

I knew my mother would get sick of my father's antics, but I didn't expect that day to come so soon. My father wasn't a horrible person; however, he had a child with another woman. I couldn't bear to face him, not now, not ever.

I didn't want to see him again. I didn't trust my actions in his presence.

"I'm serious, Damon. I don't want things going on between your dad and I to affect you so much."

I clenched my fist. "Don't you already see how much it affects me? I have a half sibling, Mom! This isn't something I can easily brush off."

She inhaled a sharp breath and I feared that maybe my words hurt her. "You're right. Damon, I am so sorry, but I don't regret my decision of leaving your father," she said firmly, although the hurt was clearly evident in her hazel eyes.

"I didn't expect you to," I muttered.

"Don't hate your father. He's still family," she sighed.

"I am not related to that filthy pig," I growled.

"Damon, you can't hate your father. It's not right."

"I don't care. He's a bastard that deserves to rot in hell."

"Damon—"

"I'm sorry, Mom. I'm just really mad," I forced out. 'Mad' wasn't even the right word to describe my emotions.

She nodded her head in understanding. "I think you should talk to your father. It might help you cope with everything."

"No," I stated. "I don't care what you say, but he's not my father anymore."

Stress lined her forehead creasing, it seemed like my mother had aged ten years more. Although her husband's betrayal from years ago cut like blades against her sensitive skin, she was a mother above all else, my mother to be exact. I was her priority.

"I… I understand how hard life has been, Damon," she choked over her own words, tears brimming her eyes. My hand instantly grasped hers. "With that fight from your old school, this move, your father's gambling, and now this. I know how hard it is."

"I don't think you know the extent of it."

Her tearful eyes met mine, her own body shattering before my eyes as all the years of fighting with Dad finally struck her. "Did you think I liked watching my son come home with a busted lip and bruises all over his body? Did you think I was happy watching hatred eat you as the days went by because of one student? I saw your future flash before my eyes. I saw you becoming just like your father, damaged and troubled."

The memory of Luqmaan pained me. "I don't want to talk about my old school. I don't want to talk about Dad."

"That's exactly the problem, Damon!" she exclaimed. "You can't keep running away when people hurt you. You can't keep searching for a release from your life problems. You even refuse to talk to your father, instead, you run away."

Damn, that hit a nerve. I couldn't contain the eruption of anger from fueling my system. Without thinking, my mouth spat fire on its own accord with my mind blinded by rage.

"Isn't that why you moved away from us, Mom? You wanted to run away, too! You didn't want to accept that your husband was fucked up. You ran away and took us with you!" I yelled, retracting my hand as I stood up, glowering down at her. "Don't tell me not to run away when you did the same thing."

"Damon, I never said I was perfect."

"Then why do you expect me to be?" I croaked. "I'm not perfect, Mom. I'm fucked up just like Dad. I'm a lost cause just like he is. Your fears were right. I am just like him."

The thought broke me. I felt my heart drop and my mind fog into a tortuous memory. I remembered that day so clearly and I relived it every night. I remembered Luqmaan's betrayal.

He had me cornered in the hallway, stalking me like a hawk. His friends came out from behind, swiping a knife right at my throat as they threatened to slit it unless I gave them what they wanted: drugs. It had all been for drugs.

Luqmaan wanted to kill me, calling me an infidel, a man who deserved to die at the hand of terrorists. He praised their work, called himself a Muslim of divine right. Our friendship was meaningless.

Until Amira happened, I believed all other Muslims were some twisted version of Luqmaan, people who wished to eradicate me from this world because I wasn't like them. I didn't realize I was doing the same thing to the Muslims.

"Damon," Mom softly said. "You're not like him."

"How would you know? I found release in immoral things, Mom. I'm not capable of loving or to be loved."

Her gaze softened. "But there's a girl in your mind, sweetheart. You care for her, don't you?"

I mutely nodded.

"So, you are indeed capable of loving and of being loved. Anyone can fall in love, Damon, but not everyone is good at maintaining their relationships. Your father was the latter."

“Maybe we both need to stop running away,” I whispered. “Maybe we should both face things head on.”

She smiled. “I think so, too. Go tell that girl how you feel tomorrow. You might not get another chance.”

“You should talk with Dad.”

That night, my mother and I made a silent pact with each other, a toast to our future. Escaping reality wasn’t an option anymore because everything in life was hidden under a veil and a touch of sorrow. Sadness didn’t have to silence the weak, not if I could face my problems with my own courage.

CHAPTER 28
Two Hearts

AMIRA SARKER

I sat down on the bleachers, watching the students train for their next soccer match. Groups of students chased after the ball, tripping, screaming, and yelling orders at each other. The sun blazed against their backs, sweat staining their uniforms. Blades of grass flew into the air, students brushing against the hard surface of the world.

Damon told me to wait at the bleachers after school, so he could tell me something. His eyes had been red and puffy like he had spent the previous night in the turmoil of an emotional rollercoaster. I didn't ask questions, but I knew whatever he had to tell me, it bothered him throughout the night.

I sat there for several minutes. *Where is he?*

"Hey!" a voice called.

I jolted upright as Damon ran toward the bleachers. He was sweating a lot. His jersey clung to his sculpted chest, touching all the hard creases on his body. Sweat beads dripped down the side of his face, falling to his shoulders. His wet hair stuck to his forehead, drenched in a hard day of work.

He sat next to me panting and trying to regain his posture. I couldn't stop the giggle from escaping my lips at the state he was in.

"Shut up," he muttered.

"Oh, don't be such a baby," I pouted.

Damon's lips slowly curled into a smile, his bright green eyes staring at me with such emotion that I was left breathless.

Clearing my throat, I asked, "So what did you want to tell me?"

He straightened, looking flustered as he tried to form the words. I tilted my head slightly, studying him with curiosity. He closed his eyes for a brief second as if trying to give himself confidence, clenching and unclenching his fists as if he was in pain or serious frustration.

What is so important that the usually arrogant Damon is now shy?

He opened his eyes, and they shined with a vivid emotion that I couldn't interpret. Maybe I didn't want to interpret it because of what it could mean.

"Promise me that if I say it, you won't run away. Okay?" he asked.

"I promise."

He looked me in the eyes. "I love you," he said softly.

I froze. He couldn't love me. Maybe I heard him wrong.

"What?" I asked, shocked.

"I said, I love you."

The three words that I desperately wanted to hear my whole life was now being said to me. I panicked instead of celebrating. Damon couldn't fall in love with me. If he did, it was going to hurt him even more when he would see me gone in the future. I didn't care what would happen to me, but I cared about Damon. It was then that I realized that I was in love with him, too.

I loved him.

"Amira," he pleaded. "Say something."

"You can't love me," I said hoarsely.

He chuckled half-heartedly. "Sweetheart, I can't control these feelings anymore. I fell hard for you and I'm still falling. I can't get you out of my mind. No matter what I do, you're always there for me. I can't even focus without you. I—I love you so damn much that it hurts," he said with honesty dripping from his every word.

"Damon, are you sure that you love me?"

"I've never been so sure in my entire life," he admitted.

I choked up. "You can't love me. You're going to get hurt."

He shook his head with a slight smile. "I don't care. I can't stop loving you."

"Damon, love can ruin you. Don't you understand? I might ruin you."

"Then let it ruin me. Amira, I'm in love with you and I can't stop it," he said softly, reaching to grab my hands. I felt tingles reach up my arms. "I need you. Without you, Amira, I am nothing."

I tried to pull away, but he only held my hands tighter in his steel like grip. "Damon, stop."

"Amira, what do you feel for me?" he asked.

The vulnerability in his eyes was what stopped whatever protests that formed in my throat. How could I answer him truthfully? I didn't want to hurt him, but I didn't know what to do.

"I can't say," I mumbled, looking down.

My limbs went limp. Damon released his grip on my hands, and ran his fingers through his soft brown hair. A frustrated expression was painted across his face.

"What are you so afraid of, Amira? I just confessed my heart out for you. The least you could do is say something. Anything!" he exclaimed.

I closed my eyes to try to release the frustrated angry thoughts in my head. *Allah, please guide me,* I thought, *please help me.*

I debated on what I was going to say, sighing as my thoughts overwhelmed me. "Damon, this is a matter of beliefs and morals. I need to keep my self-control, but it gets harder every day. You're... you're all that I want," I whispered the last part.

His eyes widened. "Are you saying that...?" he trailed off nervously.

I nodded hesitant because I knew whatever I said now would be either for the better or the worse. "I may be falling for you."

He grinned widely before he saw my pained expression. "What's wrong?" he frowned.

"The worst part is that I know I let it go too far. I'm scared," I whimpered with tears pricking my eyes, but I blinked them back.

He came close to me, hesitating on whether to touch me or not. His hands stayed limp at his sides as he looked at my state.

"Why are you so scared of showing your feelings?" he asked, quietly.

"I can't love you, Damon. One of us will be terribly hurt in the end. We can't be together. Don't you understand?"

He stayed silent for a few moments. I felt a bit relieved that he finally understood my reasons, but disappointed that I couldn't be with him.

"I'll convert to Islam," he said casually.

My jaw dropped. "Damon, are you insane? You can't convert for that! Changing your beliefs is a big thing. If you convert to Islam it has to be for the religion, not for me."

"But this way we can be together, and you won't be so conflicted."

I shook my head. *This boy, I thought.* "As sweet as it is, no. I would rather you convert for the right reasons."

He sighed. "Why are you so difficult?"

"Because I care."

"This is one of the reasons why I love you," he smiled.

The butterflies in my stomach only intensified. My cheeks burned as his loving gaze engulfed me in his ardor, a warm bubbly feeling in the pit of my stomach. As the wind bristled between us, the golden string from Greek myths led me back to Damon, back into a world of bliss where nothing could shatter my perfect perception of love.

Nothing except rationality.

CHAPTER 29
Brotherly Problems

AMIRA SARKER

I stood in front of the mirror, looking at myself through my reflection. When I looked in the mirror, I saw the flaws in me that others didn't see. I saw the imperfections that I desperately tried to conceal. I saw the truth behind my eyes.

I sighed as I looked away from the mirror. I wasn't overly beautiful, but I wasn't bad looking either. In my eyes, there was no such thing as ugly. The true ugly people were the ones with no heart and rotten personality; the ones who were blinded by selfishness who begged for attention in the worst possible ways. I couldn't help but wonder what Damon saw in me to say that he loved me.

I was covered completely in cloth. I didn't show any skin except for my hands and face. Then again, Damon didn't fall for my looks. He fell for me. He fell in love with who I am. There was that word again.

Love.

He loved me. I didn't know if I could say that I loved him, but a part of me longed to, urging me to tell him that I wanted to only be his, but my future stopped me. I wanted to save those words for my future husband. I wanted to be completely sure before I said 'I love you' to another person.

Looking at the mirror again, I noticed the soft glow that covered my cheeks, making my skin look brighter, but that didn't stop the guilt. *What happened to me?*

*   *   *

Damon was at my locker, waiting for me before school. He was texting on his phone, leaning against the lockers with a frown painted on his lips. His brown hair ruffled on top of his head, as the gray hoodie stretched across his broad chest. He seemed a little too angry this morning.

"Is everything alright?" I asked, walking up to him.

He jolted at the sound of voice. When he saw me, he grinned, quickly putting his phone away. "Just missing my girl," he winked.

I shook my head with a smile. "And the pick-up lines continue."

"Don't act like you don't enjoy them," he teased.

"I didn't say I didn't enjoy them, did I?" I playfully questioned as I put in my combination numbers.

He whistled lowly. "Not as innocent as I thought, huh?"

I opened my locker, putting my stuff in. "Whatever, playboy. I'm still more innocent than you."

He chuckled. "Man, I love you," he sighed contently.

I stopped my movements. *There he goes again and here I am like a lost puppy.* Damon noticed my movements and came up behind me, wrapping his arms around my waist. I knew it was wrong so I find myself pulling myself away until we were a couple feet apart.

Falling in love wasn't forbidden. *Allah* knew that we were only humans who couldn't help what we felt for others, but *Islam* was a religion of self-control. It was a religion that taught its people to treat others with respect, and put boundaries in our social interactions. I could fall in love, but I shouldn't act upon it.

"Hey, what's wrong?" he asked, softly.

"Nothing," I brushed off quickly.

He sighed. "This is about us that's bothering you, right?"

"I just don't know what to do."

"You don't have to do anything. Just feel."

I only nodded. The way Damon and I saw things were completely different. To 'just feel' sounded so easy and so simple. However, life was not like that. The life of a Muslim was not like that. This was a temptation. Just because his touches and presence felt right didn't mean that it was right.

He leaned over and kissed my cheek before I could even move away. "Believe me on this," he said, leaving the skin his lips touched burning from embarrassment or guilt, I wasn't sure.

Maybe both.

Ya Allah, forgive me. I can't control what he does, but help me control myself.

"What were you so upset about earlier?"

He raised a brow.

"You were looking at your phone and seemed distressed, why?" I asked.

Realization dawned upon him. "My dad was texting me," he shrugged, pretending as if it was nothing of importance. From the hidden fury behind his eyes, I knew the flames of his anger came from deep within. "It's really nothing," he continued, placing his hands into the pockets of his sweats.

"I don't think you're being honest."

"Why do you say that?"

"Because I know your father's betrayal hurt you," I said softly, "I know how much it hurts to think about."

Seeming ambivalent, he released a deep sigh, knowing it was probably best if he talked about it. "My mom and I talked last night," he admitted.

"And?"

He tore his gaze away from mine, finding the floor to be more interesting as he shifted from foot to foot. "I'm not ready to face him. I don't know if I ever will be. I know he isn't a horrible person, but this time he went too far. He hid this for years. He lived with us while knowing he had another kid with another woman, Amira. I don't know how I can ever forgive him."

My heart urged me to comfort him with my touch, to hold Damon close, but my mind screamed. I couldn't physically comfort him like that. I couldn't touch him without getting burned by my own desires. I had to stay in control.

"Maybe you should learn how to forgive," I said.

His green eyes snapped up to mine, pale face twisted in disbelief. "You've got to be kidding me," muttered Damon to himself. "How do you forgive such a man?"

"Well—"

"No, Amira. I forgave him way too many times in the past and he abused that forgiveness. He promised to change like he always did, but he never did. He isn't obviously capable of change, let alone maintaining his relationships in life."

"You don't have to believe that he will change, but don't completely shut him out. He's still your father, Damon. One day he might not be there," I said, sadness dripping off my words as I thought about the one I lost. "Death doesn't discriminate. He takes the young and the old, the healthy and the ill. You should cherish that he's still alive and that he still has time to change."

"I don't know," he sighed. "It's hard to forgive."

"Think about it," I whispered. "You should talk to him though before it's too late."

I knew I had given too much information about my past, but there wasn't a day that went by when I didn't think about all the pain death had caused. The ripple effect flowed through everyone in my household, scarring Tanwir in the worst possible ways. My mother still wept for her lost child, her eldest. We had time, but we wasted it.

* * *

I came home from school and went to search for my phone. I realized I left it at home during my math class. *I really need to organize my stuff,* I mentally grumbled. As I walked into my room, I saw Tanwir staring at my phone screen with a hard expression.

"Tanwir, what the hell are you doing?" I glared. *Why doesn't he let me touch his stuff but he touches mine? That's completely unfair!*

His eyes snapped up to meet mine. The hard expression was replaced with a scowl. "I was going to play *Summoners War* on your account since you're such a lower level compared to me, but instead I found certain messages that I shouldn't have found," he calmly stated.

Anger flared inside me. He looked through my stuff. "Why are you looking through my stuff? Do you not respect privacy anymore because the last time I checked, you never let me look through your stuff," I hissed in an annoyed tone even though my hands were shaking. *He couldn't have seen them.*

"Relax, it was in your notifications, but now I need to teach some sense in you," he growled before glaring in my direction. "What's the matter with you, Amira? Why do I see this message from a boy named Damon?"

My jaw dropped. *I'm done for.* "What message?" I asked carefully like I was talking to an angry beast.

"Allow me to read it. 'I wish you would give me a chance especially since we're both into each other.' Amira, what is this? Don't give me crap about a joke or something. Tell me the truth," he demanded.

Shame overwhelmed me. I knew I couldn't keep it a secret for long. "It's nothing."

He humorlessly laughed. "Oh, that's funny. It's nothing you say, huh? Because to me it looks like *something*."

"Tanwir—"

"No! Don't 'Tanwir' me. Amira, you know Muslims aren't supposed to date. You're not supposed to have relationships like this with the opposite gender. What don't you understand?" he reproached, eyes reprimanding me into silence as excuses melted on my tongue.

By now I was enraged. I couldn't blame him for judging me, but it still hurt to hear it aloud. "Stop judging without knowing me! You're one to talk considering you do things secretly without Mum and Baba knowing. I do understand and I know what I'm doing. I have the situation under control, unlike you."

As soon as I said it, I regretted it.

Something in Tanwir's eyes changed. The fierce flare in his eyes was replaced by an affectionate gaze. Shame streamed through my blood, painfully squeezing my heart as I watched my brother crumble before me, vulnerability was shining through his eyes.

"When you lose self-control in one aspect of life, you lose it in another. Don't be one of those girls, Amira. Don't stray away from the right path where you are in," he whispered softly.

I was shocked. This wasn't the tone I normally heard from him. I must have hit a soft spot in his heart, and the words he spoke about self-control scared me.

I felt the frustrations of life brim my eyes, quickly brushing the tears away. I opened my mouth to say something but he held up his hand.

"Don't make the same mistakes I made. Be better than who I am. I won't tell Mum and Baba because I trust you," he said before walking out of my room without a glance at me.

I fell to my knees as soon as he left. *What have I done?*

CHAPTER 30
The Journal of Truth

DAMON WINTERS

Thundering fists banged against my bedroom door. I jolted upright and looked at the clock beside my bed. It was five in the morning. Groaning, I pulled my sheets off. Whoever was knocking should better have a good reason for waking me up because if not, they were going to die.

I sluggishly walked over to my door and rubbed my eyes, opening it. My jaw automatically dropped as I saw who was in front of me. Amira, or I least that was what I thought.

I rubbed my eyes again. "A-Amira? Is that you?" I stuttered.

In front of me was not the Amira I knew. This Amira had a hooded gaze in her eyes that were filled with a passion that I was very familiar with. She had a white blouse on, wearing skinny jeans that made me want to grab her legs and wrap them around my waist, as I directed a pleasurable feel all throughout her body.

She wore midnight black heels. What really caught my attention was the silky black long hair that reached down to her hips in beautiful waves. In all, she looked breathtaking.

She giggled. I mentally slapped myself and focused my attention toward her. Oh God. Those smoldering dark eyes kept me standing still. She looked exotic and I felt myself instantly react to her.

"Damon, why are you looking at me like that?" she asked in her angelic voice as she tilted her head.

I groaned. Holy shit! She was making me so aroused and she hadn't even touched me yet. I was so screwed.

"I need you," I staggered out as my breathing became uneven with every step she took near me.

I didn't move. I had too much respect for her to do something that she might regret later, but hell, I was getting hard. Snap out of it, Damon!

Amira grinned mischievously as she closed the door and walked in. I took a step back as she took another step toward me. I felt myself against the wall with a straining bulge in my boxers, yet I still managed to keep my hands to myself even though all I wanted to do was explore her silky soft skin. She placed her hands on my chest gently, and leaned her mouth close to my ear until her hot breath fanned over my neck.

"I missed you," she whispered, pulling back to look me in the eyes.

I found myself staring at her beauty. Her cute button nose and those perfect sugar plum lips were tempting me in ways that drove me to madness. The gaze she bore upon me was not one of lust, but rather one of love.

A love I was starving for, a love I relied on to breathe, and a love that showed me the light.

I moved my arms to wrap around her waist to pull her soft body against mine. The feel of her against me was heavenly. I never felt like this before. Without hesitation, I kissed her.

As soon as our lips made contact, all reasoning and logic flew out the window. Her lips were so soft and inviting. I groaned at the feel. It drove me wild.

I switched our positions so that she was pressed up against the wall with my knee in between her legs. My mouth devoured hers as she moaned. That sound was music to my ears. I bit her bottom lip; asking for entrance into the warm haven of her mouth. She kept her mouth shut and slowly teased my lips with subtle nibbles.

I growled frustrated and grasped her behind, which ignited a small gasp from Amira. I slid my tongue in her mouth as her fingers pulled my hair. Grasping the back of her thighs, I lifted her up against the wall. I trailed kisses-

Ring! Ring!

I jumped awake as my alarm went off. *Damn it!* I had another dream of her. The bulge rubbing against the material of my boxer was pure evidence of the effect this girl had on me. Sighing, I got up to take a cold shower.

* * *

As I dried my hair with a towel, I caught sight of my reflection. I had gotten slight bags under my eyes due to the restless nights of thinking about Amira and my own family dilemma. The dreams always fell into similar patterns, my fantasies of Amira.

I suddenly felt dizzy. I grabbed the counter with both hands to steady myself, glancing up at my reflection again and realized one thing. Amira had changed me.

Her influence had made me into someone better. The thought made me smile. Any man would helplessly fall in love with her. It was that enchanting personality she had. Looks didn't matter because as soon as she started a conversation with someone, they would be taken back by her confidence and sass.

I thought about her words about forgiveness. *Could I forgive my father?* The thought kept me up for half of the night. I still hadn't properly spoken to him, my pride not allowing me to give him even a slight chance to explain himself. My jury had deemed him as unworthy of my affection, and I didn't intend to go back on that decree.

I walked out of the bathroom, whistling to myself. Searching my drawers for my clothes till I found a causal outfit, and shrugged on plaid button-up with jeans. I walked toward my bed in search of my phone, but suddenly tripped over a book.

"Fuck," I muttered, glancing at the journal on the floor. It was Amira's.

I picked the notebook up and sat on my bed, tracing the elegant pink and blue designs with my finger. This was full of riddles of Amira's past. Something happened to her a long time ago and whatever it was, affected her a lot. I could sense it whenever she gave me advice. There was this look in her eye that screamed pain.

Something either happened back then or was happening now.

Did I want to read the contents of this notebook? Absolutely.

I knew Amira was going to hate me, but she never talked about her problems. She kept in all in. Desperate times call for desperate measures, especially with how down she'd been lately. She tried to conceal her emotions, but I could see right through them like she was an open book.

With a deep breath, I leaned my back against the headboard and opened the notebook. I read the poems quietly to myself. The year was put at the top of the page. Some of them were funny little rhymes that were about crazy dreams.

As I flipped through the pages, a small smile found its way to my lips. *This is how imaginative Amira was as a child,* I thought. It was adorable. The small Amira was so carefree and innocent like an untouched pearl covered by the ocean, but suddenly the poems became more serious, more tainted in sorrow.

The next few pages were about being alone, sadness, staying quiet, and despair. They abruptly changed. Even the writing style was more matured and better written, however, one poem really stuck out from the rest. It was the most recent one, but it held such a strong meaning.

She stares blankly at the white wall,
Emotion drained from her colorless eyes,
Her body lies limply on the bed,
No movement, no sound,
The world sits in black and white,
Calls for her are silenced.
Why did the world seem so distasteful?
Her head ached like her heart.
Why is she so weak?

She could fight,
But she stays limp,
She could talk,
But she stays mute,
Coward to the world's inhabitants,
Chained to an everlasting pain.
When will it all end?
When will she see the light?
Frost crawls up to her spine,
A slave to pain,
Knives prick her soul,
She still does not move,
Drowned in her memories,
Through all the pain she sheds no tears,
Visions of her past cloud her eyes.
When will it stop?
Eaten by the harsh reality,
There is only one thing she can do,
Patience heals all,
She could endure the pain,
Or at least that's what she hoped for.

I exhaled the breath that I didn't realize I was holding in. This poem was written a few days before she dropped her journal. I felt an unfamiliar tug at my heart at the thought of Amira going through so much emotional pain that she couldn't find it in her to cry anymore.

One thing that caught my attention was that in the poem she wrote about how her heartache. That made me think that maybe she wrote that because of *me*. If that was the case that would mean—

"Damon, can I talk to you for a bit?" a deep voice asked from the door, thus interrupting my deductive reasoning.

My head snapped up and I saw my father leaning against my door frame. He had his arms crossed over his chest as he looked at me. My gaze immediately turned hard. *What did this bastard want?*

CHAPTER 31
Mistaken Judgments

DAMON WINTERS

"What do you want?" I sneered out.

I was still mad at what my father did to my mother. I couldn't understand how he could cheat on her. I couldn't imagine hurting Amira like that. That would kill me.

He looked down in shame before taking a deep breath, looking back at my enraged expression. "I was wondering if you wanted to meet your half-sister today with Percy, Daniel, and me?"

I laughed bitterly. "I don't want to meet the product of your affair."

He tensed up. "Damon, the past is past. She is still your sister," he said through gritted teeth. *Oh my, Papa Bear is getting mad!*

"Maybe by blood, but not by heart. Just like you're not my father anymore," I seethed while standing to assert my authority. Dad and I were relatively the same height. "You have some nerve to come into my room acting all high and mighty, don't you? Fathers are there for their children at all times. Where were you when Luqmaan beat me up? Where were you when I suffered a mental breakdown?"

"Damon, that's enough! I'm still your father whether you like it or not! And you will respect me! I will not have my own child disrespect me like this," he exclaimed, angrily.

"Like you respect Mom? How fucking dare you talk about respect when you couldn't even respect your wife enough to stay faithful to her?"

"Damon! Let it go! I can't change what I have already done no matter how I wish I could," he quietly mumbled the last part.

"How could you do that to her, Dad?" I asked, as my voice cracked. *Fuck emotions, I needed answers.* "She loved you. A—And you just let her love go to waste. Why? Just fucking why?" I yelled with clenched fists.

He looked down with his fists clenched to his sides. "I was drunk when I hang out at a bar with a few of my friends. She was a waitress and I just... it just happened. I didn't mean to."

"So, you just randomly ended up with another woman? Oh yeah, that makes perfect sense," I sarcastically said, clapping my hands in a mocking attitude. "Did you want a trophy for being an ass or another night with that woman?"

His head snapped up, glaring at me. "I still love your mother, Damon. More than words can describe, but I made a foolish mistake so I have to live up to it. That little girl she gave birth to is *my daughter*. She needs a father to look up to."

"*I* need a father. Daniel and Percy need a father, too. How can she look up to you if you're a cheating bastard?" I hissed. "You were never there for us, yet you think you can change all that with a new kid?"

"Damon! Stop this nonsense at once!" he demanded as he took a threatening step towards me.

"How about you listen? I know I'm just eighteen and you probably don't care about what I have to say, but if you really love someone, you respect them. You stay faithful to them and value their love. Clearly you don't, or else you would have fought to keep Mom with you," I glared, blinking back tears. "You would have fought against your gambling addiction."

"You don't know anything! I begged for her not to leave me! I went on my knees just trying to hope that she would stay *near* me! I don't want to lose her. I never want to let go of your mother," he said, as tears fell from the corner of his eyes.

Even though I hated him, I could feel the thorns of guilt prick my heart. I didn't want to feel remorse for my words, anger or my own need to hear him say that he wanted us as a family, that he wouldn't give us up for this new family of his.

"Then why are you leaving us? Her?" I asked with a hoarse voice.

He sighed. "It's because I love her, Damon. If it makes her happy to be with someone else... I-I will do it. No matter how much it will hurt me. I love her and I want her to be happy," he smiled sadly. "It's all I want for her."

I felt my anger drown among the river of guilt that followed. It wasn't the words my father said that broke me, but the way he said it. He sounded so... broken. He seemed so lost without her like his other half had been ripped, like a man who had lost everything, a man who was stuck in life, unable to move forward.

It was then that I took a good look at him. He had bags under his eyes and stress lines on his forehead. The light in his eyes was gone just like the love of his life.

I cleared my throat. "I need some time, Dad. I'm not ready to forgive you."

He nodded, turning his back toward me as he walked out. Before he left, he looked over his shoulder and said, "We're leaving soon to meet Jade, your half-sister. Please come, Damon."

Then, he left.

I flopped back down to my bed. My elbows were on my knees as I buried my face in my hands. He still loved her. *Was that what love was really about? To sacrifice my happiness for someone else's?*

As I thought about what just happened, I felt the bed sink beside me and a comforting hand on my shoulder. I looked to my side and saw my mother's kind face. Seeing her smile at me sadly with puffy eyes made me think of all the struggles in my life. I wrapped my arms around her and let tears fall onto her shoulder.

I couldn't hold it in anymore. She tightly wrapped her arms around me and stroked my hair. Life was so unfair, cruel, and downright depressing. *If God existed why did he make people hurt so much? It was so cruel of Him to do. How could Amira love Him like that when He caused so much pain?*

"Shh, my little boy. It's okay. Mommy's here now," she whispered in my ear.

This made me cry more. "I feel so weak for crying like this," I sniffled.

She pulled back and stroked my face with her gentle touch. "No, no. That's not true. Crying doesn't make you weak. It's just a way of expression. Damon, you are my strong little boy. I know you can get through with this," she smiled.

"Life is so unfair, Mom! I'm losing my family and the girl I like. Everything is just so wrong," I said frustratingly.

"That's just life, Damon. It swallows you up and throws things at you, but then you get back up and fight through the force. You fight for the ones you love," she said before looking at my tearful expression. Her smile dropped as she pulled me back for a hug. "I'm so sorry, honey. I didn't know how much this affected you. I'm so sorry."

Her apology made everything feel even more surreal like a bad nightmare that I desperately wanted to wake up from. I needed my mother's comfort right now. "Is Dad really leaving us, Mom?" I asked quietly.

She tensed. "Yes."

"Make him stay, please. Don't make him go," I begged. God, I was such a baby, but at the moment I didn't care. I wanted my old life back.

"I can't, Damon. I'm so sorry," she said with remorse.

We stayed quiet for a while. I controlled my ragged breathing, slowing sitting up and rubbing my eyes.

"Damon, go meet Jade," she said with finality in her tone.

"What?"

"Go meet Jade. She's still your sister. Even though your father made a mistake, Jade is still innocent in all this."

I sighed and got up, grabbing my sweater. "Fine."

* * *

We stopped in front of these apartments. I sighed as I got out of the car. *Time to meet my little sister*, I thought. As we walked towards her flat, Percy reached up to hold my hand, squeezing it as fear swarmed through his eyes. I smiled reassuringly even though I felt the same turmoil he did. I had to be strong for them.

It's going to be okay, I mouthed.

I glanced at Daniel who looked uncertain about everything, but he kept a brave face. I placed a hand on his shoulder for comfort, silently reassuring him that everything would play out perfectly. We had nothing to worry about when we had each other.

Dad watched us siblings with longing, but stayed silent once he saw my icy glare. For most of my life, I remember being the only fatherly figure to my siblings, the only rock in this storm of chaos.

"You're a good brother, Damon."

I glanced at him with a blank stare. "That's what I strive for," I said coldly.

We continued walking as we reached closer to their door. These apartments looked beaten down and dangerous. It did not look welcoming at all. There were mouse traps at the corners and the paint on the walls was stripping down.

Dad knocked on the door. Percy's hand tightened around mine and I squeezed it back to relax him. Some shuffling was heard from around the door and a small girl shyly opened the door. Her ginger colored hair was pulled back in a ponytail. Her bright green eyes were almost identical to mine. She has freckles sprawled across her cheeks and a beauty mark on the left side of her face.

This must be Jade.

Jade run up to my dad and hugged him. "Daddy!" she squealed as he picked her up.

"Hey, sweetheart," he smiled at her with adoration. "Where's your mom?"

"Right here," a middle-aged woman said.

She had wrinkles around her eyes and a cigarette in her hand. Her dull blue eyes looked at my sibling and I with disappointment, which I simply glared at. She had ginger hair like Jade, but with streaks of white hair.

"Megan," Dad nodded toward her.

She stepped aside to let us in and I immediately wondered what Dad saw in this lady. She had the darkest circles I'd ever seen, not to mention she looked like a drug addict. We all sat on the couch with Jade on Dad's lap. Megan sat opposite to us. She had a hard expression spelled across her visage.

The apartment was small, constricting us with the tiny available space. Glancing over at the walls, I noticed the paints were peeling off. Cockroaches climbed up the wall with their brown coats coloring the dirty white. Cute little Jade shouldn't live in a place like this, especially with a mother like that.

A bag of white powder sat on top of the television, a bottle of booze beside it. The stench of cigarettes hit my nostrils, making me want to run from the filth of the entire complex. I squinted my eyes at the hot pink toy under the table before closing Percy's eyes.

That was not a children's toy.

Dad cleared his throat. I looked at Dad and Jade as she cuddled up against Dad's chest. I smiled at the sight in front of me. *This is my little sister.* I felt a wave of protectiveness and connection wash over me.

"Megan, these are my kids. Damon, Daniel, and Percy. Kids, this is Megan," he introduced us.

I didn't care about Megan or the look of resentment on her face. My attention was purely on the little red-head on Dad's lap, who was staring at me curiously with her bright green eyes, freckles shining.

"Jade, these are your brothers," he told the little girl gently.

She gave me a toothy grin. "Hi! I'm Jade," she cheerfully chirped.

I chuckled. "Hey Jade, I'm your older brother. How old are you?" I asked.

"I'm eight! I'm a big girl," she said proudly.

"Oh yeah, well I'm ten. I'm bigger," Percy teased.

"So what? I'm going to grow up and be taller than you," she huffed.

"I beat you all. I'm thirteen," smirked Daniel.

Jade stuck her tongue out at them. "Damon's nicer than all of you," she said as she hugged me. "At least he doesn't brag about age."

Percy and Daniel started to laugh, easing the tension from their shoulders. They also were mesmerized by this little girl whom we didn't even want to go near with just a few days ago.

We all chuckled. I was shocked at first, but eventually hugged her back. Feeling her small arms around made me wonder what it would be like to have a family in the future. As I gazed down at her, I realized how much Jade would love Amira. Perhaps they would meet one day.

* * *

We said our farewells, leaving the broken apartment, and I thanked the stars that we didn't have to go back. While we drove, Percy and Daniel fell asleep. I sat in the front with Dad, leaving me no escape when he started talking.

"Damon, I want to tell you something," he said as he broke the silence.

I leaned my head against the window. "What?"

"When I found out that Megan was pregnant, I felt like the cheapest bastard in the world. I love your mom so much and I didn't want to hurt her, so I kept it to myself. When I first saw baby Jade, I knew that I couldn't leave her. I couldn't just walk out of her life. She was a part of me and was innocent in this mess. Over the years I kept providing for her family because, well, you can tell from their home that money is an issue. The stress became too much for me mentally and physically so I started to gamble in hopes of getting more money easily. As you can tell that didn't happen," he laughed heartlessly at his mistake.

"Even though I'm still mad at you, I understand what you mean. Jade is innocent and I accept her as my sister," I smiled tiredly from the lack of sleep I'd been getting. "But I'm not ready to forgive you."

"What?"

I exhaled a deep breath, straightening. "You've done a lot to hurt us, Dad. I can't forgive you just like that. I need to see you change not only for us, but for Jade as well. I'm really sorry, but I can't."

"You're a good kid, Damon. I hate to leave you guys like this, but it's for the woman I love. I will forever regret my mistakes and try making it up to you all," he promised, staring at the road. "I hope one day you can forgive me, kiddo."

I hope so too.

CHAPTER 32
An Unwanted Intrusion

AMIRA SARKER

Nanu came back from the hospital a few days ago and stayed at home with us. He had been unusually quiet, which was odd considering how much he talks. Mum reassured me that it was only because he was tired, but I knew there was something else bothering her. The reassuring smile she gave me didn't reach her eyes.

I slumped down on my bed. This day had been going so slow. I just felt so exhausted and useless.

Ever since Nanu got back from the hospital, Mum and he just argued. The constant bickering was pretty harsh on me. I hated it when people raised their voices. When I overheard their arguments, I felt so weak. I couldn't stop them no matter how hard I would try.

People didn't take teenagers seriously, even though I was more mature for my age, no one would listen. My voice just withered from their minds as a faint memory, drifting endlessly in a realm of darkness and sorrow.

Baba was usually at work or quiet throughout the whole daughter-father arguments. Tanwir didn't really see this because he was always locked in his room, completely ignoring the world around him. I was the only one who couldn't ignore the shouting, the heartbreaking screams or the broken hearts that haunted our home.

Then there was Tanwir, his words echoing my mind like a broken symphony. I couldn't sleep at night without thinking how wrong I was.

"When you lose self-control in one aspect of life, you lose it in another."

I placed my palms to my ears. *No, not again. No, please.*

"Don't stray away from the right path where you are in."

I laughed bitterly; *I'm already losing it. I bet Allah hates me.* I let Damon take the one thing from me that I kept under so much protection and resistance, but around him they all just vanished.

He got close to my heart, and now I was going to be punished for it with agony. He was going to leave me and I knew he would. No matter how many times he said he loved me, I knew he would leave me in the end.

Yet that never stopped my heart from yearning for him. It never stopped me from falling in love.

I brought my legs to my chest, wrapping my arms around them as I buried my face in my knees. I took deep breaths to calm myself down.

It's going to be okay.

I was going to fix things. If I didn't stop things with Damon soon, he might get hurt. And that was one thing I would never let happen. Besides, I had bigger things to worry about. A tragic romance was the last thing I needed.

I lifted my head, staring through the clear surface of an opened window. The soft breeze lightly twirled my hair in its embrace, wrapping me in its comfort and reassurance as if nature sought to provide an answer to my distress.

At that moment I tuned out the tortured feeling, locking it away deep within me, and just lived in the moment. The voices of the past were hushed out of my system as the wind whispered to me. I felt my body relax as I thought of a Quranic verse.

"Only in the remembrance of Allah can the heart find peace." [13:28]

I smiled slightly; *I'm going to be okay. I just have to stay strong.*

Glancing back at the darkened night sky, and saw the glimmering specks of white flicker across the black sky with their radiance reminding me of people. In their darkest hours, they needed that star, that light in their lives.

With this in mind I got up and prayed. I forgot the world around me and stayed focus on my Lord.

* * *

It was getting late as I walked into the kitchen. I walked by our living room, and paused in the hallway as I heard voices. Nanu and Mum were fighting again. I was going to keep walking, but the things they said, froze me to the core.

"How can you do that to yourself? Don't you know how hard this is for us?" Mum yelled.

Nanu laughed humorlessly. "I'd rather die. I'm getting too old to live. It's better if I died."

"If it was your time to die, don't you think *Allah* would have taken your soul by now? We're trying so hard to help you become healthy again and you deliberately eat the things you aren't supposed to, and not do what the doctors tell you to do!"

"What do those doctors know? I know best for my own body!" he countered.

"Oh really? You know best? You're a certified doctor now? Clearly, if you were you wouldn't have been at the hospital or you wouldn't have been swelling."

He slammed his fist on the table roughly. I flinched at the thundering sound, leaning my body against the doorway of the living room. My heart hammered within my chest, and I found myself counting my breaths in an effort to relax.

"I just want to go back to my home country! I'm tired of these Americans thinking they know my health! Send me back!" he roared.

"They're trying to help you! We're trying to help you! Can't you see that?" she questioned with tearful eyes. *Why doesn't he see how much pain he was causing his own daughter?*

"I want my true grandchildren to be near me," he muttered quietly.

My blood ran cold. He couldn't have just said that.

"And what about my children? Are they not your grandchildren?"

He looked away from Mum's piercing gaze. "They don't show the same love."

I stood forward. "How can you say that?" I asked with a distraught expression.

Both Mum and Nanu snapped their heads toward me. He kept his mouth in a tight line as he stared at me. Mum's eyes held sadness as she gazed upon my expression.

"We've spent thousands of dollars trying to help you. We've been researching ways to help your condition. I've sacrificed my time to stay with you at the hospital and made so much *duaa* for you. I had sleepless nights just hearing you arguing with Mum and praying to *Allah* that you would realize all we were trying to do is help you!" I exclaimed with tears in my eyes. I blinked them back harshly.

I will not show weakness.

I will stay strong.

His silence proved to be even more deafening.

"Can't you see how much pain you are causing us? Your pain is our pain that is why we are trying so hard to keep you alive! How can you say that we don't show the same amount of love? Just because I don't see you every day doesn't mean I don't love you. It just means that I'm learning the value of love and cherishing every moment I have with you," I said quietly.

I waited for a reply from him, yet he sat still. Mum reached out to hold me, but I pushed her arms away and ran upstairs. Slamming my door, I leaned my back against the door as I slid down.

Oh Allah, why doesn't he see the love we all have for him? Why did he have to say something so hurtful?

The fact that he thought distance could destroy the special blood bond that we had just broke me. Distance didn't demolish love. It just made it greater because we begin to hold every memory dear to our hearts.

We didn't think of the bad times, we only thought of the good times. It was a struggle at times, but he was my grandfather. I couldn't ever stop loving him. He was the person who had a great impact in my life and helped make me become who I am.

I sniffled a little, trying to blink back the tears, but every time I thought of what Nanu said, I would feel a damp trail down my cheek. I sighed. *How can one expect me to be fine, if I'm the one who is comforting myself?*

I was never really good at expressing feelings. I had ignored unwanted emotions for so long and now all of a sudden, I felt that the wall come crumbling down.

My phone started ringing. I got up to pick it up from my dresser, checking the caller ID. It was Damon. My face scrunched up in confusion, wiping off the last of my tears as I took a deep breath.

"Hey," his deep voice sighed in contentment.

"H-Hey," I sniffled quietly. *Damn it! Now he'll know that I'm upset.*

I heard a pause from the other line as he registered the sound of my voice. "Are you crying?" he asked with worry lacing his voice.

I mentally awed at the fact that he was worrying about me. I moved to lay down on my bed as I flung an arm over my eyes. Could I trust Damon? Yes. Would it be a good idea to tell him the reason for my sour mood? Probably not, but I knew he was going to keep pressing the matter.

"Yes," I mumbled.

I tried to control my breathing, but it came out uneven as I bit back the sob.

"It's okay, sweetheart. I'm here," he whispered softly into the phone.

My heart swelled at the way he said it. The gentle tone he used with me always made me feel welcomed and gave me a sense of comfort.

"Thank you."

"Don't worry about it. Now, tell me what has my sweet girl in tears?" he asked.

"It's really nothing to worry about," I reassured him as I wiped at my eyes.

"Amira," he said sternly, "Please tell me. It hurts to hear you cry."

I sighed into the phone, "Just a lot of bad things happening in my life right now."

"I hope I'm not one of them," he joked.

You're one of the best and worst things that ever happened to me, I thought.

I snorted. "Very funny," I said sarcastically.

"Seriously, Amira. What's wrong?"

I hesitated for a moment and then just shrugged to myself. I might as well tell him. He's offering help and comfort, something that I wasn't used to.

I inhaled a shaky breath. "Before I say it, just know that I've never been good at expressing my feelings."

He hummed in response as he waited for my answer.

"My grandpa is... really sick. He's getting better now, but sometimes he'll get worse because he doesn't listen to the doctors. He and my mom have been arguing so much lately. It's heartbreaking to see in all honesty. But that's not even the worst part," I said quietly.

"What's the worst part?" he asked cautiously.

"He thought we didn't love him. He doubted how much we care, Damon," I whispered.

He whistled lowly. "Damn. That's hardcore."

"It just hurts to know that the person who helped you shape who you are, doubts your love because you live far from each other. He thinks that, that I don't love him as much because I don't see him often," I explained.

"Distance as an obstacle doesn't destroy love."

"That's what I said!" I exclaimed.

He chuckled lowly before abruptly stopping. "You said 'bad things', meaning there's more than just that. It's plural."

I rolled my eyes. "Way to get technical, Winters."

"I'm for real here, Amira. What else happened to you?"

I froze. "What?"

"Oh uhm... oops. I think it's too early to bring this topic up," he trailed off.

"No, no. What do you know, Damon? Or a better question is how?" I asked in a cold voice.

"Amira," he started.

"Damon, what do you know?" I cut off.

He sighed and I could already imagine him tangling his fingers through his soft brown hair. "Remember when you lost your journal?"

"Yes."

"Yeah... well, the thing is..."

"Damon, just spill the beans," I snapped.

"I read it."

"Oh."

We had a moment of silence as I thought about what he just said. He read my journal. Just reading that journal took one through my entire childhood. He read through my secrets, read through all the darkness. Damon knew everything now and there was no way for me to undo time, and that terrified me. How could I have been so careless to let my journal fall into his hands of all people?

"Amira, why did the poems go from playful and silly to straight out depressing in two pages?" he asked curiously.

I stayed silent for a moment. I went through a rough time during those years. I never told anyone. I just did what I was usually used to, which was keeping things to myself until it became too much to take in. Damon had forced himself into a world he had no idea exist, and it was right around me, circling me with so many memories, so many nights of tears.

"You shouldn't have read those," I mumbled, as visions of my past clouded me.

CHAPTER 33
Depths of Broken Memories

AMIRA SARKER

"Amira, I'm so sorry," she said with glazed eyes.

"No! Please don't do this," I begged her.

She couldn't leave me. "No! No, you're going to live!" I yelled into the hospital room.

"Amira," she shook her head. "You have to let me go. My time here is done, sweetheart."

"No, no. Please. I don't want to be alone again. I can't go on like this," I cried, as I latched onto her shoulders.

She pulled away and cupped my cheeks. "Hey," she said softly, "Life will go on, okay?"

I viciously shook my head. Allah wouldn't be that cruel. Allah wouldn't take her away from me. Not my only friend.

"Amira, promise me one thing," she said, as she held my hands tightly.

"What is it?" I asked.

"Promise me that when I die, you will not blame Allah. Don't turn away from Islam, is that understood? This is a good thing. I can now be with my Lord. My one and only wish," she smiled.

I didn't realize that tears were running down my face as I let out a whimper and I nodded my head.

"I-I promise," I whispered shakily.

"Oh, Amira," she breathed out, as she pulled me into her arms tightly. Her hands were cold.

I cried my heart out as I clutched onto her, hoping that she wouldn't leave. I stayed in her room and didn't leave till her very last breath. I was young, but something changed in me that day. I became more mature.

I never thought she would die the way that she did, but then again, life is full of unexpected surprises. One may think they know how the chapter of one's life would end, only to realize they were completely wrong. Leaving the "what if's" in their minds.

* * *

"Amira?"

Damon's silk-like voice broke me from my thoughts.

"I'm sorry. What were you saying?"

"What happened to you?" he questioned softly.

I let out a shaky breath as memories of her flooded my mind, how she and Tanwir played at the playground and helped me ride the swings. I remember how painful it was seeing her lifeless, and the day that we rushed her to the hospital continued to haunt me. I knew her death wasn't my fault, but hell I wished she could have lived longer.

I wished she was there for me when I needed her the most. I missed the way her soft hands stroked my hair. I missed her beautiful white smile. I missed the way her eyes would light up seeing me or Tanwir.

I missed her.

I never told anyone how I felt. I kept it all in. Her death stole my innocence away. Life must have thrown torture and pain at her too fast or maybe she was weak, but that girl is gone and had grown into a woman. One who learned that happiness won't last and with happiness came sadness. This girl had learned realities of life the hard way.

Memories of her just kept flashing my mind. When she died, a part of Tanwir died with her. He became cold and distant. He changed, and so did I. My whole family. Everything.

"Damon, what I'll be telling you now is something that I have never told anyone. Not even Aria, Tasneem, Lucy, and Meredith," I stated with an emotionless voice.

"Okay."

I exhaled; *Here goes nothing.* "Those poems changed with me. I used to have an older sister."

"What do you mean by 'used to have'?" he asked.

"She's dead, Damon," I said in a cold distant voice.

I heard his sharp intake of breath.

"H-how?"

"She had leukemia. I was only twelve years old and she was sixteen when she died. She was the eldest daughter in my family, a year older than my brother," I said.

"Oh, Amira. Sweetheart-"

"I don't need pity, Damon," I snapped. "I have moved on with my life. I made a promise to her that I would. She was my only friend."

"I don't pity you, Amira. Don't you ever think that. You're one of the strongest girls I know," he stated fiercely.

"Thank you. Anyway, her death destroyed my family. My mom cried so much, Damon. She couldn't accept that her daughter was now buried six feet under. She prayed and begged *Allah* to keep her daughter alive." I trailed off. "My dad had pulled me out of school and we went rushing to the hospital. When we got there, she looked at me with the twinge of life in her eyes, and gave me a strained smile. She told me she loved me, and then her body went limp. The heart monitor started beeping loudly, a signal saying she was gone. My mother flung her body at her dead daughter and sobbed. She tried shaking her awake, but she did not respond. "She's gone," I said, as I hiccupped a sob.

It's been five years and it felt like it was just yesterday. I clutched my chest as I felt my heart beat at a rapid pace. My mind was reeling. I gasped.

"Amira! You're okay. Shh, baby, don't cry. Please," he begged brokenly, as if my struggle to breathe was stabbing him internally. "You don't need to finish the story. Shh, it's okay. Everything's alright."

No, it's not.

I shook my head. I had to finish. "My dad stood there trying to move my mother away from my sister. Her name was Aisha. She was beautiful. She was one of the best people I had ever known. She thought of others before she thought of herself. She was selfless in her deeds. Men would be allured by her personality. She would always smile. When she died, a piece of my brother died as well. He became cold and shallow. He stopped caring. He had no will to live," I mumbled quietly into my phone as I clenched my fist.

"Do you mean—"

"Yes. He tried to kill himself," I whispered brokenly.

"Damn," he muttered.

I closed my eyes as I told him what had happened that day. The memories were so vivid. They burned me and drove me to insanity all at once.

* * *

I walked into Tanwir's room, only to find it empty. Some kids from school had tormented me for my headscarf. One of the girls even tried to physically hurt me until the teachers came around.

They contacted my parents and got worried ever since. Aisha used to be the one to comfort me, but now she was gone. Mum and Baba were outside talking to some neighbors.

"Tanwir!" I called out. Where could he be?

I walked around the house looking for him. It was deadly silent. Something wasn't right. I felt it in my gut. It was like something was urging me to go somewhere. I shivered as an unusual feeling of dreadfulness swam down my body, and it alerted my mind. I heard a small sob and immediately tracked down to where it was coming from.

I ran into the bathroom and screamed at the scene in front of me. Tanwir sat on the tiled white floor with a sharp knife in his hand. It was grazing his skin, and the slightest movement would cut it.

When I screamed, he dropped the knife and it scratched his leg. He hissed in pain and I stared horrified at the crimson blood flowing onto the white tiles. I opened my mouth to scream again, but nothing came out. I was in shock.

Voices were around me and flying in my head. Memories of Aisha flooded my mind. I tightly closed my eyes. No! Please! Oh Allah, make it stop! Her lifeless body flashed behind my eyes. I fell to the floor.

I opened my eyes and my vision blurred. Tanwir tried to reach for me, but I slapped his hand away.

"H-How could you?" I whispered in a shattered voice.

All that consumed me was pain. My heart felt numb. My body ached to be comforted, but now I knew. Life was coming after me. Life was trying to take me down, but I wouldn't let it. I will not be weak! I will not do this to my family. I had to stay strong for everyone. My own brother...

He looked down at his leg in shame. I heard thundering footsteps run up the stairs.

"You are my only sibling left! How can you just leave me?! Why? Why would you do this?!" I sobbed uncontrollably. This pain was consuming me. It was destroying the last bit of my heart. I was breaking. No. I would not let it happen. I won't let my heart break. I will not be weak.

Mum broke down crying as she saw all the blood. So much blood. She crouched down next to me to pick me up. I kept hitting her chest to let me go. "No! Mommy! He's going to kill himself! No, please! I have to help him! He's hurt! Mommy, please!" I screamed as I thrashed around in her arms.

"Shh, no he won't. I promise," Mum comforted me by holding my small frame close to her body.

"I'm all alone. He's going to leave me too. Everyone hates me. No one wants to be with me anymore!" I yelled, brokenly.

It was then that my parents and brother realized how affected I was. It was at that moment that they realized how tortured I was. My body shook as I sobbed.

Did no one love me anymore? He wanted to leave his only sister. He wanted to abandon me. I let all my frustrations out. I was in hysterics. My head hurt.

This world was becoming a dark pit that I desperately wanted to escape from. I clawed at my chest. I wanted it to stop. I wanted to stop feeling emotions. I wanted it all to go away! Why was life so cruel? Allah, please help me.

I was going insane.

* * *

Damon was silent as I finished the story. The pain I locked away for so many years came crashing back with full force. That day was one of the scariest moments of my life. I almost lost my brother. If I didn't come in when I did... I would have been an only child.

"Amira, that's awful. You witnessed it... God damn. You held so much pain inside of you," he stated, hauntingly.

"I know. Please don't think of me as weak or pity me. I'm still Amira. If it wasn't for these incidents in my past, I wouldn't be who I am today. Yes, I faced it at a young age, but it was worth it. I changed into someone better. The past is what makes us who we are. It helps change our future."

"Like I said, you're one of the strongest girls I know. I don't know if I could have ever handled that pain. You're truly amazing, Amira," he said in awe.

"No, I'm not. I'm just a regular girl," I insisted.

He laughed softly. "You are so much more than that," he said with honesty coating every word.

I smiled sadly. I was going to have to let him go soon. No matter how much I didn't want to. It was the right thing. I sighed.

"Amira, how can you love a God that put you through all that?" he asked, confused.

It was my turn to laugh softly. "You know why I grasped onto my sanity?"

"Why?"

"Because in those dark hours of my life, He was the light. I kept reminding myself of the comforting words He tells us in the Qur'an. They were the light that broke my dark cage. If it wasn't for that light, I don't think I would be standing here alive today," I answered.

"But He hurt you," he emphasized.

I shook my head. "It's like parenting. You know how your parents sometimes say things that hurt you?"

He paused and then muttered, "Yes."

"Don't we still love our parents? Even though we are hurt, we learn things. *Allah* never gives His servants something they can't handle. It's just that sometimes we don't believe in ourselves. But He always believes that we can overcome the harsh reality of life. Yes, He causes it, but He also fixes it and provides the comfort that no one else can give better than Him. Because of this love from Him, I survived."

"I see," he trailed off.

We talked a little more till he brought up his half-sister, Jade. He told what happened with his dad and how his father told him about his love for Damon's mother. I inwardly awed. It was so sad, but so sweet at the same time. We joked around a bit and just enjoyed each other's company. I felt a twinge of guilt, but I ignored it. I will let him go, but I just want to enjoy this moment I have with him. Just for tonight.

"I love you," he said when he was about to hang up.

"I—"

"It's okay. You don't need to say it. I understand your conflicted emotions," he sighed.

"I love you too," I whispered, hanging up.

The funny thing was that I meant those three little words with all my heart. It was at that moment that I realized that pain would once again consume me. The only difference was I didn't know how badly I would hurt this time around.

CHAPTER 34
His Choice

DAMON WINTERS

"You're so whipped!" Tye exclaimed, as his jaw dropped to the ground. Not literally.

I rolled my eyes, parking my car. "No, I'm not," I muttered.

"Oh? You freaking woke me up an hour early just so we could buy flowers," he scowled while narrowing his eyes and crossing his arms.

I shrugged, innocently. "You could have just decided not to come with me. It was your choice," I smirked. He really didn't have a choice since I was his only ride to school.

"Go to hell, Damon."

"Nah. I'm good on planet Earth," I grinned, opening the car door.

I touched the petals of the roses I had just bought. They were so beautiful, but they hurt to touch with the thorns. It reminded me of Amira. She was like thorns. She hid behind a barrier to hide her true emotions for the people she loved. Not many people have taken the time to take away the thorns that surround her. Like the stem of the rose, she was easy to break, but she could still stand strong without a stem.

I thought back to when she told me about her sister. The fact that Amira had to go through all that pain and helplessly watch her family suffer made my heart tug painfully. The thought of her crying killed me. She was indeed strong to go through all that and keep a smile on her face every single day, a blinding radiance and warmth that rippled through those around her.

She made it her daily mission to make others smile even if she was down. I couldn't help but admire her more for these qualities. *She's all mine*, I thought and then frowned.

Well, not *necessarily* mine.

"I swear to God, Damon. If you are rethinking this whole stupid plan of yours, I'm going to shoot you without a doubt," Tye threatened, pointing a finger towards me. "My sleep deprived brain is angry and irritated."

"Dude, relax. I'm no coward."

"This girl better must be worth missing an hour of my sleep," he mumbled to himself.

I shook my head, jogging next to him. *She is definitely worth it.*

* * *

I waited by her locker for two minutes. My hands were getting clammy as I wondered the outcome of all this. What if she hated roses? What if she completely ignored all this? What if-

Shut up.

Now those were some wise words.

"Damon?" a sweet voice asked.

I turned towards Amira with the widest grin. "Hey, beautiful," I winked.

She rolled her eyes at me, yet there was a glimpse of smile that coated her lips. I chuckled and pulled out the roses from behind my back.

She gasped. "Whoa. What's the occasion?"

"Just thought I'd make you feel some more love from me," I smirked.

She threw her head back and laughed. "I'm loved enough. You don't have to get me anything, silly."

"But I want to," I said gently.

She quickly looked away from me with a smile gracing her luscious lips. That one action widened my grin, a hum of ease singing in my head like the tune of Amira Sarker and her lilting voice. My heart pounded against my chest, pride blooming form the effect I had on her, and it took every fiber of my being not to take her in my arms.

"Is the great Amira Sarker actually blushing?" I teased.

I was an ass.

But she loved it.

"I never blush. Why would I?" she huffed and crossed her arms.

I leaned in closer to her, which made her stumble back a little. My breath was right next to her headscarf as I whispered, "Because I make you nervous."

Her breathing wavered. She was so beautiful. Her flawless face and dark eyes seemed to hypnotize me every time I stared at them. Her innocent demeanor, her strong personality, and her valuable morals have all rubbed off on me. She made me a better person and all I wanted to do was make her happy.

I wanted to be the cause of her smile, her laughter, and her brightened eyes in every glance she took at me. Love wasn't supposed to be this overwhelming with a desire to please and comfort, yet here I was standing before a personal angel and all her wings of glory.

Someone coughed behind me. I broke my gaze away from Amira to see Tye pointing at his watch. I rolled my eyes. *How stupid does he think I am?*

"Hey, Amira. I need to ask you something."

She raised her eyebrow in question.

"There's someone really special I want you to meet," I said nervously while scratching the back of my neck.

"Who?"

"My sister."

She looked taken aback. "What?"

I sighed and interlaced our fingers. "I want you to meet her. She'll love you," I smiled, reassuringly.

"But why?" she narrowed her eyes.

"Why not?" I countered.

"You're stalling. What's the real reason?" she asked. *Is it wrong to find her undeniably adorable when she was irritated?*

"Because I love you," I said softly while holding her hand to my lips. I placed a gentle kiss on the soft skin of her hand, tilting my head to look up at her.

I heard her take a breath. Her lips were parted, as if she was waiting for a kiss, and her eyes had a glint that wasn't there before. Suddenly, all her emotions were shut off as a cold look entered her eyes, pulling her hand away from my grasp.

She looked away from me, pulling her bottom lip into her mouth. A look of uncertainty crossed her brown eyes, fear clasping over her of the unknown future with me. I knew her answer, but I refused to believe it.

People fought for love. Perhaps I could do the same for ours.

I checked my watch. We had ten minutes till the first bell. I wish we had more time together, but instead; all these obstacles were put between us. There had to be a way for us to be together. I wouldn't stop until she was mine. I opened my mouth to speak, but she cut me off.

"Damon, please. I'm begging you to move on from me. Don't do this, Damon. I can't bear to think that I'm hurting you," she pleaded to me with glassy eyes.

Sorrow and anguish filled her eyes. I realized that each word she was saying was hurting her which was unacceptable. She shouldn't have to be in pain for being in love.

"We can be together, Amira. We both love each other and I heard you last night. You love me like I love you. We'll get through this together," I promised.

She frantically shook her head. "No, we can't. You know this. We have to let each other go," her voice cracked at the end.

I felt my temper rising, but I held it back. "You want me to let go of the best thing that has ever happened to me. Are you insane?" I asked with an edge to my voice.

"Yes! I want you to let me go. You don't even know what love is, Damon! How can you say you love me if you don't even know what it is?" she exclaimed, harshly.

"I don't know what love is? Are you hearing yourself? I'm crazy for you. I would have even converted for you if you let me. Hearing you cry over the phone, and not being there with you to help was killing me. I feel lost whenever we're apart. You changed me and all I want is you. Not even want, for God's sake! I need you," I said breathlessly and lowered my voice. I reached for her hand again and placed it over my heart, which was thundering rapidly within my chest. "Feel that? That's what you do to me every time I'm near you," I whispered into her ear. We were so close to each other, but her hand was a barrier between us.

"Damon," she started.

"Do you love me?" I blurted out as I stepped closer.

She stepped back. "Look I -"

"Do you love me, Amira?" I repeated.

She stayed silent for a moment before whispering a mumble, "Yes."

I stepped back with a grin. "Then we'll be okay, sweetheart."

She sighed. "If you really love me, you'd move on."

"I love you so much to do that. I can't bear the thought of someone else having you," I said honestly.

"Please, do it for me."

I moved away from her as if her touch had burned me. My fingers were tangling in my hair, tugging at the edges as I tried to wrap my mind around her words. Amira pushed too hard this time; too desperate to cleanse her soul from my stained one. She wanted me to let her go, but how could I let the one girl I love go?

"Amira, I don't know if I can."

She looked at me curiously. "What do you mean?"

Ring! Ring!

I gave her an apologetic smile that didn't quite reach my eyes. She simply looked away.

"Come on, let's go to class," she mumbled.

* * *

Throughout the day, I kept thinking about what Amira had said. I sat at my desk, listening to my Calculus teacher, but was unable to comprehend what he was saying.

"If you really love me, you'd let me go."

I shook my head. I didn't want to torture myself like this. I continued trying to follow his lesson.

"We have to let each other go."

I dropped my pencil and pinched the bridge of my nose, but I could still her voice in my head.

"I'm sorry, Damon."

Stop. Her voice is all I hear and I couldn't concentrate anymore.

"I love you too."

I used to laugh at people who said love was real and that love was just a figment everyone had, then I met Amira. She was the one person I could trust with all my heart. I could tell her anything and she would welcome me with her sense of comfort. She was my home.

She loved me, but she asked me to let her go. It wasn't because she hated me; it was for the kind of love she had for me and I realized that it was true.

The thought of letting her go pained me to no end because I didn't want to. It felt like a knife stabbing my chest. The thought of releasing her from the prison I created tore me apart, shredding me into pieces and leaving my fragmented memories of her lost in the abyss of a thousand worries. Letting her go meant letting myself go. It meant losing the one girl who secured my heart with a lock and key forever.

She wanted to unlock it.

I rested my head on my arms. *How can I let her go? I need her so much.*

I had plans for our future, children, and family. I built my life with her in my dreams a million times. It felt so real within my grasp until I could almost touch the future. Suddenly, darkness clouded over that surreal peace, tearing it into tendrils of gloom.

Now, I would have to watch her move on with a Muslim man that wasn't me. However, if it made her happy, I would do it. My breathing wavered. I knew I was going to let Amira go.

My heart broke with every memory of her that passed my mind. The hope I once had was slowly being shredded. Every smile she gave that used to warm my heart, now felt suffocating. Her touch was forever embedded in my mind.

Why was life so cruel? I was losing Amira and I couldn't stop it. Love was the best thing that ever happened to someone, but could also be the worst. Well, in my case, it was.

"Mr. Winters, are you alright?" Mr. Baron asked, snapping me out of my depressing thoughts.

"I think I need to go to the nurse," I mumbled.

He wrote me a pass quickly once he saw my sickened expression. I saw all the kids in class looking at me as I walked up to his desk.

"Feel better," Tye whispered, as I walked by.

A nurse wouldn't make this pain go away. No one could.

CHAPTER 35
Broken Hearts

AMIRA SARKER

I started to lightly sketch out the bowl of fruits in front of me, shading gray lines across the shadows and edges of the bowl. Coloring the highlight on the apple, my mind wavered elsewhere from my drawing and onto Damon. I was currently sitting in Art class and attempting to draw. Luckily, Alexis was in this class too, along with Tasneem.

"Holy shit! I'm done. I can't draw for my life," Alexis groaned, as she slammed her pencil against the art table.

Tasneem winced. "Isn't it a little too late to give up?" she asked.

Alexis huffed and crossed arms. "It's never too late to give up."

"I think you mean it's never too late to fix your mistakes," I countered.

Alexis slammed her head against the table, mumbling incoherently. I chuckled as I lightly traced over the delicate lines on my paper. I paused, facing her and poked her side.

"Stop."

I poked her again.

"Stop it."

This time I *pinched* her side.

She sprang upwards in surprise. "Holy damn! What part of 'stop' do you not understand?!" she exclaimed with her hands in the air.

I chuckled. "Don't be such a bum."

"Shut up," she mumbled.

I laughed loudly, causing our class to glance towards us with amused eyes. Feeling embarrassed, I put my attention back to my drawing. I heard Alexis grumble under her breath and it made me grin. I always found her getting riled up to be amusing.

Time seemed to tick by slowly yet all my attention was focused on my assignment. Art class was a way to express myself. The different colors and the blank page represented a clean slate. I could erase every mistake I made; however, reality wasn't like that.

I couldn't start over with a blank canvas that easy. My canvas was splattered with different colors. Both darkness and light filled the negative spaces. Only sincere repentance could help one start with a blank canvas.

No matter how dark my canvas could get, it disappeared when I repented. *Allah* would forgive the sincerest hearts. However, the memories of the darkness still haunted me and would never leave such mistakes that I didn't ever want to repeat.

When my sister died, I thought I could never recover, but here I was now. I was living life like any other normal teenager, surviving through every difficulty Allah has given me. It still hurt oftentimes like a fresh wound. She was my sister. My own flesh and blood and I watched her slowly die. That memory will never be forgotten. She would never be forgotten.

"Could I borrow that?" asked a voice.

I snapped out of my thoughts as I looked at the newcomer. It was Sean, an Asian art prodigy. His long black hair slightly covered his left eye, while his rectangular glasses reflected the light at our table. He blew it away from his face as he stuffed his hands in his pockets.

"I'm sorry?"

"I asked if I could borrow that color," he said, gesturing with his head.

"Sure," I shrugged.

He smiled, and it was adorable in a boyish way. He was short but lean, and he had cat-like eyes that seemed to scream mischievousness. Sean was pretty awkward most of the times, but according to Alexis, he was very loud around his friends.

"Hey, Sean!" Alexis shouted.

Sean turned on his heel towards us. "What?" he asked in a bored tone.

"Well, geez. Why couldn't it be '*hello, I see you*?'" he sarcastically replied.

He rolled his eyes. His mouth twitched upwards into a smirk and slightly bowed. "Forgive me, your Highness. I did not mean to displease you," he said in a fake British accent.

Alexis raised her hand in dismissal. "Off with your head!" she said, as she clapped her hands.

Tasneem and I exchanged glances. This should be amusing.

"Oh please, your Highness. I beg of you," Sean pleaded halfheartedly.

Alexis opened her mouth to say more but Tasneem stopped her. "What is this, Medieval Times?"

Sean chuckled. "Nah she was just being retarded. Carry on with your drawings."

Alexis's jaw dropped. At this point I was doubling over with laughter. I wiped a fake tear.

"That's golden," I grinned.

"Sean! Did you just call Alexis a retard?" Ms. Nelson asked.

"Uhh... no?"

"Liar! You're such a bastard!" Alexis screamed.

"Are you trying to make me deaf? You sound like a banshee," he cringed.

"What?" Alexis deadpanned.

"I said—"

"I know what you said! I was giving you the option to rephrase your words before I kill you," she glared while clenching her fist.

"Dude, she's about to whip you," I warned.

"No joke," muttered Tasneem.

"I'm so scared. Ah! Help," he said sarcastically.

"Okay, okay, that's enough. As much as I find this amusing, I don't want to deal with a corpse today, so don't provoke her anymore," Ms. Nelson demanded.

Sean shrugged and went back to his seat. Ms. Nelson eyed him wearily, and retreated back to her desk. She was one of the coolest teachers who tolerated us more, compared to other teachers, which is probably why she's one of my favorite instructors.

I sighed, as I leaned back to admire my work. It looked good enough. I wasn't an amazing artist, but I was pretty average.

"How are things going on with Aria and Mark?" Alexis asked.

I snapped away from my thoughts. "I think Aria is starting to get over him. It's been rough on her."

Alexis scoffed. "That asshole. I can't believe the nerve of him. Like hell! He should at least have the integrity not to rub it in her face every time he sees her," she complained.

To be fair, I agreed with her a hundred percent. It was a low move.

"Speaking of boys, have you guys heard about Damon's new girlfriend," Tasneem grinned.

I sat up straight. "What?" I asked with wide eyes. "He had a girlfriend?"

No, it couldn't be. He said he loved me this morning. He wouldn't have moved on that fast, right?

Girl, who are you kidding? Of course, he would leave you. You told him to.

I know I did, but I couldn't believe it. He couldn't have. Not this fast. There was no way.

"W—Who is she?" I asked with a trembling voice.

Tasneem's face scrunched up as she thought. "Oh, I remember! Her name was Kaylie."

I felt my heart drop. It was that girl I bumped into. She was the girl that was all over Damon at that party. Was he with her? No, no. Oh *Allah*, please don't let it be.

"Are you sure they're dating?" I asked, hesitantly.

She gave me a puzzled look. "I mean they were making out a while ago. Maybe she's a *hit and run* kind of girl for him," she shrugged.

I hang off every word she said, and my mouth went dry as I felt disgust rise. It had to be someone else. There was no way that could be my Damon.

But, that's what you wanted, Amira, my inner voice reminded me.

"Whoa. Damon has a bae? Damn! He always gets the hot chicks," Alexis laughed.

I felt my body tense.

"I mean, he is a good-looking guy. Did you really think he wouldn't take advantage of what he had?" Tasneem joked.

I felt like crying; my heart was like a fragile glass, it seemed that every word shattered a piece of me and stabbed me at my chest. This pain was foreign to me, but it hurt so much. I placed a hand on top of my chest as I relaxed my breathing.

Shh, calm down, Amira. They don't know. It'll be okay. Just be quiet, I reassured myself.

"I thought there was a girl he liked for the last couple of months. No girls even bothered approaching him because he said he was off limits," Alexis stated.

That girl was me! I was the girl he liked.

I kept my mouth shut. I had no claim over Damon, told him to move on and pleaded constantly to let me go. How could I expect him to still love me after all that? It wasn't fair, but I made my decision and I had to live with it, even if it ended up hurting me the most. It was for *Allah*. I was doing this to stay faithful to my Lord.

"You think that girl is Kaylie?" Tasneem asked curiously.

"Probably. They might have just made it public," Alexis waved off as she focused on her drawing.

I bit my lip. I wanted to yell out, "It's me! Not Kaylie!" however, I knew I could not. Damon was just doing what I asked him to do and it wasn't his fault. It was mine.

I sighed, thinking about this secret I kept on hiding for so long. I did it for Damon because I loved him. The fact that he was able to move on from me in a blink of an eye, made me realize that he never loved me to begin with.

If he was in love with me, it should have taken him a little longer to get over me. I let the walls around my heart go down and he sneaked right in. However, in his case, it was like I hadn't been anything at all, like I was just another girl to string along when he needed comfort. It was almost as if the last few months were just figments of a dream that we had woken up from.

"Amira, you okay? You look like you're going to be sick," Tasneem asked in a concerned voice.

I didn't want to burden them with my pitiful love life, so I nodded my head. "Of course, I am. I'm just tired that's all," I smiled tightly.

"You know if anything is wrong, you can tell me, right?" she asked, as she held my hand.

I looked up to her with gratitude and saw how much she cared for me. All of my friends did; I just never allowed them to help me. All my life, I've been used to helping them without realizing I needed help, too.

Sitting here and watching the anxiety wash over Tasneem's face, I knew I should talk my problems out. But right now, I wasn't ready. I wasn't mentally stable enough to tell her everything that happened, not when I couldn't believe it myself.

"I'm fine, Tasneem. Seriously. A couple days of good sleep would make feel like a rising beauty," I joked with her.

She reluctantly let go of my sudden mood change, and continued her conversation with Alexis about Damon and Kaylie. I felt jealousy and agony engulf me, restricting my breaths. I wanted to break down and scream at them to stop. I wanted to yell at Damon for putting me in such a vulnerable state, but I held it all in.

I tried hard not to let them know that I am dying inside. I neither wanted to be judged nor be called 'weak'. Although my friends would never do that, something was stopping me from telling them the truth.

You're afraid, a voice whispered.

I shook my head. No, I wasn't. I know how I feel about Damon. I also accepted the fact that I brought this burden upon myself.

You're afraid of the pain you are about to endure, my inner self stated.

I put my head down on the palms of my hand as they rested on the table. That's exactly what I was afraid of. If I loved something, I loved it with all my heart. I was too careful about the people I chose to be in my life, but I've never fallen in love with a guy before. This was a new experience. Something I had no idea how to control.

This uncomfortable prickling of thorns in my chest was foreign to me. It felt like my heart was being ripped apart every time I hear his name. When they mentioned Kaylie, I thought I was going to cry a river for something she had that I couldn't have.

"Amira, seriously, what's wrong?" Alexis asked.

"It's nothing," I mumbled with my head still in my hands.

"Amira, please let us help you. Tell us what's wrong," Tasneem pleaded.

"Just a really bad headache," I said quietly.

I felt fingers wrap around my arms and pull me up. I looked at Alexis with raised eyebrows. "You're going to the nurse."

I didn't even try to fight back with her. Maybe if I rested a bit, this pain would go away. Ms. Nelson sent me away with a pass and I gathered my things. I walked out into the long, narrow hallway.

I felt myself wobble a little, and tried to focus on walking instead of this pain pounding inside me. I felt blood rush to my head, and everything went dizzy. I paused. The thought of Damon in someone else's arms hurt me so much. I didn't want to let him go, but I had to. I didn't want to see him kiss another girl when he told me he loved me.

I placed my hands on the lockers for support and took deep breaths. *Allah* will help me ease this pain. I went through a lot of difficult times and survived; I watched my sister die, and saw my brother suffer through depression. I saw people I loved leave me, and got bullied for my beliefs. I know I could surpass all these. I just had to be patient with everything and put my trust in *Allah.*

I felt a little lighter and proceeded walking to the nurse's office. However, nothing prepared me for what I saw. Damon was sitting on a bench outside the nurse's office with his elbows on his knees. His head was down and his shoulders were shaking.

Was he crying?

. We were both feeling this pain and I felt sympathy for him. The only difference was that one of us was going to get hurt more, and it would most likely be me. As I approached him, I saw Kaylie touch his shoulders. I didn't even realize she was there and I froze.

"Damon, baby, what's wrong?" she purred.

His voice was broken as he said, "I messed up."

CHAPTER 36
Torn Apart

DAMON WINTERS

Guilt trickled down my spine like claws of reminder. Kaylie's lips felt so wrong on mine and I wanted to push her away.

"If you really loved me, you'd let me go."

Her words kept replaying in my head as I bury my head in my hands. I couldn't believe I kissed Kaylie. I shouldn't have left her but I was a fucking idiot who couldn't even hold the hands of the girl I loved.

"Damon, it'll be okay," Kaylie whispered as she rubbed my back.

I pushed her hands away. "Look, Kaylie," I paused.

Across the hall, Amira stared wide eyed at me. Her eyes were glassed over as she held my gaze. Pain and confusion swirled around her dark brown eyes. Her lips trembled, yet she didn't look away from me. I scanned her face; oh, she was so beautiful. How could I let such a jewel slip away from me like this?

I cleared my throat as I felt Kaylie's gaze burning holes at the side of my face. I opened my mouth to turn her down, but she spoke ahead.

"Look, I know there's a girl you really like and she doesn't feel the same, but Damon let me help you. Let me take that pain away from you. I will love you the way she never would," she said with sincerity.

I knew Amira heard Kaylie's little speech, because I saw her body tense up and fists clench. Could I really let Amira go and be with Kaylie? Amira was a jewel. She deserved better than me but I only kept on hurting her. I couldn't save her the way she saved me. Deep down in my heart, I knew Kaylie was wrong. And Amira would love me. She did love me.

Then why hasn't she ever shown it?

I still didn't understand why she couldn't love me. She was the only person who I truly loved; like my personal angel sent to save me in darkest times; who shined brighter than the stars.

"Okay," I told Kaylie. "I'll be your boyfriend."

As soon as I said it, I instantly regretted it. My heart broke into a million pieces and I felt dizzy. I could feel my breathing come out uneven. Kaylie quickly grabbed me and I leaned against her.

Damn. Why did my chest hurt so much?

My eyes wildly searched for Amira. However, she was gone, and the spot she was standing in was empty.

* * *

In class, my mind felt numb and I was unable to focus on anything. I kept glancing back at the empty spot near me, Amira still hadn't shown up. She disappeared as if she never even existed.

The love we shared was much more than a figment, yet I couldn't see the future with a tornado of doubts to come by. Amira would marry a good man one day, one who wasn't as damaged as I was, or had the same religion as hers.

Our teacher gave us some free time at the end of the lecture, telling us to work on any missing assignments. Amira told me to leave, but it still hurts to think about it.

I didn't want our conversations and laughter to end. I didn't want to lose the one girl who made everything right with just her smile. I knew we couldn't be 'just friends,' because none of us would be contented with that.

"Damon, you alright man?" Tye asked, settling in the seat next to mine. He tilted his head with his small eyes narrowing at my sorrowful expression. "You don't seem as thrilled as you were this morning."

"Who would have thought how badly this day would turn out?" I asked no one in particular. "Life sucks."

"Doesn't it, always?" Tye chuckled, but he quickly stopped himself when he realized I wasn't laughing along with him. "So, there are some rumors."

"There are always rumors about me."

"Well, this one is different."

I raised a brow. "How so?"

Tye nervously shifted his gaze to the wall behind me, seeming afraid to even bring up rumors that he knew I hated. Tye was a curious fellow, so I didn't blame him for trying to find out the truth.

"They say that you're dating someone again."

"And?"

He snapped his dark eyes back to me with confusion swirling through them. "Guess what? I thought you were into Amira. This morning you couldn't stop swooning about her!"

"Shh!" I hissed, noticing the strange looks we were getting from the class. "Don't tell the whole world now. We have to respect Amira's privacy."

He lowered his voice. "What the hell, man? Wasn't she your dream girl? Why'd you start dating someone else that fast?"

"I'm a mess, Tye."

"I call so much crap on this," he muttered to himself.

"Why do you care so much about my love life?" I asked. "There isn't much to talk about except that the rumors were true."

Tye became silent for a while, his lips thinning with distaste at my actions. I was too far from reality to even care. The classroom was a mere buzz while my mind continued on its inward torment, where all my memories of Amira shattered against my skull, clawing at me to remember all the good times, and to fight for our love.

But she had denied me.

My friend's voice cut through my silence. The voice was low enough for my ears to hear. "Why do you let rumors and the past control you?" he asked.

"What? We're not even talking about the past."

"But you still let it hold you back. Don't you get it, Damon? You screw things up for yourself because you tear yourself down all the time. You're not a broken mess. You're Damon Winters. My best friend, a king at soccer, and a complete jerk in video games," he said softly. "Your only enemy here is yourself."

"You don't know what you're talking about."

"Damon—"

Ring Ring.

I stood up, ignoring his desperate attempt to grab my attention. I tuned myself out, falling into the pit of voices in my head instead.

It doesn't matter. This is what she wants, so this is what she gets.

CHAPTER 37
Misery

AMIRA SARKER

I felt like I got punched in the stomach after hearing what Damon had said. I ran to the bathroom, rushed to the sink and gripped the counter. This can't be happening. The air in my lungs seemed to be ripped away from me.

Breathe. Inhale. Exhale. Inhale. Exhale. Come on, Amira.

I wobbled uneasily to the wall. I pressed a palm against the cold surface while touching my forehead. Why did everything feel so slow? I was seeing blurred images as my eyes filled with tears. My body didn't seem to cooperate with my mind. I felt my knees shaking and soon enough, I lost balance.

My head slammed against the tiles on the floor. Pain seemed to be erupting from everywhere toward the center of my being; my heart. There was pounding in my head, but it was nothing compared to what I felt in my tender heart. There was emptiness that couldn't be filled. What was this?

Amira, no. Get back up. Don't surrender yourself to this pain.

The need to just lay there in self-pity was so strong, but I knew better. I had to fight back. I had to be strong. Though my vision was hazy, I pushed myself off the floor and; managed to stand up.

*   *   *

"You're bleeding!" the nurse exclaimed.

I gripped onto the doorknob as my body heavily leaned against the wooden door. *Am I bleeding?*

"Sweetie, what happened?" she asked, as she rushed to my side and I collapsed in her arms.

"I-I fell," I whispered. My head felt heavy, as if an axe was wedged into my skull. The constant pounding got worse, and it didn't stop.

Oh Allah, what's wrong with me?

The nurse pulled me to one of the beds. She told me to take my headscarf off, and pulled the curtains around us, in case anyone came in.

"Oh dear," she mumbled, as she cleaned up the area.

Her gentle hands placed band-aids on my ripped skin, applying gentle pressure to the wound. I looked at her and saw pity in her cerulean eyes. *Why does she pity me?*

"Call your family," she said, and gave me a phone. "You shouldn't stay in school in this condition."

"Am I okay?" I asked.

She nodded. "You only have a concussion. Consider yourself lucky because usually a situation like this calls for immediate medical assistance at the hospital," she explained seriously.

Damn, did I fall that bad? Wow, Allah certainly saved me today.

I eagerly took some painkillers she gave me although these painkillers wouldn't take away this sorrow buried deep within me. They only distracted my mind from it and the distraught still pressured my body. Everything felt dull and lifeless. It was like my heart was drowning in my own self-pity. *Stop, Amira. Don't do this again. Be strong.*

I sighed and dialed a number. The nurse left the room to give me some privacy. Finally, the phone rang. *Please pick up. Don't leave me when I need you most. Allah, please make him answer.* Desperation clawed me and I called my brother for help. He knows that I couldn't tell my parents, yet.

"Hello?" his groggy voice answered.

I felt tears rushing to my eyes. They streamed down my face live a river as I furiously wiped at my eyes.

"*Bhaiyah* (brother,)" I croaked with an uneasy voice.

I heard shuffling from the other line. I only called him *'bhaiyah'* when there was something wrong.

"What's going on, Amira?"

I sniffled. "Please take me home. I don't wanna be here right now," I cried. It hurt as if thorns were pricking my fragile heart.

"I'm on my way," he said and hang up.

I dropped the phone and laid my head down on the pillow. I cried with heavy sobs ripping through my chest. I knew this would happen. I should have stopped things before it got worse. I should have ignored him; but I fell in love.

The realization echoed through my mind. *I love him with a forbidden love.* I couldn't love him. He and I could never be, but somewhere inside of me had a shimmer of hope. I thought that there could be a miracle that would make us to be together. However, dreams don't always become reality if they were never meant to be.

I closed my eyes. *Allah, make this pain go away. Make it all stop. I don't want to feel so... broken.* I hated to be weak, yet, I couldn't help it. I sucked in a deep breath. I knew I had told him to move on, but why did it hurt so much?

"Amira?" a voice called.

I didn't move. My head felt heavy and I let a few more tears drip down my face and onto the pillow. My heart was desperately beating to remind me that I was still alive.

I felt a warm hand touch my wound on my head. I cringed at the contact.

"Oh my God. What happened?" he asked.

I opened my eyes and was glad to see my brother came. I felt more tears brimming my eyes, but I held it back. Tanwir's eyes softened when he saw my tear-streaked face, and quickly sat on the bed. He pulled me to his chest and I felt like everything I was holding in for such a long time just came out.

I wrapped my arms around his neck tightly and sobbed quietly onto his shoulder. It's been so long since Tanwir showed this kind of affection towards me. He's never hugged me before. The last time he did that was when I was little and Aisha was alive.

"Shh, it'll be okay," he whispered, as he tightened his arms around me.

I choked back a sob. "I—I was w—wrong. I'm s—sorry," I said shakily.

He was quiet for a moment. I felt him pull away and disappointment filled me. *Please don't let him leave yet, Allah.* I silently prayed.

He held my shoulders and wiped the tears from my cheeks. He fixed my *hijab* for me and I stared at him confused. He then gave me a sad smile.

"We're humans, Amira. We all make mistakes and *Allah* knows that. It's okay. I promise everything is going to be okay," he reassured and hugged me again.

I rested my cheek on his chest and listened to his heartbeat. "It hurts," I whispered, brokenly.

I knew he realized I wasn't talking about my injury because he tensed up. "Shh, I know, Amira. It'll get better. Don't worry," he said through clenched teeth. It was obvious that he was less than pleased about Damon.

"Please don't leave me."

"I promise I won't. I'm your older brother. It's my job to be there for you."

I didn't say anything. I didn't trust my voice.

He sighed. "Come on, it's time to go home," he said, as he pulled away.

Something in his eyes told me that we were going to have a long talk, whether I liked it or not, yet, all I could think about was that he cared. Tanwir did care about me and this time he wouldn't leave me.

CHAPTER 38
In Comforting Arms

AMIRA SARKER

Silence echoes into the room,
Fear of heartbreak fills her,
A void,
An everlasting pain that never ceases,
A shattered hope.
That has been buried under all the memories,
No one to hear her calls,
No one for comfort,
Welcoming arms do not greet her,
She's too far away.
The light has been hidden,
Alone in dark-

"Amira, stop!" yelled a deep voice.

My pencil tip broke. I looked up. My hair covered my face from my brother's angry expression. He paced back and forth in my room. His hands tugged his black hair in all different directions, as worry etched his face. I looked down.

"Stop drowning in your emotions like this, please," he begged.

I felt tears prick my eyes as I thought of Damon. Everything about him seemed so perfect to me. His eyes, his lips, his earth-shattering smile, just... everything he was left a mark on me. I felt a wet tear trail down my cheek.

My vision blurred. *Why did he have to go? Why did he do that? I thought he loved me. Don't people fight for their love?* Questions swirled through me and my shoulders shook as I let out a sob. The worst part of it was that I did all this while knowing it was wrong. I betrayed Allah.

"It's all my fault," I whispered.

Tanwir stopped pacing and stood in front of me. "What?"

I sniffled. "I said, it's all my fault. Everything I did was my fault! I wouldn't be hurt if I had just stopped talking to him! I wouldn't be crying in bed if I never met him. It's all my fault," I cried.

I felt the bed dip besides me. Familiar arms wrapped around me and I was pulled to a chest. I cried more. *Allah, please make this unbearable pain go away. Make it all stop, Allah.*

"Shh, it's going to be alright. Don't cry, tubby," Tanwir said, softly.

"It hurts so much," I breathed out as I choked on a sob.

"I know it does, but you're a strong girl. You're amazing, Amira. Don't let this get you down."

"No, I'm not. *Allah* probably hates me for this," I mumbled.

He pulled back to look at me with a fierce gaze. "Don't you ever say that. *Allah* will always love you. You're human who commits mistakes. It doesn't matter how many times you've done wrong in your lifetime, as long as you always repent. *Allah* would rather have imperfect servant."

I stayed silent and he continued.

"Stop beating yourself up about this. Yes, you made a mistake, but it's okay. You're still the strongest Muslimah I know. Everything about you, Amira, is enchanting. Don't you ever wonder why so many aunties and uncles love you? It's because of how strong your faith is. You're a good person, but you're not perfect," he finished with a whisper.

I sniffled again and gave him a sad smile. "Thank you for everything you've done to me. I'm sorry if I was a bad sister to you. I really am," I said, ashamed as I thought back to the day I insulted him in anger, when he found out about Damon.

"Hey, look at me," he said. I moved my eyes to focus on his face. "I'm your older brother. Yeah, I'm a dick sometimes, and I'm not going to say I'm never going to hurt you again because I most likely will, but I will never leave you. We're family and a family sticks together through hard times," he grinned.

I laughed as I wiped away my tears. "*Ohana* means family, am I right?"

He shook his head at me, amused. "Okay, Stitch. Now get up, you have to eat."

I rolled my eyes. "Still, as bossy as ever," I muttered.

"What'd you just say to me?" he asked with narrowed eyes. I knew he was joking from the mischievous glint in his eye.

"Oh nothing," I shrugged, innocently.

"Uh-huh, sure. By the way Mum comes back from the hospital in like an hour with Nanu."

I face palmed myself. With everything happening, I completely forgot about my family issues. *Oh, I'm such a terrible granddaughter.*

"How is he?" I asked nervously.

"He's... well, not okay, but he doesn't care. He's just too selfish to realize how much we all care," said Tanwir, angrily.

I froze. Did I hear him right? "Did you just admit to caring?" I smirked.

He opened his mouth most likely to deny, but then he closed it. "I don't know what you're talking about," he said, as he looked away.

I squealed. "I knew it! I knew you weren't a cold bastard!"

"Amira, be quiet! Geez!" he grumbled.

I chuckled. "Well, how come you acted like you couldn't stand Nanu and Nani here?" I asked, curiously.

He clenched his fists at his sides and I wondered if I provoked him. "It's... I... I just hate seeing people I care about act so selfish. I didn't want to blow up in front of them, but I can't stand it."

I nodded my head in understanding. "You think he'll be alright? I really don't want to lose him like... Aisha," I whispered her name, afraid of Tanwir's reaction.

He closed his eyes as if he were in pain. His body tensed when I mentioned her name.

"I miss her sometimes. Makes me wonder who else we'll lose like that," I said softly.

"I miss her too. A lot has changed hasn't it?" he laughed humorlessly. "I sometimes wish that she was still alive; that I didn't try to end my life that night," he looked at me with a grief.

I walked up to him and hugged him. "We'll be okay. Allah will take care of us, right?"

"Yeah, *In Shaa Allah* (If God wills it)."

* * *

Tanwir and I were playing an intense chess match. Currently, he was winning, but I was determined. I moved my King and realized my mistake. Fudge.

"Haha! Checkmate! I told you I would win!" he gloated.

I glared at him. "Shut the hell up. You got lucky."

He stuck his tongue out at me. "It ain't luck. It's called skill," he smirked.

"Nonexistent skills you mean," I muttered.

"I heard that!"

"I wouldn't have said it if I didn't want you to hear it."

"Ouch, why don't you love me?" he asked playing hurt, as he placed a hand over his heart.

I gave him a sly grin. "Oh, baby you should go and love yourself," I sang.

"Amira, shut up!" he begged, as he put his hands to his ears.

I kept going until I heard the front door opened. Tanwir and I exchanged glances as Mum walked in with sagged shoulders with Baba not too far away from her. The bags under their eyes seemed to have deepened in the course of a couple of weeks yet their eyes drooped more than ever like they were trying not to faint form their worldly struggles.

"What do we do?" she asked.

Baba gripped onto a paper tightly as he spoke. "We have to talk to them."

"What's going on?" Tanwir asked.

Baba sighed. I felt anxiety consuming me as I waited for his answer.

"Your Nanu destroyed both his kidneys. He needs dialysis, but it's over a hundred thousand dollars," Baba said through clenched teeth.

I gasped.

"A hundred thousand dollars?!"

"How the hell are we going to pay that?" asked Tanwir.

Baba looked away. His silence told me the answer. We couldn't pay for it. That amount of money was more than our parents could make in a whole year. Hell, a doctor could make that much because it's a highly-paid kind of job.

"But what happens if we don't?" I asked with a hint of fear.

"We lose him," Mum said quietly.

We all went silent as if trying to comprehend what was happening. Nanu might die.

CHAPTER 39
Happily Never Afters

DAMON WINTERS

I drove my car to Amira's house. I was getting anxious by the second, having no idea what compelled me, yet, there I was in the middle of the road, struggling to get to her house without making her freak out.

The sun began to set as I turned on the road. The air was breezy, but the animals were as silent as the foreboding night. The golden orb fell down the horizons, slowly sinking into the depths of the Earth as a pomegranate pink sprayed across the sky.

My eyes landed on a girl with a scarf wrapped tightly around her head, wearing a long black garment, and I pressed on my brake.

Pushing my car to reverse, I waited for her to pass by me and followed her. Amira kept walking and as I got closer, I realized the furious way her feet hit the pavement. The wind softly brushed against her golden skin with the last remnants of sunlight kissing her gently.

I parked my car and got out. Amira stood still as I walked toward her, slowly. She didn't run or scream. Everything was eerily silent that I could only hear her heavy breathing. When I got near her, she spoke instantly freezing me.

"Leave me alone, Winters," she said in a voice without emotions. I felt chills crawl up my spine as she used that dead tone of hers.

"Amira," I breathed.

Stepping closer, I hesitantly turned her around to face me, ignoring the slight tension that coiled around her shoulders. I felt guilt come at me with a harsh force that threatened to drag me down.

Her eyes were glossy with tears and I saw a drop trail down her cheek. Instinctively, I held her face gently in my hands and wiped it away. My fingers lightly caressed her cheek and she didn't push me away. She didn't hit me.

Tye's words came crashing back. *Your only enemy is yourself.*

Suddenly, she slapped my hand away and glared at me. "Don't touch me," she said.

I put my hands up in surrender. "I'm sorry," I whispered.

I missed her so much and I wanted her back; her beautiful smile, the teasing playful side of her that never failed to amuse me, her adorable giggle at one of my stupid pick-up lines, and how her eyes lit up whenever she ranted about something. However, most of all, I wanted her love back.

She snapped her fingers in front of me, which grabbed my attention. "You don't get it, do you?" she asked.

I gave her a puzzled expression.

She sighed. "Damon, please. Leave me alone. Don't talk to me ever again and stay away from me," she said, biting her lip. "I mean it this time. Leave. Me. Alone."

"What?" I asked with narrowed eyes.

"You heard me."

I scoffed in disbelief. "You're kidding, aren't you?"

She gave me a blank expression. "I'm serious."

"Amira, listen to yourself! You're telling me to basically forget about you!"

"Well, maybe that's what I want!"

"Well, maybe I don't!"

"Stop yelling at me!"

I stopped my retort, clenching my jaw. "Amira... Don't test my patience tonight," I growled in anger. She was unbelievable.

She crossed her arms over her chest. "News flash, Damon. The world doesn't revolve around you."

"What's the matter with you? Can't you see that I'm actually trying right now? It's like you think I'm always going to be here waiting for you to love me back," I practically exploded. "I don't even know why I bothered. I should have just left you alone. I knew you'd do this."

I saw her eyes widen for a second before she composed herself. My words cut deep enough to trigger something from within. Amira truly believed that there was nothing left for us except a typical tragedy, a typical high school sweetheart that shredded as years went by. She didn't believe that our love was worth it and I didn't believe that our love would survive.

But why do I still want to try?

"You're insufferable! Guys like you make me want to stab them for their clueless brains. You don't know anything!" she hissed with her dark brown eyes burning with fiery spirit. "You don't know what I feel. You don't know how hard this is for me? You think it's all fun and games, but it's not. It's not a fairy tale for me, Damon. It hurts. Everything just hurts."

"Why won't you admit anything to me? How will I know your feelings if you don't tell me?" I asked, softly.

"Because I told you to move on, Damon. I deserve this," she said.

"No, you don't. Love isn't supposed to hurt you."

"Yet, it's the worst kind of pain. I don't want to sin, Damon. I don't even want to go near it, but I can't… I can't…" she struggled to say as her chest began to heave. "I can't do this. I just can't."

The sun went down with a new night arising from its debris and a galaxy of stars were waiting to be revealed behind the black curtain of darkness. The fire that had fueled us had been extinguished, releasing a blanket of cold air around us. It was bittersweet. We weren't good for each other, but we were like magnets constantly being pulled back whenever we were apart.

"Amira," I whispered, "I love you. All I want is for you to feel the same."

The despair had only heightened the corners of her eyes, a river of pain threatening to spill. "You can't do that to me, Damon. Have more mercy in your soul than that. Don't do this to me," she begged as she took a step back, eyes wide with fear.

"What's wrong?"

"You can't claim to love me and kiss another girl. That's not how love works. Please, don't mess with my feelings like that. I don't know how much more I can take," she whispered, bringing her hands to cradle her head. Her body trembled like an inharmonious ricochet off her thoughts.

"I'm not messing with your feelings! I really do love you," I spoke, defensively.

"When will you stop lying to me? Just... go away."

"No."

"What did you just say?"

"I said no," I repeated, crossing my arms over my chest.

"Damon, stop this nonsense." she sighed.

"Not until you tell me how you really feel."

"Damon—"

"Amira, why? Why are you angry at me when you told me to move on? Why are you pushing me away?" I blurted out the questions that were deep inside my mind without realizing it.

She looked taken aback. It was like realization finally dawned to her. Her shoulders slumped, her head hanging low, hands lying limply at her sides. My mind was yelling at me to go and beg for her forgiveness, but I stayed rooted to my spot. I had to know.

"You're right," she muttered, casting her gaze away as if in shame. "I have no right to be angry. It's all my fault."

I stayed silent. The wind howled around us, and it felt as if time was going by slowing. The crickets chirped, filling our silence in their constant tune. My mind seemed to be working overdrive as I tried to puzzle Amira together in my mind.

Several moments of silence stretched between us. It seemed like neither of us knew what to say. The atmosphere was thick. The cold night air seeped into my skin, crawling up my arms. When she suddenly spoke, my muscles had immediately tensed upon hearing the slight chill to her voice.

"I'm sorry for my actions, but I'm not sorry for my behavior. You knew the reasons why I had to let you go. I did it for you. Don't you get it, Damon? I did all this because I love you," she gave me a sad smile.

I stood there awestruck. It was out in the open now. She loved me.

"I didn't want you to be hurt and I knew if you were with me, you would be hurt. Life is blissful for a while, but eventually we will end up hurting each other," she said softly.

Without knowing what I was doing, I rushed over and pulled her into my arms with joy seeping through my pain. There were no thoughts about all the wrongs in my life because I finally had something that was right, a girl who felt too right to be in my arms. I was at my high indestructible peak at the tallest mountain.

Amira loved me.

She pushed me away. "Damon, you realize that nothing changes now, right? I still can't be with you," she frowned.

Not yet. I wanted to say, but I had to be patient with this. "Yeah, I know."

She nodded her head, seeming a bit suspicious of my intentions, but nonetheless left it alone. "Right. Okay, well I should get going."

I grabbed her arm. "Let me walk you," I smiled.

"Please don't. My parents would kill me."

I winked at her. "Trust me I'm slick."

She reluctantly agreed.

* * *

"You know you don't have to keep hurting like this, Amira. We could still be together," I said.

She shook her head. "Allah comes first," she stated.

I rolled my eyes. *Not again with this religion crap.* "Religions seem too constricting," I shrugged.

"They're really not. It's like a safe haven. Like a guide towards a content life."

"Yeah, okay," I said, sarcastically.

"I'm serious. Why don't you learn about some religions? Even if you won't convert to them, it's a good idea to have some basic knowledge. That way you can understand people better."

I gave her a sideways glance. "I don't know."

"Ignorance isn't always bliss, you know. It can cause a lot of hurt, a lot of hate crimes, and a lot of unnecessary disasters that could have easily been avoided if people had educated themselves," she said, a faraway look in her eyes. I knew she was talking about the recent jump in hate crime statistics that had dominated the news media from bold headlines to nonstop coverage.

"I suppose you're right."

When we got close to her house, she paused and turned to me with a smile as if she was welcoming me towards a realm of knowledge. "Think about it," she had said. "It might change how you see the world."

I watched her walk to her house. She waved at me one last time before she unlocked her door and vanished from my vision. I stayed nearby for just a minute longer, wondering why everyone kept telling me to learn more on my own about other cultures and religions. *How do I make things right again?*

I heard the Muslim prayer call, faintly from Amira's house.

Allahu Akbar Allahu Akbar.

It was like a light bulb went on in my head.

CHAPTER 40
Damn Damon

AMIRA SARKER

I gloomily walked to my science class which was biology. Teachers shouldn't give tests on Mondays. What was life at this point? The worst part of it all was that Damon was in that class.

I wanted to just go hide under a rock whenever I saw him. Ever since Friday night when we had that deep conversation, I just felt empty and awkward near him. I didn't want to face him and his *girlfriend*. That thought itself made me cringe.

I scoffed. He said that he loved me.

"Amira!" Ana exclaimed when I opened the door.

"Huh?" I asked, confused.

"Aye, it's my best art buddy," Sean grinned.

I placed my binder on the table, and put my backpack down on the gross looking science class floor. I noticed that Sean was in my seat. "Hold up, you're in this class now?"

His grin grew more. "Hell, yeah I am. My schedule changed."

"Well, that's great for you, but like you mind getting out of my seat?"

He crossed his legs on the table and put his arms behind his head. "Yeah, no. I'm pretty comfortable here," he smirked.

I laughed. "Aw, how cute. You thought I was asking. No, sweetheart, it was a demand not a request so move."

His jaw dropped at my remark, while Ana held her stomach from laughter. "Well, damn, Amira. So bossy," he muttered.

"Did someone say 'damn Daniel' here?" Thomas asked as he came up to our table.

Just then Damon walked into the classroom as well. His 'girlfriend' was nowhere in sight. I couldn't help but feel pleased at the thought but I quickly reminded myself to stop.

Sean had a mischievous glint in his eyes, a gaze that even *Shaytan* (Satan) would scurry in fear from. Ana and I exchanged nervous glances at each other. *This can't be good.*

Sean shrugged. "Hey, we don't have a Daniel but we have a Damon," he winked at me as Damon was walking past us.

I hid a giggle behind my hands, careful not to alert Damon of Sean's plans. If only our teacher was here to enjoy it with us. The *'Damn, Daniel'* was a joke from a 2016 viral video. These two guys made a collection of Snapchat stories that brought them to internet fame due to one of the boys exaggerating his friend, Daniel's, outfits.

Damon stopped his steps as he heard his name. He slowly turned around, knowing the sense of dread almost instantly from Sean's wide smile. "I swear to God, Sean. If you say—"

"Damn Damon! Back at it again with the fancy Jordans!" Sean hollered.

Damon looked down at his athletic shoes as a sigh escaped his lips, lifting his head to glare at Sean. Ana, Thomas, and I cracked up from laughter, the melodic sound of entertained students echoing down the halls. The rest of our class filed in, excited to see what the hype was this morning. We probably sounded like psychopaths.

"Damn Damon!" Thomas repeated in a nasal voice.

"Oh, my freaking God. Shut the hell up. That is the stupidest thing I've ever heard of. Honestly, that kid didn't even deserve a scholarship. I swear there's something wrong with this country," Damon scoffed in annoyance.

"Definitely. I hate how Josh, you know the guy who was saying 'damn Daniel,' only got a surfboard while Daniel got all this attention for legit doing nothing. His clothes weren't even that great," I said, referring to all the coverage the meme had gotten.

Damon grinned at me, leaning against my table with his arms crossed over his chest. I could see his biceps move with the motion and strained against his black t-shirt. I drew my gaze back to his face and saw him smirking at me, probably realizing that I was checking him out to some degree. I quickly looked away.

What happened to lowering your gaze, Amira?

Sometimes I really hated my conscious mind.

"At least Amira understands how annoying that stupid video is," Damon muttered.

"Hey, man! That's quality work right there. You can't tell me it's not funny-" Sean started to say but was interrupted.

"Oh my God, Sean. Shut up already!" exclaimed Ana with the ghost of a smile still feathering her lips. She enjoyed riling him up.

Thomas, Damon, and I stifled a laugh. Sean glared at all of us and then leaned back against his chair, which was right next to Ana's now, and propped his legs onto the table. He had changed seats during our argument. I shook my head, amused. Where were his manners?

"Okay boys, time to go back to your side of the classroom. Me and Ana have to get acquainted with our new... group member," I said, feigning distaste. I even scrunched up my nose to add an effect to my words.

"Hey! What the— Why are you saying it like I'm a disease? I swear, I'm harmless," he pouted.

Ana and I exchanged troublesome glances at each other. *Oh, she definitely knows what I'm thinking.*

"Well..." we both trailed off with a shrug.

Sean dropped his legs from their careless position and slammed his fists onto the table. "Well, fuck you guys!" he yelled, annoyed.

"Watch your profanity!" Damon and I said simultaneously.

We looked at each other, shocked.

I felt the corner of my lips tug upwards as I said, "Yeah, look who's talking, Mr. I-Like-To-Curse-A-Lot."

"Ouch. My princess wounds me," he said with a strange edge to his voice, which made him sound genuine.

I felt myself tense. Our playful mood shifted to serious in a matter of seconds. I realized our other three friends were quietly watching us.

"Maybe the princess doesn't want a knight in shining armor," I retorted while trying to keep a blank face.

Please, don't see my emotions. I don't want you to know.

"Maybe she's just scared of falling in love with him."

I hated how cheeky he looked as he said that. I hated that irresistible spark that lit his green eyes like shimmering stars. I hated how my stomach would flip whenever he gazed at me with such ardor.

"Maybe—"

"Good afternoon, class!" greeted Ms. Lyons, completely ruining the hypothetical world Damon and I had created.

We all took our seats as class began. I felt someone nudge my shoulder. I looked to my side to see Ana's concerned expression.

"You alright?" she asked.

I hesitated. Was I alright?

No, I'm not.

I nodded my head. "Yeah I'm fine, just stuff at home that's been bothering me. Nothing too serious," I smiled reassuringly.

She didn't look too convinced, but nodded her head anyway. "Just know that I'm here for you. All of us are," she said as she gestured with her hands the friends we have in this class.

My heart warmed at her words. She was right. My friends are all here for me. I just have to open up to them and let them play therapist for a change. On most days, I would be the healer of their wounds whether they be physical or emotional, I had been their guide to redemption. I had inspired them yet I never took my own advice.

I chose to hide in my shell, and that would be my destruction one day.

"Thank you. It means a lot to me. Love you, buddy," I winked.

She chuckled. "Yeah, I know I'm great," she said as she flipped her hair over her shoulder.

I rolled my eyes. "Yeah okay, McCocky."

"McCocky? Really?" she asked with elevated brows.

I shrugged. "What can I say? My nicknames are that great."

She simply shook her head, amused, and returned her attention back to Ms. Lyon's lesson.

From across the room, I could see Damon's eyes on me. He wasn't even trying to be discreet. I ignored him. I couldn't deal with that longing look in his eyes. I wanted to hate him for having a girlfriend and for telling me he loved me when he held another girl in his arms yet I couldn't bring myself to.

One day, I was going to have to face all these problems, maybe even alone. I was extremely grateful to have my friends by my side that genuinely loved me. *Allah* could take anything away at any given time, no matter the weather, no matter the day, *Allah* had the ability to test us whenever He deemed it to be a good time.

I was grateful for everything *Allah* had given me in my life, regardless of all the suffering it had taken me to be at this point in my life. Yes, like every other human being, I was greedy for more, greedy for love, greedy for Damon and his unwavering attention.

Help me, Allah. Save me from this temptation. If Damon and I were meant to be, make a way for us. If not, then put obstacles between us. Ameen.

I brought my mind back to planet Earth and focused on my assignment, leaving my previous thoughts in the back of my mind.

* * *

I was at my locker packing up to go to Tasneem's house. No one was home and Tasneem's family offered their place to me until someone was home. As I walked to Tasneem's car, I noticed two familiar figures talking in hushed voices at a corner.

I squinted my eyes and saw that it was Damon and Thomas. The two tensed as Kaylie skipped towards Damon. Damon was pale as ever and nervously laughed at something she said. He whispered something in her ear, much to Thomas's dismay it seemed, and she giggled. She grabbed his jaw and kissed him hard on the mouth for a second and then left him standing there bewildered.

I quickly shielded my eyes from the scene. I felt familiar pricks of pain touch my heart. I gasped a deep breath. *Oh Allah, why is such a pain so unbearable that I can't even breathe? I've heard and seen Aria go through heartbreaks yet I never imagined they'd feel this bad.*

The fact that I had kept all these conflicting emotions inside me for so long was starting to bring me closer and closer to insanity. I didn't know how much more I could take before I burst.

I proceeded to walking to the front of the building. I saw Tasneem, Lucy, Meredith, and Aria standing there, chattering. I ran up to them, leaving all contemplations about Damon and his girlfriend behind, and all thoughts of heartbreak in the debris of my awaiting night ahead.

"Hey!" I waved.

"Amira! Okay, everyone is here, so let's go to our study session, people. Aria, could you take Lucy and Meredith with you? I have to talk to Amira," Tasneem said.

Uh oh. She wants to talk to me. This can't be good.

"Sure, no problem. Let's go guys," Aria gave me a reassuring smile as if to tell me 'this talk' wasn't going to be bad.

Tasneem and I got in her car. As she started up the engine, I caught a glimpse of Damon's car. Thomas and him seemed to be having an intense conversation in his car, and by the look of controlled anger on Damon's face, he was not pleased. I wonder what was up with them now.

I heard that they had a fight last week, which was odd considering how nice of a guy Thomas was and how close their friendship was. Come to think of it, Damon was said to have gotten into a big argument with Jacob earlier today.

There you go again, listening to rumors. Stop.

"Do you like Damon?" asked Tasneem, bursting my bubble.

I blinked. "What?" I asked.

She took in a deep breath. "Do you like Damon?" she reiterated.

"No."

She looked taken aback. "You don't?"

I shook my head. "I think what I feel is more than *like*," I said softly.

Just like that, my vision blurred from the memories that consumed me.

CHAPTER 41
The Letter

AMIRA SARKER

I choked up. "You can't love me. You're going to get hurt."

He shook his head with a slight smile. "I don't care. I can't stop loving you."

"Damon, love can ruin you. Don't you understand? I might ruin you."

"Then let it ruin me. Amira, I'm in love with you and I can't stop it," he said softly, reaching to grab my hands. I felt tingles reach up my arms. "I need you. Without you, Amira, I am nothing."

That adrenaline that ran through my blood vessels, as I heard him say those words was something I never felt before. Everything about him, even if it was small, made me fall in love with him every day. The worst part was I couldn't stop these feelings, even if I tried too.

I wanted more of his love and I wanted to be selfish. Just once, but I knew I couldn't be *that* selfish, at least not with my religion and sanity on the line.

"Amira?" Tasneem's voice brought me out of my dark thoughts.

I hummed in response.

She sighed. "Are you sure you love him? You're only seventeen. You don't know what love is! How can you be so sure?" she asked, tiredly as if she were speaking down to me.

Something snapped inside me. Did she really think I'd rush to a conclusion like that if I wasn't sure? "I know what I feel is true. You know that I'm immune to playboy antics and looks, it's just not me. I choose personality over appearance, and if he had a rotten personality, I wouldn't be sticking around him as much as I do. I know I love him. I tried to deny these feelings, Tasneem. I really tried. I know it's wrong, but I'm only human. I-I don't know what to do anymore," I stuttered as I blinked away the tears from the pain I felt, knowing that my own sister in Islam judged me too quickly.

Tasneem stayed quiet for a while as I inhaled uneasy breaths to calm down. After several moments of stretched silence, she spoke in a hoarse voice like she was ashamed of herself.

"But Damon? Out of all people, you choose him?" she asked, incredulously.

"When do we ever get a choice in how we feel about others? I can't just close off all my emotions. Besides, I didn't do anything out of bounds with him. I told him to leave me alone and move on," I muttered, annoyed at her for making me feel guilty.

"Amira, that's not what I meant. I'm only looking out for you."

"Well, friends don't judge others like that. Do you have any idea on the amount of pain I was going through all this? I know it's wrong for goodness sake! I know that he and I aren't meant to be; but tell me, how does one just ignore something like that? How do I make the right decision when temptation is pulling me closer to it? Do you have any idea how guilty I am? On how many nights I cried and prayed to Allah to save me from *Zina* (unlawful intercourse)?" I asked her hysterically. "Do you have any idea?"

It hurt. It really did hurt to know that even my friend was turning against me because I fell in love. It was like everyone expected me to be perfect, but didn't realize that I wasn't perfect. I was still a teenager. I had mood swings and had crazy moments. I was just a girl trying to figure out life. Why should I be judged for one mistake I made?

"I'm sorry. I admire you, Amira. I really do. I can't imagine how much pain you must have felt for letting something so precious to get away like that. Oh, my Allah. We all even talked about Kaylie right in front of you," she gasped as realization dawned upon her. "Amira, I'm so sorry. If I had known-"

"Hey, relax. It's okay. You didn't know. Don't feel bad," I said, gently.

"Yeah but—"

"*Tasneem*," I pleaded. "It's really okay. I'm fine. Don't worry about it," I smiled reassuringly.

"Stop saying that!" she exclaimed as the car came to a sudden halt on the side of the road. I jerked forward. "Amira," she said, strained. "I know you. I know how hard you try to conceal all your feelings. I know how much you care for people, even more than yourself, but you have to realize that we all care for you, too. Listen to your own advice, Amira. Let us help you carry your burdens. We're your friends. You helped Meredith, Aria, Lucy, Alexis, me, and a whole bunch of other people through the most difficult times in our lives. It's time for us to take care of you," she said softly as she held my hands in a tight grip.

I was stunned and became speechless. Here with me was not just a friend since I was twelve, but my sister in Islam. She made a point. I did refuse to take help when I really needed it.

"I guess I can't always be the therapist, huh?" I asked with a smile.

The corners of her mouth twitched upwards. "Even a therapist needs help sometimes," she said.

"I'm sorry. You're right. I need to take my own advice before I destroy myself emotionally."

"Hey, it's okay. There's always room for improvement even in some of the strongest minds."

I laughed. "Start driving, you fool. The others are probably worried," I urged her as I pulled my hands away.

"Not until you promise to be more open with me and the rest of our friends," she bargained.

I hesitantly nodded my head. *Well, why not? Allah is giving me an option to help me, might as well take advantage of it.* "I promise."

With that said, we continued our way to her house.

* * *

It was around 8 pm when I came home. I told my friends about Aisha and a little about my crush on Damon. I only said I liked him because it didn't feel right to tell the whole world about Damon and our conflict. I just wasn't ready yet. It felt a lot better to tell someone about my own stresses in life like a weight was lifted off my shoulders, and I could finally breathe again.

Thank you, Allah, for blessing me with such amazing people in my life, I thought.

For once, in the last couple of months, I started to feel lighter and happier. Yeah, life was rough, but there were always good memories to shine through the dark ones.

Knock Knock.

I jumped. *Geez, why does that always scare me?*

"Come in."

Tanwir's head peeked from the side of the door. "Yo, there's a letter for you. I just thought I'd deliver it," he said with a bored tone as he handed me the letter. He looked around my room with distaste. "Why is your room so messy? You know cleanliness is part of our faith, tubby. You should practice it."

I rolled my eyes and opened the letter. "Jerk," I mumbled.

He glared at me. "Say that to my face, chicken head."

I looked up and smirked. "Now, where's the fun in that, my dear brother?" I asked in an overly sweet tone.

"Just read the damn letter, loser," he sighed in annoyance.

I grinned at him playfully and read the contents of the letter. I felt my eyes go wide as I reread the letter again. *Oh my Allah.* My jaw dropped.

"What? What's going on? Why are you looking at the paper like that?" he asked.

"Oh my God! Tanwir, I got in! They accepted me to my first choice university! I got accepted! Alhamdulillah (thanks to God)!" I screamed, happily.

"Wait! Lemme see that." He grabbed the letter and skimmed through the contents. A slow grin spread across his face. "Congratulations! I knew you could do it," he said smugly.

I playfully rolled my eyes and thundered down the stairs to tell my parents. "Mum! Baba! I got in! I got in! Look!" I exclaimed through the halls.

"What?" Baba asked as he lowered the TV volume.

I saw Nanu and Nani look at me inquisitively. I ignored them momentarily, showing Baba the letter. Tanwir followed me down and leaned against the wall with crossed arms, a look of pride was written across his calm visage. I eagerly waited for Baba to finish reading the letter. I couldn't stand still.

My grandparents smiled, knowing the contents of the letter had clearly lifted my spirits again.

Baba's frown deepened as he finished reading it. I felt my own facial expression reflect his, Tanwir was tensing behind me. Baba slowly put the letter down with his unreadable eyes.

"You can't go," he stated firmly.

"What? Baba, this is one of the best universities for students that wish to pursue a career in the medical field. I have to go to this school. It's my dream," I desperately pleaded in front of him.

He scratched his beard, a habit of his when he was thinking, and shook his head. "I can't let you go. This university is so far away from us. I refuse to let my daughter move into a dorm, where she could have a male roommate. I'm not letting you go," he repeated with finality in his tone, leaving no room for arguments.

"Baba, please. Rethink this decision. There are all girl dorms or I could rent out an apartment. Please let me do this," I begged him. *Oh Allah, please let there be a way.*

He opened his mouth to say more, but Tanwir cut him off. "I'll graduate in a couple of months. My friend's father has a big company for electronics and he needs full time cyber security majors. I could rent out an apartment with the money I have saved and watch over Amira," he explained.

"Tanwir, she's just our little girl. We can't let her leave us and go into a world like that," Mum said softly as she wrapped her arms around me.

"Mum, I'm almost eighteen! I would have to face the real world eventually. Please let me go with Tanwir."

My parents exchanged glances with each other. I gazed at Tanwir with a face full of panic. He nodded at me, our sibling bond speaking louder than words.

"Baba, can I talk to you, privately?" he asked.

Baba nodded and followed Tanwir to a separate room upstairs. I waited in agitation as Mum tried to convince me out of my decision. I shook my head. I had to do this.

When I was little, I promised Allah I'd become either a doctor or medical researcher to help those in need, and use that money for charity. I wanted to complete that dream and promise of mine. I wanted to follow my own ambitions, and I was determined to accomplish this one. If I went to this university, I'd have the best chance.

After, what felt like several hours, Baba and Tanwir emerged from their "private talk."

Baba smiled at me. "I will give you one year, Amira. If you don't get mostly A's in that year, I will make you come back here. You will stay with Tanwir, call us every day and visit at least once a month. If not, we can use *skype*. Is that understood?" he asked, seriously.

I gulped, straight A's for one whole year. I barely got a 4.0 GPA every quarter in high school. Could I really make it in college? Well, it was a risk I'm willing to take. "Understood, Baba."

Mum looked warily at the two men in the room, but then sighed in defeat. "Don't you ever stop being my little girl," she whispered into my hair as her arms around me tightened.

"I won't, Mum. I promise," I whispered back and rested my head on her shoulder. I felt her tears on my left shoulder.

I will always be your little girl, Mum.

CHAPTER 42
Break Ups

DAMON WINTERS

"Damon! Wake up! Wake up!" a voice squealed.

I groaned and buried my head in my pillow. "Go away," I grumbled.

"Damon! You promised I'd meet that pretty girl you talk about!" Jade exclaimed.

I lifted my head up and looked at the time. It was only eight in the morning. *Oh, great! I'm sleeping.* "Jade! It's so early go away. Let me sleep in peace!" I groaned as I fell back against my pillow, tugging the covers over my head to ensure darkness.

Jade was staying with Dad for a while since her mom was visiting family in Canada. Dad moved out of the house and I was visiting him this weekend. I felt a little body jump onto my back.

"Damon, stop being a jerk! I wanna see her," she pouted.

Her ginger colored bangs covered her forehead as she looked at me with wide puppy dog eyes. Her curly hair bounced on her shoulders as she jumped on my bed, flopping on it with a small giggle. I felt the mattress shake underneath me, thus ruining the last bit of sleep I had left in my eyes.

"God damn it," I muttered as I gently pushed her off. I sighed as I rubbed a hand over my face.

"Damon?"

"What?" I asked impatiently, looking for decent clothes.

"What did you say?"

I froze. *Dad is going to kill me if he finds out!* I quickly turned around and gave her a nervous smile. "Never ever say that word again, understand?"

"But you just—"

"Jade," I sent her my pointed glare.

Jade looked down, ashamed at getting scolded. I saw tears glazing her eyes. "I'm sorry," she said quietly.

I sighed, realizing I hurt her, and embraced her to my chest. Her tiny arms spread around my waist, pulling me closer. Her small face buried itself in the fabric of my white shirt.

"I'm sorry, little one. It was my fault. Don't cry," I whispered.

How could something so precious be my little sister? It all seemed almost surreal. As I looked down at the little figure, I realized how my dad couldn't have just abandoned her. Jade was so innocent. She needed someone there for her, especially with her mom being a drunken drug addict, not to mention a pain in the ass.

I hated to send Jade back to her. It wouldn't be long until her mother started to take her anger and frustrations out on Jade. Her home was unstable. Jade told Dad about how her mom whipped her as a child.

The fear I had for Jade's well-being was immense. She's my little sister. We may be half-siblings, but she was still my sister, my own flesh and blood. I couldn't leave her defenseless like that. As an older brother, it was my job to protect and cherish her when our families were falling apart.

I felt Jade push me away from her, and I raised my eyebrows at her.

She gave me a disgusted look while pinching her nose with her two fingers. "Your breath smells," she gagged.

I chuckled and rose to my feet. "Of course it does. I just woke up.".

She laughed. "So what? That's no excuse," she playfully scolded.

Jade was eager to meet Amira. I talked about Amira and her hilarious moments in class. Jade loved her. She even asked me how beautiful she was and I responded with no words to even describe her beauty. She was drop-dead gorgeous.

Unknowingly, Jade pushed me into the bathroom, slamming the door on her way out. I couldn't erase the smile that graced my lips. Once I had accepted Jade as my sister, another sibling didn't seem cruel.

Maybe Mom and Amira were right. I really did have to seize the opportunity to be optimistic whenever it was possible.

* * *

"Damon! Thomas is at the door!" Dad yelled.

"Coming!" I hollered back.

I slipped on a shirt and some jeans. As I walked to the living room, I was drying my hair with the towel. Jade was eating cereal and watching *My Little Pony,* while Thomas sat next to her going off about how lame the show was.

"It's the best show ever!" Jade exclaimed.

Thomas chuckled deeply. "Nah fam. It's so girly," he retorted.

"Says the one who played with the merchandise with his sisters as a kid," I smirked as he quickly turned to me horrified.

Jade giggled.

"We promised not to talk about that!" he glared at me as a faint tint of pink coated his cheeks.

"Dude, I don't make promises I can't keep," I shrugged, a look of mischief crossing my eyes.

"Whatever," Thomas mumbled as he rolled his eyes, which earned him more moments of humiliation from Jade and I.

Thomas and I left Jade alone in the living room and joined my dad for breakfast at the dining table. Thomas and I were talking about the latest *promposals.* I thought they were lame. I mean it was just prom, not like the guy was actually proposing.

"Speaking of *promposals,* Damon aren't you going to ask out your girlfriend?" asked Dad as he sipped on his coffee and continued to look at newspaper.

Thomas choked on his milk. "G-Girlfriend?" he sputtered as he wiped his mouth with the back of his hand. "I thought you were gonna break up with her."

I shot a warning look at Thomas. My father liked Kaylie like his own daughter. I didn't know how he would react if he knew I liked a Muslim girl. He wasn't very fond with Muslims due to all the negativity in the media and the Luqmaan incident. His brain was brainwashed like the average American.

Then again, he was an average American, so that would make sense.

Dad's head quickly snapped up to meet my sheepish expression. He narrowed his eyes, placing his paper down slowly. "You were going to break up with her?" he asked, carefully. I could already hear the masked anger in his voice.

Thomas was looking anywhere else but at Dad and I. *This is going to be a long conversation.* I slumped in my chair, sighing.

"Dad, I… I don't like Kaylie like that. I'm thinking of breaking up with her cause I can't keep leading her on. I already hurt someone. I can't hurt another," I said sadly as I diverted my gaze to the floor.

"What did you do?" he asked slowly.

Thomas cleared his throat, interrupting us. "I'm gonna go watch TV with Jade," he smiled nervously at my direction. Even my friend felt pity for this conversation.

Well done.

"I broke her heart."

He leaned back against his chair and crossed his arms. "Wait, so you broke a girl's heart, decided to date Kaylie and now you're going to break her heart too? I'm clearly missing something," he wondered out loud.

I face palmed. "No, Dad. I used Kaylie as a way to get over someone. I don't like Kaylie," I bluntly stated as if it was obvious.

Dad's eyes widened. "Damon Hayden Winters! What's wrong with you?!" he yelled as he stood up.

I huffed. "What? I didn't do anything wrong," I mumbled. Kaylie offered it, and I already told her I liked someone but she didn't care. She just wanted to be with me.

Dad paced back and forth as he pinched the bridge of his nose. "Damon," he sighed. "That girl really likes you and you're just using her?! I thought you got over this phase," he said, disappointedly.

I felt the anger rising within me. *What the hell is he talking about?* "I'm not playing her, Dad. I told her what I really felt and she was okay with it," I gritted out as my fists clenched.

Dad gave me a blank stare. "You cannot be that blind," he denied as he shook his head.

"I told her my intentions," I mumbled.

"Damon! She's a girl! Come on. You lived with your mom for eighteen years. You should know that they hide their feelings!" he exclaimed.

I paused. "*Kaylie actually likes me?*" I muttered as realization took over.

"I need to talk to Thomas real quick," I rushed out as I walked to the living room and grabbed Thomas by the collar and pulled him into my room.

"What's wrong, dude?" he asked as he shook me off him.

I sat down on the bed with my face buried in my hands. "I'm such a retard," I muttered.

"Yeah, we already knew that," Thomas lightly chuckled. I lifted my head up to see his hands in his hoodie. "So what you gonna do?" he asked, casually.

I leaned back against my arms. "I don't know man. Fucking hell! How did I not see that Kaylie actually liked me? I don't need that drama in my life."

"Just break up with her already! It's so simple!"

"No, it's not! What if I hurt her more?" I asked, terrified. I was done hurting people just because I was hurt.

Yet you keep hurting the ones you care about.

"You need to stop this nonsense and get yourself together. It's either Kaylie or Amira, Damon. I suggest you make the right choice because one of them will be hurt in the end. It's inevitable," he told me seriously.

"I know. I just... don't want to hurt anyone," I confessed as I directed my gaze to the floor.

Thomas sighed and sat down next to me. He put a reassuring hand on my shoulder and squeezed it as a way of comforting me.

"Listen dude, life is about hurt. You can't avoid that in every situation. Hurt isn't always a bad thing. People learn from it. It's okay, man. It's all going to be okay," he said softly.

In that moment in time, I realized what Amira had meant all those months ago when she told me to be grateful. Family and friendships kept a person's sanity. Here I was, afraid to hurt another person, and he was trying to guide me towards a good decision. No matter what happened in life, people like Thomas, Tye, Jacob, and Sean would always stick by me.

These friendships I had were a blessing, and I had taken it for granted for too long.

"I'm sorry," I said.

Thomas raised his eyebrows at me in a questioning glance. "For what?"

I smiled. "For not realizing how important our friendship means to me until now. Thank you, Thomas. I'm grateful for everything you've done for me, even if you had to beat me up sometimes," I chuckled as I recalled the memory of Thomas yelling at me after school once for dating a girl like Kaylie like all my other friends in our little group.

He laughed. "Well someone has to beat the hell out of you when you're being an ass. I like to call it balance. I'm just maintaining it," he smirked.

I rolled my eyes. "I hate you."

"But Damon, weren't you just confessing your love for me?" he asked with his smirk still perfectly painted on his lips.

"No, I was expressing my gratitude for your lameness because it makes me seem cooler," I retorted.

"Well damn then. Be a dick about it," he pouted.

"Shut up, you big baby. Now toss me my phone."

"This is why you and Amira are perfect for each other. Both bossy as hell," he muttered as he passed me my phone.

I ignored his comment as I dialed Kaylie's number.

"So, who are you choosing?" Thomas asked.

I turned to him with a ring. "The girl I went to a mosque for," was my simple reply. Before he could say anything else, Kaylie answered.

"Hello?"

"Hey, Kaylie. We need to talk," I said nervously. I saw Thomas give me a thumb up.

Wait for me, Amira. We'll be together soon.

CHAPTER 43
Promise Me

AMIRA SARKER

I smiled at my neighbors, waving at them as I walked to the lake. Children were running around throughout the neighborhood while their parents were hosting family gatherings. The sun's radiance sparkled in their eyes and everything seemed so perfect.

No one was judging each other. No one was yelling; no tears and no heartbreaks except happiness. Smiling faces and gentle voices greeted me as I walked down the street. My neighbors were congratulating me for being accepted at the university.

As I approached the lake, I frowned. *Where is he?*

Damon told me to meet him here and I realized I might as well tell him the great news. I nervously bit my lip. How was he going to react?

He won't care, I thought.

I saw a spot underneath the shade of a tree, so I walked over, settling myself on the bed of grass that enveloped me. The wind bristled through my peach-colored hijab, gently shaking the branches, and allowing a few leaves to fall on my lap. The birds sang their song around me, calling out to their own children and family. I was mesmerized by the call of nature and all its glory from the small daffodils at my feet to the soaring birds above.

Memories of the past flooded me as I found myself desperately trying to relive those times again. Her smile was forever in my mind. It seemed as if time had frozen. Suddenly, I felt intense longing weigh down on my heart as I remembered Aisha.

*   *   *

I giggled as I ran into the forest. "You won't catch me!" I yelled.

"Amira! Be careful!" Aisha yelled as she picked up her pace.

I stopped running as I came across a wondrous sight. The trees gently moved with the wind. The sun beamed down upon the crystal clear water. It looked like diamonds were underneath the clear sheet of water. I slowly walked closer, kneeling beside the lake where my reflection greeted me. Small colorful fishes swam around in a hurry.

I swirled my finger around the water as the underwater creatures scurried away from me. Curiosity strained against me, and I wanted to catch the pink fish, but of course it was too fast for me.

"There she is," I heard a familiar voice pant out.

I quickly turned to see Tanwir and Aisha holding onto a tree as they caught their breaths. Tanwir looked up and glared at me. "Amira, you know you're not supposed to run off like that," he scowled.

"I'm sorry," I mumbled quietly as I looked to the ground, ashamed. I felt tears brim my eyes. I didn't mean to get in trouble. I thought we were just playing.

Tanwir opened his mouth to say more, but Aisha elbowed him. He winced and chose to be quiet. Aisha pulled me to her chest, lifting me onto her hips. My arms instinctively wrapped around her neck, burying my head in the floral scent of her hijab.

"Shh, he didn't mean it. We were just worried. It's okay, sweetheart. Don't cry," she whispered gently into my ear as she stroked my hair.

I tucked my hair into her scarf covered neck. "I'm really sorry. I didn't mean to," I cried.

I felt another presence loom over me. I looked up. Tanwir smiled at me reassuringly and brushed my tears away. "Amira, it's okay. Stop crying now. Let's go look at the fishes, okay?" he asked softly.

I eagerly nodded my head and Aisha put me down. I was only seven years old and I began to realize the importance of family. My parents and siblings would never leave me. They reassured me thousands of times that they would always stick by me. Baba used to always tell me how Islam made family a priority and that we should never take it for granted because one day we might just lose it.

"Aisha, why do some people not like the way we dress?" I asked her, referring to her abaya and hijab.

Tanwir scoffed. "They're all just racist scumbags," he said bitterly.

Aisha slapped his arm.

"Ow! What was that for? I'm just telling the kid the truth," he grumbled.

She rolled her eyes. "She's only seven! Don't feed her misconceptions. Not everyone is that bad," she argued.

"How can you see the good in people who call you a terrorist every day? Open your eyes already. This world isn't all cupcakes and butterflies. It's cold and cruel. We're already labeled as killers by society, yet you sit there and defend the people that have done you wrong?" Tanwir angrily exclaimed.

I felt fear creeping into my veins. Please, make them stop yelling, Allah. I cuddled closer to Aisha's chest due to the fact that I was seated on her lap. I hated when they argued. Something bad always happened when people were angry. Suddenly, I felt her arms embrace me tightly in a comforting gesture.

"Stop it. You're scaring her," she warned him.

Tanwir's gaze softened as he looked at my shaking figure. He sighed and ran his fingers through his dark messy hair.

"It's not fair, Aisha. It's just not fair. Why am I judged for another's crime? Why am I told that I don't belong here because I'm a Muslim? Why do they hate us?" Tanwir asked, brokenly.

I had never seen my brother act so confused. He usually had this confident demeanor and upbeat personality. It was like nothing anyone could say would ever bother him.

Aisha gestured for him to come closer. He silently obeyed and she embraced both Tanwir and I. "It'll get better, I promise. Everyone is just shook up over 9/11. In a couple of years you'll see the Muslim population skyrocket," she said as she pulled away.

"Allah gives us hardships in life. Not being accepted by society is one of them. Remember that no matter what anyone tells you, you are not a terrorist. Society doesn't determine who you are and who you can be. You are both individuals that are meant to do great things. Don't ever forget that or lose hope, okay?"

I finally understood the harsh realities that I would eventually have to face. I was different. Not everyone would like me. People had fears of Muslims and the only thing I could do is show them that there was nothing they had to fear about me. I was just like a normal human being. That was what Aisha taught me. She taught me that I was more than what society made me out to be and for that I would forever be grateful.

* * *

I felt a shadow loom over me. It felt familiar and somewhat comforting. My eyes slowly fluttered open, blinking to adjust. I noticed bright emerald eyes filled with elation as I gazed back at them. Damon had his usual charming smile planted on his face. His light brown hair brushed over his forehead and he flipped it back. Longing buried itself within my chest as I realized one day that smile would be for someone else who wasn't me.

"Hey, beautiful," he smiled.

I shook my head with a ghost of a smile crawling onto my lips. "Hey, loser," I smirked.

He feigned hurt. "My princess doesn't appreciate my kind gestures. I'm wounded," he said as he placed a hand over his chest.

"I thought I was your princess," a childish voice chirped behind him.

We both turned to the intruder of the voice. It was a little girl with ginger hair in a high ponytail. She had the same colored eyes as Damon and freckles across her pale cheeks. Somehow, she looked extremely familiar. *Where had I seen her before? Wait a minute.*

"Emmy? Is that you?" I asked, hesitantly.

Confusion rang through her mind. Slowly, realization crossed her face and she jumped into my awaiting arms. Her arms tightly held onto my neck as I embraced her lovingly.

"I missed you, Amira!" she exclaimed, happily.

I laughed and pulled away. "You've grown up so much, Emmy. I remember when you were a baby."

"What the fu-I mean heck?" Damon covered up his profanity with a cough. "How do you know each other? Emmy? What kind of a nickname is that?" he scoffed.

I rolled my eyes. "My mom used to babysit Jade when she was a baby. I called her Emerald because of her eyes and eventually shortened it to Emmy. It's a great nickname," I said smugly.

"I never knew that you were the girl Damon liked. To be fair, you're way better than his other girl. She's too awkward," Jade whispered in my ear. I giggled. *This girl is like a mini me, I swear.*

"Jade, go look at the fishes for a bit. I need to talk to Amira," Damon said sternly.

Jade gave him her adorable pout, which he seemed unaffected by, and stubbornly trotted away to the lake. Damon sighed as he sat next to me beside the tree. A silence fell upon us and I didn't know if I should break it or not. All that could be heard were the birds chirping and Jade's excited squeals as she chased squirrels.

"I broke up with Kaylie," Damon said.

"What?" I asked, shocked. *No way. He broke up with her?*

He bitterly laughed. "Funny isn't it? I hurt two people because I'm selfish. I couldn't even keep the girl I love."

"Damon—"

He held up a hand. "Let me finish."

I nodded.

"I miss you, Amira. I miss you so fucking much that it drives me crazy. You're beautiful, smart, gentle, sarcastic, funny, and so much more. I was a fool to let you go. You're perfect for me. I just need more time. Can you give me that?"

I shook my head. "I can't be with you unless you're a Muslim. We can't be together. I'm sorry," I said.

"That's why I said to give me more time."

"You're thinking of converting?" I asked, appalled.

He slowly nodded. "I don't know yet, but I'm willing to learn about other religions and Islam. I'm willing to change," he firmly stated.

I felt happiness bubble within me. Could Allah possibly giving me a chance at a future with Damon? My mind conjured up different images of Damon and I. I imagined a wedding day, our pointless arguments, kisses, and even children. I imagined the impossible dreams that I refused to acknowledge, even though they haunted me in my sleep. Our future in my eyes looked so bright, but the cruel reality hit me out cold with a rock.

"Damon, I'm going to another state for college. I'll be living there with my brother for four years. I don't think you want to wait that long."

He stayed silent, visage blank like a white canvas just waiting for an expression to seep through. Disappointed, I looked down at my hands that limply sat on my lap. I knew it was too good to be true. The earlier hope I had was slowly withering away.

"Promise you'll come back to me? You're not going to leave me without a goodbye. Can you promise me that?" he asked, nervously, as if he was afraid I'd say no.

I sighed in relief. "I promise," I smiled.

Maybe this really was the sun after a storm.

CHAPTER 44
A Nightly Surprise

DAMON WINTERS

The chorus of students cheered as the principal announced the festivities for prom. *Is senior year really almost over?* It seemed like just yesterday that I was gaming with my friends and teasing Amira for her chastity, a quality I now admire. I smiled to myself. Things certainly have changed.

I gazed at Amira from across the hallway. There she was, the girl of my dreams. She threw her head back and laughed loudly at something Aria said. It was almost lunch time when our principal decided to call us seniors down to the auditorium. It was basically a way to start the prom hype, which I thought was lame.

"Sup' man," a voice called as he hit my shoulder.

I turned around and was met with Tye wearing a shark costume. I laughed uncontrollably, knowing no doubt that he had been pulled into *promposals* without his consent. Tye glared daggers at me.

"What t-the hell are y-you wearing?" I wheezed out.

"Shut the hell up, asshole. I'm being a good friend to Jacob," he grumbled.

I tamed down my laughter. "For a *promposal*?" I asked.

"Yup, it's so corny. Basically I'm the shark trying to eat her and he plays the hero. He even got a boat as a prop."

"Damn, did he have a poster?"

"Of course he did! It was the stupidest shit ever. Literally it said, 'It would be jawsome if you would be my date to prom.' I was so close to murdering him." said Tye, huffing and puffing like the wolf from *Three Little Pigs*.

I stifled a laugh. I could not take Tye seriously with that shark costume on.

Tye rolled his eyes. "My masculinity is at risk," he mumbled to himself.

Sean strolled around the corner, carrying a large instrument case on his back. He whistled to himself, casually walking the hall until he spotted me. His eyes brightened and he jogged over to us.

"Damon! I brought your guitar back," Sean trailed off as he examined Tye's attire. His face broke into a grin. "Nice outfit man. It looks sexy for sure. Bet all the ladies are drooling," he playfully winked and nudged Tye.

Tye scowled, "Fuck you," and walked away.

Sean wiped a fake tear from his eyes. "Why didn't I take a picture of him?" he questioned himself.

"Because you're an idiot."

He narrowed his eyes at me. I shrugged with an innocent smile plastered on my lips. "Ya know, just because you have a dick doesn't mean you have to act like one," he said dryly.

"Get used to disappointment, kid."

"Ouch, this is bullying."

"How?"

"Because you're not being nice to me," he whined.

I rolled my eyes. "Shut up, you big baby. Give me my guitar back," I said with an outstretched hand.

"So bossy," mumbled Sean and he passed my guitar to me.

I ignored his comment and gestured for him to follow me to the courtyard. Sunlight seeped through my lashes, a realm of green awaiting me. Once my eyes adjusted to the brightness, I was met with a group of my friends, laughing and eating around a table.

Their white teeth shone against the rays of yellow and orange, eyes glittering with mischief.

As we walked closer to the bench, Thomas waved at Sean and I.

"Finally you guys are here," he said.

"Yeah, sorry dude. We got sidetracked," Sean said with a devilish glint in his eye.

"Yeah. We saw a shark," I played along.

Thomas looked between us, confused.

"And his name was Tye," Sean said.

Realization dawned on Thomas's face. "Wait he dressed up as a shark?" asked Thomas.

"It was the funniest shit ever. I can't wait to see it in the yearbook," Sean grinned.

"Damn it! I wanted to see the fool humiliate himself. See the sacrifices I make for you, Damon. Be grateful," he scoffed.

I chuckled. "I am. Now tell me if this song sounds good for her."

The boys hushed as I softly strummed the guitar strings. I let the music flow through me and listened carefully to each beat. I wrote this song for the woman I loved, for the muse to my life: Amira. She deserved so much more than me.

She deserved to be treated like diamonds, and cherished for the rest of her life. She deserved better than me.

As I sang the lyrics I wrote for her I realized, that this girl was the reason why I came to school smiling. She was the reason why I even bothered to look into Islam. She was the girl who taught me how to become a better person. For that, I'd be forever grateful to her.

My past demons vanished in her presence, and the angels had blessed me instead with opened eyes and an optimistic look towards the future.

I stopped strumming, "What do you guys think?" I asked my friends.

Their jaws were dropped. I nervously scratched the back of my neck. Was it that bad?

"Holy shit, Damon! Where did you learn to play like that?" exclaimed Thomas, shocked.

"My dad taught me when I was a kid," I said.

"Dude, Amira is gonna love this," cheered Sean.

"I hope so," I whispered to myself, looking down at the guitar.

* * *

Me: *Meet me at the lake today at 6*

I quickly sent a text to Amira. I sighed as I put my phone down. She was going to be gone. *Gone*, for four years, I couldn't imagine it. Images of her figure retreating from my embrace stabbed my heart. *Four years,* echoed my thoughts. She would be gone for that long. She would be away from me. Could I survive?

Take the chance and learn about Islam.

Islam was something I never thought I'd actually take time to learn about it. To me, Islam was an unfair religion that valued men over women. It was a religion that was based on terrorism. Many people feared it, and feared people in the religion. It was like we viewed them as mass murderers instead of human beings.

I was so terribly wrong.

It wasn't until I met Amira that I understood how misunderstood Muslims were. The stuff that was on the media, of Muslim terrorist groups brutally killing thousands, was not what Islam was. It was a cover up. *They* did not represent Muslims. *They* were not symbols of Islam. *They* were criminals, liars, and killers.

Muslims though... they weren't anything like that. Amira wasn't like that. She was one of the most admirable women I knew. Muslims are portrayed as evil for following a religion that supports terrorism when in reality it was never that.

Every Muslim I met at the mosque this last month or so were kind-hearted people. I was an Atheist, someone who didn't believe in God, and they welcomed me with open arms. No one judged me or made me feel uncomfortable. They made me feel like I belonged.

Ever since I dropped Amira home that one day and heard the Muslim call to prayer, I visited the mosque the following day. I figured if anyone could help me learn, it would be the head of the mosque. The guy in charge of the mosque gladly let me borrow some books, and I had been reading them the past couple of weeks. Any questions I had the Imam (leader of a mosque) would answer it.

Beep.

I jerked towards my phone. It was Amira.

Amira: *Sure I'll see you there.*

I packed my guitar in the case and sprinted out the door. Nerves bundled inside my stomach. The fear of her not liking the song I wrote for her scared me. I wanted to treat her right. I needed to show her how much she meant to me; how much I loved her.

* * *

As I parked the car, I saw her tempting figure walk through the trees, towards the lake. I quickly got out and called her. She spun around and smiled.

"Hey," I said.

"Want to explain why you're not at prom?" she questioned with a smirk playing at the corner of her lips.

I leaned close to her and whispered, "Because my girl wasn't going," and pulled back to look at her tinted cheeks. I felt pride blossom in my chest for having her react to me like that.

"Whatever," she mumbled.

"Awe, are you blushing?"

She glared. "I don't blush," she said and crossed her arms, "I just felt hot."

I snorted at her remark. "Well," I said slowly, "you are a very beautiful woman. The sun was just reflecting that beauty of yours." I placed a hand on her cheek, gently. "The sun in my universe," I said softly.

She gazed up at me with ponderous eyes. There was a strong emotion her eyes held. It was buried deep within yet she blinked it away. It was like she didn't want me to understand her. She gently pushed my hand away, ashamed of herself, but I snatched her hand.

"Amira," I warned.

"Damon," she sighed, tiredly, "You know we can't."

I let out a frustrated growl. "I'm trying, but I can't do anything if you don't let me in."

"I'm not doing anything."

"Yes you are."

"Nope, I'm not."

"Amira."

"Damon."

"For fuck's sake, can I just show you the surprise now? We'll discuss this later," I said, defeated.

She grinned, "Could have just asked," she shrugged, innocently.

I shook my head at her methods on getting under my skin. I led her to the lake, and pulled out my guitar. I wouldn't screw up with her this time. I strummed the guitar strings and felt her unwavering attention purely on me. Tonight was about her.

CHAPTER 45
Goodbye

AMIRA SARKER

I felt tears brim my eyes. *Is he really singing a love song to me?* His voice was silky and deep. It was almost comforting and somewhat soothing, his voice sensual as he sang the words. The way he was looking at me made it seem like I was the only girl in the world.

Damon's fingers thrummed against the strings of the guitar in a gentle movement. Then we made eye contact, and I swear my heart stopped beating as I gazed into those beautiful green eyes. I could see every single emotion that rushed through his veins. Every single word he sang matched perfectly to what I was feeling- the feeling of contentment and love.

I slightly swayed my head side to side, following the rhythm of the song.

Damon grinned at me as he continued. It seemed as if no one else but us existed. It was just us. That term, 'us,' was something I forbid myself from ever believing in. I shouldn't love Damon, but something about him lured me in more and more as if I was the human the siren hunted after.

He was perfect. From his flawless face to his incredible personality, it was almost surreal. I shook my head. I could wish all I wanted for him to be mine, but he'd never be mine.

I didn't want to sacrifice my religion for something like love. No matter what happened in this life I would always choose my Lord, my Creator. That was the promise of a Muslim, to put *Allah* above all else. People left, people died, but *Allah* never abandoned His servants. *Allah* would always be there, and I would be a fool for choosing someone other than Him.

But how could I abandon the boy who serenaded me underneath the sunset like something straight out of a movie?

I closed my eyes.

Just once, Allah. Just this once, let me have this moment, let me be with him one last time before I leave.

I let go of all the stress and drama I felt and just focused on his lulling voice. Memories of senior year with Damon splashed waves across my mind. I thought about all the times we laughed, we argued, we cried, and even the time when we confessed our feelings. *Am I really just about to just leave all that?*

Damon abruptly stopped playing, and I slowly opened my eyes at the loss of sound. His eyes were red and glassy. The creases on his forehead made themselves known, lips trembling at the force of inner turmoil. Immediately, concern rippled through me.

"What's wrong?" I asked, worried.

"A lot of things are wrong, Amira," he laughed, humorlessly as he looked down at the ground.

I moved closer to him until I was right next to his crouched figure. I nudged his shoulder with mine, even when guilt prickled at my heart. I wanted to comfort him one last time. "Come on, tell me."

He sighed. "I can't tell you."

"Why not?"

"Because it's just going to hurt me more when you leave," he whispered.

"Damon, this is our last night together. Don't let me leave with regrets."

He looked so torn, lost, and broken. I'd never seen Damon so heartbroken. The ocean of guilt seemed to drown me under its harsh waves. Ever since he met me, his life fell at a faster speed than gravity, weighing him down with all of his family struggles and our tragedy of a romance. He'd been misleading himself for something that could never be.

"You're going to leave," he choked out, "and that makes me scared about how you'll feel for me in four years."

I stayed silent. Even I didn't know what could change between us these next four years, only *Allah* knew that. Damon and I could be completely different from what we were now. We might not even be friends. The thought alone saddened me. Out of everything, this friendship was the least I could offer Damon. It was one of the most refreshing part of senior year.

He was someone who pushed himself through my mental walls, no matter how many obstacles stood in his way. He was someone who tried his best to make sure I was smiling every day, no matter what I did or how many times I told him to leave me alone, he was always there for me at the end of the day. For that I'd be immensely grateful to him for the rest of my life.

"You know, four years go by really fast," I said quietly into the sunset.

The sun sprayed its vibrant colors across the skies. The birds imitated their own love songs and a gentle breeze danced between us. Orange and pink hues painted the canvas above, a distant car honking in the background away from our safe haven. We had each other in a world of mysteries, and although we'd go our separate ways, this was our last bittersweet moment.

It would be hard to leave him, but I had to. My dreams awaited me, a part I was meant to play, a world I would one day change with my own research. I couldn't let love hold me back.

"I'm gonna really miss you," he said as he brought his knees to his chest.

"I'm going to miss you too."

"Man, who would have ever known that the Muslim girl who sat in front of me was going to mean the most?" he chuckled half-heartedly.

"Love finds us at the most unexpected places."

"I'm glad I found this love. When you come back, you're going to see a new me. I promise that," he swore.

"What?" I asked, confused. *New him? What does that mean?*

I turned to look at him as he leaned back again the trunk of the tree. "I went to the mosque."

My eyes widened. "Wait back up! You did what?"

He grinned. "I said I went to the mosque."

"Why?"

"Remember when you told me I should look into religion?"

I nodded.

"Well that's what I'm doing. Islam seems like such a widely talked about religion in the media, but it gets so much negative attention. I won't lie, before I met you I wasn't very fond about Muslims, but you weren't like that. You weren't what the media depicted you to be. At first your beauty did hit me hard, but it wasn't looks that attracted me. It was this atmosphere around you. I can't describe it, but it was like pulling me to you," he said softly.

"I'm pretty sure you hated Muslims."

He chuckled. "Yeah, I did. But then I met you, and Tye, Thomas, Jacob, and even Sean. If I hadn't met any of you, then I probably would still be stuck in my dark hole."

"By the grace of *Allah*, you met us," I smiled. "Not hating Muslims is a bonus to that."

"I know. It really bothers me now because the Muslims at our school and you aren't ISIS crazy followers. They're not extremists. They're normal," he said, gazing at me with an apologetic look in his eyes. "It was wrong of me to judge you only because of Luqmaan. I never should have let the past control me like that, but I'm slowly getting over everything."

"I'm glad you can finally find some peace."

"Honestly, I'm thinking of converting."

My mind swirled as I tried to comprehend what he said. If Damon converted, we could be together.

Didn't you want a Muslim man who was religious and would lead you in salah (prayer)? Besides how would all the aunties react to a convert who didn't know how to recite the Qur'an? And your parents? My inner voice chimed.

I could teach him those things. *There was a possibility of it working out for us, right?* I mentally shook my head. There was so much judgment that would come on me. I shouldn't care, but a part of me does. Besides there are a lot of Muslim scholars that are converts, it wouldn't be that bad.

"I know what you're thinking, that I won't be that amazing religious guy from the start, but give me a chance, Amira. Give us a chance. Maybe... uhm... *Allah* is showing you an opportunity," he suggested.

I hesitated; could I give him a chance? All those dreams I had of us being together one day in the future could become a reality. It was all depending on whether or not I wanted to.

I stared into Damon's mesmerizing green eyes. They were so sincere and gentle like the breeze that surrounded us. His lashes flickered; lips stretching into his breathtaking smile that made my knees go weak. His features were as perfect as his heart. I'd be a fool to let him go.

"Okay, but don't convert for me. Convert when you fall in love with the religion."

He winked at me. "I'm one step ahead of you."

CHAPTER 46
I Love You, Mum

Amira Sarker

I glanced around in fear. There was something odd in the air and it was almost as if Allah was giving me a sign that something bad about to happen.

The hallway was dark. My footsteps echoed off the walls. I didn't know what I was looking for, but my feet were dragging me somewhere. Where was I? I raised my hand to the wall. The wallpaper wrinkled under my touch. I had the urge to sneeze from the dusty air.

"Mum! Baba! Is anyone there?" I called out into the darkness.

Silence.

Suddenly, I saw a spark. At the end of the dark hall, there was a bright orange flame and I started to run towards it.

The bright flame flickered to the left due to the blowing winds. If there was a blowing wind, it meant that there was a window to escape from. I felt relief flood me as I came closer to the flame. As my running halted to a stop, the relief I previously felt before was gone.

The flame ignited into many more.

I backed up a little, horrified, until I felt a door behind me. I turned around, quickly. My wobbly fingers tried to turn the knob.

It was locked.

I glanced behind me. The flames started growing bigger and the temperature in the room seemed to have gone up a hundred degrees. I frantically tried pushing and hitting the door.

"Somebody, please! Help me!" I screamed, helplessly.

I could hear my heart pound against my chest. There had to be an escape. I looked around but there was nothing but flames that kept growing and growing, coming closer to my sweating skin. I tried breaking the door, pushing, pulling, and tugging at the knob.

It was no use. 'This is the end,' I thought as I slid down against the door. The fire was going to devour me. I would never see my family or Damon again and it felt like it was the last chapter of my life. I felt tears slid down my face as I saw the fire crawl closer.

"Mommy, please help me," I whimpered.

I just wanted my mother; to feel the warmth of her arms around me, her delicate hands run through my hair, to hear her soft voice tell me I was going to be okay and to hug her one last time before I die.

"Amira!" I heard a familiar voice shout.

I wiped the tears from my eyes and yelled, "Mommy! I'm right here, Mommy! Please help me! I'm scared!"

"I'm coming!" she yelled back.

Mum broke down the door and frantically searched for me. As soon as her eyes laid on me, she ran to me and pulled me into her arms.

"Alhamdulillah! You're okay. My baby is okay. Oh Allah, thank You so much," she whispered as she peppered kisses all over my face.

I sobbed as I held onto her, not believing that she was real.

"Come, we have to go now," she said as she grasped my hand and started running.

I had no idea if we were going to survive this, but I knew that Allah had granted me my wish. I got to hold my mom one last time. With her tightly gripping my hand, I felt safe. Her comfort and gentleness engulfed me as we ran from the fire.

We stopped running after a while and found a window. Stars filled the sky and I heard people shouting down below. They were waiting for me and my mother. I looked back at her. She smiled sadly at me with wet streaks sliding down her cheeks.

I tilted my head. "Why are you crying? We're going to be okay, Mum."

She shook her head and kissed me on the forehead. Her lips lingered there for a bit as she bit her lip to hold in a sob.

"You're going to be okay," she breathed out.

My eyes widened as I realized what she meant. "No, no, no. We will. I'm not leaving you!" I yelled.

She picked me up and said, "I love you, my little girl," then she dropped me out the window into the awaiting firefighters and safety sheets.

I fell down, screaming, as I watched my mother be taken away from me. No, this couldn't be happening to me. It had to be a dream. I couldn't lose her. No!

I jolted awake. A layer of sweat drenched my body. For a second, I even forgot how to breathe. I started to look around my room, terrified. *Is the nightmare over?* My eyes fixed on my bedroom door, and slowly my mind started to calm down as I familiarized my setting.

Dreams usually tell people that something in their minds refused to acknowledge. Did that mean my mother was dead or about to die?

I quickly scrambled out of bed and ran to my parents' bedroom. My mother's back was turned to me and her long curly black hair rested against the pillow peacefully. I couldn't tell if she was breathing or not, so I hurried to her side. I put my ear close to her body and heard her soft breaths.

I sighed in relief. *She's alive.*

I backed up against the wall of their bedroom. I felt myself lose strength in my knees and I slowly slid down the wall. I brought my knees to my chest and wrapped my arms around them. The shock and horror of the dream collapsed on my mind. Haunting images from the nightmare overwhelmed me.

I leaned my head back against the cold wall. Tears slowly fell from my eyes. My vision blurred and I just couldn't think straight anymore. My heart ached. The thought of losing my mother felt as if my entire body would shatter into pieces.

She was the woman who took care of me, loved me, taught me, raised me, and was there for me even when if it felt that the entire world was against me. She was the person that would love me no matter what. Nothing in the world was as strong as a mother and child's bond. *I couldn't lose her, Allah.*

I covered my mouth as I felt a sob shake through me. I couldn't lose her. I was still a kid and I wasn't ready to face the world on my own. Could that dream have really foreshadowed her death?

I heard shuffling from the bed. I froze. *Don't move,* I thought.

"Amira?" she asked in a groggy voice.

I cleared my throat. "Yeah, Mum?"

She sat up, stretching her arms over her head. She looked at me, confused. "Why are you sitting on the floor?" she asked with a yawn.

I couldn't find the words to speak. All I could think was, *she's alive and breathing. She's not taken from me.*

I saw her lips move, but I couldn't hear a thing. *She's alive. She's not gone. She's really alive.*

I leapt up and ran over to her. I caught her by surprise as I wrapped my arms around her in an embrace.

"What's wrong with you today? Wait... are you crying?" she pulled me away and looked at my tear streaked face.

Her eyes gleamed concern and I opened my mouth to say something, but all that came out was a sob. I sniffled once more and said, "I-I had a n-nightmare."

"About?"

"Losing you," I whispered.

Mum pulled me back in her arms and rested her chin on my head. "Shh, it's okay. I'm right here. I'm okay," she whispered calmly.

"W-what did it m-mean?" I cried into her chest.

"I think it's about you leaving for college soon, but it's just a thought."

"I'm not going if it means I lose you," I sniffled as I held her tighter.

She pulled away and held me by the shoulders. "Listen to me, you follow your dreams, okay? Don't let a nightmare stop you. Maybe it was just Allah trying to show you how much I mean to you," she said softly while stroking my hair.

I paused. Maybe Mum was right. *Allah* might be trying to tell me how important my mother is to me. That nightmare didn't have to mean that I'd lose my mother. It could just be a little life lesson.

Mum wiped the tears from under my eyes. "Now, let's go do something that'll take your mind off that awful nightmare," she smiled.

"How about packing?"

"So much work," she sighed, sarcastically. "Let's get it over with."

I rolled my eyes at her, playfully. "Mum, you love housework," I laughed.

"Shh, if you tell your father, he'll tease me for it."

"My lips are sealed," I said, pretending to zip my lips.

As my mother and I packed, I realized just how important she was to me. I couldn't bear to lose her. I glanced back at my mother, who was folding my clothes.

I love you, Mum, I thought. *More than you will ever know.*

CHAPTER 47
Bromance

DAMON WINTERS

"Should we wake him up?" a voice asked that sounded like Jacob.

"Don't. He's probably still upset about his breakup with Kaylie." I bet that was Thomas.

"Oh boo hoo. Breakups happen all the time. He'll get over it, but our day of fun cannot wait." Yep, that was definitely Tye.

"Guys, it's not Kaylie. It's someone else," said Jacob.

"You mean, Amira?" Tye asked.

I wondered if they realized that I was awake.

"Duh. Who else, dumbass?" Thomas whispered as I heard a whack followed by a muffled "ow," most likely from Tye.

It was time to make my presence known. "Shut up. I can hear you guys," I grunted into my pillow. "Let me sleep, assholes."

Ever since Amira left, I had this empty feeling in my chest. I started to miss talking to her, hanging out with her, and just absorbing her presence. Hell, I even missed the way she smiled at me. With all the shit that happened in life, Amira was the type of person to share every detail with from the most gruesome to the most erratic. Being separated from Amira felt as if my heart was torn in half, my soul being a diseased part of me.

There were some things that I had only told her, things I didn't want to share with anyone else. She was there when I needed her, and now I had to live without her, the love of my life.

"Damon, wake up!" Tye yelled.

"No."

"I don't have all day for this bullshit," Tye grumbled.

"Holy molly! Are you on your man period? Damn, get a tampon or something," I said, sitting up with a deep frown.

"How did you know?" Tye grinned, obviously joking.

Thomas, Jacob, and I all groaned at Tye. His grin had only widened at our displeasure at hearing him speak. I had promised the guys a day of video games at my mother's house while she took my younger siblings out.

It was odd how all I wanted to do was think about Amira until I drove myself insane. Shaking my head, I tried to forget about her at least for today. I couldn't keep wallowing in my own pity. I had to keep moving forwards in life, keep pushing against the currents and desperate thoughts to be with her at college.

She needed her space, and I needed mine. I had to figure out whether Islam was right for me.

"Tye, get lost," Jacob glared.

"Well, damn you guys, are the stupid people I call friends. At least show some decency to me," Tye said sarcastically.

I raised a brow. "Is decency even a concept among us?"

Thomas shrugged, bright blue eyes shining with jest. "Among us? Nah. We haven't evolved to that level yet."

Jacob threw his head back in a deep chuckle. "Right," he smiled. "Our only form of sophistication is through teasing Tye."

Tye rolled his eyes, throwing a pillow at Jacob. "Very funny," he muttered before brightening up again. "Now, hurry up. I need to assert my dominance through gaming."

Maybe this will keep my mind off her.

* * *

My friends and I, sat on my living room couch as we played some video games on my Xbox. The room had filled with laughter, a joyous sound ricocheting off the walls and into our ears, a new memory forming to keep the picture of friendship everlasting in my mind. A feeling of euphoria settled against my eyes, and I never wanted it to end.

Soon, these friends, these brothers that I had met would be gone just like Amira. They would climb the highest peaks, the highest mountains to chase their dreams, forcing themselves through every wall that trapped them. They would find happiness in a world where they could make a difference.

I only hoped that I could join their journeys in the same way.

"When are you guys leaving for college?" I asked them, putting my controller on my lap.

"In a week," said Tye.

"I'm going in like a month, I want to spend time with my girlfriend first," said Thomas.

"Thomas got a girl," Tye cooed.

"Shut up and play the damn game," Thomas retorted.

I rolled my eyes. "Maybe we should find Tye a girl."

"Nah, I'm good. The single life is the best life."

Jacob nodded in agreement. "I can't say that I disagree with him."

I exaggeratedly gasped. "Jacob and Tye are agreeing with each other? Man, college hasn't even started yet and I already sense the changes."

"Shut up!" said Tye, pushing my shoulder. "I have a reasonable amount of charm that makes Jacob gay for me."

I shook my head. "Absolutely not."

"If you can pull Amira, I can pull whoever I want. It's the twenty-first century, man. Anything is possible, and I mean *anything*," he emphasized.

"You know, I think he's onto something here," Jacob acknowledged, scratching his chin with a free hand. "I'm definitely seeing the evolution of Tye."

Tye groaned. "How do we always come back to that?"

"It's okay, Tye. It's just a natural instinct in us," Thomas smirked.

Tye glared. "1v1 me, scrub."

"You're so on," Thomas said with a mischievous glint in his eye.

"Hey, Jacob, wanna help me make food?" I asked.

"Sure," he said as he put his controller down.

Jacob and I walked to the kitchen. Dad took Jade on a business trip with him, so I'd been at Mom's house, trying to help her in any way that I could. Mom has been really busy lately, and decided to use her day off to take Daniel and Percy to an amusement park. Daniel was still a pain in the ass while Percy just sat in his room all day, wallowing in his own pool of misery as the divorce ate away at him *every single day.*

"You alright there?" Jacob asked while slicing tomatoes.

I snapped out of my thoughts. "I was just thinking about Percy."

"What about him?"

I sighed, leaning against the counter. "My parent's divorce is really fucking with him."

"Well, obviously. He's a little kid who looked up to his dad," Jacob said as started cutting the lettuce for our sandwiches. "By the way, where are your brothers?"

"They went to an amusement park with Mom and their friends."

"What? Why not us?!" he exclaimed, turning to me with a horrified expression.

I raised my eyebrows. "Aren't you like an adult?"

"By law but not by heart, which means I can act like a child if I want," he huffed proudly as he went back to his sandwich making. Not going to lie, Jacob makes amazing food.

"Bitch," I muttered under my breath.

"Sometimes I wonder how Amira even likes you."

The mention of her name brought a smile to my face. "She's… different, special, and all kinds of amazing."

Jacob gave me a sly glance. "I'm glad you finally realize how much she means to you. I'm still grossed out by the fact that you have a girl you're crazy about."

"Why?" I chuckled.

He shrugged. "I never saw it coming in all honesty. Remember what you were like when you first came here?"

"Oh, God. That feels like ages ago."

"Doesn't it? Time seems to be going by so fast now. I don't think I'm ready," he admitted, a faraway look in his dark eyes.

"Me neither."

Suddenly, Jacob began laughing to himself as a memory played a reel in his mind. "You used to hate Muslims, and now you're in love with one. Isn't that ironic?"

I smiled. "Shut up. I know it is."

"Have you talked to Luqmaan again?"

I shook my head. "Some things are better left unsaid."

"Oh?"

"I just…" I paused, exhaling a deep breath. It still hurt to remember what he did, and I had a feeling that lingering pain wouldn't be gone anytime soon. "Honestly, I don't want to put myself in a situation where my curiosity gets the better of me. There are so many things I want to know about why he did what he did, but it's better for me not to know, to live my life away from his toxicity, to focus on my future instead of the past. Luqmaan is a part of my past, and I don't want to revisit it."

Jacob slowly smiled. "That's a big thing to say, Damon. I'm proud of you."

"You don't think it's cowardly?"

"Of course not. You want to move forward with your life, and you should. Don't ever hold yourself back because of one person. No one should ever have that much control over you."

"Thanks, Jacob."

Right as I said that, Thomas yelled, "You, goddam liar! I trusted you!"

"That's what you get!" Tye shouted.

Jacob and I looked questionably back at the two boys playing video games.

"We better feed them before they kill each other," I cringed.

"Seeing the preppy Thomas get worked up like that really is a treat," Jacob chuckled.

"You have no idea," I shook my head, laughing as we brought out the tray of well-made sandwiches.

* * *

The four of us sat around the dining table enjoying our lunch, while listening to Tye and Thomas bicker about their game. Jacob and I, had questionably glanced at one another as their trash-talking escalated. They had not stopped. Not for one second.

"I call that foul. You cheated!" Thomas accused, pointing a finger at Tye.

Tye scoffed. "It's not cheating; it's called using my resources."

"That's bullshit," Thomas said.

"Can we *please* talk about something that isn't your stupid game?" Jacob asked, finally annoyed at their petty argument.

We had to listen to them argue for the past twenty minutes. I didn't blame him for being annoyed.

"I can't believe we're actually about to go to college," I said, changing the topic.

"I know. It seems too fast," Jacob said.

"I think it's pretty good timing. I get my freedom," Thomas shrugged, seeming unfazed by the sudden turn of events.

"Won't you miss your family?" I asked.

"I mean yeah, but sometimes I want some space from them, you know?" Thomas justified.

"Maybe I'm just too family oriented," I chuckled.

"That's a good quality to have," Jacob pointed out.

"Really?" asked Tye, shocked.

"Yeah, dumbass," Thomas said as he whacked Tye upside the back of his head.

"Ow! Quit hitting me!" Tye scowled.

"Not until you stop being dumb," countered Thomas as he whacked Tye again.

"I swear to God, you're going to give me a concussion before sundown," Tye said while rubbing the back of his head.

"That's the point, smart one," Thomas said.

Tye glared. "Sometimes I really want to punch you. A nice, heavy punch to the gut."

"The bromance is real, right Damon?" Jacob asked as he leaned back against his chair and crossed his arms, amused.

I chuckled, leaning my head against the palm of my hand as I watched my best friends continue to insult each other, my conversation with Jacob muted by more trash talk. "It's great."

And I hope it will always be great.

CHAPTER 48
Consequences of Hatred

AMIRA SARKER

The sun was starting to set in its marvelous hues of orange and bright red, spraying in vibrant rays, as the last remnant of light slipped past my eyes. The Muslim prayer engraved itself into a believer's heart. Cars honked as everyone prepared to go home, the people outside oblivious to the sign of worship, to a Muslim's instinct to remember *Allah* through their daily prayers. The *masjid* (mosque) called the *athan* (prayer call) and Muslim women gathered around to pray their *sunnah* (voluntary prayer).

Women of all colors; white, black, Indian and oriental Asians sat in the masjid. With shoulders side to side, foot next to foot, small and tall, they stood before their Lord, they stood before *Allah.* The women wore their long skirts and black *abayas* with their scarves wrapped tightly around their heads. It felt comforting to know that they were Muslims like me in this densely populated city, who reminded me of home.

Tanwir and I, had just finished moving all our stuff into our new apartment. It felt weird knowing that for the next four years. my older brother and I. would be living together without our parents. Some of our neighbors didn't even like us either, especially with the upcoming elections.

Islamophobia had been at its prime this year. People were afraid of men with beards or women wearing *hijabs.* I didn't even think that the presidential elections would be extremely complicated and that the presidential candidate who hated Muslims would even win the primaries but clearly, I was wrong.

Anyone who swore to value the Constitution and had no rational judgment might soon use every legal power in their hands to eradicate those they disapproved of. While America had a system to check against such people, I just wished that whoever would take the position would go for equality regardless of race and beliefs.

The *imam* called the *iqaamah* (second call to prayer) and I lined up with the rest of the congregation. I carefully listened to the *ayahs* that were recited, feeling a wave of tears in my eyes as my heavy heart drenched with my loneliness. I had never been so far from home, and I desperately wished to be back in my mother's arms.

Oh Allah, please protect my family and don't let them worry too much about Tanwir and I, I prayed silently.

With that, I returned my focus back to my prayer.

* * *

After we finished, the girl that was praying beside tapped my shoulder. I turned to her and was greeted with a wide smile.

"You're new around here, aren't you?" she asked with her voice as chirpy as the birds that sat outside our apartment window.

"Yeah, I am."

Red, subtle velvet flowers decorated the outer layer of her *hijab* and deep rose that complimented her pale complexion. Her nose was long and straight, eyes with a deep shade of maple brown, lighter than mine but darker than most light-skinned people with that skin tone. I wondered if she was of Middle-Eastern or European descent, maybe both.

"I thought you were. Our Muslim community is pretty tight, so I didn't recognize you. Are you a college student?"

I nodded. "I graduated high school like a couple weeks ago."

"No way!" She exclaimed. "I did too! Wait, which university are you going to?"

"The one that's like five blocks away from here. It's a school for premedical students."

"Oh my *Allah*. I'm going there, too! Yes! I have a friend to go with me now! This is great news," she grinned, excitedly.

"Aren't your friends going there?" I asked, confused. I thought everyone would go to the university closest to them, especially if it was a good university.

She smiled sadly as she shook her head. "I'm afraid not. Everyone was so eager to leave especially the Muslims."

"Why?"

She sighed and leaned back against the wall, closing her eyes like a memory that pained her had flashed before her eyes. Slowly exhaling, her eyes blinked open. Her gaze was hard, and I felt as if the room suddenly got a degree colder.

"There was this...incident here not too long ago," she said, bitterly.

I sat quietly and listened more attentively.

"This Muslim boy was playing basketball. Oh, he was such a sweet boy. He had a clean record in school like straight A's, volunteered at the *masjid*, helped the elderly, and even led *halaqas* (religious gatherings) here. He was even supposed to get married! May what happened to him not happen to any other youth," she hauntingly whispered.

I swallowed the lump in my throat, not liking the chill of her voice. *Please, don't be what I think it is.*

"What happened to him?"

She looked me dead in the eyes. Tears glazed her dark eyes. Pain swirled in spirals as she said the words that I feared the most, "He was murdered."

I gasped. "A Muslim man was murdered here?"

She nodded. She held back a sob as tears rolled down her face. "He...he was," she hiccupped, "my fiancé."

I was appalled.

"T-This man, he killed him," she whispered. She roughly wiped the tears from her face. "His name was Musa. He did nothing wrong and he killed him!" she cried.

I felt my heart break into pieces as I watched this girl fall apart. She was going to get married and right when she found the perfect man for her, he was taken.

I pulled her into my arms, embracing her tightly. She sobbed into my shoulder, completely torn apart from her past events, holding me tighter like I was her lifeline in her turmoil of chaos, her personal disaster that ripped an innocent man away from her.

"Shh, it's okay. Everything is going to be alright. Calm down, I'm right here," I told her gently as I stroked her head.

Her cries shook her shoulders as she kept all her pain out. She was so strong to be able to go through that. She must have held all the anguish back, just like I did. She held it back all the way to the point where it consumed her.

"Don't cry. It's okay, shh."

Moments after, her sobbing decreased. She started to breathe heavily, trying to control her breaths. Once her cries ceased, she said in the most broken voice I ever heard, "He stabbed him to death."

I pulled back a little to wipe her tears. "*Allah* will help you, don't worry. *Allah* will take care of him, remember?" I tried my best to give her a comforting smile.

She sniffled. "Yeah, I remember." She sat up straight, rubbing her eyes with her left hand, gazing at me apologetically. "I'm really sorry about that. I just… miss him."

I placed a comforting hand on her shoulder. No words were needed. She had suffered a great loss for the community, for her family, and for herself. Life was only painted in colors for her, yet all that drained as hatred poisoned dull, gray colors into a once beautiful community. Hatred expelled love.

And the Muslims had ran.

It was strange how we were strangers sitting in a masjid yet at that moment I felt like I knew her my entire life.

* * *

Kanza, the girl from the *masjid*, and I stayed and talked about school and our dreams. We also talked about the riots going on around here.

"It's quite difficult for Muslims in this area, but this is our fight. It's not fair that people vandalize our mosques and physically hurt our community. That's not right," she said, as she shook her head.

"I know what you mean. I wish people would understand that Muslims are human, too. Just like the whole Black Lives Matter movement, our lives matter, too. All of our lives matter, all colors, sexuality, or religion. Everyone's life matters."

"We're compassionate, which is why I didn't want to leave like a lot of other people. When times get rough, we have to stick together if we want people to change," she confessed.

That was quite honorable of Kanza to say. Her words were really motivating and I could already see a bright future for her. Safe to say, I was inspired.

"Hey, Amira?"

I turned my attention back to Kanza. "Yeah?"

"Why is there a crowd in front of the *masjid*?" she asked, uneasily.

I furrowed my eyebrows and looked out the window. There was a protest outside against Muslims. "How hateful are these people?" I asked, appalled.

She cringed." You don't want to know." Kanza pulled my arm. "We have to leave now."

Fear snipped at me. I started to feel anxious as I said, "How? The front door is blocked by the crowd!"

The other Muslim sisters held their children close to their chests. The babies started crying as the crowd shouted cruel chants. Their voices got louder, stronger to the point where all I heard were earth-splitting yells and screams. The crowd fueled off of their hatred. They relished our fear.

"Go back to your country!"

"We don't want terrorists!"

"You deserve to burn in hell!"

I felt trapped. Why were they all here? The community here was just praying! They didn't do anything wrong. They worshipped God. How was that a crime?

"Someone call the police! We need to leave!" a sister shouted.

Kanza rapidly dialed 911. I'd never been in a situation where I feared for my life as a Muslim. This was terrifying. At that moment, all I wanted was my mother. I wanted her to tell me I was going to be safe, but she wasn't here right now. She couldn't make all this go away, and if help didn't arrive on time, I wouldn't be alive to hold her one last time.

I had to calm down.

"Sisters! We're going through the back door," Tanwir shouted from the door.

"We can't! They surrounded the entire building!" another brother shouted.

"Tanwir, what do we do?" I asked, afraid.

He saw the terror in my eyes. He placed his hands on my shoulders. "We're going to be okay, Amira. Just make a lot of *duaa* until the police come."

The *masjid* was chaos. Tanwir went back to the brother's side to help the brothers find a way to calm the crowd before it got dangerous. The sisters tried to calm the children down and were praying, begging *Allah* to protect them.

Kanza and I watched the crowd from the window.

"How long till the police get here?" I asked in a whisper, wincing as something was thrown at the building.

"I don't know. They said they were on their way," she whispered back.

I saw something shiny and silver in one of the protester's hands. Immediately, I felt my blood go cold. *Oh Allah, please don't let it be what I think it is.*

Then, he pulled it out.

"Fudge," I muttered.

"What is it?" asked Kanza, urgently.

"It's a gun."

Right after I said that, we heard a gunshot.

CHAPTER 49
Their Greatest Fear

AMIRA SARKER

The *masjid* was silent after we heard the gunshot. No one moved. No one spoke. A deadly silence fell over the Muslims, a distant gasp and a hoarse cry for help. It was from the brothers' side.

Kanza and I, were trying our best to keep the sisters where they were and not go outside, especially if a man had gotten shot. My eyes welled in tears, the anguished cry for help had only strengthen, and the brothers were scrambling to him the fallen man.

Not you, Tanwir. Please, don't let it be you.

Tears streamed down my cheeks, a sob ripping from my chest as the lump in my throat only grew. He couldn't be dead nor could he be injured. We were bonded by blood, bonded by our parents, bonded by our forefathers. He was my brother, and I needed him alive.

Not now. Please, Allah. Protect him. Save him.

I couldn't lose him, no matter what. Calming down, I looked outside the window again; the crowd was hitting the doors, their thundering fists banging against the feeble wooden gates, each punch louder than the next.

A crash followed after. Kanza and I, yelped in surprised, our backs pushing against the only entrance to the sister's side just in case. The chanting outside only escalated, the slurs becoming a mass of twisted lies and bloody threats. Fear latched onto me, pulsing my veins with adrenaline as if this moment was a flight or fight situation.

"Where are the cops?!" Kanza shouted.

"They're going to kill us. Oh Allah, help us," a sister cried.

I sat next to her and embraced her. "It's okay. *Allah* will protect us. Don't lose faith," I reminded myself and them.

"How can you say that when we're on our deathbeds right now? The police aren't here. The brothers are trying to hold the crowd off and in the midst of it. Someone has been shot!" she sniffled, as she wiped her tears with the back of her hand.

The sister was young. She looked like she was still in high school with dark coal-like eyes that were wide with terror. Her eyelashes were long and thick with a hint of jet black eyeliner on her waterline. She seemed as anxious as a wild animal trying to run away from hunters.

She was petrified.

"I can say that because Prophet Muhammad (peace be upon him) was in situations worse than this, and *Allah* helped him. *Allah* helps the believers and will never stop helping us. *Allah* loves us, we just need to have faith in that," I spoke softly, trying not to frighten her more.

"But—"

"Amira is right. *Allah* never lets us down. Right now the world is in chaos against the Muslim *ummah* (community), but in the end our struggles will be rewarded. We just can't lose sight of our religion right now, so we must have faith in Allah," Kanza reiterated.

Allah always came through for believers. Whatever happened was for the best. When Aisha died, I thought it was the worst thing to ever happen. I truly believed that my life was cursed. That wasn't the case. Aisha's death taught me how to be a grown up early. It gave me a maturity that not many people possessed at my age.

Aisha's death made our family bonds stronger. Death was a scary thing, but sometimes beautiful lessons were born from it.

The girl sighed. "You guys are right. I'm just scared."

I held her shoulder with one hand in a comforting gesture. "We all are, but we have each other to protect."

She smiled at me. "Thank you for helping me calm down."

Before I could even respond, the clamoring of an ambulance was heard nearby, sirens ringing like bells as they pushed through a crowd of inked hate.

Immediately, all the sisters ran to the windows, eyes wildly searching for their rescuers. The brothers instructed that we stay in the masjid for our safety. The crowd started to calm down, but the question still lingered through the air.

As paramedics rushed into the building, a stretcher was wheeled out with a middle-aged man on it. His beard was tainted in his own blood and a bullet wound that drowned itself on his forehead. His body didn't move, nor wince when the paramedics began to stick tubes in his mouth.

I felt my heart drop, recognizing the honorable man who led the previous prayer, the Imam. Soon enough, the paramedics shook their heads, knowing it was too late. He died.

My body shook. I had heard a lot of hate crimes, seen anchors on TV's give their condolences to the dead, but nothing compared to had actually experiencing it and became a victim of another person's animosity. Perhaps my dream the other day had nothing to do with my mother, but of me and how close death had come to snatching my life.

The blade of a short life threatened my existence, and this crime that I experienced may have killed another. It all happened so quickly, so fluidly like a motion in water that I didn't realize how life flashed before one's eyes, how I could have been the Imam.

Knock Knock.

"Come in."

Tanwir appeared with tear stained cheeks and crystal eyes. "It's safe now."

"Will the Imam be okay?" Kanza asked.

He solemnly brought his gaze to the ground. "Only *Allah* knows," he said.

A sob was heard behind us. We turned around to see a woman crying. Some sisters surrounded her, offering their shoulders for her to cry on, but the woman was too grief-stricken. She seemed to be mumbling about her husband.

Realization dawned on me, the wife, that woman lost her husband.

Before I knew it, I was in front of her. I took one of her hands and held it firmly between my palms. Her face was tear-stained, and her breathing was uneasy. She had pale skin, and large eyes that lined with sorrow as she stared up at me, searching for someone to tell that it was all a nightmare, that her husband would be waiting for her when she came home.

My heart broke.

"I know it's hard right now, but he died fighting for Islam. May *Allah* reward his bravery. He died protecting his community and I don't know what's more honorable than that. We can't do anything for him now except make *duaa* (small prayer). May *Allah* grant him the highest place in Jannah and reunite him with his family in the Hereafter," I prayed. "Amen."

Shattering before my eyes, her legs had given out as the truth settled within. Following my instinct, I wrapped my arms around her when she collapsed and let all her sobs out.

"No. I-It can't be. Somebody, please! T-Tell me it's not real!"

"Allah knows best," I whispered. "Shh. Everything will be okay. I promise."

No one knew when they would die. Only *Allah* knew. Death was painful, almost unbearable at times. The heavy ache on one's heart was hard to ever forget, however, good came out of everything. *Allah* would take care of this widow and her family because *Allah* never abandoned us when we needed Him.

He would always be there.

*   *   *

Silence fell upon every one as we all walked down the steps of the *masjid*. The crowd started to act up again. Jabbing taunts and racial slurs at us yet we didn't care as we tried to comprehend how the day started off peacefully and ended in something that put our faith to the limits.

The police yelled and shouted at the crowd to disperse, but their attempts were futile. Hatred could not be silenced. It was a reckoning force that would always exist, one that couldn't be diminished even with the holiest of waters and the purest cause. It would always threaten to shoot the weak.

What happened to the world? How can human beings continue to hate when the damage already took effect? How do we allow such injustices to happen?

Those were questions that didn't linger in the minds of politicians or bystanders. They were hopeless echoes to people but not after today. Voices needed to be heard, and I was going to do everything in my power to make my voice heard.

CHAPTER 50
The Real Terror

DAMON WINTERS

I casually sat on my bed in my new place to live. My cousin let me live with him while I went to university because dorm rooms were so expensive. First year college students didn't have much money unless they get a small "loan" of money from their parents.

Anyway, I sat on the couch flipping through channels, bored out of my mind. My cousin, Aiden, was out on a date with his girlfriend so I was home alone. I decided to watch the news, which had been entertained with America's new leader. It was a puppet show for dummies.

I angrily watched his victory speech. The stuff he said about minorities, African-Americans, Muslims, and the Hispanic/Latino community really boiled my blood. I couldn't understand how my country could let him win. Didn't they care?

I started to remember my father. He had similar views, but didn't agree with everything the crazy man said. However, the election itself hasn't scared me at all. I was more worried for all the hate crimes, especially revolving around Muslims.

Amira was a practicing Muslim girl, making her a bright target for demented people. I stayed awake at night consumed with fear for her safety. There had been terrible men that would go up to

Muslim girls and tell them that they deserve to be attacked for covering or even believing in God.

Muslims were their scapegoats. Once upon a time, I had thought the same. I thought Muslims deserved to be hated, but like my friends had taught me, not all Muslims were Luqmaan. Many were average Americans who were just trying to get by another day of hard work. They weren't any different than the rest of us, but this president made me see the horror of my old beliefs.

Man, he made me seem like an angel.

Amira didn't deserve the hate. With the increase in hate crimes, I could only pray for her to be safe. I never really prayed, but the Imam at a local mosque nearby told me about *duaas*. They were like short prayers, so maybe if I said some to *Allah*, He'd protect Amira.

Speaking of Islam, it seemed as if I fell in love with the religion every single day. Yes, it did require a lot, but it was reasonable. The Muslims had the most propaganda for years, but the more hate the community got, the more people learned about the *real* Islam.

Honestly, it was so inspiring to hear the Imam Zakir talk about it. He spoke with such pride in his religion that I felt it through his every word. He told me about Islamic history from the Prophet to the empires. He told me about the discoveries that shaped the world, the science in the Qur'an, and the history of Algebra.

Muslims were far more impressive than I gave them credit for.

After a couple minutes of searching through channels, a specific heading halted my movements.

"Currently, a mosque is being surrounded by Anti-Islamic mobs that are armed. Authorities are on their way as we speak," the news anchor said.

I squinted my eyes. What I saw made the hair on my arms stick up. Amira was there. That was the state she was in right now. I pulled out my phone quickly and dialed her number.

Please be alright, I thought as the phone rang.

After an eternity of ringing, she picked up.

"Hello," she whispered.

Relief flooded me. "Amira! Are you okay? Are the cops there? What's going on?" I asked, as I put my coat on, grabbing my keys. I'd be damned if I let anything happen to her.

"I have to go. I'm sorry," then she hang up.

Something about her voice really worried me. Her voice sounded like she was talking about the death of her sister. It was monotone and dead, void of the bubbly personality that I was used to. If anything, I knew Amira was terrified, which meant something really bad happened.

I got in my car and sped off.

God, if you're there, please protect Amira, I silently prayed.

* * *

The crowd was still shouting as I pushed my way through them. My sanity would be gone unless I found Amira.

"Amira!" I shouted.

I wildly searched for her. When I saw the paramedics drag a body that was covered in a white sheet, I felt my heart sink.

It couldn't be.

Where was Amira?

Was she alive?

My thoughts raced against time and I frantically searched for her. Did this angry crowd take away my love? Were they responsible for her death? Anguish was replaced with anger. Even if it wasn't Amira, they took the life of an innocent individual. Who were they to judge someone they didn't know? My fists clenched and unclenched.

These Muslims weren't evil, the crowd was.

I stood up at the top of the steps. "All of you shut up!" I shouted.

The crowd kept their ongoing roar. At this point, my mind went into overdrive with rage. All I could see was red.

"Could I borrow that?" I asked an officer next to me, gesturing to his speaker.

He nodded.

"I said, be quiet!" I yelled loudly into the speaker, my voice emulating the sound of violent thunder.

Slowly, one by one, the differing faces in the crowd quieted down to hushed whispers. All of them gazed at me in wonder, some in anger for interrupting their protest while others seemed indifferent. Police officers and investigators were at the scene and arresting people, however, even they seemed to halt and look up at me.

I took a deep breath. *Allah, please let Amira hear this.*

"I used to think this country was golden. I used to think that anybody had a real chance here, not just white people. The American Dream was said to be for everybody. Everyone is supposed to be treated equal here. America is the land of the free, yet we've oppressed those searching for freedom. "

Silence fell upon the crowd. Even the news reporters hushed.

"Do you guys understand what you've just done? You killed somebody. Your hatred caused the end of someone's life. Not just anyone, but an important member within the Muslim community. What if he's a Muslim? He's still a human being. Whatever happened to human rights? Doesn't the Ninth Amendment of our Constitution guarantee that? Yes, you all exercised your right to protest, but all of you also managed to violate another right." I said, disappointment lacing my words.

Shame fell upon some of their faces. The others scoffed as if Muslim didn't deserve the rights I just mentioned.

"I'm sure everyone is wondering why I'm defending Muslims, but the truth of the matter is I used to think like all of you, until I met a Muslim. Their religion isn't teaching about terrorism. It's not teaching them to kill and rape people. It's teaching them how to be good families, loving neighbors, nice friends, amazing parents, and how to achieve paradise in the afterlife. How is any of that wrong?

"We're the ones prosecuting them. We're the ones destroying their countries. We gave the weapons to terrorist groups during times of war. We trained those terrorist groups because we thought they were for democracy. Don't you all understand? We created terror organizations. They run on hate, and now we run on hate too. How are we any different?" I asked, softly.

Murmurs went around. I scanned the area looking for Amira, until my eyes caught the stare of beautiful brown eyes that seemed to beckon me to her. Arms were wrapped around her quivering body. The man holding her reassembled Amira. I slowly smiled at them both, much to Amira's surprise. *Thank you, Allah, for keeping her safe.*

"Today, the real terrorists weren't ISIS or Al Qaeda. Today, it was the Americans. Until you all take responsibility for your actions, you have the blood of that Muslim man on your hands. Let it be a reminder to all about the consequences of hatred," with that I stepped down the steps.

I ignored the reporters and walked through the crowd. My head was held high as I heard some people in the riot yelling, others still throwing stuff at me. I knew I did the right thing, and I did it for the whole world to see.

It wasn't enough to change people, but it was enough to give Muslims hope. It was enough to give me courage to take the biggest step of my life. It was time. No more stalling or excuses. It was time to become a part of the Muslim community.

CHAPTER 51
A New Path

DAMON WINTERS

To say I was terrified was an understatement. I had no idea what life would be like after I did this. *Will my father disown me? Will my brothers cry that I left their religion? Will I even be considered family anymore to my relatives?*

Thoughts like those overwhelmed my mind as I continued to press the gas pedal, feeling the thrill of speed and wind slap against my car. Like my hazy mind, the trees blurred behind, taking my past with it because I was blinded by my potential future. My heart thumped loudly in my chest, a thundering rhythm racing with my car's speed, chasing after it as questions and confirmations swirled within my mind. A constant beat that drummed louder and louder as my thoughts pierced my heart with negativity.

Your parents won't care for you if you convert.

I pulled over.

They'll disown you.

My knuckles turned white on the steering wheel, biceps straining against my shirt and my chest tightening. My father was going to be so disappointed in me. He hated Muslims.

He believed all the bullshit the media reported. He believed all Muslims were extremists. He believed that Islam was backwards, a religion that lost its time long ago.

I used to be just like him. It was the only thing we had in common, the only idea that brought us together, the only father and son moment we shared. My eyes burned, thinking of all my errors, all my mistakes. I had labeled Amira and all her Muslim friends when they had done nothing wrong.

I was no different from my father.

If I told my family about my spiritual predicament, they'd destroy me. I'd be alone again in this cruel world, where the weak were silenced and the strong prevailed through any means. My voice would be among the crushed voices of other Muslims. I'd be the scapegoat. I'd be the one everyone deemed as an extremist.

The struggles the Muslims faced would soon be mine as well. If I converted, my whole life would change.

"Oh God, tell me what to do?" I whispered, as I leaned my head against the wheel.

Was converting to Islam really worth everything I might sacrifice in the end? Could I honestly make this decision and not regret it?

"Please, help me," I begged to *Allah*.

Would He even hear the prayer of a non-Muslim?

Knock! Knock!

I lifted my head from the steering wheel, meeting the blurry image of an elderly man with a long graying beard and white hat sitting proudly on his head like a crown. Amira called it a *kufi* once, something Muslim men would wear to prayer. I noticed the silky white garment that fell to his ankles, a sharp collar lining his neck and cuffs at his wrists.

He gently tapped on my window, moving his mouth even though the sound was muffled through my windows.

I rolled them down.

"Sir, your car has smoke coming out of it," he said with concern etched on his face.

I got out of my car. The old man was right. Smoke was flaring out like wings around my car and the dark gray clouds were drowning us in their toxic scent. We both coughed as it intensified. The engine was burning, and the car made unusual groaning noises like something was about to break.

"Shit," I muttered, dialing my car mechanic.

"What do you want, Damon?" he answered, groggily.

"Sorry to bother you but I need a favor."

* * *

My car mechanic, Michael, told me he'd send some guys down to bring my car to his shop. Chances were my car would be wrecked for quite some time, leaving me with no options for transport. I wanted to scream at my misfortune, but held myself together.

Stress was wearing me down little by little, until I was just a shell of a human soul who wandered helplessly on haunted streets of shattered and confused people. Luckily, the elderly man offered to take me to wherever I needed, his small act of kindness another reason I felt guilty for ever treating Muslims as horribly as the average American.

I had given them the cold shoulder, the sleeting ice of my eyes, and the freezing touch of my anger. A person like me didn't deserve to be redeemed by the Muslims, let alone be on the same playing field with them, but my heart still longed for the peace that awaited me, the absolute certainty that came with being faithful in one's beliefs and holding true to their morals.

"I'm sorry about your car," he said with his eyes on the road ahead.

I shrugged. "It's fine. I guess I was so distracted that I didn't even notice."

"My name is Dawud."

I smiled. "I'm Damon."

The car stopped at a traffic light. Dawud looked at me oddly like I was a strange creature from another planet, dark brown eyes scrutinizing my features. He was as pale as I was, yet he looked different from me, acted different. This man may have looked just like me, but he had wisdom and knowledge far beyond my years.

"Sorry, you look like that white guy from the news earlier. You know the one who defended the Muslims?"

I chuckled. "That *was* me."

His eyes widened. The car started moving again as Dawud asked, "Why did you defend Muslims the way you did?"

I looked out the window. The sky was turning into a dull hue of gray, previous storm clouds slowly shifting, and a brilliant orb of light was revealed in its mass of luminosity. I relished the warmth, the pleasing atmosphere after such a traumatic day of worry and uncertainty. Maybe this was Allah's way of helping me be sure of converting.

"I don't know. I just remember how immensely angry I was at that crowd. It wasn't right. That man didn't deserve to die. Those Muslims did nothing wrong. People will always hate what they cannot understand, but it doesn't mean they should attack people for their differences."

He nodded in understanding. "I just haven't seen young boys like you defending an entire community of Muslims to people who most likely don't agree with our beliefs."

I crossed my arms, leaning against the seat. "I think it was mostly because I learned about Islam. I've been studying it and I know that Islam isn't what Westerners think it's about," I said softly. "Islam is a blessing from Allah to help mankind maintain their morality, especially during the times where morality has no meaning. Of course, not everyone will agree with that, but it's just how I've come to see it."

Dawud eyed me for a second before breaking into a grin. "If I didn't know any better I'd say you were ready to convert."

That caught me off guard. "What?"

He smiled warmly at me. "You believe that *Allah* is the one and only God, right?"

"Of course."

"Do you believe in the many prophets and their books that Allah sent down to guide us?"

"Yes."

"Do you believe in the Qur'an?"

"Absolutely."

"Do you believe Muhammad (peace be upon him) is the last messenger of *Allah*?"

I hesitated. Did I believe in Muhammad (peace be upon him)? It was as if my heart already knew the answer. "Yes, I believe that he is the last messenger of Allah."

"Congratulations, Damon. You're now a Muslim. You just have to say the *shahada*. It's the testimony of faith," he grinned widely, showing his pearly white teeth.

I pursued my lips, scratching my neck nervously. "I don't know if I can be Muslim," I sighed.

"What's stopping you?" Dawud frowned, sensing my hesitation.

"Is Islam worth everything I might sacrifice from converting? My family is going to hate me if I become Muslim," I said disappointed. "How can I sacrifice the people I love for *Allah*?"

"Damon," he started softly, "do you want to be a Muslim? If there was no complication, would you become a Muslim for the sake of *Allah*?"

"Yes, I would become a Muslim for *Allah's* sake."

"Then, don't worry about your family. *Allah* will help you sort out that problem. As a parent, it's impossible to hate your child. Children are a parent's most precious treasures. Even in anger, our children will be the very soul of our being until the day we die. That's how large a parent's love for their child is," he said with a distant look in his eyes. "Anyway, if you believe Islam is right, then don't hesitate. Become a Muslim first then deal with the aftermath. There is no reason to wait if your heart already believes."

I paused. Did I love Allah enough to be a Muslim? Of course I did.

Studying Islam ever since Amira came into my life taught me stuff I never thought religions believed in. The Qur'an has the answers to everything. Yes, it dictated a Muslim's daily life, but everything that was obligatory for Muslims maintained their sense of morality. It kept their faith strong. Surely, *Allah* did this to keep His creations pure from a tainted society like today.

In modern era, freedom was throwing their life down the drain as golden pleasure consumed their eyes, a lust for wealth overpowering proper business transactions. In the modern era, people believed that their pride should always be protected if threatened, even if they had to go through great lengths to do it.

Women and men refused to reconnect with one another, a compromise buried within the depths of their polarized mindsets. In Islam, they were taught to communicate, to respect one another because in the eyes of Allah, everyone was equal. No one would have an advantage and no one deserved to be treated disgracefully.

The idea of freedom and modern day had taken a new form. People no longer respected themselves or others. They were not open-minded to people. Stemming from the long lists of mental illnesses, many people were not happy nor were they content when they had everything they ever wanted.

They were depressed, lost, confused.

They had no direction, no purpose, no light in their dark lives.

Islam gave such people a purpose, an end goal to strive for, a comforting prayer for those days when everything was falling apart. Time and time again, religion had been proven to support those who needed it.

Everything made sense now.

"Could you take me to a *mosque*?" I asked.

"I thought you'd never ask."

*   *   *

"Say *Ashadu Anlaa,*" the imam instructed.

"*A-Ashadu Anlaa,*" I repeated, nervously.

"*Illaha,*"

"*Illaha,*" I said. I was really doing it.

"*Ilallaah,*" he continued.

"*Ilallaah.*"

"*Wa ashadu anna.*"

"*Wa ashadu anna,*" I continued.

"*Muhammadur Rasoolillaah,*" he finished.

"*Muhammadur R-Rasoolillah,*" I repeated. My hands were shaking. This was the biggest moment of my life.

The imam grinned. "There is no God but Allah."

The imam smiled at me encouragingly as I said, "There is no God but Allah."

"And Muhammad is the messenger of Allah."

I took a deep breath. After I said this, I would be a Muslim. "And Muhammad is the messenger of *Allah.*"

The imam embraced me in a bear hug. "Welcome to Islam, Brother Damon," he grinned.

Other Muslims, men and women, clapped. Brothers one by one were coming up to congratulate me, clapping my back, hugging me, and speaking to me with such pride in their voices that I was left speechless. The imam had given me books about how to pray and the basics of being a Muslim. At that moment, I couldn't contain my happiness.

This warm welcome, it felt so refreshing and genuine, a brotherhood that tied the bonds of faith with its unbreakable strength and irrevocable faith in *Allah*. Like those before us, we were a connected community, and I was its newest member. Everyone's beaming faces reminded me of home, my *new* home.

Dawud was right. There was no reason to wait if I already believed.

CHAPTER 52
Five Years

AMIRA SARKER

I scribbled out some words on my paper as last minute studying for my final exams. When I'm done, then I would officially finish my degree.

Had it really been five years since I graduated? It feels like just yesterday that Tanwir and I moved here. Over the years, Kanza and I, had become inseparable. Of course, I stayed in touch with my high school friends as well; however, Kanza was my first friend here. If it wasn't for her I wouldn't have survived college. Now, in a couple days Tanwir and I would be home.

Home.

Now that was a word that I wished I heard sooner. I didn't realize how much my family meant to me until I moved. It had been hard to only see my mother through the screen of a phone, to only dream of my parents' loving embraces, and to only hear their voices for short minutes within a day.

Sometimes, I'd stay awake at night wondering why I ever left them. My family meant more to me than life itself. Like a lion pride, we had always stuck together. I was the little bird who left the nest and I paid the price of missing my family for it. It had been worth it, but the dull ache in my chest always came back whenever I heard their soft voices, reprimanding me as if I were in front of them.

"Amira? You ready?" Kanza asked.

I focused my attention back to my notes. "I need like two more minutes," I said, quickly skimming through my writing.

She rolled her eyes at me. "Girl, you're literally going to kill yourself before you even take the finals."

"Shut up," I glared.

She smirked as she hooked her arm to mine and dragged me away.

"Kanza!" I whispered since we were in a library.

Obviously, she ignored me.

"Kanza, buddy, don't you want me to pass?" I asked, innocently.

She stopped and gave me a flat look. "I want my friend alive. Now, less talking more walking,"

I groaned. This girl was more bossy than Mum. That alone said a lot.

* * *

I face palmed as I read through my notes outside of class.

How did I get that wrong?

The one thing I didn't study for was on the test. *How is this even possible?*

I hated when teachers said something wouldn't be on the test and then that same material ended up on the test. It made my head explode. *Oh Allah, I'm pretty sure I just failed.*

Kanza walked out of the class with slumped shoulders. I opened my mouth to tell her I failed too, but she held a hand up at me. "I swear by *Allah,* if you say you failed I'll throw a fit," she threatened.

I instantly closed my mouth.

She leaned back against the wall, sighing, "Ah, the sweet sound of silence."

I snorted. "You were just in a quiet room. Shouldn't you want to hear—"

Kanza covered my mouth. "Why are you ruining such a blissful moment?"

I shoved her hand away. "It's not blissful if you're in it," I said, playfully.

She narrowed her eyes at me. "Isn't that a little harsh for the *sweet* Amira?" she taunted back.

"Nothing's too harsh for me," I grinned.

"Oh really?" she smirked, playfully. "Not even tickling?" she asked as her fingers suddenly attacked my sides, forcing uncontrollable laughter to escape my lips.

"Stop! You know I'm ticklish!" I exclaimed.

She stopped, smiling brightly. "That's why I did it, she winked. Kanza walked a couple paces ahead of me until a thought popped back into her brain. She turned back to face me. "Oh, before I forget. Amira, could I have your brother's number real quick?"

Well, this is new.

"Excuse me?" I asked, as I raised my eyebrows in question.

She shook her head with a small smile. "I swear, it's not what you think. It's just that our *Imam* wants to speak to him about something and told me to give the number to your brother."

I breathed a sigh of relief. "Thank goodness. For a second there, I thought you had a crush on Tanwir. "

"Y-Yeah, that'd be weird," she said, nervously.

I gave her a blank stare. "There's no way."

"What?" she snapped with her arms crossed.

"You like Tanwir, don't you?"

"Pfft no," she huffed.

I gave her a sly grin. "Mhmm. That's what they all say."

"Leave me alone, dork," she grumbled, as she nudged me.

"I'll text the number to Tanwir."

"After you're done, let's get ice cream to celebrate."

"Why?" I asked, confused.

Kanza's jaw dropped for a bit as if she couldn't believe what I just asked. "Girl! We just finished our last final. Hello! This calls for a celebration!" she cheerfully exclaimed.

* * *

Kanza and I, were giggling over the funny pictures we took at the ice cream parlor, reminiscing the times where we had come to the colorful store whenever our mood was in need of being lifted like during final season or excruciating homework days. We tumbled up the stairs of the apartment complex like we were the drunkards of the neighborhood.

We were too engulfed in our friendship to care about what others thought when they heard our foolish laughter.

When I opened the door to the apartment, I was greeted with Tanwir, grinning widely while rapidly speaking on the phone as if he couldn't contain his excitement.

"He sure is happy," whispered Kanza whispered.

"I know. It's kinda weird," I said quietly, stifling my laugh.

"You're a terrible sister," she joked.

I winked. "Nah, I'm the best."

I gestured for Kanza to go to my room while I made some food for us. Luckily, she complied. I walked over to the kitchen and started making tuna sandwiches, flipping through the fridge for all the ingredients. I softly hummed a tune that was stuck in my head until I heard parts of Tanwir's conversation. Although his voice had lowered upon seeing us, certain words had caught my attention, and I was reeled into whatever he was talking about, trying to puzzle the mystery man in my mind.

"I can't believe he's a Muslim now. When did this happen?" he asked, excitedly.

Whoa, Tanwir is hardly ever that happy.

"*Subhan Allah* (glory to God)! Five years already? This boy works fast," he chuckled.

My hands stilled. Who converted? Instantly, my mind wandered to Damon. Even after five years, Damon still haunted my mind like the ghost of my past. A familiar ache settled itself onto my tender heart, prickling me with inklings of regret for leaving him behind. I had to move on, but I couldn't.

We had shared our deepest secrets to one another, helped each other change towards a different direction, and encouraged each other to follow our dreams with nothing holding us back. Love would always be there while opportunities flew past.

I remembered his teasing smiles, his husky voice, his forest-green eyes that always managed to knock the air right out of me. I remembered the song he sang for me, the shattered appearance of him when I told him I'd be gone. Islam had always come first, and I still stuck by that belief.

No matter how much my heart longed for Damon, I would have to hold the reins to my self-control. If it was meant to be, Allah would pave a way for us.

"Amira's going to be so happy. I can't wait," Tanwir said.

I leaned against the kitchen doorway, clearing my throat to grab my brother's attention. Tanwir turned around, startled. Slowly, the corners of his lips tugged upwards, glowing brown eyes beaming with glee.

"My sister deserves someone like that because she's worth more than anything in the world. She deserves the world and more."

I shook my head with a smile as I walked up and embraced him. My brother was the only one to say that. I still could not believe how much he'd changed. He used to be so cold and distant like a glacier from afar, but with time, the ice had melted around his heart, and the old Tanwir I knew when we were kids was finally back.

He said *salaams* to whoever he was talking to and hung up. "Hey, tubby."

"Was that the Imam?" I asked, completely ignoring his childish nickname for me.

"Yeah, it was. Guess what?"

"What?"

"You got a marriage proposal!" he said, elated.

I gave him my blank stare. "Again?" I asked in a bored tone.

I'd gotten plenty of marriage proposals in the past, but none of the guys seemed to suit me. Some of them didn't even have a sense of humor or weren't even that practicing. I wanted a man with a kind heart, someone who wouldn't be afraid to argue with me and someone who understood the importance of having *Allah* remembered not only in our minds, but in our hearts. Baba didn't even like some of the guys that proposed to me before.

He glared, rolling his eyes. "Okay, very funny. This one is special. He's a convert."

This caught my attention. "How long since he converted?"

"Five years."

That was a pretty long time. Could it be Damon?

He did defend Muslims after that riot years ago. He defended Islam on live TV. It was all over the newspapers and many Muslims talked about for months. I had to admit, whenever people talked about Damon, I'd always feel a surge of pride pulse through my veins. I taught him about Islam, and now he was a defender of Muslims, armed with knowledge and his sword of morals.

"What's his name?" I asked, desperate to know if it really was Damon.

Tanwir pretended to zip his lips. "Not saying. It'll ruin the surprise."

"You can't put stress on me like that and not tell me."

"Too late, I just did," he shrugged. "By the way, our parents are coming over tomorrow, along with the Imam and the guy."

"Great. You don't tell me about the guy and you throw the bomb of a fancy dinner at me. Just great," I muttered under my breath.

"Heard that!" he shouted, walking away towards his bedroom.

"Good! I hope you feel bad about not telling me!" I yelled back.

"I have no remorse!"

How did I get stuck with such a pompous brother?

CHAPTER 53
Proposals and Suspicious Fathers

DAMON WINTERS

My leg shook up and down, anxiety pulsing my veins like a fire set to gasoline. I bit my nail as I looked out the window, searching for some divine sign that told me I was overreacting, anything to prove that I was fine and all would go well.

The sunshine mocked my nerves.

I rehearsed everything I was going to say to Amira's father for hours, talking until my voice was sore and my lips were dry. Now, I forgot everything.

Take a deep breath, I told myself. *It's not like my entire future with my dream girl will be ruined if I screw up.* I face palmed. Man, I had horrible prep talks to myself. I wasn't even nervous.

I was petrified.

I remembered Amira told me how overprotective her father was. Being a Bengali-Muslim father didn't make anything easier. It only made my collar feel tighter, and my throat feel like sandpaper. I doubted that her parents would be pleased to see a white guy at their doorstep asking for her hand in marriage.

I knew I shouldn't think this way, but we lived in a world where interracial couples were still new, especially to the Bangladeshi community. Not to mention, my father hated me for doing this.

Sad to say, Dad did not take the news of my conversion to Islam well. He threw a table at me. Imam Zakir had advised me to be patient with my parents because it wasn't easy for them to find out that their eldest son converted to a religion they had prejudices against. Of course, I listened to him.

Zakir had been the imam that converted me. He spent the last five years being my mentor and best friend. He taught me the Arabic alphabet, Quranic grammar rules, pronunciation, how to pray, and most importantly he taught me how to read the Qur'an.

Regardless, my mind was still consumed by thoughts of the girl I loved. There wasn't a day that went by when I didn't think of Amira. My future was planned around her, and it included her in every aspect of my plans for my life. It didn't matter how far the distance between us is or how many years we are apart; I would keep on loving Amira.

She was the one. She was the queen of my kingdom, the light of my eyes, the muse to my voice, and the other half to my *deen* (religion).

"Hey, Zakir?"

"Yeah, man?" he asked, a little distracted by the road.

I inhaled deep breath. "You're Bengali, how do you impress Bangladeshi parents?"

Zakir glanced at me with an amused grin. "You don't."

"Say what now?" I asked with wide eyes. *No way. Did I just dig my own grave?*

Zakir chuckled. "I'm kidding."

"You scared the crap out of me," I breathed out in relief.

"Listen, Damon. When I got ready to propose to my wife, I was scared to death. Her father had just died and her brother was the most overprotective man I'd ever seen. I was for sure that I was a goner. Actually... I didn't even have the guts to ask for her hand in marriage for a long time," he said softly.

"So what gave you the courage to do it?"

He gazed at the road ahead with a longing expression. "*Allah* gave me the courage. I'd get nightmares of losing her or dreams about my future with her. I guess it was *Allah*'s way of guiding me. Eventually, I heard about a guy proposing to her and that drove anger all over my body. At that point, I knew I had to ask for her hand in marriage before I lost her."

I let out a low whistle. "Damn, that's deep."

Zakir shook his head with a small smile painted across his lips. "Damon, relax. If this was meant to be, Allah will guide you. Allah is the best of planners just trust Him," he assured me.

I trust Allah.

*   *   *

Zakir and I, sat on the couch of the small apartment. Tanwir and Zakir were chatting it up about politics. I occasionally joined in, but Amira's dad was glaring at me, a murderous frown sent directly at me.

When the suffocation became too overbearing, I nudged Zakir in the arm. He ignored it. Rolling my eyes, I kicked his shin.

"Ow!" he hissed. "What?"

"Her dad is killing me here," I whisper-yelled back.

Zakir nervously smiled and cleared his throat. Amira's dad briefly glanced at him before bringing his eyes back to my terrified self. Even Tanwir looked uncomfortable as an awkward silence fell upon us, stretching between the tension and uneasiness.

"Why does a white man want to marry my daughter?" her dad questioned as he narrowed his eyes at my small beard.

Zakir and I, exchanged glances. Damn, her dad was rough. I didn't want to mention his rudeness because in Bengali culture being blunt probably wasn't rude. At least he was being straightforward with me.

"Brother, Damon converted to Islam five years ago. He was the man who defended Islam when the riots against the masjid happened. I've been his mentor for those years," Zakir said.

Her father eyed me again. "Damon, why do you want to marry my daughter?"

I looked at Zakir and he shrugged at me. I mentally groaned. *Allah*, why did You make this so horrifying for me?

I took a deep breath, *just talk from the heart, be blunt, and tell the truth.* "I've heard your daughter was very religious. I would like to have a wife who follows Allah's commands and the *sunnah* of our beloved Prophet Muhammad (peace be upon him). I know that I am still a new convert to Islam, but sir, I have never known the peace religion gave to one's mind and soul. *Allah* has brought me to the straight path and I would like to continue this religious journey with my lifetime companion, my spouse, my wife."

Her father's harsh expression softened as he asked, "Why did you convert?"

Tanwir gave me an encouraging nod with his head. "When I was in high school, I thought all religions were stupid, especially Islam. I was brainwashed by the lies the media fed me and my personal experience with one deranged Muslim. Then I met a *real* Muslim, who taught me through actions.

"This Muslim was patient with me when I asked rude questions or judged Islam. This Muslim helped me through the most difficult times in my life. This Muslim opened the doors to Islam for me when I didn't have the courage to do it myself. Through this person, I learned that Islam wasn't sent as a punishment, it was sent as a blessing to mankind," I finished softly as I remembered Amira's words.

Amira's father smiled at me. "Good answer," he grinned.

I felt my own lips curl upwards as I returned the smile. Zakir nudged my side. I raised my eyebrow at him as he gestured me to talk more.

"Oh right," I mumbled, realizing I still had to propose. "I know it's weird to see a white guy like me to propose, but sir, I would be honored if you let me marry your daughter. I need a woman who will help me become a better Muslim and keep me on the right path. So, may I have your daughter's hand in marriage?" I asked with a tight smile, worried that after all this he would still say no.

Amira's father gestured with his hands at the door behind him. My jaw almost dropped at this woman's beauty. She was dressed in a purple salwaar kameez (Bengali traditional dress) and a hijab wrapped tightly around her delicate head. Those familiar brown eyes stared back at them with the exact love and adoration I say before she left.

The love of my life stood right in front of me. *Amira.*

She was as beautiful as ever, time a gentle caress that only amplified her beauty throughout the years. Her eyes were lined with black kohl, giving Amira a seductive yet subtle look to her. My arms begged to hold her after all this time apart, to cradle her cheeks and kiss those inviting lips, but I held myself together, tightening my control.

A voice cleared behind me and I quickly lowered my gaze. I probably ruined everything now by staring at her right in front of her father.

"Amira?"

"Yes, Baba?" her velvet voice said innocently.

God, she was still so pure and perfect.

"You heard everything, so what do you say to the marriage?" her father asked with a knowing smile.

Amira glanced up at me. "Yes."

My heart stopped. Did she just say, 'yes'? I pinched myself. This had to be a dream but to my delight, it was real.

Her father nodded. "Yes, you may have my daughter's hand in marriage."

Cheers erupted around us as the females who were waiting in the other room came out. I silenced everyone out as I narrowed my vision in on the girl in front of me. The urge to touch her was so strong, but I knew I had to wait. I've gotten this far, now I had to just wait a little more.

"Told you that I'd make you mine, beautiful," I smirked.

CHAPTER 54
Her Fairytale

AMIRA SARKER

"Amira!" Tasneem yelled as she held the eyeliner pencil. "Look up or else I might poke your eye."

"Sorry," I mumbled, fidgeting with the sleeves of my red bridal gown. "I'm just nervous."

Kanza laughed from the couch across the room. "Oh, you're funny. Good joke." She shook her head amused, muttering something about me being a jokester under her breath.

She had been swiping through her phone, checking her social medias for the new vlog she posted yesterday. Over the years, Kanza had become fond of YouTube, and was actively posting humorous skits and vlogs during the week. Kanza figured my wedding day would be a fun time to pull the camera and record the "blushing bride" for a couple minutes.

I stared at her blankly. This girl made everything a joke.

She put her phone and camera down. "Listen, you are the most confident girl I have ever met. You give speeches and presentations like it's no big deal." Kanza examined her nails. "All you gotta do here is sit there and look pretty. Honestly, Amira, it's not that hard."

"That is not all I have to do," I said, crossing my arms in a challenge.

Kanza raised her eyebrows at me. "Oh?"

"I have to give my testimony of agreement in front of the witnesses, sign papers, and then have that awkward staring phase with the groom," I scoffed.

"That sounds so hard," Kanza said sarcastically.

"You know you guys do a great job of calming nerves on my wedding day," I mumbled under my breath.

I must have not noticed that I moved because Tasneem slapped my arm lightly. "I told you not to move!" she exclaimed.

"You're asking for a lot when you tell me not to move."

Kanza stifled her laugh as she fixed her *hijab*.

"Very funny, Amira. I'm trying to make you look like a queen, but my God you are so difficult," Tasneem sighed.

Tasneem was an amazing makeup artist, making my face the golden canvas of her work where shimmering eyeshadow, intense eyeliner and bright lips created a mesmerizing mask of beauty and made me a glowing bride. I asked her personally if she would do my makeup, which she squealed in delight after hearing I was getting married.

"That's right, Amira. We have to give Damon a heart attack when he sees you," Lucy joked, playfully when she walked into the room.

"Lucy! You're here!" I smiled and ran up to hug her while Tasneem groaned in annoyance.

"How many times do I have to tell you? Stop moving!" Tasneem scowled, pulling my arm back down on my chair. "Sit, child."

I rolled my eyes. "Yes, Mom."

Tasneem glared at me. "I'd be nice to me if I were you. I can still make you look like a clown," she threatened.

"Alright, I'll stay still."

Lucy sighed. "Ah, nothing like good ol' friendship banters before a nikkah."

Lucy was dressed in a black *jilbaab* and a *niqab*. I felt so proud knowing that I witnessed her journey to Islam from the first day. Lucy converted way back in high school, but she increased her Islamic knowledge day by day, her thirst for knowledge growing more and more. In fact, Lucy was studying to be a teacher so she could teach at an Islamic school.

"I can't wait to see Damon's face when he sees you," Kanza giggled.

"Trust me, when I finish applying this red lipstick on Amira, he's going to be putty in her hands," Tasneem said with a determined look on her face.

The girls were chatting as Tasneem finished my makeup. I couldn't help but wonder if all this was real. Was I really about to marry the boy who I thought would never be mine?

I smiled. *Allah* definitely didn't lie when He told us to be patient for good things to come. I couldn't get this giddy feeling out of my system. Damon was going to be my husband. He was really going to be mine.

I started to remember the days and nights that I spent crying in my room. All the pain and misery I felt, the dark abyss of guilt that withered the stem of my faith for a short amount of time, the trembling sense of regret that haunted me during those lonely nights. At the same time, so much good came out of that suffering.

Tanwir stayed by my side. He comforted me in my darkest hours, being the noor (light) that protected me against the universe. His need to play hero had saved me from wallowing in my self-pity because every time I lose myself to guilt, my brother was there to remind me of the true meaning of a Muslim.

Muslims always come back to *Allah*, no matter how many times they messed up or how many times they felt lost in a sea of their own emotions, the chaos would disappear as we stood in prayer, unity and faith bonding us to Allah.

Thank you, Allah. None of this would be possible without You, I thought.

"Girls," Mum said as she opened the door.

She froze when she looked at me. Nani was right behind her. Their eyes widened, jaws dropping as disbelief and pride swirled their dark, kohl-lined eyes.

Mum's expression filled with sadness, lips trembling as she held back a cry. My heart lurched for her, wanting to hold my mother in my arms again, to revisit those days when I was young with a dream to be married and be successful in life.

Tasneem and my other friends moved to give Nani and Mum space to walk towards me. Tasneem grinned widely and gestured for me to smile.

Mum's hand went to her mouth. "Is this really my daughter?" she asked while keeping her gaze locked to mine.

Her brown eyes ushered with tears as Tasneem replied, "Yes."

Nani held my face in her palms, lips twisting into a sad smile. "I never thought I'd live to see the day when you would get married," she choked on her words as she pulled me into a tight hug. "Thank you, *Allah*. Thank you so much for blessing me with such a beautiful granddaughter," she kissed all over my cheeks.

I heard a quiet sob from behind Nani and we both looked. There stood my beautiful mother in her purple floral abaya, wrapped in a magenta *hijab*, crying. She cried out of happiness and loss. Having her youngest daughter get married wasn't easy for any parent. It was a sign that I had grown up, that I was ready to face the world on my own, that my duty now would be to care for my parents like they cared for me.

I stood up.

With every step I towards her, my heart felt heavy. My own eyes started to well up in tears, as I focused on my mother. I inhaled a sharp breath as I stood in front of her, our identical eyes locking with one another, tears glistening them with their clarity. My chest tightened as I saw myself through her eyes.

Instantly, her arms came around me and I was greeted by her motherly warmth. I held her onto her as if I might lose her at that second, as if I would be leaving her if I let go. I couldn't stop the tears falling from my eyes and onto her hijab.

"I-I'm sorry," she cried in my neck. "I just… I can't let you go like this. You're my b-baby," she sobbed.

"I know," I whispered.

She pulled back and wiped my tears with the back of her thumb, exhaling softly. The emotions those eyes contained broke my heart in pieces. I knew it wasn't easy for a mother to let their child get married, especially the daughter she spent years protecting.

My wings would soar when her hand left mine, a new beginning was waiting for me through married life, my childhood nest far from my mind with a lingering touch of nostalgia.

She closed her eyes for a moment as if to calm herself down. I gripped her abaya tightly in my hands, scared to let her go, scared to let her accept the fact that I was no longer a kid. My former self was a shadow compared to the educated, confident, and strong Muslim woman I had become, where my faith stood proudly on its pedestal, my main priority in every action that I accomplished.

I could hear the quiet sniffles around me. I knew this was very emotional for everyone in this room.

"Amira?" Mum asked with her eyes still closed. She was breathing deeply.

"Y-Yes?"

Mum opened her eyes. "Promise me something."

"Anything," I nodded quickly.

"Promise you won't forget about your family." Tears still stained her cheek.

"I promise," I smiled sadly as I wiped her tears away just as she did with mine only moments ago. "I won't ever forget my family. I won't forget about you, Mum. I'm still your little girl, forever and always."

Her lips trembled. "Oh, Amira," she hugged me again, her face resting on my shoulder as her tears started again. I gently patted her back and sniffled once more.

She needed this moment more than she ever did.

I looked around the room and saw everyone wiping their own tears. Glancing at Tasneem apologetically, I realized I probably ruined my makeup.

Tasneem caught onto my thoughts because she simply said, "Good thing I brought waterproof makeup."

I've truly been blessed with amazing people in my life. Alhamdulillah (thanks to God).

* * *

I had given my agreement to the witnesses and signed the marriage contract. Taking me out of the room, I was placed on the stage that was decorated in cloths of gold and red, the classic colors of a *desi* bride. I sat perched upon the cushions like a princess of royalty, watching the women file into the room, colorful lights flickering above like fairy lights in mystical realms.

I was sitting beside the divider that separated the males and females. I hadn't even seen Damon yet. The anxiety of how he would react to me was eating me up inside, nerves bundling like the first time he told me he loved me, like the night I left, and like the day he proposed.

I glanced at the silver embroidery that decorated my gown in intricate vines of floral rhinestones and complex designs that emulated a traditional style. Heavy weights of hold rested against my chest and collapsed onto my wrists with disparate bangles of gold.

"Oh my God, Amira," Kanza laughed with two little kids following behind.

"What?"

"We have fulfilled the *desi* tradition," she announced in a proud voice.

I face palmed, knowing all too well what that meant. "Don't tell me you made those kids steal his shoes while he prayed."

She grinned, broadly. "Yeah, I did."

"Kanza, what am I going to do with you?" I sighed, pinching the bridge of my nose.

Kanza stuck her tongue out at me, which I ignored. I glanced at the little girl with her jet black hair in a pretty braid down her back. She was wearing a purple lehenga (Bengali celebration gown) and shifted from foot to foot as she stared at me, eyes wide with curiosity.

"You're a really pretty bride," the little girl said sheepishly.

"Mash Allah (God has willed it)," Kanza chimed.

I smiled at the little girl. "Not as beautiful as you will look when you're older."

She giggled.

Her brother, on the other hand, was dangling Damon's shoes on his fingertips. He had midnight black hair like her, but his stopped at his neck, thick waves of black falling over his sun-kissed forehead.

"What do I do with these?" he asked.

I shot Kanza a warning glare.

"Relax, Amira. He's going to knock on the dividers and ask for them soon," Kanza said, rolling her eyes.

As if on cue, someone knocked on the dividers. It was Tanwir. "Guys! Give Damon his shoes back!"

"That comes with a price," Kanza yelled back.

"She's kidding! I'll send the little boy with them now!" I shouted, signaling the little boy to return Damon's shoes.

"Aw man," Kanza pouted.

"Kanza, this is a wedding not an investment."

"A girl could hope," she shrugged.

Aunties gathered around the tables. Some were congratulating me personally while others stood on the sidelines, snapping quick photos of me to share with their relatives or to capture a peaceful moment.

Children ran around playing games with their mothers hot on their trail. Some of the teenagers began to take selfies in every corner of the room with their friends. Cameras were flashing and aunties were murmuring *duaas* as they kissed my forehead.

A microphone made an eerie sound and everyone cringed, their conversations halting. "Sorry," said Tanwir, clearing his throat. "May I have everyone's attention, please?"

People started to quiet down. My friends had settled down in their seats, thus leaving me alone on the bench.

"This is a very special day. I mean it's not every day that my younger sister gets married," chuckled Tanwir. "I wanted to say a few words about Amira. She's one of the most important persons in my life. My sister is the reason why I became a better Muslim. She's not an ordinary girl and I think the Muslim community noticed that when she was young. She's different. Amira is the type of Muslim that is always conscious about her deen. She knows when she does something wrong and she learns from it. Along the way, she teaches others. If there's one thing about my sister, it's that she always puts others before herself."

The aunties nodded as they smiled at me. I immediately averted my gaze away from the attention.

Tanwir continued. "When I was a teen I got caught up in the western ideologies and the American way of life. I neglected my faith, but Amira changed that. She was also so curious about Islam even from a young age. She'd ask my father nonstop questions as if to grasp the reason why she was a Muslim. She wanted to believe with all her heart, which she now shows in her every action."

The crowd reacted with awe as they heard Tanwir's heartfelt speech. A slow smiled played onto my lips, and I tried so hard to resist it, but I couldn't contain the pride that blossomed at hearing my older brother's appreciation of our time together from childhood to adulthood. He had always been aware of my presence, of my likes and dislikes, of my journey to knowledge and love for Islam.

"Usually, the older sibling finds the truth of Islam in their hearts first and guides the younger sibling. In our household, it was the opposite. Damon, you're a lucky guy. Not too many guys can get a wife that's a diamond in Islam," he finished.

I was in awe. That was my brother, my own flesh and blood. Friends came and left, but family stayed for life. If someone had asked me five years ago if Tanwir would ever say a speech about me, I would have laughed in their face.

People started clapping and cheering. My heart swelled with pride. *Tanwir really is the best older brother.*

* * *

"Amira, Damon's going to come to the girl's side for pictures. You cool?" Tasneem asked.

"Not really," I sighed, fidgeting in my seat.

Tasneem sat down next to me, holding my hands in hers. "Amira, don't you remember high school? Damon loves you. He defended Islam all those years ago. Allah brought Damon to Islam for a reason, and that all started with you, Amira. You changed his life for the better. You inspired him because you're a practicing Muslim. You show people the light of Islam by just being yourself," she said softly. "With that said, I'm pretty sure he's desperate to see you after a whole month since he proposed."

"I guess you're right," I laughed a little. "Thanks for being there for me."

"Amira, you're like a sister to me. I'll always be there for you."

Our conversation stopped as children started chanting, "The groom is here! The groom is here!"

Tasneem winked at me and got off the bench, her Smartphone camera pointing directly at me. I shook my head at her. Some things never change.

I gazed up towards Damon. He was staring right at me, eyes widening. Slowly, he walked towards me, ignoring the flashing lights behind and luminous shadows of guests.

His beige garments resembled an Arabian prince, the hat of a sultan sat proudly on his head with the wrapping of silk shaping it. His eyes never left mine, a mixture of disbelief and awe settling in the iridescent glow that radiated off them.

As he stood in front of me, I felt my heart thumping against my chest. Heat rose to my cheeks from his never wandering gaze. He sat down, quietly. Nothing came out of his lips. Did he regret marrying me already? I didn't even do anything yet. I idly stared at my henna stained hands until a larger hand clasped onto my own. I focused on our interlocked fingers, refusing to look at him.

Damon leaned in close to my ear. "Look at me, beautiful," he said, as his hot breath blew against my veil.

I did as he asked.

He gave me his breathtaking smile that seemed to put my heart in cardiac arrest. Soon, I felt myself smiling back. This was real, not a figment of my imagination. We were married. I could touch him and hold him and kiss him all I wanted now. We were married, tied together under the grace and mercy of *Allah*.

As if the thought ran a course in his mind, his smile widened, showing his pearly white teeth. "I swear; no girl will ever be as perfect as you."

"Damon, you don't have to flatter me," I laughed, lightly. "We're already married now."

He moved his face closer to my own, squeezing my hand. "For the rest of our lives, I will tell you how perfect you are," he said, as his lips brushed my cheek.

Girls cooed at us and started snapping even more pictures.

"I can't believe this is real," I whispered to him, keeping the bright smile on my face.

He wrapped his arm around my waist. "Neither can I."

"Did you really wait this long to be with me?" I asked, curiously.

Damon smirked. "You really thought I wasn't going to marry you?"

"Just a little bit," I said as I gestured with my fingers how little it was.

"Amira Sarker, you are mine. You came into my life, and now there is no chance that I will leave you ever again."

I leaned my head against his shoulder as he pulled me closer. "You sound like a dictator now," I joked.

He chuckled, kissing my forehead. "Only for you, sweetheart."

At this point, I think we killed half the girls in the room because their fangirling became too much.

"My ship has officially sailed!" Tasneem yelled in happiness.

I lifted my head off Damon's shoulder, shaking my head at my friends in mocking disappointment. My friends made a wedding into a comedy. In all, Damon found it amusing, still keeping his arm around my waist and refusing to let go.

"Oh, the feels!" Kanza exclaimed, dramatically falling into Tasneem's arms.

"I can't believe these are my daughter's friends," muttered Baba, joining us on the bench for a family photo.

Mum, Nani, Nanu, and Tanwir soon followed. Damon's mother and brothers also stood on the stage with us.

"Damon?" I asked.

"Yeah?"

"Where's your dad?"

He gave me a tight smile. "My dad... isn't coming," he said sadly.

My parents' eyes softened, staring at the man who risked everything to step towards Islam and dedicate his life to being a practicing Muslim. His father had clearly given him a hard time, and Damon tried to hide the effects of his father's disaster towards his own son.

"You're a part of our family now, Damon," said Baba. "We'll be here for you as well as long as you take care of my daughter."

"Y-Yes sir," gulped Damon.

"He better take care of my granddaughter. I'll beat him if he doesn't," Nanu huffed in Bangla, making my family and I laugh.

"Your family sure is protective," Damon commented.

"Yeah, that's why they added you to the bunch," I said.

Tanwir hit Damon's shoulder. "You're a part of the Sarker Family Protective Club over Amira," he jokingly said.

I rolled my eyes at Tanwir.

"I already love your in-laws, Damon," his mother laughed. "Such welcoming and humorous people aren't they?"

Damon smiled, gazing fondly at me. "Yeah, they are to have raised such an amazing daughter."

Our conversations halted as Zaynub, Imam Zakir's wife, held her camera. "Smile, everyone," Zaynub said.

Snap.

"I love you, Amira," whispered Damon in my ear.

"I love you more," I whispered back.

"Not possible."

In hardships, there was always ease. That was what made this fairy tale worth everything Damon and I went through. Now, we had the rest of our lives together. *Forever.*

CHAPTER 55
Finally His

DAMON WINTERS

I was awakened by an *athan* (call to prayer). I reached over to my bedside night stand to turn off my alarm, turning over to see Amira peacefully sleeping beside me. Her long, silky, black hair cascaded around her in waves, perfect lips slightly parted as she gently exhaled.

I couldn't help but smile. She was so beautiful. I thought about last night, our Nikkah.

Amira's family definitely cared a lot about her. I'd never seen a family as overprotective as hers. Her father silently cried as I took Amira back to the hotel. It was understandable because right when she was about to live with her parents again, I married her. It must have broken her parents' hearts.

As I stared at her, I thought, maybe I should buy a house near her family. I landed a job in cyber security in the exact same company as Tanwir's. I knew I wouldn't be able to propose to Amira if I didn't have a stable job first, so I practically begged Zakir to use some of his contacts to aid me.

Gently stroking Amira's cheek with my finger, I traced over her delicate features. Amira stirred. I stalled my movements. When she relaxed again to my touch, she snuggled closer. I placed a hand on her hip, molding her tempting body against mine, ignoring the burning need to keep her in bed for a couple more hours.

"Wake up," I huskily whispered, lips nipping at her earlobe.

"No."

I chuckled. "You're awake."

She opened her eyes, revealing her dark brown eyes. "I've been awake since you thought that tracing my face was a good idea," she smirked.

"I have no regrets."

"I didn't expect you to."

I pulled away and said, "I'm going to take a shower before I pray."

She nodded and snuggled back into the sheets. They fell over her curves, giving my mind mental images of her naked figure. Damn, she was a sight to see. "You're welcome to join me," I winked.

"I'm still sore," she whined, playfully.

I tensed. "Did I hurt you?" I asked, worriedly.

"No. I'm just a bit sore," she said then she waved me off. "Now go shower. You stink."

I rolled my eyes as I picked up my clothes and walked to the bathroom.

* * *

After we both prayed, Amira and I relaxed on the bed. We still had two hours before her friends would come in and kick me out. Today was going to be our Walima (marriage banquet). We were going to leave right back to my place afterwards.

I inwardly groaned, *I have to drive the whole way.*

"Hey, Damon?" asked my wife's soft honey-like voice as she absentmindedly traced circles on my chest.

I looked down at her as she leaned against my arm. "Hmm?"

Her finger tracing stopped as she asked, "Why doesn't your dad come to our Walima?"

I felt my body go rigid. This was a topic I wanted to avoid because I knew it would hurt Amira if I told her the truth. "It's... complicated."

Her dark brown eyes stared into my green ones. She bit her lip. "Is it because you're a Muslim?"

I looked away from her. "Yes," I mumbled.

I felt shifting beside me. I could no longer feel Amira resting on my arm. I sighed. I knew she'd be hurt by the fact that her own father-in-law refused to meet her. I felt slender fingers tilt my chin as she rested her other hand on my cheek.

We were so close that I could feel her minty breath hovering my face, my heart thumping against my chest. Her exotic eyes lured me in like a lost man, promising me her undivided love and attention, promising me a future of laughter, promising me her loyalty.

I wanted to kiss her like I did last night. I wanted to ravish her and feel her soft body against my hard one. Under my sweat, I could feel a familiar stirring. Her plump lips were begging me to bite them. Images of the previous night flashed through my mind, but her eyes pinned me to stay still. She was so beautiful, it killed me.

"I know it hurts that your dad won't come, but I promise you that *Allah* will send good things your way if you're patient with your father. Why don't you call him and ask him to come one more time?" she asked.

We were still talking about my father? Man, I was so mesmerized by her that he completely slipped my mind. I held Amira's wrist when she was about to pull away.

"Allah already sent good things my way," I told her softly.

"What?"

I chuckled deeply, pulling her to my lap and wrapping my arms around her small waist. "You. Allah gave me you. You complete me, Amira. My dad can hate me as much as he wants, but at the end of the day I'm the luckiest man to ever live because I have *you*."

Then I kissed her.

My Lord, her lips were so soft. They made me crazy, moving perfectly against mine. I bit her lip, asking for entrance. She opened her mouth to me and I felt myself groan at the feel, firmly holding her hips as I flipped us over so she was under me.

I trailed my kisses down to her neck, hearing her gasps of surprise. I spent some time in one particular spot on her neck gently nibbling and biting down on the tender skin. I skimmed the shirt that covered her alluring body from me, losing my control by the second.

"You're so gorgeous," I whispered into her ear. "So beautiful."

She gripped my arm tighter. "I know," she smiled.

Nuzzling my face into her neck, my hands trailed down her slim body. Memories of our tangled limbs and breathless words played in my mind, toying with me and tempting me to continue, to make her mine again.

"Damon," she said breathlessly. "We can't."

"I want you now."

She shook her head, "We have people coming over soon."

I grunted in annoyance as I got off her. "They're cockblockers," I muttered.

"Damon!" she exclaimed with her jaw dropped.

I chuckled. "What?"

"You're so insufferable," she huffed.

"And you are extremely sexy," I huskily said.

I saw the small tint of pink on her cheeks and I leaned over to kiss her cheek, unable to control myself. I kissed her forehead and her other cheek. When I pulled away, she tilted her head to the side, visibly confused.

"What was that for?"

"Well, since I can't do what I want to do to you, that's going to have to suffice for now," I said. I didn't add the part that I left a hickey on her neck. "I'm going to call my dad."

As I walked away, Amira got up and looked at herself in the mirror. "Damon Winters!" she yelled when she saw what I had done.

I was already inside the bathroom by the time she figured it out.

* * *

Amira's friends kicked me out of the hotel with all our stuff packed in my car. I had my close friends driving me as I tried to fix my tie in the car. Zakir was driving. Thomas, Tye, and Jacob were in the back with me. Ibrahim, my friend from college, sat in the seat adjacent to Zakir.

During college, I had made new friends, Ibrahim becoming my closest one. There weren't many Muslims at my university, but I had seen the mysterious pale guy in the back of an economics class, dark eyes as powerful as his intimidating stare.

I remembered how girls admired Ibrahim from afar, loving his classy attire and cool personality. He barely talked unless it was required, but the calculative nature of his potential business affair sparked a curiosity in me. I always saw him at Jummah (Friday prayer), and he would always be the last to leave, standing in worship until his feet swelled.

I admired him, so I took the initiative to start a friendship even when he pushed me away. He was a lonely soul, who experienced true horrors in Turkey, his home country. It left him with the inability to trust anyone. That was until I brought my friends to him, showing Ibrahim the wonders of a true brotherhood.

"What's the point in marriage anyway?" Ibrahim asked in his casual pessimistic tone.

"It completes half our deen," said Zakir, keeping his eyes on the road.

"Your point?"

I shook my head. "Trust me, man. I thought marriage was stupid for a long time."

Ibrahim looked through his window with longing in his eyes. My worry was dragged away when Tye punched my shoulder.

"Yeah, that was until he met Amira," Tye winked.

"Damon got whipped after that," Jacob called out.

"Our little Damon is so grown up," Thomas cooed, pinching my cheek.

I slapped his hand away. "I'll bite you."

"Kinky," he winked.

The guys all laughed as I face palmed. *Dear Lord, help me.*

*   *   *

Amira and I, were told to walk in together, so I waited by the door for her. What was taking her so long?

Ibrahim leaned against the door frame. "Girls take too long," he grumbled.

Just as he said that, Amira and Tasneem walked in. I was completely shocked by what I saw. Amira stood in a baby blue lehenga that emulated the clear skies above.

Her hijab was wrapped delicately around her head in the same shade, rhinestones and glitter decorating the ends. The lehenga fit around her like a glove. Her eyeliner gave her dark brown eyes this seductive look like a temptress from another world, sent to steal my heart at any means. Her lips were a perfect shade of classic red just like the wedding.

"Surprised?" Tasneem smirked.

I couldn't take my eyes off Amira. "Wow," I breathed.

Amira blushed. "Our audience awaits us," she smiled.

I grabbed her hips, pulling her close to me. "I can't wait to strip you tonight," I murmured so only her ears could hear.

She lightly slapped my chest, hiding her grin. "Pervert."

I noticed that Ibrahim and Tasneem looked at each other, confused as hell and slightly angry from Tasneem's side. "You're the girl from that café," he stated, shocked.

"You two know each other?" asked Amira.

"No," Tasneem said with an icy glare.

Ibrahim narrowed his eyes at her. "I got some business to attend to Damon. I'll see you inside," he said with one last lingering look in Tasneem's direction.

He left soon after, pulling his phone out. A flash of hurt spelled in Tasneem's eyes as if the two had a history that the rest of us were blind to. Amira mirrored my worry for both of them.

"You guys go in. The guests are getting impatient," Tasneem smiled tightly.

We could find out what happened later. Tonight was about us.

I took Amira's hand in mine. "To the rest of our lives?" I asked.

She grinned. "To the rest of our lives."

Then, we walked hand in hand into the ballroom. She was finally mine.

BOOK YOU MIGHT ENJOY

FACES OF LOVE
Lily Orevba

A bond stronger than all; a bond that has always been tied as one.

It was supposed to be the most wonderful thing in the world when two mates meet. But for Patience, it was the opposite. She was rejected by her destined mate, and it hurt like hell.

Instead of moping around, she decided to join the yearly hunting game in hopes to find her chosen—a mate who will fully accept and love her.

When Patience met Titus, her new mate, she learned about his terrible past and was trapped in yet another set of troublesome situations. How is she going to face all the problems life had thrown at her?

Come and join Patience as she frees herself from a major heartbreak and creates memories with the new love of her life.

For all werewolf readers out there, this is one new story you should read. Grab a copy now!

BOOK YOU MIGHT ENJOY

AMOR ETERNO
Mara Lynne

"I can't wait to sell this property, then I could go back to Japan to do my own thing!"

Xander Montejo, a young, successful professional photographer and painter, finds himself in his grandfather's hometown all because of an inheritance that he needs to claim.

He is prepared for a boring stay in the mansion, but what he didn't expect is that his grandfather's home isn't ordinary at all and boring is not a word to describe it.

When he uncovers the first mystery, he is hindered speechless. He is looking at the empty diary that he threw out the other day only to find it in his table the next day. No longer empty.

Clarissa, a young woman from the eighteenth century, is too excited to write again in her diary; a gift from her late grandmother. But, when she opens it, another entry, one that is surely not hers, is written on it.

How is it possible for two people from different times to communicate with each other through a diary?

What other mysteries are hidden in the Montejo Mansion?

And is love possible when both are centuries apart?With mysteries, gods and goddess, curses, and unconditional love, you will surely get hooked with this one of a kind story.

Grab a copy and uncover the mysteries that surround Xander and Clarissa as they battle their way to happiness and as they try their best to defy their fate.

ACKNOWLEDGEMENTS

I will always be grateful to Allah that I was given the opportunity to write a book that would help others increase their faith in whatever way I could. This book was written for the sake of breaking stereotypes, but many people helped make this dream a reality.

First, to my amazing publishers and editors, who worked day and night to edit and market my book. Even when their own lives offered stresses and grievances, they managed to pull through as a team and treat my work to the best of their ability. Thank you for believing in this small story from Wattpad and bringing it into a paperback book.

Along with my publishers, I owe a lot to my parents and brother. I kept my writings a secret for a very long time because I was afraid of rejection and ridicule, yet when my family heard about my books for the first time, they cheered me on through every step and were more excited than I was. Without my parents or my seemingly annoying but great brother, many of these characters wouldn't exist either nor would my understanding and love for my religion. They taught me day after day about how incredible Islam is, and I wanted to share that to the world.

Let's not forget about those who helped me write in the male perspective. Stone, if you hadn't edited some of my chapters and told me how ridiculous they sounded, the male characters in this book would have been very bland and two-dimensional. He followed my book from the beginning and became the reason why Damon's character was so unique.

Another person who impacted my writing style is a favorite teacher of mine, Mr. Zemel. Thank you for being a harsh grader with essays because I pushed myself even harder to apply everything you taught me to all my writings, especially in the descriptions.

I saved the best for last. A huge JazakAllah to my readers from Wattpad who have followed this book from the first day I published it on Wattpad. You guys are the absolute best, and deserve all the best in life. Without your continuous support or encouraging words, none of this would be possible and I can't say it enough. Thank you.

AUTHOR'S NOTE

Thank you so much for reading *A Diamond In Islam*! I can't express how grateful I am for reading something that was once just a thought inside my head.

Please feel free to send me an email. Just know that my publisher filters these emails. Good news is always welcome.
s_nahar@awesomeauthors.org

Sign up for my blog for updates and freebies!
s-nahar.awesomeauthors.org

One last thing: I'd love to hear your thoughts on the book. Please leave a review on Amazon or Goodreads because I just love reading your comments and getting to know you!

Can't wait to hear from you!

S. Nahar

ABOUT THE AUTHOR

Shadia Nahar is a full-time student that finds time to write whenever she's free. Shadia writes for her school's newspaper and has written several books on Wattpad. She was born in Maryland to Muslim Bangladeshi parents. Her works mainly focus on the stigma surrounding Muslims in America, where she tries to break stereotypes and change the status quo. When she's not writing or studying like a maniac, she can be found playing League of Legends, reading her favorite books, or debating politics among her peers.